HEROES
OF THE
EMPIRE

BOOK 1: THE CAVALIER

HEROES
OF THE
EMPIRE

ISRAH AZIZI

Published in the United States of America by
PageTurnerPress LLC. Visit page-turner-press.com
Title: Heroes of the Empire/ Israh Azizi
Other titles: The Cavalier
Cover design by Damonza
Identifiers: Library of Congress Control Number: 2022910999
ISBN: 978-1-958688-02-1 (hardcover)
ISBN: 978-1-958688-00-7 (paperback)
ISBN: 978-1-958688-01-4 (ebook)

Printed in the United States of America
10 9 8 7 6 5 4 3 2 1
First Edition

For my mom.

You've always been my hero.

PRONUNCIATION AND
CHARACTER GUIDE

Aslo (Oss-low) — Stable hand

Awal (OW-aal) — Deedans, the Tariqin army

Ayleth (EYE-leth) — One of the four kingdoms

Aylis (EYE-less) — Savorian woman

Bear — Winston's right-hand man

Blayton — Horse master who trained Velamir

Bloody Fools — Tavern in Namaar

Boltrex Vaz (Bol-TREX) — General in Verin

Borderlands — Defensive place holding Prolus back

Cadellion (KED-el-lee-on) — Emperor Malus's bodyguards, wielders of four blades

Casr (CAH-sir) — Jax's uncle

Chishma (Chish-muh) — Prolus's elite soldiers and graduates of the Chishman Academy

Coralie (Cora-LEE) — Woman Velamir meets in Verintown

Covskin – (KOV-skin) — Advisor in Verin

Cselnsor (SELLIN-soar) — Savorian name written on the chest in Velamir's room

Dale — King of Verin

Dauntess (DON-tess) — Winston's Ondalarian warhorse

Deedan (DEED-aan) — Soldiers in the Awal, rejected from the Chishman Academy

derinium (DER-een-nium) — Savagelander metal

Derolos (DER-roll-us) — Boy Cora rescues from kidnapper

Destin — Advisor in the Grand Palace

Devorin (DEH-vorin) — Kingdom of Snow, one of the four Imperial kingdoms

Docks, the — Lawless city containing mercenaries and illegal trading ports

Doer — Common Shadow Manos ability, crafter and able to enhance poison with their blood

Dralex Valent (DRAY-lex VALL-ont) — Prince Draven's brother, deceased

Draven Valent (DRAY-ven VALL-ont) — Crown Prince of Ayleth

drivy (DRIV-ee) — Long protective wall in the Borderlands

Elise — Natassa's first handmaiden

Evinshore (Eh-VEEN-shore) — Commander in Verin, joust participant

Falus (FALE-us) — Emperor Malus's father, former emperor

Finnean Colleda (FINN-ee-ahn COLE-eda) — Verin soldier

Flondin Woods — Woods in Verin

Fortin — Imperial Captain

Fortress Kalea (KAAL-ay) — Chishman Academy in Tariqi

Frumgan – (FRUM-gen) — Shadow Manos in Tariqi

Galvasir (GAAL-vasir) — High-ranking soldier in the Empire

Gavin — Thorsten's decoy

Graga (GRAA-gah) — Grand Palace librarian

Harold — Chishma, undercover as a tailor

Hearcross (HEER-cross) — Capital of the Karalik Empire

heeln (HEEL-in) — Imperial for spoiled

Hesten Hartinza (HES-tin HEART-inza) — Natassa's eldest brother, deceased

Honder — Imperial Captain

Honzio Hartinza (HON-zee-oh HEART-inza) — Natassa's older brother, Crown Prince of Karalik Empire

Jaxon Tana (JAX-en) — Velamir's close friend, Shadow Manos

Jevin Loster (JEV-een LOST-er) — Verin Galvasir

Joster – (JAW-ster) — King of Ayleth, Draven's father

Jyorm (JEE-yorm) — Mentor at the Chishman Academy

Kalex (KAY-lex) — Imperial Captain

Karakan (kara-KON) — Rumlok twisted into a savage beast

Karalik Empire (KAARA-lik) — Land of the remaining four kingdoms

Kasdeya Vosta (Kas-DAY-a VOZ-ta) — Krealyn's twin sister, Natassa's decoy and handmaiden

Keelo (KEY-low) — Imperial Captain

Kej — True Manos

Kisto (KEES-to) — Boy Velamir was reputed for killing

Koseer-ja (KOH-seer-jah) — Joust Master

Kostos (KOS-toz) — Head Advisor in the Grand Palace

Krealyn Vosta (KREE-ah-lin VOZ-ta) — Kasdeya's twin
    sister, Natassa's decoy and handmaiden
Lady Flivane — Natassa's teacher
Lady Blayton — Latimus's mother
Latimus Blayton (LAT-ih-miss) — Blayton's son
Lil' Jimmy — Gatekeeper in Namaar
Lilly — Jax's cousin
Lissa (LISS-ah) — Cadet at Kalea Academy
Liston — Advisor
Lore — Latimus's younger brother
Lorgont Cavenshaw (LORE-gont KAV-in-shaw) — Joust
    participant
Lure — Rarest Shadow Manos skill, able to bend a
    person(s) to their will
Madame Clion — Possible Shadow Manos living in
    Hearcross
Malus Hartinza (MAL-us HEART-inza) — Emperor of
    Karalik Empire
mavaalin (MOV-aw-lin) — Savorian farewell meaning
    wind in your sails
Mordon (MORE-dawn) — Galvasir, General Boltrex's
    son
Namaar (Na-MAR) — Town in Verin
Natassa Hartinza (NAT-ossa HEART-inza) — Princess
    of Karalik Empire
Nildon (NEEL-din) — Imperial Galvasir
Ondalar (On-DUH-laar) — One of the four kingdoms
Oslavit Day (Ozz-la-VEET) — Celebration in memory
    of the Imperial's victory over the Savagelanders
ovaline (OH-va-line) — Deadliest flower in existence
Ovi (OH-vee) — Natassa's mother, deceased

Ovus Fye (Oh-VUS fi) — Legendary Chishma

Pass of Namaar — Pass in Verin

Pit, the — Wasteland on the outskirts of Ondalar

Prolus (PRO-lus) — Lord of Tariqi, the Empire's enemy

Qistool (KISS-tool) — Long wall enclosing a kingdom in Tariqi

Quintus — Cadet at Kalea Academy

Red Eagle Forest — Forest in Verin, surrounding Winston's manor

Renegade — Mordon's lancer horse

Rolix (Roll-ex) — Commander

rumlok (RUM-lock) — Wolf/bearlike creature

Salvador (SAL-va-dor) — Vykus's henchman

Saphira (Sef-ira) — Winston's wife, deceased

Savagelands — Arid environment housing tribal groups

Savoria (SAAV-oria) — Large island conquered by Prolus

Seer — Rare Shadow Manos ability, able to see past, present, and future

Shadow Manos — Person marked with a phoenix birthmark, withholding a type of shadow

Talon — Chishma, Velamir's mentor

Tarin (Tear-in) — Captain in Verin

Tariqi (TORIH-qee) — Realm consisting of nine kingdoms, eight of which used to belong to Karalik Empire

Thander — Captain, Honzio's guard

Thorsten Hartinza (Thor-stin HEART-inza) — Natassa's older brother

Tolsfin (TOLE-es-finn) — Captain in Verin

True Manos — Imperial healer

Velamir (vel-uh-meer) — Cadet at Kalea Academy

Vandal (VAAN-del) — Velamir's lancer horse

Verin (VER-in) — One of the four kingdoms

Vykus (VI-kiss) — Renowned mercenary

Wallington — Town in Karalik Empire

Welix (WELL-ix) — Advisor in Verin

Wernis (Wer-nis) — Chishman mentor at Kalea Academy

Winston Raga (Win-ston Raw-ga) — General of Tariqi, Velamir's guardian

Xeni (Zen-EE) — Shadow Manos once disguised as a True Manos

Zamanin Sulari (ZAAMON-in SOOl-ari) — Waters of time

zat (ZAAT) — Crimson wine-like drink

zelont (ZEL-lont) — Imperial for monster

Zenrelius (ZEN-rel-ee-us) — General of Ondalar

A DEPICTION OF
KARALIK EMPIRE
and SURROUNDING
TERRITORIES.

AS DRAWN BY
IMPERIAL CARTOGRAPHER
MASTER MUSTOLE

Savoria

PORT OF

Lagrima Sea

Verin

Ondalar

Port of Ayleth

Ayleth

Karakan

Flondin Wo

Wallington

The Pit

H

The Ja Sea

The Savagelands

The Ja Desert

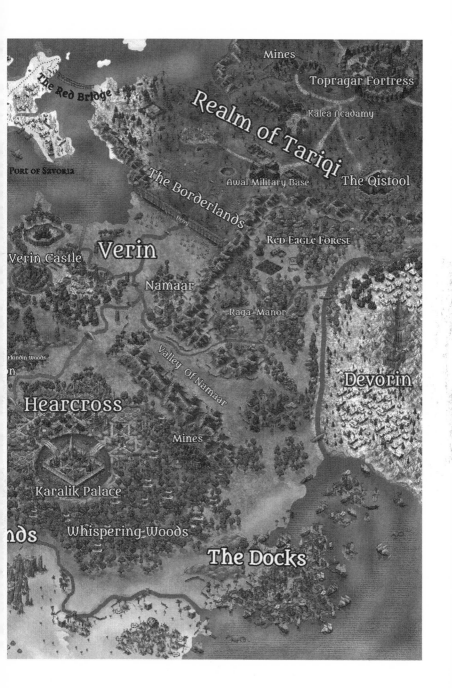

PROLOGUE

WINSTON STARED AT the fortress ruins surrounding him. Injured men lay groaning everywhere he looked. Winston swallowed, suppressing the anger that consumed him. He'd won but lost everything achieving victory. Winston inhaled the sharp odor of sweat, and smoke invaded his nostrils along with it. He eyed the entryway and the pile of burned corpses, the charred faces angled his way as though screaming for help. But it was too late for them and many of the others.

The sky was growing dark, clouds gathered, and rain fell. Droplets landed on his face, rolling down his cheeks, as if the sky was mourning for the dead. He ran the back of his gloved hand across his forehead, his lip curling in disgust when the leather came away with smears of blood and dirt.

"Quite the battle," Winston muttered and glanced at his right-hand man.

Bear was already staring at him, his broad arms crossed over his chest, his gaze blank, withholding emotion.

"It must remind you of Savoria," Winston continued, noticing Bear's cheek muscle flex in response. Winston slapped his worn glove against Bear's arm. "I'm sure your family is fine. Prolus is ruthless, but he's not heartless."

Bear's jaw clenched. "I heard some say he is soulless as well."

Winston barked a laugh, which died abruptly as his eyes narrowed. "You should be careful with your words. His whisperers are everywhere. If he hears what you say of him . . ." Winston shrugged and motioned with his blood-covered glove across his neck.

"I'm well aware of his whisperers." Bear's voice was low, almost inaudible.

Winston stared at him a moment more, until the thud of approaching boots drew his attention away. He watched his soldiers near, towing a young child with them.

"Commander, we found this boy hiding in a bedchamber," one of Winston's men said.

The soldier pushed the boy, who couldn't be older than four years, Winston's way. The youth stumbled toward Winston, who reached out, placing a steadying hand on his shoulder. He was wiry and small, his brown hair dull and darkened with grime from lack of wash, something the rain was repairing as it poured in faster drops. The boy looked up at Winston with dark green eyes. His gaze was strong, unwavering, but filled with unshed tears.

"Are you going to kill me?"

Winston shook his head and got on his knee, holding the boy's gaze. "No, lad, I saved you."

The boy was doubtful. "You are Prolus's men." He pointed at Winston's armor, where a symbol of a horned mask adorned the center of his chest plate.

"There's no reason to fear. We defeated your fortress's attackers. Prolus is the reason you are still alive." Winston waved a hand at the injured men in spiked black-and-gray livery. "We arrived as they were attacking."

The lad glanced at the men, his eyes filled with hate.

"If you wish, you can punish them." Winston smiled, unsheathing a dagger strapped in place behind his back.

The boy took one look at the dagger and grabbed it. At the same moment, lightning burst across the sky, casting a bright light over the child. Winston felt something ominous pass over him, but he shrugged it off and laughed at the lad's enthusiasm.

"That's the spirit. Tell me, what is your name?"

The boy opened his mouth to answer, but then his brow furrowed. "I don't . . . know."

Winston smiled. "Where I come from, we have a word in our tongue. In your language, it translates to courageous. Would you like to have a name like that?"

"What does that mean?"

"Courageous?" Winston inquired, and at the boy's nod, he said, "It means someone who is brave, who never gives up. Someone who would take up a dagger to avenge his family."

The lad glanced down at the dagger in his small fist and back at Winston. "I want that name."

"Very well, you shall now be called Velamir."

VELAMIR
FIFTEEN YEARS LATER
THE REALM OF TARIQI
KALEA FORTRESS
CHISHMAN ACADEMY

"WHAT MAKES UP the Realm?"

The cadets shifted, standing in a circle around their mentor. There were a dozen answers to that question, and yet only one was right, according to the academy's teachings. Velamir glanced to his left, not surprised to see Jax's hand lifted, his finger pointing upward. Chishma Wernis spotted him and nodded.

"In the past, Tariqi was a small kingdom with its own customs and language. Then the Empire came, and the emperor enforced his rule over Tariqi, along with twelve other kingdoms that had sworn fealty to him. Lord Prolus conquered Tariqi and eight kingdoms, saving many lives from the injustice of the emperor. The Realm is now a place of tranquility, and peace continues to grow as Lord Prolus's campaign furthers."

The people now had peace, but they lived in destruction. Velamir recalled all the places in Tariqi he had seen. They were desolate, poor, desperately attempting to rebuild destroyed cities, ruined homes. But as his guardian, General Winston, always said, everything has a price, liberation most of all.

"A brief answer would have sufficed," Chishma Wernis admonished and turned to another cadet who addressed him.

Jax's bright face dimmed. He glanced down at the floor, his shoulders caving in. Someone across from them let out a snort, and Velamir's eyes flew in that direction. Quintus leaned forward, sneering at Jax. He made a sad face, pulling his bottom lip over his top, and trailing a finger down his cheek like an imagined tear. He nudged his friends on either side of him, and they snickered, although they stopped as soon as they saw Velamir's expression. Quintus was the only one who continued staring at Jax with mock pity. Velamir had enough when Quintus lifted his hand and crossed his forefinger over his middle one, aiming it toward Jax. The meaning was clear—*bastard*. It was an Imperial symbol, but they all knew it, as most of them had been born in Imperial kingdoms before they had become part of Tariqi's land.

Velamir stepped forward, but Jax's hand shot out, clamping over his shoulder. "Forget it, Vel."

Velamir gave Quintus another withering glare and turned to look at his friend, his only friend, really. They'd met as children, and when Velamir had seen Jax away from the other cadets, he felt a bond form between them. Though all the children had been orphans, Velamir and Jax had been the castoffs, the most unwanted.

"Forget it," Jax repeated and released his arm. "It will only make it worse."

Quintus scoffed, and Velamir looked back at him. Quintus's lips lifted in a smirk, and his eyebrows rose. He mouthed, *I dare you.* The other cadets grew alarmed and whispered for Quintus to stop. Velamir took another step forward out of his place in the circle just as Chishma Wernis turned away from the cadet he had been speaking to. Quintus composed himself in a flash, all signs of amusement gone. Chishma Wernis's eyes fell on Velamir.

"Is there something you wish to share with us, Cadet Velamir?"

Velamir cleared his throat and shook his head.

"Then unless you need to use the loo, I suggest you stay in your place."

If it had been anyone else Chishma Wernis had spoken to, the class would have been in peals of laughter, but there was no laughter as Velamir fell back into the circle. No one ever laughed at him because of his horrifying reputation in the academy.

When he had arrived, the cadets nicknamed him *heeln,* Imperial for *spoiled.* The cadets used Imperial phrases as insults, making the barbs more potent. General Winston had sent Velamir to the academy, as his adoptive son, for training. Most of the cadets didn't have someone to call family and they never would. They were in the academy for one reason and one reason alone—to become Chishmans, the elite soldiers in Prolus's force. And soldiers' lives didn't have happy endings.

One child had shoved him against the wall and beat him while the others watched, expressions of glee on their faces. Jax had been the only one to stop it, stepping in front of Velamir. That had infuriated the bully, and he attacked Jax too. His punches held a viciousness, his eyes an anger that masked pain that would never heal. He sought joy in bringing others down. The Chishmans in the academy had separated the bully from them, but he didn't receive punishment. Or so they had thought.

The next morning, they found him hanging from a noose at the academy gates. The rope bit his neck, his feet dangled limply, and his body swayed in the light breeze. His dark eyes had been black, lifeless. Someone had plucked them from his head, leaving behind empty sockets. Tears of blood had dried on his face. Velamir received a new name. *Zelont*. Monster.

The name chased Velamir through the next years, whispered in shadowy corners as he walked by. The rumors spread. That he had a strange power that could suck the life out of a man. That he could glance at a person, and they would fall unconscious. That he was so lean because his power took all his energy. These were all speculations, but for growing children who had nothing but combat drills and history lessons engrained in their heads, a fantastical story was exactly what they needed.

The classroom doors flew open and slammed against the stone walls, the banging sound echoing in the room as all eyes fastened on a heavy-breathing cadet.

"Chishma Wernis! They brought spies!"

An audible gasp flew around the room. Velamir and Jax exchanged a wary glance. Chishma Wernis clapped his hands.

"Excellent." He motioned for the cadets to lift their arms.

Velamir reluctantly did so, dreading what was coming after the lesson. Chishma Wernis held out his arm and pulled his sleeve up to his elbow. A scar shaped like a crown with three spikes at the top stood out against the pale skin of his forearm. The cadets mimicked Chishma Wernis's movements, pulling back their sleeves to expose their not-yet-branded arms. The symbol represented the search for the Golden Crown and Lord Prolus's determination to claim it. The cadets would earn their mark when they proved their loyalty to Lord Prolus and his cause.

Chishma Wernis lifted a finger, tracing the first spike.

"Wisdom," he said.

"Wisdom," they recited after him, most in a monotone voice, sick of the routine, while others said it quickly, wanting to get to the main square in the academy's entryway.

"Power."

"Power," Velamir repeated. He wondered if the Golden Crown really existed. If it truly gave its possessor these unnatural abilities.

"Eternal." Chishma Wernis followed the last spike. After they copied him, he said in a loud voice, "Long live Lord Prolus! Long last Tariqi!"

The students shouted after him, and he nodded with a smile.

"Slowly but surely, you are becoming strong Chishmans."

A smile crossed Velamir's face at the praise. Although Chishma Wernis addressed them all, Velamir felt it keenly, like all the hard work he was doing was paying off. Chishma Wernis exited the classroom, his long cloak billowing behind him. A horned mask, Lord Prolus's primary symbol, was emblazoned across the back of the cloak. The students filed out behind him, and after navigating through the academy, they stepped out into the square. The sky was somber, as it always was in Tariqi. A strange mist seemed to hover in the air, ghostly hands reaching out to snatch one's soul and retreat into the darkness. At least, that was Velamir's take on it.

Velamir focused on the captured spies held before them. Chishmans stood behind the spies, their hands placed on their shoulders, forcing them to their knees. Velamir took in the stern expressions the Chishmans wore. They were the ones who kept watch on the Borderlands, their cloaks mostly black, few pieces of red fabric to be seen. Velamir wasn't sure what Chishma role he would fill once he passed all the lessons. It was either patrol or infiltrate. He only knew that he was grateful to be a Chishman cadet and not part of the Awal. The Awal was filled with inferior Deedan soldiers. They were the ones who fought first and died fast.

Velamir caught sight of two other mentors coming to stand beside Chishma Wernis.

"Imperial spies," Chishma Jyorm spat. "The rats crawled into our Realm." The combat instructor was thick-chested with broad shoulders. Combined with his shorter height, he appeared bulky.

"This one is a Galvasir from Verin," Chishma Talon said with a rare grin, motioning to one of the kneeled men. "Imagine King Dale's rage when he sees the head of one of his best soldiers."

The man roared and attempted to get to his feet. It took three Chishmans to hold him down. Velamir glanced at Jax to see his reaction, but he wasn't even watching. Instead, he was staring at one of the cadets. Velamir followed his gaze. Lissa crossed her arms. A smile played at her lips as she observed the captured Imperials snarl and writhe against their captors. Her eyes connected with Velamir's, and her lips lifted higher at the attention. Velamir wrenched his gaze away. There was something disconcerting about her, the purple shade of her eyes, the agile way she moved, like a predator.

"Lissa's looking this way." Jax's whisper was so hopeful Velamir had to close his eyes against his optimism.

He had told Jax many times that she wasn't worth it, that she didn't care, but Jax had insisted she liked him. After all, why did she always hang around them? Velamir hadn't the heart to tell him that her eyes hadn't been focused on him. Velamir was the one she hunted, the one she stalked behind.

"Line up!" Chishma Wernis's voice was sharp.

Velamir moved in unison with the others. He was so used to taking orders, he didn't even have to think about what he was doing as he stepped back, taking his place in the long horizontal line.

Chishma Wernis paced in front of the cadets,

eyeing them with contemplation. Finally, he called out, "Quintus!"

Quintus stepped forward, his head lifted and chest puffed out. "At your order, Chishma!"

Chishma Wernis motioned to the first Imperial spy. "Your task."

Quintus walked forward, an evil glint in his eye as he faced the kneeling Imperial. "How do you wish to die? Sword, axe, or bow?"

The Imperial's face was pale, and his hands shook by his sides, but he gave no response. Quintus shrugged and glanced at Chishma Talon. Talon nodded at one of the Chishmans, and he stepped forward, extending a strung bow to Quintus. Quintus took it and waited expectantly.

"An arrow?"

Chishma Talon shook his head. "Use the string."

Quintus approached the Imperial until they were a foot apart. Velamir's gut clenched when he realized what Quintus was about to do. The other Imperials struggled, desperate to help their comrade who was at death's door. Quintus stepped behind the Imperial, placing the bow-string against his neck. Quintus moved fast, turning the bow over so the string twisted, closing in on the Imperial's air flow. He placed his knee on the man's back and leaned away. The Imperial choked, and spit flew from his mouth. He reached up, trying to pull at the string, but it was no use. His face darkened to a deep red, and Velamir's disgust grew when he saw the chilling smile on Quintus's lips. He was enjoying this.

Velamir struggled to keep his expression impassive. They were doing this for the betterment of the world.

For the sake of all the starving orphans hiding away, fearing Emperor Malus's cruelty. Lord Prolus would take the rest of Karalik Empire and make it a better place. A glorious reign.

The life drained from the Imperial, and he sagged forward, his eyes dull. Quintus released his hold, his breathing heavy from exertion.

"Well done. Back in line," Chishma Wernis ordered, and Quintus bowed his head, slapping the palm of his hand onto his forearm, where the Chishman symbol would soon be, and returned to his place.

Chishma Wernis eyed them again and then said, "Lissa."

She swept forward, agile as always. "At your command, Chishma." Even her voice was slick, concealing her true thoughts.

She repeated the same question to the second Imperial. He accepted his death bravely, choosing a sword. Lissa thrust it into his heart without mercy, but she didn't smile in satisfaction as Quintus had. She simply completed her task. The Imperial sank to the floor, his blood staining the cobblestones. The color transfixed Velamir, the crimson pooling against the black stains on the dead man's uniform. Black and red, Lord Prolus's colors, fitting.

Chishma Wernis made his final rounds, and Velamir saw the moment his attention landed on Jax. Jax's blue eyes grew wide and his face pale. Would Jax be able to follow through if chosen? He'd once refused to kill a rabbit during a training exercise and suffered through days in a cell without food or water. Weakened and desperate, Jax had finally given in and killed the rabbit with tears streaming down his face. Taking lives was a soldier's duty, but Jax hadn't been born for this kind of life.

Chishma Wernis opened his mouth to speak, but Velamir interrupted, stepping out of the line.

"Give me the honor of this task, Chishma."

Jax sent him a shocked stare that Velamir ignored. Chishma Wernis eyed Velamir and smiled. "Proceed, cadet. May it be blessed."

Velamir nodded his thanks, though he felt sickened for such an act to be called a blessing. He strode toward the last Imperial, hoping to ward off any hesitation. The probing eyes of the cadets bore into his back. Velamir wouldn't be surprised if they burned a hole through him with their intensity.

"Sword, axe, or bow?" Velamir said, as was custom.

"Go to hell," the Imperial spat, his dark brows making a V shape as they lowered.

Velamir had been looking at the ground, trying not to stare at the man's face. It was easier to kill someone without looking at them, to pretend they weren't human. But now he looked up, taking in the rough angles of the Imperial's face, the hardness in his eyes. Maybe he had a family waiting for him in Verin, a family who did not know Velamir was about to take their father from them. Velamir glanced at Talon and saw the Chishma watching with arms crossed.

"You said he was a Galvasir. Maybe he has useful information."

Talon shook his head. "We know everything there is to know in Verin. Our spies there send us news regularly."

"*Prolus'den besin*," the Imperial snarled. *Prolus's phantoms.*

"What's your name?" Velamir asked him.

"What's it to you?"

"He's Galva Jevin Loster," Talon informed Velamir, his brow creased, likely wondering why Velamir was wasting time.

Velamir stared at Talon a little too long. The Imperial used that moment, jumping to his feet and out of the grasp of the surprised Chishmans holding him. He flew at Velamir, hands reaching for his neck. Velamir reacted on instinct. He grabbed the sword from a Chishma standing beside him and sliced it across the Imperial's throat. The Imperial stumbled. His hands went to his neck, attempting to stop the shower of red. He coughed out a stream of blood.

"Zelont," the Imperial wheezed. It was his last word before he collapsed onto the ground.

Velamir didn't flinch. He didn't feel the pain that usually came with the word, because it was true. He had become a monster.

2

NATASSA
KARALIK EMPIRE
HEARCROSS, THE CAPITAL OF THE EMPIRE
THE GRAND PALACE

"WHO IS IT?" Krea asked, examining the painting.

Princess Natassa's brow furrowed in concentration as she dabbed smudges of deep brown color to make layers of hair for the subject of her painting. She smiled, glancing at her handmaiden, who leaned closer.

"It's not another portrait of your brother, is it?"

Natassa laughed. "Since when does Thorsten have green eyes?"

Krea rolled her eyes and motioned to all the finished paintings hanging around the chamber, several of which were the prince. "You seem to paint no one else these days."

12

"I'm worried about him," Natassa whispered.

Prince Thorsten Hartinza, Galvasir and prized soldier of the Empire, third son of Emperor Malus Hartinza, was stationed at the Borderlands, the current most dangerous place to be. It was the first line of defense against the Dark Lord Prolus's attacks. The Borderlands were defended in segments, each section led by a man of noble blood. The leading positions changed every few months. It was a fair law, the only fair Imperial law in Natassa's opinion, because nobles and commoners both fought. No one was exempt from the duty.

"You received his letter last week," Krea assured her. "He wrote the attacks had stopped. Perhaps Tariqi has settled for the land they have already stolen from us."

"Perhaps." Natassa refocused on her painting, adding bronze color to the cheeks. She took a step back to examine the portrait. The boy looked as she remembered him, with slight adjustments to make him appear older, how she imagined he looked now.

"Prince Draven arrived an hour ago," Krea informed her, and Natassa's hand tightened around the brush. "Your father might send for you soon."

"He was busy torturing those Savorians. I doubt he will remember." Natassa paused in the middle of a stroke, closing her eyes against the image of the Savorian boys being whipped for answers they had no knowledge of. She could still hear their screams as their skin was torn open, but the worst part of the memory was her father. Emperor Malus had reclined on his throne, tossing back a goblet of zat that might as well have been blood from the way the crimson-colored liquid trailed over his lower lip. His face delighted as he soaked in the torture.

"I can go in your place," Krea offered, dragging Natassa out of her morbid thoughts.

"You know my father won't fall for it."

"If he realizes, I won't let him harm you," Krea told her. "I will take the punishment."

This time. The unspoken words hung in the air. Natassa's empty hand went to her wrist, trailing across the bracelet she always wore and resting on the skin beneath her thick sleeve, where a ring of bruises surrounded a healing wound.

The sudden blaring of the city horns pierced Natassa's ears. Her brush dropped from her hand, and she exchanged a glance with Krea. They stood frozen, tensely waiting for it to sound again. Natassa's fingers moved under her paint-splattered apron, inching to her belt, reaching for one of her small knives. If the horn blew once, it meant they were under attack, twice for returning troops, and thrice to signal an evacuation. They released a sigh of relief when it blew a second time and then stopped.

"Troops have returned," Natassa said and paused. "But the position change isn't for another month, and there weren't any soldiers sent out to replace them."

Krea's voice was strained. "Something is wrong."

An abrupt knock sounded on the chamber door, and Natassa's attention shifted to it, her hand sliding a knife free and holding it lightly. Her door swung open, and a palace guard burst in, his face red as he took rapid breaths.

He stared at Natassa for a second, taking in her paint-stained apron before turning to address Krea. "Your Highness, Emperor Malus orders you remain in your chamber for the next hour."

"What is going on?" Natassa asked, and the guard's eyes popped open, realizing he had been addressing the wrong person.

"Princess." He bowed deeply, but before he could say anything further, Krea's identical twin sister rushed inside. Kasdeya's eyes were wide. "Prince Thorsten's contingent has returned!"

Natassa moved without hesitation, thrusting her apron aside and sweeping past the guard, her handmaidens mere paces behind her.

"Princess!" the guard called. Desperation coated his voice, but Natassa ignored him, hurrying down the halls.

When she stepped into the courtyard, she was taken aback by the chaos. The large double entry doors leading out to the city were wide open, and the portcullis raised, exposing the drawbridge. Worn-through soldiers littered the area, ripped pieces of cloth wrapped around their arms and legs, dried blood crusted onto their hands and faces. True Manos tended to them. The healers were the only ones who had a rhythm in the disordered mess. They moved calmly, calculating each wound and tending to them with decisive care. Natassa admired their work. They saved lives, and nothing could be more important than that.

Fear flashed through Natassa as she scanned for her brother among the disarray. A small smile formed when she spotted a man with his back turned to her. His hair was dark and cut close to his head, his skin bronzed from the sun. She rushed to him, her relief immense as she grabbed his arm. Her heart plummeted to her stomach when he turned and she realized it was her brother's decoy, Gavin.

"Where's Thorsten? What happened?"

Gavin winced as her grip on his arm tightened, and she released him after glancing down to see a row of stitches lining his forearm.

Gavin frowned. "Princess, you shouldn't see this."

Natassa followed his gaze to a wooden plank. A body rested on it, covered by a long sheet. She shook her head in disbelief. "No."

Natassa moved past Gavin, falling to her knees beside the board, reaching out with a shaking hand, her fingers brushing against the sheet. She barely noticed the scuffed boots of a soldier standing beside her, murmuring something in a low tone.

"Natassa," she heard one of her handmaidens tell her. "Turn around."

She shook her head. *They don't want me to see his lifeless body.*

"I must," she told them, tears blurring her vision as she dragged the sheet down. She blinked them away and was startled to see short blond hair. She pulled the sheet down farther, exposing the noble face, prominent cheekbones, and firm chin. His eyes were closed, and from the stillness of his chest, it was evident that he was no longer breathing.

"Natassa," the soldier standing beside her said, and she realized he had been saying her name all this time.

Natassa whirled toward him, a wild laugh ripping from her throat. "Thorsten!"

She rushed into his arms. He grunted, and Natassa released her tight hold on him.

"Where are you hurt?" She stepped away, searching for a True Manos healer.

"It's not bad, arrow wound. Gavin cauterized it. The pain is minimal now."

Natassa narrowed her eyes at him, knowing full well he was making it sound like a breeze. She glanced back at the body on the board. Overwhelming guilt crashed into her when she realized she was happy he was dead and not her brother. Thorsten followed her gaze.

"Prince Dralex died in the attack. He was stabbed in the heart. We brought him to the palace to give him a proper ceremony before sending his body to Ayleth so his family can bury him."

The thought of his family sent a shiver through Natassa. "Draven is here."

Thorsten's jaw clenched. "Pressuring for the betrothal, no doubt."

Natassa nodded in agreement. "The last thing he expects is a dead brother. What is going on, Thorsten? Why have you returned?"

His expression grew somber. "We lost, Natassa. The Borderlands belong to Tariqi."

The twins gasped from behind Natassa. She closed her eyes at the news, dread sweeping over her.

"They attacked at night. Prolus's phantoms suddenly appeared. We weren't prepared." Thorsten grimaced.

"We were no match for them. Whoever survived retreated to their kingdoms. The rest are dead."

"I don't understand why, instead of rallying the kingdoms, he obsesses over something that doesn't exist," Natassa said, and Thorsten nodded at her words.

As if on cue, the emperor's voice rang out, "You had one job."

Natassa turned, watching her father cast livid eyes around the courtyard. "And you failed." He snapped his fingers, signaling the True Manos to stop their ministrations. They bowed low and fell back into the palace.

"My father, Emperor Falus, was weak," he told the soldiers. "When his men were unable to accomplish their missions, he continued to give them chances. But what happens when you overlook mistakes?" He paused. "They thrive. They spread like a disease."

The soldiers murmured discontentedly, realizing the emperor's intent to remove them. A roar of protest rose. "You can't do this to us!"

Natassa couldn't believe what was happening. Thorsten raised his voice over the protests. "Father, you must allow them to be healed first."

One man stepped forward. "We have families. We cannot afford to lose this position."

Emperor Malus's bodyguards gathered around him in a tightly knit group. The Cadellion, wielders of four blades. They held a long weapon in each hand, the ends sharpened on both sides. They were always in groups of six, trained to protect the emperor and the emperor alone.

"This is absurd," one of the soldiers growled.

The emperor's hand twitched. It was a subtle movement, but Natassa had seen it enough times to know what it meant. *No!* Her frustration and anger mounted. She could do nothing to stop the oncoming storm.

The Cadellion moved in unison, their blades flashing. The soldiers attempted to fight them, but they were no match for the Cadellion's ruthlessness, and they had no energy to withstand them. One by one, the soldiers fell, blood spurting from their bodies. Thorsten stepped forward, but Natassa grabbed hold of his arm, shaking her head. The Cadellion wouldn't know the difference between him and the others. A sob racked through her as the final soldier fell to his knees. Malus walked toward him and stared down at him.

"You're as vile as Prolus," the soldier spat, and a speckle of blood landed on the emperor's face.

The emperor's teeth clenched. He wiped the blood away with a rough motion before holding his hand out. A Cadel placed a dagger into it. The emperor thrust the dagger into the soldier's heart.

The soldier wheezed, and the emperor leaned closer so he was staring at him eye to eye. "No," he said. "I'm worse."

He kicked the man in the chest, shoving him to the ground, the dagger still pierced into his heart. Emperor Malus glanced around at the bodies in distaste. "Failure to accomplish your duty means you are nothing more than a rodent to me, and I have no room for an infestation." He called out, "Take the bodies to the Pit and burn them."

Palace guards started dragging the bodies away to a large cart for transport to the infamous wasteland on the outskirts of Ondalar. The Pit was filled with the dead, mostly Savorian slaves. Natassa's eyes were still rooted on the last dead soldier, on his prone figure. They had to stop this, or the emperor would destroy his people before Prolus ever could.

"Why did you do that?" Thorsten asked, disgust coating his voice.

Emperor Malus turned his vicious stare upon him. "If you wish to continue as a prince of the Empire, I suggest you remain silent."

He focused on Natassa, and his expression darkened further. He advanced toward them, and Natassa recoiled. Thorsten squeezed her arm in assurance. Her mother's voice echoed in her mind, *You are Princess Natassa Hartinza. You will face your fears.* She tried to focus on the memory, but her terror was strong and difficult to overcome. Emperor Malus didn't stop until he was directly before her, the Cadellion trailing behind him.

"You disobeyed my order," he hissed, his brows lowered over dark eyes. "And so you must be disciplined. Prince Draven is waiting in the sitting room. You will speak with him and then remain in your chamber for the rest of the week. No donations to the *poor* or *city brats.*"

Natassa felt Thorsten's eyes flash to her, but she didn't look at him, instead lowering her head in the image of a meek daughter, exactly what Malus wanted.

"Do you understand?"

At her small nod, he conceded and turned away, storming back into the palace.

Natassa breathed out, her rigid posture easing.

The servants rushed out carrying pails of soapy water. They held mops and rags, scrubbing at the bloodstains, wiping away evidence of the soldiers' existence. It sickened Natassa to think of the men who had dedicated their lives to the Empire only to be killed by the ruler of the very place they fought for.

Thorsten stepped closer to her. "I won't let you face Draven alone."

"You've always been fighting my battles for me, Thor, but I cannot allow you to keep shouldering that burden," Natassa replied, tearing her gaze from the servants.

"What are big brothers for?" He tried to tease, gifting Natassa with a small smile that didn't conceal the worry in his eyes. It didn't lift the mood either. In fact, it darkened it further.

"I've had my fair share of older brothers." Natassa sighed.

Realization dawned on Thorsten's face. "What did Honzio do?"

Natassa glanced up at him, looking into his compassionate brown eyes, and shook her head. "Nothing, he does nothing. He never speaks to me, he never acknowledges me. It's like I don't exist." Her voice broke at the last word.

"You know his injury changed him. Give him time to heal."

Natassa glared. "He started changing before the injury, and you know it. He's turning into Hesten, listening to Father blindly and following him like a fool. He's crown prince, and yet he acts like a puppet. How will he rule the Empire when he doesn't use his own mind to rationalize?"

"*Natassa.*" The one word was loaded with meaning. "We've had this conversation before. We agreed not to mention Hesten anymore. It's not right to speak ill of the dead."

Natassa looked away from him, watching as men wearing purple livery, Ayleth's color, lifted Prince Dralex's board and began walking with it up the palace steps. "I'm afraid the same thing will happen to Honzio, that he will be assassinated, and I will be consumed by regret that I didn't try harder to get through to him."

"That's the reason Father hired decoys. So something like that wouldn't happen again."

Natassa tilted her head, looking past him. "Really? And where is your bodyguard?"

Thorsten gave a guilt-ridden shrug. "I ordered him to the infirmary. He had a leg wound that needed to be looked at."

Natassa shook her head, frustration mounting. Thorsten spoke. "Look, it's not the same for Gavin and me. We don't have the pleasant relationship you have with your bodyguards." He motioned at Krea and Kasdeya, who were waiting a short distance away. "He reports everything I do to Father. I cannot breathe when he's around."

"I know," Natassa said, sympathizing with him. "But he is there to protect you. If something happens to Honzio, you are the next heir. You cannot risk your life so recklessly."

"My life was sold the day I was born. As a prince, I'm bound to nothing beyond orders."

Natassa knew his words were true, and she agreed with them, but Thorsten played with his life. He gambled it away when he took part in every jousting tournament their father held.

Thorsten cleared his throat, changing the subject. "What did Father mean when he said you cannot give charity to the poor and children? Does he—"

"He doesn't know," Natassa interrupted him. "I told him I'm giving food to the poor in honor of his upcoming birthday." She glanced at a guard who picked up a body near them. She lowered her voice. "The shelter is safe."

"And our ally?"

"He stopped coming last week. I haven't been able to send anything since then."

"Don't worry, I will take care of it." He shook his head. "I'm astonished Father fell for that."

"You shouldn't be. He thinks the world revolves around him."

Natassa looked up at the palace steps and remembered her father's command.

Thorsten sensed her change in mood and said, "Have one of your decoys take your place."

"We tried at the last celebration Father hosted when you weren't here. He noticed at once and . . ." Her voice trailed off as her fingers drifted over her sleeve.

Thorsten tracked her movement and his eyes narrowed. Natassa hid her arm behind her, not wanting to burden Thorsten with the fading bruises. She smiled, glancing at her handmaidens. "But Father's been the only one to notice when they take my place. I'm lucky to have them."

Natassa recalled the first time she had seen them. It had been like looking into a mirror. Hazel eyes, brown hair, oval faces. They could've passed for triplets. It would take someone close to her to spot the differences.

"Well, it's time to greet the dragon." Her lips curled into a sarcastic smile. Fans of his jousting often referred to Draven as the Invincible Dragon.

Thorsten's brows lowered, his eyes darkened, and he didn't move. For a moment, he looked like a replica of Emperor Malus. It terrified Natassa, how similar and yet how different they were.

"It's only a matter of time," Natassa told him, knowing he was feeling guilty about the plot their father was embroidering for her. "Father wants to marry me off to the highest bidder, and in this case, it's Draven."

Thorsten gripped her arms. "I won't let it happen. As long as I draw breath, I will not allow you to be taken by that monster."

Tears welled in Natassa's eyes at his fierce loyalty. She blinked them away. "It's not in your hands, Thorsten."

He shook his head in fierce determination, and she continued with a bitter laugh, "All the citizens want to be us. They think titles and riches give us freedom, but they don't understand that we are more trapped than they will ever be."

Thorsten looked away. The regret written on his face proved her words were true. Thorsten couldn't help her, no matter how much he wanted to. He was perhaps even more a prisoner to their father's steel-like mandates than she was.

"Now that you've returned, will we be able to practice again?"

"Soon," he replied. "I will send word with your handmaidens."

Their conversation was interrupted when someone rushed toward them through the open gates, panic accompanying his jerky movements. One of the palace guards stepped in his way, holding him back. The man clawed against the guard, drawing the attention of the other guards tossing bodies into the cart.

"Prince Thorsten! Please, you must help me," the man begged.

His accent was thick, and as Natassa examined his short black hair and dark skin, she realized he was covered in some sort of powder. She could see some parts of his hair were blond and certain patches of skin on his neck pale as snow.

"He's Savorian," she whispered.

"I know," Thorsten replied, his face stricken. "Leave him be!"

The palace guard holding the Savorian glanced over in confusion, and the guards approaching froze in place.

Thorsten nodded at them. "Continue with your work. I will see to him."

The guards exchanged glances before one of them shrugged. The one holding the Savorian released him with a shove, and he stumbled toward Thorsten and Natassa. Thorsten caught the threadbare sleeve of his worn tunic and hauled him to his feet before he fell.

"Have you gone mad?" Thorsten spoke harshly,

keeping his voice low. "Do you want to end up back in the prison?"

The Savorian shook his head. "I heard you returned. I have no one else to go to."

"What's wrong?"

"It's Aylis," the Savorian said. "They've caught her."

Alarm flew over Thorsten's expression. "What?"

"They are trying to sell her in the new market."

Thorsten traded a glance with Natassa, an inward debate raging across his face.

"You must help them, Thor. I can take Draven alone."

Thorsten was torn, but Natassa gave him a confident smile.

"I will be fine."

Thorsten wrapped an arm around her shoulders in a quick hug. Then he was gone, following the Savorian across the drawbridge. Natassa stared after them for a moment, wondering who Aylis was. She had to be someone important at the shelter to elicit such a reaction from her brother. Natassa saw the guards staring at her and realized she was standing in the middle of the courtyard as they attempted to work.

She nodded at her decoys and walked up the palace steps like a soldier on a mission. Natassa braced herself, ensuring all her emotions and fears were hidden away. She wouldn't allow Draven to see anything other than a demure princess. Despite that, a feeling of dread swept through her as the sitting room drew nearer. It appeared to her as the entrance of a cage, and if she entered, she would be trapped, bound to the most despicable Prince Draven.

VELAMIR
TARIQI
KALEA FORTRESS
CHISHMAN ACADEMY

VELAMIR STUMBLED TO the gates ahead. The shadows seemed to close in on him, and the mist grew thicker. He wasn't home any longer, he was a stranger in this new world. He tripped over a root obscured by the fog and fell forward. A firm hand wrapped around his arm and hauled him up.

"Careful, lad." Winston stared down at him, brow wrinkled in concern.

"Why did we come here?" Velamir asked, his voice small and afraid, sounding as though he were six instead of a twelve-year-old boy.

"You are here to train, to become a Chishma, one of Lord Prolus's elite warriors."

"Like you?" Velamir asked.

Winston's blue eyes darkened in the haze. His nose was long and straight as he peered down at Velamir.

"You will be like me, one day," Winston replied.

"Why can't we stay home at the manor? You were training me there." Velamir didn't like the whiny tone of his voice, but he was desperate. He didn't want to lose the only father figure he knew.

"You are a fast learner, and I enjoyed teaching you, but Lord Prolus calls me away on missions. I have no time to provide you with the best tutelage. This is the greatest place for it." He motioned toward the gate, the entryway to the academy.

Winston stepped past him, and Velamir reached out, gripping Winston's arm. "You will come back, won't you?"

Winston's smile was gentle as he slid Velamir's hand away. He moved forward, disappearing into the mist. A tear streamed down Velamir's cheek. It was hot against his skin, like the blood that had soaked the back of his shirt when Winston rescued him all those years ago. Velamir couldn't remember whose blood it had been, only that it hadn't been his. Velamir walked through the mist and froze. A boy hung from the gate, a rope circled around his neck with horrifying familiarity. His empty sockets peered down at Velamir. Velamir's breath caught in his throat. *How is he here? He's dead.*

The boy faded, and the gate changed into a long winding hall, the academy entryway. He stepped forward, peering into the dimness. White mists floated by. Ghosts of children who had been rejected from the academy. They were Deedans, the sacrificial army, the slain who weren't good enough to be Chishmans. Velamir saw the academy doors fly open; a man barged into the hall. He shoved a young boy forward, yanking him by the collar of his shirt. The boy was wide-eyed, and his blond hair fell in ragged curls. *Jax*, Velamir thought.

"The other soldier brats are waiting outside to be tested," the man said.

Chishma Jyorm wasn't impressed. He crossed his arms. "Vykus, to what do we owe the pleasure of your visit? I'm used to seeing your cronies."

"I want double for this one." He glanced down at the boy. A sneer curled his upper lip, revealing a gold tooth. "He's marked."

Chishma Jyorm's brow lifted. "I will be the judge of that. If he is as you say, I will notify Talon and you will get your coin."

"I brought you Shadow Manos before. I don't know why you Chishmans doubt my abilities."

"It's not your ability, it's your word we doubt," Jyorm replied.

Vykus and Jyorm faded away. Time flashed before Velamir's eyes, and he saw himself sitting beside Jax on a narrow bench. They were older, perhaps thirteen.

"My uncle gave me up as soon as Vykus came," Jax told him. "He didn't want to be caught dead with me. Giving a Shadow Manos a home is considered treason in the Empire. When my father died, my uncle came to take his house. Little did he know I was there too." Jax's smile was resigned. "Let me show you something."

He lifted his sleeve, exposing the birthmark on his arm. It was the shape of a phoenix, its color a deep purple, resembling a bruise.

"Your shadow mark." Velamir had never seen one before. "What is your gift?"

"Gift? My shadow is a curse, Velamir, a curse that follows me wherever I go."

Velamir stared at him. "You are no longer in the Empire. You're safe in Tariqi. And you're not alone. I've got your back."

Jax's smile was grim. "We've got each other."

Velamir held out his hand. "Brothers?"

Jax hesitated for a moment and then returned the gesture. They clasped each other's forearms.

"Brothers," Jax repeated.

Jax slowly disappeared, and his arm turned into the hilt of a sword in Velamir's palm. Energy trailed over his skin, and the wolf's head on the sword's pommel opened its jaws, releasing a haunting howl that echoed around Velamir. He spun, noticing he was in a dark cave.

"Help me," someone called, and Velamir's heart jumped.

The whispers taunted him, a female voice pleading for his aid.

"Velamir, please."

Velamir spun in a circle inside the cave, searching for the bearer of the words. "Where are you?"

There was no answer, and Velamir continued seeing black until he heard a voice.

"Galva Jevin Loster."

Chishma Talon's voice continued, echoing, "He's Galva Jevin Loster."

Then Velamir's surroundings changed. He stood in the square, leaning over *him*, the man he had killed. The

Imperial rose from the ground, his neck sliced open and blood pouring out. His eyes were black like a demon's, and he advanced on Velamir.

"Zelont," he seethed.

This is a dream. I must wake up.

Velamir was frozen. He closed his eyes to block the sight. Cold fingers curled around his neck, strangling him. *Wake up!*

Velamir's eyes flew open, and he sat up, breathing heavily. His shirt was plastered to his chest and back with perspiration, and the thin blanket that covered his body weighed him down with a wave of heat. He flung it off and stood, running a hand through his sweaty hair. Velamir navigated past the other beds in the dimly lit dormitory and walked over to the basin in the corner of the room. He cupped water from the basin and splashed it onto his face, the cold relieving his senses. The nightmares used to be rare, but they had been coming more frequently, tormenting him with his worst memories and wild imagination.

Velamir made his way back to his bed, taking a candle with him to light the way. He paused at a square object on the ground. Velamir bent down and picked it up. It was a journal. Velamir stood, bringing the candle closer. The small flame highlighted the plain leather cover. Velamir flipped the journal open, knowing without a doubt who it belonged to.

Jaxon Tana was inscribed inside. Why was Jax's journal on the ground? Velamir's fingers tightened on the binding. Unless . . . Velamir went to Jax's bed at the end of the dormitory and held the candle over it. It was empty. He quietly exited the room, careful not to wake any of the cadets. Their snores followed him into the hall. Velamir had a terrible feeling in the pit of his stomach, and he hoped his suspicions were wrong. He wished he held a sword or his dagger instead of the small candle, but all the cadets' equipment was locked away, and the only time they were allowed to use them was in the arena.

Velamir crept down the hall. The glow of his candle flickered, and looming shadows grew around him. Velamir continued on until he heard a distant yell coming from one of the classrooms. He rushed toward the sound, and the voices became clearer the closer he came.

"Thought you were something special, huh? That you were smarter than the rest of us? Well, get this in your head."

There was a thump and a grunt of pain.

"You are nothing but a weakling. Being a Shadow Manos doesn't make you better than us. The only reason you get private lessons and attention is because you're tainted, possessed." He heard another thump.

"It's not like private lessons with Frumgan is something special." Someone else laughed. "He's crazier than anyone I know."

Another voice hissed, "Don't you know what Frumgan can do? I wouldn't speak that way about him unless you want to piss blood and puke your guts out."

"The man's nearly deaf." The first voice chuckled. "And Jax here won't tell him a word about this, will you?"

Velamir heard another punch and groan as he neared the door of the classroom.

"Feel better?" That was Jax's voice, and though he sounded groggy and weak, he was still attempting to make a joke.

"Prove to us you are valuable to the academy!"

He recognized Quintus's voice as it rose in volume.

Velamir busted through the classroom door. Five heads swiveled his way. Lanterns lit the classroom. Two of Quintus's friends held Jax's arms back. Quintus was across from Jax, and by the cloth wrapped around his fists, it was apparent he was the one doing the beating.

Jax peered at Velamir through swollen eyes. "Hello there, Vel," he said as cheerily as he could with a split lip. "Came to join the party?"

"No," Velamir replied, placing the candle onto a side table, eyeing Quintus with disgust. "I came to start it."

Quintus's shock faded and was replaced by a condescending smile. "You think now that you have some muscle, you can fight?" He shook his head with pity. "You are still the same orphan brat that first arrived here." He said the word *orphan* as an insult, as if he weren't one as well.

Quintus continued, "I don't believe that story. About you killing Kisto. I saw how much effort it took for you to kill that Imperial today. You don't have it in you."

"Instead of making assumptions, why don't you find out?" Velamir shot back.

"Bring him to me," Quintus told his friends.

They stared at each other with apprehension. Velamir smiled, none of them wanted to mess with the zelont.

"There's just one of him!" Quintus said, exasperated.

Finally, two of them approached Velamir, leaving one

behind with Quintus to keep Jax in check. They stopped a few paces away, their hesitation clear. Velamir lifted his hands and beckoned them forward. They glanced at one another and attacked in unison. Velamir ducked under both their punches and felt the air whoosh over him. They stumbled past him. He spun, grabbing one by the back of his shirt and kicking him behind the knee. The cadet grunted, falling onto the ground. Velamir clapped his hands on the cadet's ears and wrenched him up and then down, smacking the cadet's face against his knee. There was a crunch followed by a groan of pain. Velamir released him and turned to face the other attacker.

"Velamir!" Jax warned.

Velamir spun and dodged Quintus's left hook. He slammed a fist into Quintus's stomach. Before he could advance farther, arms wrapped around him from behind, propelling him backward. Velamir saw Jax elbow the cadet holding him and reach for Quintus. They grappled with each other as Velamir slammed his head back against the cadet holding him. The arms dropped from around him, and he turned, watching the cadet slump to the ground, blood pooling from his nose. Something struck the back of Velamir's head, and pain exploded throughout his skull. Hands grabbed him and shoved him against the wall.

Through his blurry vison he made out Quintus dropping a small side table to the ground and lifting his fist. The punch rocketed across Velamir's face, and more blows rained upon him as Quintus's other friend joined in, pummeling Velamir until he saw stars. He felt like a child again, unable to defend himself. Then, quite abruptly, they stopped. Velamir sank to the ground, his face swelling and his stomach sore. He looked up, trying to see what happened through his hazy vision. Lissa was behind Quintus, holding a knife to his throat. Chishma Talon stood by the door, his arms crossed.

The cadet who had gotten hold of Jax released him and raised his hands, stepping away. "We were just playing."

"It doesn't look that way to me," Talon said bluntly.

The other two stepped away from Velamir. "Quintus forced us to do it," one of them said, holding a hand over his busted nose.

"Shut up," Quintus hissed.

"Quintus, Velamir, and Jaxon will come with me," Talon ordered and glanced at the three cadets who had helped Quintus. "You will return to the dormitory and not breathe a word of this to the other students. Have Frumgan look at your nose."

The cadet with the broken nose grumbled and touched it gingerly.

Talon pointed toward the door. "Move along."

After they left, Talon motioned for Lissa to ease off on Quintus. "Stay on our rear, Lissa. Keep an eye on them."

Lissa smirked, sliding the knife away from Quintus's neck, leaving behind a thin slice in his skin trickling with blood. Quintus put distance between them, wiping at his neck. Lissa twirled the knife between her fingers.

"At your order, Chishma," she told Talon.

In the back of his mind, Velamir wondered why Lissa had a knife when none of the rest of them were allowed one. Being Chishma Talon's daughter had its benefits, apparently.

Velamir pulled himself to his feet. The room turned around him, and he almost fell again. He blinked to clear his vision and followed Talon with the others out of the room. They walked down the quiet halls, and it soon became clear that Talon was taking them to the Head Chishma. Velamir sighed. They were going to be punished. He only had a few months left before his training would be complete. This would derail everything. He would be forced to make up for the trouble he had caused. They reached the Head Chishma's office, and Talon stopped.

"Velamir will go first," he informed them and swung the door open.

Velamir walked inside, his trepidation building. The door closed behind him. The Head Chishma's chair was turned away, and Velamir could only see the back of his head. Thick blond hair, half of it pulled back into a knot. Velamir blinked, unsure if Quintus had punched him harder than he thought. The Head Chishma wasn't blond. Then the man stood and turned to face Velamir.

"Bear." Velamir smiled, realizing it was his former Savorian mentor.

Bear approached him, engulfing him in a hug. "Stormy seas! What happened to you, lad?"

Velamir winced at the pain that rushed through his bruised midsection. "I thought that was why I was called here, to receive punishment."

Bear shook his head in bewilderment and pulled back. "No, lad, I'm here to take you home."

Natassa
Karalik Empire
Hearcross
The Grand Palace

NATASSA ENTERED THE sitting room to find Advisor Kostos seated on one of the elaborate, embroidered cushions. The remaining rays of sunlight shone through the arched windows, bathing the room in soft golden light. The advisor widened his eyes in feigned surprise and stood, his smile overly wide and false.

"Your Highness." Advisor Kostos waved his hand dramatically and lowered his upper body into a bow.

She nodded. "Where is Prince Draven?"

"We shall get to that," Advisor Kostos said and paused a moment before continuing. "It has caught my attention that Prince Thorsten left the palace shortly after arriving. I wonder the reason for that."

"That's none of your concern."

"Too right you are, but as the head advisor, it is the emperor's wish that I inform him of everything in the palace, especially concerning his *children*," the advisor replied, his mustache twitching.

Advisor Kostos had a maddening obsession with ruining Thorsten's reputation. It started when Thorsten made him look like a fool in front of the council. Thorsten had been fifteen years old, below the age of attendance, but because Honzio and Hesten had both been unable to attend that day, the emperor brought Thorsten to the council instead. Thorsten had watched in silence as the councilmembers discussed defense strategies against Dark Lord Prolus's ruthless attacks. Advisor Kostos had suggested they retreat from the Borderlands.

"It's a lost cause," he'd said. "Without any form of defense, they will easily break through our lines."

Natassa remembered his words. She had been hiding behind one of the thick curtains blocking the grand windows.

"Why don't you build a drivy?" Thorsten's voice had been youthful but full of confidence.

Natassa had peeked past the curtain, watching as every head wheeled to stare at him.

"It will hold them back while leaving gaps for us to attack them."

The councilmen murmured, some eyeing the boy with a new look.

"It would take years to build a wall of that strength

and size, and we don't have the resources to form the incinerators," Advisor Kostos had said.

"We could employ Shadow Manos," Thorsten proposed.

An uncomfortable stillness filled the room, and Advisor Kostos spat out, "Have you lost your senses, boy? We do not work with Shadow Manos, ever. It was their greed that made us lose kingdoms to Prolus!"

"Silence!" Emperor Malus boomed, and everyone's attention turned to him. "We will build the drivy. The Shadow Manos can work for us or continue being slaughtered. They know they are not accepted as it is and will jump at this chance. We can ban their cult when the job is done."

Advisor Kostos sputtered, "But they practice witchcraft. Their work is despicable. We can—"

"You will suggest nothing. I am the emperor. My word is final." The threat behind Malus's voice was evident.

"As you wish, my emperor," Kostos said with meek surrender, but Natassa saw his hands clenched at his sides.

Natassa blinked the memory away, returning her attention to Advisor Kostos, who was staring at her with expectance. Natassa took a step forward.

"I've heard a rumor," she began, "that our head advisor was spotted at Madame Clion's home."

Advisor Kostos paled. "That is preposterous!"

Natassa nodded. "I thought it was so strange, because I know how much you despise the Shadow Manos."

Advisor Kostos looked away. "Madame Clion is not a Shadow Manos."

"The fact that you are defending her makes me think the rumors may be true," Natassa said slyly. "I wonder what the emperor would do should he hear of it."

"The emperor has collaborated with them in the past." Kostos stuck his nose in the air with an irritated sniff. "No doubt he would cast aside such gossip as rubbish."

"Not if it came from his own kin. All I want is for you to leave Thorsten alone."

Kostos's eyes narrowed. "Are you blackmailing me?"

"Is that what this is?" Natassa widened her eyes. "I was going to say a friendly warning."

He focused on something behind her. "I see you have brought your lovely decoys."

Natassa glanced back at the twins. Krea and Kasdeya wore light gray dresses, the normal color for handmaidens. Each had their hair pulled back from their face in an elaborate swoop, ending in a swirling bun behind their head. It created the illusion of long hair, which the twins lacked but Natassa had plenty of. They wore an intricate belt that fell in a V shape over their hips. Attached to both sides of the V were sheaths with what Natassa would bet were the sharpest daggers in the Empire. Krea, the one who provided her with the latest gossip on Advisor Kostos, shot her a wink. Natassa sent her a small smile before turning back to face the advisor.

"How do you know I am not a decoy?"

Advisor Kostos stared for a long second before smiling and pointing at the other side of the room. "Prince Draven is waiting for you."

Natassa gave him a lingering warning look and swept past him, walking in the direction he pointed. She stepped out onto the balcony off the side of the sitting room. Prince Draven Valent, Galvasir of the Empire and crown prince of Ayleth, stared down at the city. Hearcross was a grand sight, especially when night fell. The sun was setting, and darkness was creeping in. The lights—some say the emperor forced a member of the infamous Shadow Manos to make them— hung in every part of the city, making it appear extravagant and afflu-ent. It was one of the many things her father wasted his time on. What was the point of decorative lights when the Empire was falling kingdom by kingdom?

Natassa stood beside Draven on the balcony, pasting a somewhat passable smile onto her face. The prince turned her way, his blond hair slicked back with oil and his cold gray eyes unsettling. Because of him, longer hairstyles were coming into fashion in the Empire. He smiled, revealing perfect white teeth. Many women thought him handsome, but Natassa felt repulsed every time she saw him. Because she knew what he really was, she saw the darkness in his eyes and the wolf that lurked behind that smile.

Draven examined her, his eyes trailing from the tips of her shoes all the way up to her face. Natassa felt as though a snake crawled all over her, and she longed to drench herself in a bucket of clean water. She fought to keep her smile in place, knowing better than anyone that he hadn't been taught manners, only arrogance and the expectation of servitude from everyone around him.

"Princess," Prince Draven said in a slippery voice as he bowed over her hand and kissed it. He eyed her bodice, which was exceedingly modest for his tastes. "You look well."

Natassa was relieved that she'd worn gloves. "Prince Draven," she replied, pulling her hand from his and curtsying in reply to his bow.

He grinned in approval and reached out, touching a stray lock of her hair. Natassa stepped back, placing more room between them. Draven's hand hung suspended for a moment before he returned it to his side, his cool air of authority remaining despite her obvious rebuff of his attentions.

Draven's proximity often brought Elise to Natassa's mind. Elise, Natassa's first handmaiden, first companion, first friend. Elise's low whisper, filled with anguish. *I . . . I made a mistake.* Her brown eyes haunted Natassa to this day. *He called for me, and I went to him . . . You must help me. I'm pregnant.* Natassa, young and naïve, had pulled away. *With Draven? The man you know my father intends for me to marry? How could you?*

Elise, found in a storage closet, a knife in her fist and her throat cut. A note close by, written in her hand, saying she lost the will to live. Natassa blamed herself for Elise's death. It didn't matter that she had seen Draven standing with the shocked onlookers when they found Elise's body. Or that fresh blood dripped off the side of his boot. Natassa would never forgive herself for not being there for Elise, for being selfish.

"Are you feeling all right?"

Natassa's gaze snapped back to Draven. One of his eyebrows rose, and his mouth lifted in his classic side smirk. If his arrogance were transformed into rope, Natassa could have strangled him with it a thousand times.

"I was thinking of your brother. I'm sorry for your loss," Natassa told him, and she was sincere. From what she had seen, Prince Dralex had been a much better prince than Draven could ever be. "His pain is no longer, his glory remembered."

"His name stronger, his honor forever," Draven replied, as was custom. His sarcasm was so thick Natassa could have painted a wall with it.

Dralex had been a little nobody beside Draven, but when he was stationed at the Borderlands and sent the Tariqi running with his tactics, his fame grew. It had infuriated Draven. Natassa had seen how he acted whenever his brother's name was mentioned. He was glad Dralex was dead, and she knew it. He was glad to have any future threat removed.

Draven withdrew a small decorative box from the pocket of his elaborate outfit, his cape billowing around him although there was little evidence of wind in the air. Natassa held back a scoff. It wasn't fair that he could exude such perfection to hide his dark soul. She hated the thought of all the poor girls who fell for his charm.

"What is this?" Natassa asked, accepting it with hesitance.

Draven smiled, moving to stand behind her. "You will have to open it and see, won't you?"

Natassa's body pressed against the railing, and her panic rose. Another dreadful night flashed through her mind.

He's going to ask me to marry him, Lady Genevieve had said haughtily. *He asked to see me on the balcony tonight.*

43

I wouldn't be so sure, Natassa had responded. The ballroom was full to the brim, and she felt like escaping, not only from the conversation.

You are jealous because you thought he would ask you. Genevieve spun away, giddiness in her every step as she nearly flew to the balcony.

Natassa wondered many times what Lady Genevieve had thought while standing on that balcony. Had she known she was pushed? Did she regret not listening? Would she have chosen a different man if she knew her fate was to be splattered across the palace cobblestones?

Natassa's hands shook as she held the box. Did Draven feel any remorse for the lives he'd ruined? Likely not. Natassa breathed in, remembering her mother's words. *You will face your fears.* Besides, it was not as if Draven could kill her when her bodyguards and the advisor were present.

Natassa started opening the box, willing her fingers to stop shaking, a gasp of alarm slipping past her lips when she saw what it contained. A gold necklace with the words *Princess of Ayleth* engraved on it.

"I don't understand."

Draven moved closer until his chest was touching the back of her head. He leaned down to whisper in her ear. "I should think that it's quite obvious." His breath fell against her neck as he spoke, and she stiffened.

He reached around her, his arms closing her in and hands lifting the necklace from the box. Her heart raced, fear and panic at war with her common sense. Draven brought the necklace to Natassa's neck, but she took it from his hands and shoved it back into the box. She turned around, her back now pressed to the railing and her body facing his. She raised a hand in warning when he tried to reach for the necklace again.

She spotted Advisor Kostos watching them with an amused smile near the balcony entrance.

"That necklace is for your future wife," Natassa told Draven.

"That is the point, Your Highness," Advisor Kostos said, stepping closer. He seemed eager to speak, trying to get back at her for her words to him earlier. "You have much to discuss."

"What do you mean?" Natassa asked, though deep down she knew the answer. Her hands clenched into fists at her sides, her nails digging half circles into her skin.

Advisor Kostos's smile was large, eager to share the news. "With the betrothal signed, you will be married in less than a month." He lifted a paper stamped with Emperor Malus's symbol, her father's signature written with a flourish at the bottom.

Natassa could not conceal her dismay. "What?"

"You will be marrying Prince Draven."

Natassa looked over at Draven. He was smiling down at her, eyeing her like she was a delicacy he'd never tried. He licked his lips, his tongue flicking like a snake. Darkness clouded her vision.

You will marry Prince Draven sooner or later. Learn to accept it. Her father's words from years ago rang in her ears.

Learn to accept it. Accept it.

The blackness covered her vision, and Natassa's last thought was, *I'm going to fall.*

5

VELAMIR
TARIQI
KALEA FORTRESS
CHISHMAN ACADEMY

"I'M HERE TO take you home," Bear repeated, his grin widening at Velamir's befuddled expression. "The general needs you, lad. Prolus has given him a new mission."

Velamir stood motionless. Winston needed him. After all these years, he finally sent word. Velamir had yearned to return to the Empire, to the home General Winston had provided for him. Although it had been years since he'd been there, he remembered the wide fields and pastures as though it were yesterday.

"What mission?"

"Patience." Bear looked around the room with a heavy sigh. "First, we must leave this den."

Velamir shook his head in amusement. Only Bear would call the Head Chishma's chamber, the finest in the academy, a den.

Bear's gaze returned to Velamir, and he appraised him with approval. "You've grown up. The scrawny Velamir I knew is nowhere to be found."

Velamir motioned to his bloated face, at the bruises forming. "And these?"

Bear punched a hand into his fist. "They are trophies of your valor. You won the fight?"

Velamir winced. "I was outnumbered."

Bear patted his arm. "You have my sympathy, lad."

"You have mine as well," Velamir replied mournfully.

Bear frowned. "And why is that?"

"You have aged, Bear. I hardly recognized you." Velamir could only keep a straight face for a moment before a wide grin broke through. His grin died off as soon as it pulled against the swelling in his cheeks.

Bear waved a finger at him and chuckled. "Ha! Let that teach you not to make fun of your elders."

Bear looked almost the same as he had the first day Velamir had met him. He was a tall man, towering over most, and his shoulders seemed just as broad. His stitched tunic appeared as if it would explode because of his physique, and his tangled, shoulder-length hair contained few gray strands.

Their banter was cut short when the door opened. Talon entered with the Head Chishma. The Head Chishma's robe was rumpled, his hair limp and eyes bleary. His mouth pressed together in a thin line, he wasn't happy to be roused from his slumber.

"You're dismissed," Talon told Velamir. "Inform the others to return to the dormitory. I will have a word with them later."

Velamir stepped into the hall, closing the door behind him. Three pairs of eyes were riveted on him.

Jax broke the silence. "What happened? Who did you speak to? We just saw the Head Chishma enter."

Quintus and Lissa looked just as eager as Jax to hear what Velamir had to say. "It was someone I knew from the past."

"We won't be punished then?" Jax asked.

"It wouldn't be your fault anyway," Velamir replied, glancing at Quintus. "Talon said we should return to the dormitory."

Quintus crossed his arms. "What a waste of time. Why were we called here?" He turned to Lissa. "You were with Chishma Talon. What did your father say?"

"I left to retrieve him when I heard you screaming and clawing at each other like wild animals, but he was already up, coming for Velamir."

"Just Velamir?" Jealousy marked Quintus's face. "For what?"

"I don't know," she replied, her voice gaining a sharp edge.

"I wish we knew what they were saying," Jax said.

"Maybe if you would shut up for a second, we could find out," Lissa snapped, glancing at him and Quintus before reaching out and twisting the knob. She pressed her boot against the door, pushing it. The door opened a slight bit, enough for them to hear the voices within.

Jax's face was pained at Lissa's harsh retort. The

effect along with his busted lip and swelling eyes could tug at heartstrings. Jax mouthed to Velamir, *I'm making progress.*

Getting Lissa to yell was not progress, it was more likely to land a person on her *To Be Executed* list. Velamir moved closer to the door with the others, hoping to get an earful of the conversation.

"Quintus has caused more than enough trouble. He must be punished, not rewarded, for it." The Head Chishma's voice was icy.

"Better to get him off your hands then, aye?" Bear suggested.

"General Winston asked for the best," Talon interrupted, his voice low and direct. "Quintus and Lissa are two of the best Chishman cadets, and Frumgan says Jaxon is skilled."

"They must be evaluated. I will not send mere trainees on a mission."

Velamir exchanged a glance with the others. They all stared back with bafflement.

"If you want to refuse, take it up with the general."

"They are free to enter the general's service after finishing their last year." The Head Chishma was firm. "Can he not wait a few more months?"

"If I may," Talon began. "I can hold their tests. Lissa is ready for it."

"And the others?" the Head Chishma asked. "Jaxon, Velamir? Are they ready?"

There was a long pause, and Velamir could imagine the Head Chishma shaking his head. "If I allow this, Lord Prolus will not be pleased when I send my report."

"Let that be the general's burden," Bear replied.

"I put this in your hands, Chishma Talon." The Head Chishma reluctantly agreed. "Hold the tests, but if they fail, they are not going anywhere."

Lissa reached out, taking hold of the knob, and gently closed the door before turning to face the others with a scowl on her face.

"The fates never seem to be in my favor." Quintus scoffed. "I can't imagine a worse nightmare than being stuck with shadow weakling and *zelont*." He sent a look at Lissa, rubbing the cut on his neck.

"You trapped yourself into this because you can't control your bullying addiction." Lissa crossed her arms.

"No, you heard what he said," Quintus shot back, his smile smug. "I'm the best Chishman cadet."

"He was talking about all of us," Lissa said.

"Is it so bad to go on a mission?" Velamir asked, and they turned to look at him. "We will be out of here, making a difference in the world, righting the wrong the Empire has done."

Quintus laughed, holding his stomach. "Look at him, pretending to be a hero. Listen, *zelont*, the stories you hear about the incredible Chishmans will only be dreams for you." He snarled. "You are trying to make yourself a leader, but I will never work under you."

Velamir felt Lissa's eyes on him. He glanced at her and saw her staring at him intently.

"Pass the test," she began, stepping close to him, "and I will follow your lead."

She reached out and stroked his face. Velamir recoiled, and she smirked before walking away, disappearing into the shadows of the dark hall. Quintus rolled his eyes and left as well, leaving Jax and Velamir alone. Jax's thumb brushed against the stubbed end of his pinky finger, something he did when he was restless.

"What the hell was that?" Jax asked, the hurt in his voice unmistakable.

Velamir raised his hands in apology. "I don't know why she did that."

"You had to encourage her for her to touch you like that."

"You know how I avoid her."

"That's why you warned me away from her. You could have told me the truth."

"There's nothing between us," Velamir protested. "Believe me." Jax backed away, and Velamir called, "Where are you going? I'm trying to explain."

Jax paused halfway down the hall. "There's no need for further explanation."

Velamir stood alone, his thoughts filled with the oncoming testing and the situation with Jax. He went to the place that always brought him peace of mind. The archery chamber was empty and quiet. Velamir wasn't even supposed to be there if it wasn't time for a lesson, but he had broken too many rules that night to care.

He lifted a bow from a rack that held dozens. After fetching a quiver of arrows, he stood before the row of targets. A lopsided sketch of a grotesque-looking man was pinned into the target facing him. One of the cadets must have put it there after the last lesson as a joke. Velamir approached it and tore it off. *Emperor Malus* was written in barely legible text.

Tariqi was supposed to bring change to the callous Empire. Velamir couldn't condone the acts of the cadet who had drawn this. It was low, something the Imperials would do. The first step to victory was to be nobler than the enemy. Velamir crumpled the sketch in his hand and set it aside. He returned to his spot and took up his bow again. He pulled the string back until his fingers brushed his cheek. Velamir winced as he closed one eye, the surrounding swelling paining him.

"You should have Frumgan look at that."

Velamir flinched at the deep baritone. He lowered his arms, holding the bow in one hand and unhooking the arrow with the other. He turned to look at Bear leaning against the doorway.

"I'm fine," he said in response. "Besides, I'm sure Frumgan is occupied."

"Being the only Shadow Manos mentor keeps him busy, but you know as well as I do Winston requested a position for Frumgan so he could keep an eye on you," Bear reminded him.

Velamir shrugged, rolling the arrow shaft between his fingers. "You know how he is."

"Frumgan?"

Velamir nodded, and Bear said, "He's a mite bit strange, but the man can't help it. I think nearly being set ablaze at a stake would drive anyone mad. I don't agree with killing them, but their talents make me wary."

Velamir frowned. He had nothing against Shadow Manos—after all, Jax was one—but it was Frumgan in particular who set his nerves on edge. Velamir lifted his bow again, nocking the arrow on. He drew the string back, and his eyes grazed over the mark engraved into the tip—Lord Prolus's horned mask. Velamir might have made this. He had made hundreds of arrows, dyed the fletching on the ends until his hands were colored in red and black. Blood and death.

"What's on your mind, lad?" Bear asked him.

Velamir let the arrow fly. It thumped into the center of the target. "The test."

Surprise flitted through Bear's face. "You listened to the conversation. You might as well know that Talon is holding it tomorrow."

"Tomorrow?"

"Do me a favor, lad," Bear said, pulling away from the door. "Go see Frumgan, so at least your wounds won't affect your performance."

Then he was gone. Velamir returned his equipment and left the archery chamber, navigating through the academy. Before long, he stood in front of a door, and a memory flashed through his mind.

Velamir walked to the boys' dormitory with Jax. They'd had a rough day. Combat class had been tough, Chishma Jyorm testing the extent of their stamina. Jax looked over at Velamir and frowned.

"You're bleeding."

Velamir looked down at his arm and saw a deep cut on the top of his wrist. He closed his eyes and grimaced. He'd have to see Frumgan now. He separated from Jax and walked to the Shadow Manos's chamber. Once he reached the door, he knocked and entered. It was dim inside. Jars filled with animal parts and other things Velamir couldn't name lined the shelves. It was a small chamber, a large pot in the center taking up a good portion of it. Velamir spotted a table on the side. There were a few bandages and a bloody basin. Obviously, someone else had been hurt. Velamir glanced around the room. There was no one in sight. He turned to leave when a strange feeling went up his spine.

He looked toward the back of the chamber, eyeing a closed chest. Something was there. Velamir could feel it. He approached slowly until he stood in front of the chest. It was wrong to open someone else's belongings, but he felt something there, calling to him. He opened the lid halfway, reaching in with one hand. He brushed against something solid and wrapped his fingers around it. It was cold metal. Velamir dragged it from the chest . . .

"What are you doing?"

Velamir's hands flew back, and the chest snapped closed. He spun around, his heart racing wildly at the sound of a hysterical voice. There stood Frumgan, his eyes glazed and crossed, his beard falling to his waist.

Velamir rushed past him, running to the boys' dormitory and not looking back. He ran inside the room, fresh sweat pouring down his face. The room was empty except for Jax, who was writing in his journal. As soon as Velamir had entered, Jax thrust the journal under his pillow.

"Oh, it's just you," Jax said, his voice heavy with relief, and he edged the journal out. "What happened? Did he fix the cut?"

Velamir shook his head and glanced down at his wrist, seeing that it was still bleeding. He wrapped his hand around it to stem the flow. "He is something else."

"Frumgan?" Jax snorted. "Why are you so alarmed? You've seen him before."

"No, I mean he has something. There's something . . . was something else."

Jax was perplexed. "What are you talking about?"

Velamir shook his head again, not knowing how to describe the sensation coursing over him when he reached into the chest.

Velamir traced the scar on his wrist, remembering the horror he had felt as a sixteen-year-old. He had never gone back to Frumgan's chamber since that day. He couldn't believe he stood before the door now. But if he wanted to pass the test, he had to be ready. He gave a sharp knock and turned the knob.

6

NATASSA
KARALIK EMPIRE
THE GRAND PALACE

S HE HEARD HER name in the distance. Someone
was calling to her through the gloom. Natassa
stepped through the shadows, trying to find
a way out. Her mother's shrill voice sounded near
her ear, and Natassa spun to her right.

"You will not touch her!"

The shadows melted away, and she spotted her
father looming over her mother, his face thunderous. With a sharp ache, she saw herself behind her
mother, clasping a large book to her chest, her
face pale and stricken with fear.

"She must learn how to behave!" the
emperor growled. "She cannot go parading
about the marketplace. We aren't even in the
palace but in a kingdom foreign to her."

"She's just a child," her mother replied. "Hurting her won't make her obedient."

"I was forced to explain her actions to the king. I was in a defensive position before a man who should grovel at my feet. I couldn't have Dale thinking my daughter had snuck out from the castle, so I convinced him it was her maid. I will not look like a fool before my people, Ovi. I will not."

Natassa stepped closer to the scene, her lips trembling. She knew what happened next. Before her mother could stop him, the emperor snatched the book from Natassa and lifted it, his eyes blazing as he read the cover.

"*The Book of Prophecies, The Hero's Call.*" Emperor Malus shook his head. "What is this blasphemy! I said this tome would not be found in the Empire! How could you give it to her?"

Natassa's mother straightened, lifting her chin. Natassa saw herself in that exact position every day, desperately attempting to be brave against the torment.

"Because one day it will come true, and Natassa should know it. Everyone should."

"I am the emperor. My word is law," he growled and tossed the book into the crackling fireplace beside them.

"No!" young Natassa screamed, scrambling toward the flames, watching as they bit into the pages, eating them in hungry gulps.

"Why are you so unfeeling?" Natassa's mother asked.

"You need to rein her in, or I will."

"She is not a horse, she is a person," her mother responded.

"She's learning from you, the running away habit,

the disobeying." Malus laughed, a chilling sound. "Maybe she isn't even mine."

Her mother gasped. "How could you suggest that?"

"That mark isn't natural," Malus bit out, pointing at little Natassa.

Natassa flinched at the word *natural*.

"You know who has those marks." His voice was low, a harsh whisper.

They were the only three in the guest chamber King Dale had provided for their visit.

"One of the most powerful empresses was one of them, your ancestor," Natassa's mother told him. "It runs through your blood."

"Spare me that nonsense," he boomed. "I do not have the blood of witches within me."

"You have the blood of noble people. You could be like them. Fix the changes your father and grandfather wrought upon the Empire." Her mother's voice was hopeful.

"Don't tell me what to do!"

Natassa saw her mother close her eyes, and when she opened them, they were resolved. "I will not be returning to the palace, and I'm taking Natassa with me."

"Back to your lover? Is that what this is?"

"I've never betrayed you, despite knowing how many times you've betrayed me," Natassa's mother said softly. "You've changed, Malus. The man I met is gone."

He glowered at her. "You're not leaving."

She lifted her chin, her posture defiant. "I am."

Malus ground his teeth and reached out, gripping

her arm in a harsh hold. He shook her roughly. "You are not going anywhere!" he repeated.

Young Natassa turned away from the fireplace and screamed, "Stop!"

Her mother let out a sharp cry, and Malus released her. She clutched at her chest and gasped for air. Natassa saw something she had never seen in her father's expression—fear. Terror covered his face as he reached for her mother, gently this time.

"Ovi?" he whispered.

She collapsed, and he caught her, sinking to the ground with her in his arms. Natassa cried in time with her younger self. Though it was years ago, the pain was stronger than ever before. It felt fresh, as if someone had squeezed lemon juice over an open wound, excruciating.

"Ovi!" her father yelled, his crown slipping over his forehead as he looked down. He flung it across the room with an agonized shout.

Her mother glanced at Natassa and reached for her with a shaking hand. Young Natassa dropped beside her and took her hand, holding it to her cheek. Ovi brushed her skin with her thumb.

"I love you, precious," she whispered. "Never forget, never forget who you are. Say it with me."

"I am Princess Natassa Hartinza," young Natassa said through sobs. Her mother whispered along with her, her face tight with pain. "I will face my fears."

Then Ovi stopped shaking, stopped moving entirely. She lay still, staring up with lifeless eyes.

"Mama!" young Natassa screamed.

Natassa bit her lip to stop it from quivering. She

watched the moment young Natassa turned to her father, needing his comfort. Needing his protection and guidance. She was met with cruel eyes, cold as the mountains in Devorin, the Kingdom of Snow, as it was often called. She would receive no help there.

Natassa!

The voice again. Natassa searched for the source and felt hands slapping her cheeks. She raised an arm to deflect the blows, but they kept coming, light enough not to be painful but still sharp enough for her to wince. They brought her to the present. She opened her eyes and blinked to adjust to the lantern shining near her face. She was lying on a soft mattress, and it took her a moment to realize she was in her own room, on her own bed. Natassa's brow furrowed, trying to remember what happened. Prince Draven had proposed, well, not really proposed, and then she had fainted.

Kasdeya stood above her, holding the lantern and looking down at her with a frown. Krea sat on the bed, worry creasing her brow. She smiled when Natassa's eyes landed on her.

"She's awake," Krea called to someone over her shoulder.

An elderly man. Natassa recognized him as one of the True Manos as he stepped into view. He was holding a bowl in his hand, mixing the contents into what Natassa assumed was a tonic. He waved the sisters aside and leaned over her, examining her eyes and placing a heart timer over her chest. The heart timer was another device the Shadow Manos had created, although few Imperials knew that. Emperor Malus had given the glory of the invention to the Imperial healers along with the name True Manos. *True Gift*. By true, he meant untainted by power.

There was a low hum, and the True Manos lifted the heart timer from her chest with a nod. "Your heart is in good condition, Your Highness. It appears your mother's genetic complications will not afflict you." He smiled. "And you have passed your eighteenth birthday just recently."

Natassa knew she should smile back, but she couldn't summon one in place. Her mother's heart had always been unstable, as had her grandmother's and great-grandmother's, and perhaps many of her ancestors before her. It started showing signs when they reached eighteen years of age. The thought of being afflicted with her mother's condition had plagued Natassa all her life. It passed down mother to daughter for generations, leaving them with short lives. Emperor Malus made sure that knowledge of the condition stayed contained. He didn't want any potential spouses—or rather, benefactors, as he called them—to know the princess might die before long.

"It seems you simply had a bit of a shock today," the True Manos mused. "Nothing serious." He pulled out a couple of vials. "Manos Kej ordered me to give this to you."

Natassa nodded at Krea, who took them from him. They were tonics for sickness, meant to help with head-aches and pain. Natassa requested them all the time, although not for herself.

Despite her father's attempt to quiet the heart condition in their family, rumors still circulated about her. That she was weak, that she was sick, that she only lived because of the medicine the True Manos provided. She was the reason these rumors spread, because every time more vials were sent to her, more gossip was passed around as well.

"Hours of rest and relaxation should restore you," the True Manos informed her and bowed. "I shall give my report to the emperor."

"Thank you," Natassa told him and waved her hand, dismissing him.

When the door closed, Krea scooted closer to Natassa, the bedsheets rustling as she moved. "I nearly fainted myself, Natassa. When you fell . . ." She trailed off, shuddering as the horror of the memory resurfaced.

Kasdeya smirked, placing the lantern on Natassa's vanity. "Luckily, we are forged of steel as bodyguards and not prone to such weakness as fainting."

Krea agreed and said, "But you should have seen Prince Draven's face when he caught you. He seemed so worried. Natassa, do you think you are wrong? Maybe he's not such a bad person."

Natassa glanced away, her jaw clenched as the voices of the murdered woman flitted through her mind. "He's a good actor."

"Natassa has told us many times what he's done," Kasdeya admonished her twin. "How can you speak about him this way?"

Krea shrugged guiltily. "I'm sorry, but when I saw you, half of your body toppling over and then him reaching out to catch you. His face desperate and yours solemn, eyes closed. Him holding you for a moment in the evening light, your features brightened by lanterns. It just seemed . . . well, it seemed like one of those stories you used to read to us."

"In case you've forgotten, Natassa isn't poetic," Kasdeya said dryly, "so I would stop with the flowery phrases."

Her handmaidens had been instructed to learn Natassa's mannerisms to the core, from the books she read to the way she walked and ate and acted. It was all a game, to convince the nobles or a potential assassin to believe in a false princess.

Krea rolled her eyes. "Can't I do something that is just me for once?"

Natassa felt as though a stone had dropped over her chest at those words. Her handmaidens were forced to act the way she did, without a choice on how to run their own lives. Krea said it as a joke, but Natassa knew deep down she meant it. Their futures were sacrificed for the sake of Natassa's well-being. It didn't matter if it was because of her father's orders. If she hadn't been the princess, if there hadn't been a princess of the Empire, they wouldn't have been forced into this.

"How were lessons this morning?" she asked Kasdeya, changing the subject.

"Lady Flivane tried to contain her annoyance when I couldn't balance a stack of books on my head." Kasdeya huffed, still standing by the vanity. She ran her fingers along its smooth surface and reached for the hair extensions she had used that morning, plying the long pieces into a braid mindlessly. "She moved on to the next subject rather quickly. We studied the royal line, starting from your great-great-great-great-grandparents."

Natassa smiled. "You can actually balance books incredibly. I remember when we first tried it together before a lesson."

Kasdeya shrugged and stared at her through the mirror. "Whether I am good at it doesn't matter. The fact is you aren't, which means I have to do the same."

"I'm sorry," Natassa whispered, the guilt pricking at her again.

Krea reached for her hand. "This is our duty, Natassa. Why are you sorry?"

"I'm sorry that every day you are forced to pretend you are someone you're not."

"That's no different from you," Krea told her. "You wear a mask, more than we do. You are always performing, playing the role of a princess and nothing else to the public."

Natassa searched her gaze, and then she glanced at Kasdeya, whose arms were crossed, her face grim. There were a few moments of silence before Natassa's chamber door flung open abruptly. Emperor Malus strode inside with the heir to the throne, her older brother Honzio, following behind. Startled, Natassa stared at them.

"Father?"

"The True Manos just informed me of what happened. You think I'm a fool? I know you were using the faint as a ploy to avoid conversing with the prince." Her father seethed.

"Father—"

He held up a hand to silence her.

The emperor motioned with his head to her handmaidens. The order was clear. Krea and Kasdeya exited the room.

"You will be wed to Prince Draven by the end of the month, and there will not be any chance of escaping the marriage. Do you hear me, girl?"

Natassa stood from her bed and faced him. "I want you to know that by doing this, by signing that contract with him, you are also signing away my life, because I won't survive a marriage to him."

Her father's face grew red. "You will marry him, and you will do your duty by providing him with an heir. If you hold your tongue and be silent as a woman should, he will be content with you. And soon you will thank me for my kindness, when you realize how happy and secure you are."

"Happy? As Mother had been?" Natassa never brought up her mother, but she knew it was the only way to pierce his harsh exterior, the only chance to make him see how this would destroy her.

Pain flashed across his face so quickly it was almost indiscernible. But she saw it, and she also saw the moment a blazing anger took its place.

"Never. Speak. Of. Her," he said through gritted teeth. "I am only thankful I took you away from those vile books you used to read or else I don't know what kind of wretch you would have become."

She stared away from him, focusing on a painting hanging in her room. It was a trick she learned when she was young, and it helped her not to hear his cruelty.

He scoffed, glancing around the room, taking in the canvases that lined the walls. "You were spoiled here.

When you are married, there will be no chance of painting. You will take up embroidery or something more suited to a prince's wife."

He turned and walked to her chamber door. Before he reached it, he turned back. "My birthday is in four days. You will behave appropriately."

What he really meant was, *You will blend into the lavish decorations, there to be attractive, but useless besides being admired.*

"I've invited all the nobles from the other kingdoms, as usual. This party will mark my grandness. It will be a large celebration, a night to be remembered." Emperor Malus continued, "As you know, the long-awaited Karalik Joust will commence a few days after my birthday celebration. I have decided to host your betrothal ball the same day as the joust. Do make sure you are ready." And with that, he slammed the door behind him.

There was an awkward silence.

Honzio looked at her. For a moment, it seemed as if sympathy swirled in his gaze. Natassa's eyes dropped to his arm, a now twisted and malformed limb, and empathy filled her heart. One of the True Manos had set his arm wrong after he had broken it in a joust, leaving it in that strange, bent position. Her father employed another True Manos after the incident, and the original healer had been found dead, drowned in the moat.

Honzio's eyes darkened when he noticed her gaze upon his arm. He turned without a word and left, trailing after their father. Natassa stood alone, remembering how her father had spoken about her books and how he destroyed them, but he didn't realize she had memorized the passages word for word, that she hid them within herself, where he could never take them. Where he could never burn them because they were a part of her.

He had also forgotten to mention one thing. His birthday celebration was a mourning day for her because it was the day before her mother died. Natassa walked over to the family portrait she had painted years before, staring at her mother, of the smile she had painted on her face that had never existed in real life.

I feel as though there is something locked within me . . . I don't know how to explain it. I want to tell you, but I can't, she had said to her mother long ago.

Then paint it, her mother had replied, knowing her affinity for the art.

Natassa lifted a hand and touched her mother's face. A face that she had inherited. Sometimes she wondered if that was why her father hated her so much, because she looked like her mother. Natassa left her hand on the painting, tears welling in her eyes.

"I need you here, Mama. I don't know what to do. I can't explain my thoughts to you once again. I'm lost for words."

Then paint it.

The words sent a rush of determination through her, and she pushed back her tears. Walking over to her easel, she removed the unfinished portrait of the boy and replaced it with a fresh canvas. After readying a few mixtures of paint, she lifted her brush and focused on the canvas. *A night to be remembered,* her father had said. She trailed her brush across the canvas, swiping in the first trace of color. She intended for the night to never be forgotten.

7

JAX
TARIQI
KALEA FORTRESS
CHISHMAN ACADEMY

WEAK, FOOLISH, SENSELESS.
Those were the words Jax had heard all his life. He heard them so often that he was starting to believe they were true. The first time his shadow had come, he'd been in his uncle's barn, moving hay bales. The shadow crept over him, engulfing him until he'd felt the power in his birthmark. Energy flooded through the barn, cracking the beams holding up the hayloft. His uncle had rushed into the barn, horror clouding his features.

Senseless! his uncle had cried out. *You cursed burden!*

His uncle had treated him like the plague after that day, knowing what he was. He was a Doer. His shadow increased his normal abilities, enhancing his strength and mind. But once the shadow took its leave of him, it left him weak and barren, like a forgotten tomb. There were two other types of Shadow Manos: Seers and Lures. Seers could see into the future or the past and even the present, the lengths of their power dependent on their shadow. Jax had only seen one Seer in his lifetime, but he had never seen a Lure. They were the rarest Shadow Manos, able to manipulate minds. Out of the three types, Doers were the most common. Their blood had unnatural capabilities, which could enhance a poison or aid a healing tonic.

Because of Jax's interest in crafting different contraptions, he'd once blown a hole through the arena roof. It had been late at night when his experiment went wrong and awoke the whole academy.

Foolish! Chishma Jyorm had spat, shaking his head.

An instance of his shadow abandoning him was when he attempted to bring a heavy log to the chopping block with Velamir. He'd felt strong at first, and then slowly the strength seeped out of him, and the log had slipped from his hands, nearly breaking Velamir's back. Jax had panted, hands on his knees, calling for Velamir to wait, but he didn't, carrying the log the rest of the way alone.

Weak, Quintus had muttered as he brushed past him.

Jax learned the hard way that the shadow was not a friend, it was a controller. It came when it wanted, and it left when he needed it most, almost like it was toying with him.

Jax admonished himself now as he sat in a wobbly

chair in Frumgan's chamber. How could he have been so senseless to not see that Lissa hadn't cared for him in the least? How could he have been so foolish to not realize that Velamir cared for her too, and how could he be so weak to surrender to unreciprocated feelings for her in the first place?

The liquid in the vial before him bubbled over, spilling onto the table. Jax groaned and covered his face with his arm, careful not to touch his skin with his gloves. Frumgan stepped beside him, his eyes gleaming an unnatural shade of blue.

"*Bero*," the Shadow Manos said, jerking his hand at one of the ingredients resting in a small bowl near Jax's gloved hand.

Jax nodded, knowing that Frumgan was telling him he had used too much of the ingredient. Frumgan's communication skills were hard to decipher, especially lately with the toll his shadow was taking on him.

The liquid continued running, nearing the edge of the table. Jax collected an empty bowl and used a towel to drag the liquid into it. Then he tossed it into the refuse bin along with the towel and his gloves. Even if he had failed in making the correct version, poison was still poison.

"It's time! Time for my tonic!" Frumgan exclaimed, and Jax looked over at him. His robes were loose over his skinny body, and they were adorned with a shocking number of holes. Frumgan's nose was running, mucus pouring over his lip. He grabbed the sleeve of his robe and wiped at it, adding the mucus to the other disturbing stains lining the fabric.

Frumgan was ill. He had been for as long as Jax could remember, and though Frumgan knew many forms of healing, he wasn't skilled enough to cure the sickness festering within him. Jax wasn't sure anyone could. After wiping the table down, Jax placed fresh gloves on his hands and set out new ingredients. He searched the shelves for the final part of the tonic but couldn't find it. Frumgan searched beside him, humming a tune.

Frumgan was a Doer as well. He had learned almost every poison there was at the age of ten. Jax watched Frumgan sing to himself, his eyes glazing over as he shuffled things around on the shelves. His bony, ungloved hands carelessly traced over jars containing poisons that could end a life. Frumgan stilled, his blue eyes darkened to a deep black, and he mumbled to himself. It was his shadow invading his mind. It had been happening a lot more recently. When Shadow Manos first learned to contain their shadow, they could hold them back, releasing them when necessary. But as years passed, the shadow became the master once again. Jax knew someday that would be him. It was the curse of being a Shadow Manos. Eventually, toward the end of his days, the shadow would triumph and take the last of his life and sanity. Frumgan snapped out of the shadow's control and snatched a jar containing a rich powder and lifted it into the air with a cry of victory before bursting into a fit of coughs.

"You're going to need to restock soon," Jax told him, accepting the jar.

If they didn't, they wouldn't be able to continue making his tonic, and he would die slowly, painfully.

But maybe it was better that way, to be taken by the poison before the shadow. Years before Velamir's guardian, General Winston, rescued Frumgan from certain death, Frumgan had known the Imperials would attempt to kill him. He tried to end his own life using a poison made with ovaline, the deadliest flower there was. He had almost died, but his mentor, a man now long gone, prolonged his life using a tonic seeped with his blood. It had saved him, but only temporarily. The only way he could have cleansed his body of the ovaline would have been to make an antidote with the same flower. The flower was death and life. But by taking the tonic his mentor had made, Frumgan had signed himself to a life of torment.

Jax completed the mixture and handed it to Frumgan, who took it in rapid gulps, his chest easing once he finished. Jax watched him with worry. Frumgan had taught him everything he knew, and although he was certainly strange, there was a part of Jax that would hurt if the old Shadow Manos passed on.

"Where is the most potent ovaline found?" Jax asked.

"In the Empire, in the Karakan's lair." Frumgan's expression darkened as his thoughts trailed away. "I took the ovaline from there long, long ago."

"What is the Karakan?"

"It was a rumlok once. But it was experimented on too many times. It grew larger than the others and turned on the Handlers. Prolus caged it and ordered the Chishmans to bring it to the Empire. It broke through the protective barriers in the Borderlands and killed many Imperials until it finally made its home in the cave."

"Why did the Doers help the Imperials? That was their chance to run, to be free. But instead, they made the drivy and kept Prolus out."

Frumgan stayed silent, picking at herbs and just when Jax thought he wouldn't respond, Frumgan said in a hoarse voice, "We didn't have a choice."

Jax's hand touched his sleeve, his fingers lingering over his birthmark. He could feel power pulsing beneath his skin. He had gained more control of his shadow in recent years. It had wanted to come out during his fight with Quintus, but he had contained it. It was a small victory. Quintus had a special vendetta against him. Shadow Manos had killed his parents. It didn't matter that Jax wasn't the one who murdered them. Just the fact that he was part of the *cult* made Quintus furious enough to go through with the beating.

"You didn't join me so early in the morning for breakfast, did you?" Frumgan said, removing a boiled egg from the large pot in the chamber.

Jax shuffled his feet. After his argument with Velamir, he hadn't known where to go. He had unconsciously gone to Frumgan's.

Before Jax could reply, there was a knock at the door, and it swung open to reveal Velamir. Velamir paused when he saw him, and Jax witnessed the moment that guilt crossed his face. Remorse filled Jax too, and he almost forgave Velamir for betraying him, but he had to keep up the resentment for a while longer so Velamir would get the message that he wasn't everyone's respected hero.

"What are you doing here, Velamir?" Jax muttered as he went back to cleaning the supplies.

He caught Velamir wince when he said his full name, which he only used when he was speaking about him to someone else or when he was angry.

"I came for a healing tonic."

Jax glanced at him and looked over the black-and-purple bruises covering half his face. Jax had taken a healing tonic as soon as he came to Frumgan's.

He wordlessly scoured the shelves for a tonic while Velamir turned to greet Frumgan. Even though Jax knew Velamir was hesitant to be near Frumgan, he didn't back down. It drove Jax crazy sometimes when he watched how Velamir conversed with people. With respect and kindness, even when he received none. And if someone brushed him off, he assumed it was his fault. He thought no one liked him, that everyone feared him, but Jax saw the way the others stared at him. With admiration. When Velamir walked into a room, he commanded it. It was what made Quintus jealous of him and, if Jax was being honest, himself too. Because Velamir looked like a hero from the storybooks. Tall, strong, handsome. But he wasn't arrogant or prideful, and that made people like him more. Jax was jealous of him, and he hated himself for it, especially since Velamir was the only one to consider him a friend.

Jax reached up, taking a tonic from the shelf, and began mixing it harder than necessary, remembering when the tables in the dining chamber filled near the area he and Velamir sat. No one used to sit near them because of Velamir's reputation as a child killer, but after a few months, when Velamir started filling out and looking tough, many of the cadets, especially the girls, edged closer, hoping Velamir would notice them. He never did, but Jax had, and it made him feel more unwanted than ever before.

"Velamir!" Frumgan said, his voice high, a result of being deaf in one ear.

Velamir fidgeted. It was clear he was uncomfortable under the old man's stare. Jax approached him, sparing him. "Drink this."

Velamir took the tonic and smiled. "Thanks," he said, swallowing a sip. He coughed and grimaced, his reaction so humorous that Jax had to smile.

"This is horrible."

"That means it's working."

Velamir drank some more, and Jax could see the effect working on him as he slowly straightened to his full height, the pain no longer weighing him down.

Frumgan was munching on the egg, shell and all. It was underdone, the yolk still soft, and the yellow thickness poured down his chin, tangling in his beard.

"Not bad at all, cadet!" Frumgan screeched at Jax as he appraised Velamir.

It didn't escape Jax's notice that Frumgan called Velamir by his name, whereas he always called Jax cadet, or student, or learner. Velamir cleared his throat, seeming uneasy at the proximity as Frumgan crept closer.

"Velamir," Frumgan said, his voice scratchy and coarse when he spoke in a level tone.

Jax crossed his arms, watching with slight amusement as Velamir stared at Frumgan's face. Standing so close to him, Velamir could probably make out all the little critters running through Frumgan's beard and possibly swimming in the egg yolk. Jax glanced at Frumgan's ear, where his phoenix birthmark rested. When he'd first met the Shadow Manos, Jax had mistaken it for ear wax because of its deep yellow color.

"Can I help you?" Velamir finally asked.

Frumgan smiled. It was as wide as the grins Quintus would give when he was plotting something wicked.

"It is I who will help you." Frumgan gave a merry laugh and flew toward the back of the chamber, to his chest. Jax had never seen the contents of the chest, and his anticipation grew. Frumgan lifted the chest open, freezing for a moment to admire whatever was inside.

"Aha!" Frumgan cried out, pulling something covered in leather halfway from the chest. Frumgan, who Jax knew was agile for his age, attempted to raise the leather. He groaned, his eyes closed in effort. He managed to lift it and approached Velamir with shaking arms.

"Take it." Frumgan's eyes watered from the weight.

Velamir grabbed the leather, brows raised. Frumgan rested a hand on his lower back and heaved recovery breaths. He motioned for Velamir to unwrap the leather.

"Getting old, huh, Frumgan?" Jax told him, attempting to jest while hoping the strain wouldn't bring his sickness back faster.

Velamir tugged the leather free, his fingers stilling at what he saw underneath. Jax leaned forward and peered at a long, intricately constructed sword. He assessed the sword from the pommel, which was designed into a howling wolf with a crown upon its head, to the bottom of the embellished leather sheath containing it. Elaborate engravings spread out like wings on the cross guard. Velamir took the sword in his hands with a dreamlike expression, and Jax knew he didn't even notice when the leather wrapping fell to the floor with a slight thump.

Frumgan pointed at it. "The blade is made from derinium metal, forged in the Savagelands. It is much stronger than a typical sword."

"Perhaps you should step back," Velamir warned as he wrapped his hand around the hilt again.

"What—" Frumgan started.

Velamir drew the sword in one fluid movement. It swished through the air, nearly severing Frumgan's beard. Frumgan hurriedly retreated, but Jax took no notice of him as he stared at Velamir's new sword.

Velamir cleared his throat, glancing at Frumgan. "I'm afraid to ask, but where did you get this?"

Jax smiled, wondering what underhanded methods Frumgan had used to gain such a unique sword.

"Within these stone walls," Frumgan said, waving his hands. He began humming again, hopping away to check his inventory without further explanation.

A knock startled Jax, and he glanced at the door as one of the other Shadow Manos entered.

The cadet paused. "I must have gotten confused with my schedule." He glanced at Velamir and then at the sword.

Jax shook his head. "You're good. We were just leaving."

Velamir led the way, and as soon as they entered the hall, Jax pulled the door closed. Velamir placed his new sword back into its sheath and held it in one hand.

Jax stared at Velamir, deciding to ignore his resentful thoughts about him and Lissa for a moment.

"You know I won't pass the test, Velamir."

"You will. I know you will."

"I'm not ready."

"Hell, you are better at archery than all the other cadets."

"Besides you," Jax replied. It was meant to be a joke, but it came out bitterly.

"You will do it, Jax. I believe in you," Velamir said.

It made Jax feel guilty for even holding a grudge, and after what felt like a minute of silence, he told him, "You're good for each other, you and Lissa. Both strong, both fierce, both brave."

Velamir closed his eyes. "Jax, like I told you before. There is nothing between us."

Jax remembered the way Lissa's fingers brushed Velamir's face. His stomach tightened, and he glanced away from Velamir.

"Trust me." Velamir's face was earnest, and when Jax looked back at him, he realized his friend wasn't prone to lying.

"I believe you," Jax said. "You were right about her all along. I should have listened."

"I hate to be the bearer of bad news"—Velamir smirked—"but I'm always right."

Jax chuckled. "I wonder why that's so hard to believe."

Velamir laughed and said, "I heard the cooks prepared a large cake."

Jax's eyes widened.

"Only for the Chishmans, not the cadets."

"Oh." Jax looked down in disappointment, but then his gaze flew up to meet Velamir's amused one.

"Are you up for an adventure through the kitchen?"

Jax knew the moment they walked into the kitchen, the cooks would gladly cut a slice for Velamir, the boy who did tasks for them without having to be asked, the boy who never requested a different food than the one they prepared. The boy who inquired about their welfare and families. They wouldn't be snatching any cake, they would take it in full sight of the cooks. But still, it sounded daring, as everything was when you were around Velamir.

Jax nodded with a grin. "Sounds like a plan."

Velamir held out his hand. "Brothers?"

Jax nodded, his smile large as he reached out to clasp Velamir's arm. "Brothers."

8

NATASSA
KARALIK EMPIRE
THE GRAND PALACE

NATASSA HEARD HER chamber door close and glanced over her canvas. Kasdeya came into view, her jaw dropping at the sight that met her eyes.

"A little help?" Krea asked, holding up two canvases.

Kasdeya rushed forward and assisted Krea, placing the canvases in the few empty spaces left in the room. There were paintings everywhere. Natassa returned to her canvas, continuing to work, although her motions were stilted and her eyes unfocused.

"How long has she been like this?" Kasdeya whispered.

"She was at it when I came," Krea

responded. "Where were you? You were gone the whole night."

Instead of responding, Kasdeya tidied the room, fluffing the pillows, picking up the used paint palettes lying around Natassa's vanity. When she reached for a fallen brush, Krea caught her hand and stared at her.

"Don't tell me you were with Thander."

Kasdeya tore her hand away. "So what if I was?"

Natassa's arm stilled in the middle of a stroke.

"You always warn me we are Natassa's bodyguards, that we must honor the rules set for us. That we don't have a choice in how we act." Krea was incredulous. "And yet the moment you catch the eye of one of Prince Honzio's personal guards, you've completely lost your senses."

"The last person who should speak about common sense is you," Kasdeya sneered. "You're constantly spouting poetry and happy tidings, trying to praise Natassa so she can hold you in good light."

Krea snapped back, "You told me yesterday how we had to act a certain way, and now you are doing as you wish."

Natassa looked up, catching Kasdeya roll her eyes. "Leave me alone."

"I won't, not until you promise me you will stay away from the captain, Deya." Krea's usually light and cheery voice was desperate.

Before they could say anything further, Natassa walked around her easel. They startled, seeing her attention on them. Kasdeya cleared her throat, her gaze uneasy.

"Prince Thorsten sent word. He's coming to see you."

Natassa nodded and wondered if she should ask Kasdeya about the captain she was apparently fascinated with. But when she saw Kasdeya's guarded expression, she brushed her questions aside. She could ask her when she was ready to answer.

"I will meet him in the hall," Natassa said after glancing around her room. "I don't want him to see this."

"What is *this*?" Kasdeya asked, staring at all the newly painted canvases.

"A gift," Natassa said simply and attempted to fix her flyaway hairs.

She held up the mirror that rested on her vanity, peering at the dark circles under her eyes that spoke of a sleepless night. Her skin was waxen and pale, and the braid Krea had done for her the day before was coming undone. Thick strands of hair had escaped it, framing her face. Natassa's lips spread in a small smile. It was no wonder people thought she was sick.

When she walked out of her chamber, she instructed Krea to stay behind and guard her door alongside the other royal guards.

"Don't allow anyone in," she told her and walked down the hall with Kasdeya. Before she turned into the next corridor, she stopped, hearing raised voices.

"The emperor deems it so," said a nasally voice that could bore a person to death. Natassa sighed in annoyance. Advisor Kostos wasn't taking his duties lightly.

"Did he also deem it wise to harass me in the hall? You know I'm not a man to be trifled with." That was Thorsten speaking.

Advisor Kostos made a noise of protest. "But of course not, Your Highness. He simply wanted me to inform you not to leave the palace, especially in the late hours."

"Now that you have imparted his words, you may go."

Natassa waited to hear his footsteps retreating, but it seemed Kostos would not be deterred. "I can only imagine how you are feeling, returning to Hearcross to inform us of such a heavy loss." She could hear the gleeful smile in his tone. "You have my sympathies."

"We fought hard to retain the Borderlands," Thorsten replied, "almost as hard as you fought to keep your seat as head advisor. I should congratulate you. I was surprised Advisor Destin lost."

"We are close friends, Destin and I," Advisor Kostos said. "It was a friendly competition."

"So, the fact that your daughter eloped with his stable boy has changed nothing between you? I'm happy to hear that." Thorsten's laugh was low and harsh.

"My daughter is none of your concern, Your Highness," Kostos said through gritted teeth.

Natassa knew if she didn't act soon, the barbed words might become an actual attack. A sharp ache swept through her head, and she placed her fingers to her temple, closing her eyes with a grimace.

"Natassa?" Kasdeya asked, stepping closer.

Natassa shook her head. "I'm fine."

She dropped her hand and walked into the corridor.

"Thorsten!" she called. "I was looking for you! You know I've been wanting to speak to Father about something important and need you to come as well."

Both men turned her way. Thorsten seemed confused and Kostos alarmed.

"Ah, Advisor." She nodded at him. "I didn't see you there. You seem to have forgotten our agreement."

He mumbled, his brow furrowing, "I don't recall—"

She angled her head and he stuttered to a stop when she tilted her lips in what Thorsten once called her intimidating smirk.

The advisor attempted to smile, but it came out stiff. "If you will excuse me?" At their nods, he flicked his cloak and strode away.

"What was that about?" Thorsten asked as soon as the advisor was out of earshot.

"Nothing." Natassa shrugged.

He shook his head in amazement. "It astounds me how you do that."

"What?"

"The way they react to you and listen." He sighed. "I have tried many times to emulate you, but it never works."

Natassa laughed. "It takes practice, I guess." She motioned to her handmaiden. "Kasdeya said you wanted to see me?"

Thorsten nodded and stepped forward, placing his hands on her arms. "I heard you nearly fell off the balcony during the meeting with Draven. What happened? How are you?"

"I'm fine," Natassa assured him, hoping to dispel the worry in his eyes. "In fact, I have good news. Mother's illness didn't pass on to me."

A smile grew on Thorsten's face. "That is amazing

news!" He hugged her. "I can't explain how relieved I am to hear that."

"I am too," Natassa admitted and focused on him. "Did you save the Savorian?"

He glanced around and spoke in a lowered tone. "I did. Aylis is tough. She was almost out of her captors' grasp by the time I arrived." He winced. "But she was wounded in the escape."

"Is there anything I can do to help?"

"I'm glad you asked. Did you receive any new tonics?"

"Yes," Natassa affirmed. "One for pain and a few others for headaches."

"We are going to need all you can send."

Natassa's eyes widened. "How badly was she hurt?"

"There's a deep slice in her arm. She's being cauterized in the shelter as we speak."

Natassa grimaced at the thought. "How will we get it to her? Have you found our ally?"

"He was killed, Natassa. I suspect it was Father's work. He had him captured last week and interrogated him, but our ally didn't say a word about the shelter. He sacrificed his life for our cause."

Natassa closed her eyes. "His pain is no longer, his glory remembered."

Thorsten nodded, his grief evident. "He was a good man." After a long pause, he continued, "I would go myself with the tonics, but I cannot so soon after I returned. Father suspects I am up to something. He will know for sure if I persist in leaving."

"What shall we do?"

"Graga," Thorsten said and then waited as a guard

walked past them, making his rotations. "She can deliver it."

"Are you sure we can trust her?"

"We don't have many options. She knows some of the Savorians. She will get it to one of them, and they can bring it to Aylis."

Natassa nodded, agreeing to the plan. "I will deliver it to her right away." She glanced at Kasdeya, who was lingering behind her. "Retrieve the tonics."

Kasdeya inclined her head and hurried back to Natassa's chamber.

"The library should be empty, so you will be able to give it to her without witnesses." Thorsten handed her a pouch of gold. "For her silence."

Natassa slipped it into the hidden pocket stitched in her skirt. "Is it that early?"

The only time the library was without visitors was in the early mornings. Thorsten nodded and grimaced at the sight of something behind her.

"Gavin is coming," he informed her. "I need to be on my way. Good luck with your mission." He winked.

Natassa smiled and waved him off. He strode away as fast as he could.

Gavin passed her a moment later, calling out, "Your Highness, Prince Thorsten!"

Natassa walked to the library. Kasdeya stepped into her place behind her when she had nearly reached the double doors.

"I brought the tonics," Kasdeya whispered, holding out a sack.

Natassa rummaged through them and took the

strongest one out, planning to give it to Graga with instructions. When they reached the doors, Natassa was surprised to see it was devoid of guards.

"Strange," she muttered at the oddity.

"Let me check inside," Kasdeya offered, but Natassa shook her head.

"Stay here, I will call if needed."

With the potent tonic vial in one hand and the sack containing the rest in the other, she entered the library. It was quiet, Natassa noticed, more quiet than she'd expected. There were no pages flipping or footsteps. The lighting was dim, and fewer candles were lit. She stood by the doors for a moment, breathing in the scent of books. A sense of calm surrounded her heart. When she was little, her tutors would try to engrave proper ladylike etiquette into her behavior. She had tired of it and would run away to the library. There was a small closet near the back where she would hide. The smell of books would stay with her for hours as she waited for her tutors to give up searching. The library was her safe place.

She walked toward the back, where the librarian's bureau stood. Her brow creased when she saw Graga wasn't there. Distant voices met her ears, and she walked farther. The voices came nearer, and she realized they must be a few bookshelves away. She had almost reached them when a hand encircled her wrist and jerked her to the side. Natassa stumbled, managing to keep hold of the sack, and opened her mouth to cry out. The hand released her wrist and lifted to her mouth, stifling her protest. She peered through the dimness and, with a start, realized it was Honzio.

He dropped his hand from her mouth and lifted a finger to his lips in a gesture of silence. Natassa nodded in confirmation and attempted to steady her galloping heart. As her eyes adjusted to the gloom, her ears focused on the voices.

"Are you sure there's no one here?"

"Very. I sent them all out along with the librarian. No one can disobey the orders of a prince." The second voice was smooth and condescending. Prince Draven.

"That better be true. I was assigned here by my betters, and if you make a stupid decision, I will pay for it."

Draven laughed. "You could disappear before anyone catches you. Isn't that what Chishmans are known for?"

A wave of fear crashed through Natassa. Chishma. The Chishmans were Prolus's phantoms, stalkers of the night, killers of kings, destroyers of kingdoms. How was one in the palace? She tried to steady herself, but she was shaking.

"What is your next move?" the Chishman asked instead of answering Draven's question.

"My father is a fool. I can remove him if I wish, but for now, he can keep his throne. My brother is dead, so he's out of the way."

Shock poured over her at the way Draven spoke about *removing* his father as if he were contemplating going on a picnic. She glanced at Honzio. His lips were pressed in a thin line, and his eyes focused on the cracks between the shelves, trying to glimpse the prince and his companion.

"The princess then?"

A deep chuckle followed that. "She is very delicate, weaker than I thought."

It took Natassa a moment to realize he was speaking of her—after all, Ayleth had no princesses. Anger coursed through her.

"She bears no threat to me. I will marry her, and once she gives me an heir, I will handle her."

Natassa's grip on the sack and vial tightened, and she glanced at Honzio again, noticing his jaw was clenched. So, he had a heart, then.

"We need to remove the brothers. It's the only way I can take the Empire."

Natassa couldn't hold back the small gasp that escaped her. Her suspicions about him were correct. He was after the throne. Honzio reached out, placing a hand on her shoulder in silent comfort or perhaps as a signal to remain quiet. Natassa would never know with him.

"Hesten was easy, but the others will be more complicated. They have bodyguards that follow them like a second skin."

Hesten was easy.

The words ricocheted through Natassa's mind. It had been Draven who issued the order. Draven had aligned with Prolus and used a Chishman assassin to kill her eldest brother. They thought they had been holding Tariqi back at the Borderlands, but Prolus's reach was already in the heart of the Empire. She felt numb. Her hand shook, and before she knew what was happening, the vial fell from her fingers, shattering into millions of tiny pieces.

9

VELAMIR
TARIQI
KALEA FORTRESS
CHISHMAN ACADEMY

VELAMIR RAN A brush over Vandal's mane. "Good boy."

He stopped grooming for a moment, and Vandal nickered, lowering his head and giving his mane a playful shake. Velamir chuckled and resumed brushing, the cross ties holding Vandal in place. Not that Vandal would move. As all lancer horses were bred for their distinct connection traits, Vandal was very obedient to Velamir.

Velamir returned the brush to its place and stepped before Vandal, smiling when his horse nudged him, searching for a hidden treat. Velamir reached into his pocket, probing for the sugar cube. He lifted it, and Vandal's muzzle tickled his hand, his soft breath brushing Velamir's skin as he snatched the sugar cube off his palm. Velamir eyed the irregular blaze that ran down Vandal's face. It fell in a crooked line, reminding Velamir of his own scar. Velamir's hand went to his neck, his finger trailing his scar while his other hand drew upward against Vandal's blaze.

"We are the same, you and I," Velamir whispered.

Vandal's ears pricked forward, listening. His head ducked down, sniffing for more treats. Velamir remembered how distraught he had been when he separated from Vandal. It was one reason he hadn't wanted to come to the academy. But then one morning, before classes, Velamir heard a loud clamor from the entrance of the academy. When he went out, he saw all the cadets murmuring among themselves. The Chishmans tried to bring the situation under control. Velamir saw Vandal standing in the middle of the entryway, his bay coloring shimmering despite the dark sky. His head tossed when he caught sight of Velamir, throwing his thick mane into the air. A Chishma who had brought the horse on behalf of Winston tried to control Vandal, gripping the lead rope. Vandal broke out of his hold and trotted to Velamir. Velamir met him halfway, wrapping his arms around his neck. The Chishma had given Velamir a note written in Winston's hand.

My stable is destroyed. He must have been looking for you.

Velamir chuckled in recollection of the letter as he threw a saddle over Vandal. He removed the cross ties and finished bridling him. The academy horses stared from their stalls, their hooves clomping as they moved between their food pails and looked around nosily.

Velamir mounted Vandal, urging him forward with the press of his legs. The test was nearing. Velamir had been released from his studies, along with Jax, Lissa, and Quintus. *Practice*, Chishma Wernis had instructed them, giving them time to work on what they wished.

Velamir decided to go riding to clear his mind, although he was sure horsemanship skills would not be a part of the test. The test didn't worry him as much as what came after. The cadets who became Chishmans together were bonded until death. Velamir wasn't sure he wanted to be stuck with Lissa or Quintus for that long.

He rode Vandal to the academy entrance, and the Chishmans stationed there gave him a brief nod before they opened the gates. Velamir dipped his head in acknowledgment and nudged Vandal into a canter, passing through. He rode past the shadowy trees and darkened caves until he reached the top of a hill. He dismounted, holding Vandal's reins in his hand, and stared at the view.

"Curious, isn't it?" Velamir said to Vandal. "I want Prolus to conquer the Empire to prevent more innocent lives from being taken. But if Tariqi invades, won't we be causing more bloodshed? Won't we be creating more orphans? Won't we be doing the very thing we are fighting to stop?"

The silent wind brushed his face as he stared at the broken-down town and crumbling castle in the distance. Something seemed to weigh on his hip and he glanced down, staring at the new sword hanging from his belt.

He touched the wolf's head with his fingers, lingering on the crown. A strange feeling overcame him. The same feeling he had felt when Frumgan had given it to him and when he'd held the sword in his dream. Velamir drew the blade, his reflection staring back at him.

"Velamir!" a voice called, *her* voice, the woman he had been hearing in his dreams.

"Help me." The whisper brushed his ear, and he spun wildly, searching.

The wind grew hungry, snatching at the overlarge leafless trees and tearing at the dying grass. Strands of Velamir's hair blew into his eyes, blocking his view. He pushed his hair back as the crunch of boots drew his attention. Lissa approached him, one of the academy horse's reins fastened to a tree at the bottom of the hill. He sheathed his sword.

"It's going to rain," she said as she neared.

"It always does," Velamir responded.

"I'm glad we found time to talk." She reached out to touch his arm, but Velamir moved away, closer to Vandal, his motion so smooth, she probably thought he hadn't seen her try to touch him.

"When you looked at me as you left the stables, I knew it was a signal to follow you."

Velamir frowned. "I didn't see you at all."

Lissa rolled her eyes and stepped closer to him. "Sure," she said. "So . . . why did General Winston choose you?"

"What do you mean?"

"The other cadets. They wonder how you could have been so lucky. Sometimes, I even see the mentors looking at you with a question in their eyes." Lissa stopped when she stood mere inches from him, the mist darkening her purple eyes to a color resembling black.

"Why are you so fascinated with what they think of me?"

She laughed, light and amused. "Because you are my task, Velamir."

"I don't know what you're talking about."

Lissa's lips formed a half smile. "Then let me explain. My father and the general have a strong friendship. When the general sent you, he didn't trust the academy to keep you safe. But he trusted my father, and who does my father rely on?"

When Velamir didn't reply, she waved a hand at herself.

"Me. Who do you think had your back all those times the other cadets were bullying you?" She leaned in. "But there was a problem. I didn't know I would fall for you."

At Velamir's alarmed expression, she spoke faster. "I couldn't allow anyone to hurt you. You became my obsession. When you stalked down the hall to check on Jax, I had been sitting by the boys' dormitory door, waiting, watching for you. I heard them beating Jax, but I waited for you, because I wanted to see you, and I wanted you to see me helping you."

"You allowed them to beat Jax? Don't you know how much he cared about you? How could you do something like that?"

Velamir turned to Vandal in disgust, his hands reaching for the pommel of the saddle. Before he could mount up, Lissa grabbed hold of his arm, her long nails digging into his sleeve, piercing his skin.

"This isn't about Jax. This is about you and me."

Velamir shook her hand off. "That doesn't exist."

She scoffed. "Are you telling me everything I did for you was for nothing? I killed for you, Velamir! My first kill was for you!"

Velamir panicked as her voice became hysterical. He was alone with this woman who had lost her senses.

"What are you talking about?"

"Kisto!" she screamed and swallowed a sob. The wind snatched her hood back, whipping through strands of black hair.

Velamir's blood froze. That name never left him. It lingered over his head as though Kisto had returned to haunt him.

"I killed him, Velamir, a young boy." She sank to her knees in the lifeless soil. Her hands gripped the limp grass. "I plucked his eyes out. I thought he didn't deserve them if he could only see the worst in people."

It chilled Velamir to the bone, hearing her words. All these years, people had blamed him, and he had said nothing to refute their claims. He had taken the burden on his shoulders.

"I killed him . . ." Lissa sobbed, her face angled to the ground. "I killed him for you."

Velamir dropped to one knee and placed his hands on her shoulders. "Get up, Lissa. You made a mistake. Everyone does."

The wind whipped their hair, and Lissa's black locks mixed with Velamir's brown ones. Her head snapped up, and Velamir almost stumbled back at the sight of her bloodshot eyes. There was hate there, and any sign of remorse was gone.

"You said we don't have a chance together. That everything I did for you was for nothing. Hear me now, Velamir." She got to her feet, and Velamir dropped his hands. "If we don't pass that test, if we don't become bonded as Chishmans, I will make your life so miserable that you will wish you were as dead as Kisto."

Then she turned and walked back down the hill, mounting the horse she had come with, cloak billowing in the gust. As the horse's hooves thundered away, Velamir winced. They sounded like drums announcing his doom.

10

NATASSA
KARALIK EMPIRE
THE GRAND PALACE

NATASSA REACHED FOR Honzio's arm. He moved without resistance as she pulled him to the back of the library.

"Who's there!" Draven called.

She heard a curse and racing feet and knew it was only moments before Draven caught them. She spotted the closet ahead of her and ran faster. Natassa opened the door and shoved Honzio inside before stumbling in herself. She closed it softly, leaving it open just a crack. The bag full of tonics rested in her fist. She leaned forward, pressing her eye to the crack. Draven came into view. He was staring at the bookshelves several feet away from the closet.

His companion approached him. He was wearing the disguise the Chishmans were known for, the fabric of his clothes specially made to blend with the background. Natassa wouldn't have known he was there if he had been wearing a mask. His face was slim, with a black mustache and dark hair flopping over his forehead. The Chishma held up a shard.

"Glass," he said.

Draven cursed again. "Someone was here."

The mustached man lifted a mask made of the same fabric over his face, obscuring it from view. "We should leave."

Draven shook his head. "We must find the sneak first, or he will tell everyone what we spoke of."

The Chishma's voice was agitated. "We've been here too long. Someone is bound to come, and what explanation will we give them?"

A storm brewed in Draven's face, and it continued darkening with every word the man said.

"We will look," Draven bit out and proceeded to search the library. The Chishma hesitated but followed his lead.

Natassa tried to even her rapid breaths. The closet was smaller than she remembered, but then again, for a child, everything looked large. Honzio crowded the space, leaving her little room. She kept watch through the crack. Draven glanced in their direction a few times but never inspected the closet. After a long while of searching, the Chishma finally convinced him.

"They probably escaped into the hall while we were searching for them. We are losing precious time."

Draven nodded. "Perhaps. Let's search the hall."

Natassa closed her eyes, fingers tightening as she

thought of them encountering Kasdeya by the door. After Draven and the Chishma left, Honzio reached out to open the closet. Natassa grabbed his arm.

"Wait," she whispered. "It might be a trap to lure us out."

He nodded in silent acknowledgment. Natassa noticed a sheen of sweat coating his forehead and felt a slight tremble in his form.

"Honzio?"

"I'm fine," he said through gritted teeth. "Just not fond of confined spaces."

They waited in the closet until Natassa said, "Draven is planning to kill you and Thorsten. We must tell Father."

"Father suspected him of such ruthlessness."

Natassa scoffed. "And he was going to make me marry him."

"That was the entire plan. You marry him so he would be subjected to our rule and not get any ideas. So we could keep Ayleth under our thumb."

Natassa stared at him. "And you approved of this plan?"

"Of course I didn't. That's why I'm here. I've been following him for a while. I've heard enough to know that a marriage will not deter him. He won't be satisfied until he rules the Empire."

"Then we must stop him."

"Father will still attempt an alliance. He will sacrifice anything if it means he stays on the throne," Honzio told her. There was a bitterness to his voice. As if he hated what the emperor did. It surprised Natassa.

"We must do something. Draven is allied with Prolus, Honzio. Who knows how much power he has with the Dark Lord on his side."

"I will take care of it." Honzio opened the closet door, inhaling a sharp breath. "We've waited long enough."

Natassa stepped out and glanced around. When no one jumped at her, she brushed the closet dust off her dress.

"Why did you come to the library?"

Natassa looked back at him, moving the tonic bag behind her skirt. Honzio's eyes flashed to it, and she knew he had seen it.

"I wanted to speak with Graga," Natassa said.

"And who is that?" Honzio raised a brow.

"The librarian. As crown prince, you should at least know the names of the people in the palace," Natassa admonished.

Honzio shrugged. "I don't see why. They are beneath me. They do their job, and that is all I will acknowledge."

Natassa didn't even know why disappointment filled her. She had already known what Honzio had become after years of their father molding him into himself.

"They are your people, and their lives are important. You cannot treat them as though they are rubbish to be tossed aside."

Honzio grumbled under his breath, ignoring her words. "We're late. A few nobles have already arrived for Father's party. Father decided to host a grand breakfast for them."

Natassa breathed in, attempting to be patient with him. "Then we better get going."

Honzio didn't respond. He started walking to the library doors. Natassa huffed to herself. *So, he's back to the silent treatment.* When they exited the library, Natassa expected to see Kasdeya waiting in the hall, but she was nowhere in sight.

"Natassa!" someone called, and she turned to see Kasdeya rushing to her.

"You shouldn't allow them to call you by your name," Honzio advised.

Natassa lifted her chin. "It's a choice for me to make, and it's not like we are in public."

"This is a public palace hall. Anyone could be lurking in the shadows." He gave her a meaningful look and turned away, heading to the throne room where the breakfast was being held.

Natassa turned back to her handmaiden. Kasdeya was breathing fast.

"I apologize, Natassa, but the emperor sent word that he expects you in the throne room. I had to retrieve one of your new dresses from the seamstress."

"Did you see anyone leaving the library?" Natassa asked.

Kasdeya shook her head. "No. I left a few minutes after you entered."

Natassa smiled in relief, glad that Draven hadn't spotted her. Kasdeya eyed her with confusion, but Natassa spoke before she could. "I need you to do something for me."

She handed the bag of tonics to Kasdeya along with the coin purse Thorsten had given her. "Give this to Graga." And then in a quiet tone she told Kasdeya to explain the situation to Graga and have her deliver the tonics to a Savorian. Kasdeya spun away, searching for Graga, while Natassa returned to her chamber.

As soon as she walked inside, Krea was bursting with excitement. She undid Natassa's dress and brought out the new one Kasdeya must have been speaking about.

"Isn't it beautiful?" she gushed.

Natassa stepped into it, and Krea pulled it up. Natassa slipped her hands into the sleeves. The dress felt airy. The sleeves hung in loose flares around her wrists. Natassa felt as though she could take flight. She wished she could.

Krea rubbed oil into her hair, and Natassa breathed in the ovaline scent that reminded her of her mother. She glanced at Krea through the mirror and noticed thick gloves over her hands. Krea caught her gaze and flexed her fingers.

"I started wearing these because I've had a strange irritation when I apply the oil. I must be allergic."

Natassa was immediately concerned. "Don't use the oil any longer. Purchase a new scent."

Krea protested. "Natassa, it's nothing, really. It might not even be the oil."

Natassa tried to convince her, but Krea wouldn't hear it. Her decoy continued working on her. She twisted her hair into an elegant bun, adding butterfly clips for extra dazzling effect. All the while, Natassa stared at her lap, thinking over Draven's words.

"You look beautiful." Krea smiled, lifting Natassa's chin to look into the vanity mirror.

Natassa stared at herself and saw a tired, confused

girl trying to play the part of a princess. Krea grabbed the back of the dress, taking hold of the laces. Kasdeya entered, nodding at Natassa, telling her without speaking that she had completed her mission.

"The Ondalarians have come!" Krea informed Natassa, trying to make conversation. She was never one who could stand silence.

Natassa sucked in a breath when Krea tightened the laces. "They always come."

"But they usually send one envoy to convey their respects. This time, General Zenrelius has arrived with a few of his men." The way she whispered the general's name in such an awe-filled tone made Natassa glance at her through the mirror.

Kasdeya's brows shot up in amusement. She stood behind them, ready to assist Krea. "You should have heard what Lady Flivane said about him. She was quizzing me on war tactics a few days ago, and every example she gave was about him." She changed her tone and lifted her shoulders in imitation of Lady Flivane. "He is the very epitome of manliness."

An unladylike snort burst from Natassa. "Did she really say that?"

Kasdeya nodded in confirmation, and Krea giggled. "Lady Flivane is silly, but one cannot help but admit admiration for the general. I mean, he is possibly the only reason the Empire still stands."

Natassa muttered, "I wish Prince Draven could hear those words. Maybe he would stop being so arrogant."

"And that guard, Captain Thander, he should hear it so he learns he's not the only man in existence," Krea added.

Kasdeya sniffed. "Leave it alone, Krea."

Krea stepped toward her sister, and Kasdeya followed her movement. They looked ready to tear each other to pieces. Natassa held up her hands.

"That's enough."

They froze and looked at her with guilty expressions.

"We can discuss this at another time. But for now, I'm late to the breakfast."

Krea nodded in agreement, and Kasdeya looked away, annoyance still marking her face. Natassa turned and strode from her chamber. She continued to the throne room, knowing her handmaidens would follow her, as they always did. But she could not help but wonder, how far would loyalty go?

Emperor Malus bestowed a vicious glare upon Natassa when his eyes landed on her. Natassa glanced away from him, scanning the crowded throne room. The view was not much better. A sharp ache stabbed her mind seeing the bright purple Draven's entourage was wearing. Ayleth was like that, colorful and never-ending parties, distractions to curtain the darkness within its leaders. She sat at the head table beside Honzio and across from Thorsten. Her head spun when she caught sight of Draven a few seats down, on the opposite side of the table speaking with a noble lady from Ondalar. His gaze met Natassa's and his smile fell, his eyes narrowing into something that looked like suspicion. Did he think she had been in the library?

Natassa swallowed the bile rising in her throat and

tore her gaze away. She touched her head, a gesture that was becoming painfully regular, and closed her eyes. *Stay calm*, she told herself. Something bumped her arm, and she glanced at Honzio.

"What are you doing?" he asked her.

His expression wasn't concerned but wary. He looked past her at their father. She knew what he was thinking. *A Hartinza never loses their composure.* It was a stern command from their father. Honzio gestured to the plate before her.

"Eat something."

He turned away, and she stared down at the intricate breakfast the cooks had prepared. The thought of taking another bite made her want to heave. She stood, fearing she would lose the contents of her stomach should she stay a moment longer. Honzio pretended not to notice her exit, and Thorsten tilted his head in question. She shook hers, but he still watched. *There* was the concern that was missing in Honzio. It reflected in Thorsten's eyes. Natassa glanced at her father. Emperor Malus was too busy laughing with a nobleman to pay her any mind.

She walked to one of the side tables where goblets of freshly squeezed juice and pitchers of water rested. Natassa reached for a glass of water and drank, hoping to remove the dryness in her throat. A hand landed on her shoulder, and she turned, befuddled to see one of the Ondalarian guards. She set her glass down and faced him.

"Can I help you?" she asked.

He leered, his uniform revealing him as a lower-ranked guard. What was he doing in the throne room? Her gaze slid behind him to the open door that led to the hall. At least six goblets crowded a window ledge in the hall. Not only had he snuck in, but he was drunk on zat as well.

"Let's dance," he slurred, grabbing hold of her hand.

Natassa snatched her hand out of his. "You are not in your right mind. Leave me be."

The man wrapped his arm around her waist and drew her to him. Natassa pushed against him, overcome by the heavy scent of zat on his breath. He was ripped away from her. Natassa turned, expecting to see her bodyguards, but was alarmed to see Thorsten. He shoved the man into a pillar.

"Stay away from my sister!" Thorsten's chest heaved.

Natassa looked past him to see Krea and Kasdeya wincing at the spectacle he'd made. *Oh, Thorsten.*

He should have let her handmaidens handle it. They knew how to be discreet. The people at the breakfast table and lower tables hushed, all eyes on the scene. Thorsten stared at the man, death in his eyes. Someone stepped in front of him. A tall man in his forties, with neatly combed black hair, a well-groomed beard, and intelligent eyes.

"I apologize, Your Highness." He bowed his head in respect to Thorsten and then to Natassa. "He will be disciplined."

"A man like that shouldn't be here. If you can't control your own guard, why bother showing up? It hardly equals respect if you don't know the meaning of the word."

Shocked whispers flew around the room. Natassa knew who he was before she heard the murmurs of his name. Zenrelius, the general of Ondalar.

The general's cheek flexed in response to Thorsten's insults. The drunk man lifted himself off the pillar and rushed forward with a roar, intending to strike Thorsten. Natassa opened her mouth to cry out a warning, but her voice failed her. In lightning-fast movements, Zenrelius unsheathed a dagger and thrust it behind him without looking. It stabbed the man in the chest, and he wheezed. Zenrelius yanked the dagger out without hesitation, not even blinking at the blood that streamed onto his hand. The drunk Ondalarian collapsed like a sack of rocks. Zenrelius flicked his dagger down with mastered efficiency, returning the blood coating it to its owner.

The silence was as heavy and still as a graveyard.

"He won't bother you again," Zenrelius said and motioned for the palace guards at their posts to remove the body. "All is well. Settle down," he told the horrified guests.

As his eyes scanned over them, tension seemed to release from their bodies. Some of them even nodded and smiled. When Zenrelius's gaze reached her, he stopped, searching for something. Natassa stared back. His eyes appeared black and as deadly as his dagger. His brow creased as he continued looking at her. Her father broke the connection when he stood from the head seat, anger seeping from him.

"Everyone is dismissed!" he shouted and turned furious eyes on Thorsten. "I will see you in my chamber."

Thorsten stiffened, and Natassa stared, horror filling her, because once again someone would suffer because of her.

11

VELAMIR
TARIQI
KALEA FORTRESS
CHISHMA ACADEMY

"WHAT ARE A Chishma's three strengths?" Velamir listened intently, turning in circles as he tried to pinpoint Talon's location based on the sound of his voice. The blindfold tied across his face bit into his nose. Velamir held his hands out before him, as a sightless man would.

"Sense, speed, sight," Velamir replied.

"Very good." Talon continued, "Now, in order to pass the first part of the test, you must avoid Chishma Jyorm's blows. If he lands a hit on you three times, you fail the test."

Velamir squashed the nervous feeling within him. He inhaled the musty smell of the arena, reminding himself of the drills he had done repeatedly over the years.

"Begin."

Velamir listened for Jyorm but couldn't hear him. He moved left and right, his boots shifting on the dirt floor. The punch came from nowhere, straight into Velamir's nose. Velamir grunted, pain shooting through his face. Blood trickled from his nostril and trailed over his lips. He wiped it away.

"Two more chances," Talon announced.

Velamir tried to steady himself and pay closer attention, but Jyorm got him again, this time with a hard blow to his stomach. Velamir groaned, the contents of his stomach swirling, fighting to come back up.

"One last chance."

I can't do this, Velamir thought, panic rising as he circled wildly, blind to his surroundings.

Breathe, Velamir.

It was Winston's voice echoing in his head from when he was twelve years old. When the Borderlands had prevented them from entering Tariqi and they had gone through the underground tunnels to reach the academy.

Breathe.

Velamir stopped moving. His thoughts trailed away, and he simply listened. The air shifted to his left, signaling Jyorm's presence. Velamir stepped to the side, and less than a moment later, he felt a whoosh of air across his face.

Jyorm stumbled, and Velamir could sense him retaliating. Velamir dropped, and a loud grunt sounded as Chishma Jyorm's punch sailed over his head. Velamir avoided four more of Jyorm's strikes. Jyorm brushed near him, and Velamir reached out, grasping Jyorm's arm and twisting it until he cried out.

"That's enough," Talon barked. "Remove the blindfold."

Velamir released him and pulled off the blindfold. He blinked a few times to focus as everything came back into view. Jyorm stood before him, holding his arm, wincing as he shook it out. Talon was standing near the observation seats, where the Head Chishma and other mentors watched. Lissa sat in an extra chair behind them. She had been the first to be tested.

"Now you must face the second part of the test," Talon told him.

Talon called out sharp commands, and a few Chishmans rushed to them from the corners of the arena. At Talon's order, the Chishmans set two heavy bricks a foot apart and placed a block of metal over them.

"We borrowed the metal from Frumgan per the Head Chishma's request. His Doers were experimenting with it, enhancing it. Frumgan said it's not likely to cave under any pressure. Shall we prove him wrong?" Talon approached him, holding out a hammer.

Velamir accepted it and held it lightly, feeling its weight. He glanced at the metal. "It's derinium, isn't it?"

Talon was taken aback for a second. He appraised Velamir and nodded. "Yes, it is derinium. You will need speed for this one." He gave Velamir a thin smile and gestured to the metal. "When you are ready."

Velamir approached it, his fingers clenched around the hammer's handle. His shoulders tensed as he lifted his arm and, with a brutal swing, brought it down. It smacked into the metal, but the derinium did not budge. Velamir continued swinging without pause, and soon his strength faltered. For a moment it seemed as if the metal wavered, the center of it lowering farther than the sides, creating a bowl shape. Velamir smiled, sensing victory close at hand. He pounded harder. But then the metal reshaped itself back into a solid block. Velamir stared in astonishment. His breath released in heavy pants, and sweat poured down his face.

The Head Chishma spoke, his voice loud enough to reach Velamir's ears. "I was right. He's not ready. He's not good enough."

The words were sour, and Velamir recoiled inwardly, feeling as though he had a healing wound and someone had cut open the stitches binding it together. Anger replaced the pain, and Velamir faced the derinium again. A renewed vigor filled his bones as his strikes rocketed with the swiftness of the fire in his veins. Sweat dripped from his hair into his eyes, the saltiness stinging his vision, but he didn't stop. Perspiration filled his shirt, and it clung to him like the hot anger burning inside. *He's not good enough.*

"Velamir!" he heard someone shout and realized they had been calling his name for a while.

He lowered his hammer, shock sweeping through him when he saw that not only had he crushed the derinium to pieces, but he had also destroyed the bricks. He glanced at Talon, who was watching him with a new level of caution. Velamir's heart beat rapidly. He tossed the hammer aside.

"Do I pass your test?" he asked, a hint of sarcasm entering his tone.

Talon cleared his throat and expression before saying, "You have one more."

Velamir didn't think the next part of the test could be worse than the one he just did.

"Retrieve Cadet Jaxon!" Talon called out.

When Jax came in, his gaze found Velamir's, and he raised his brows in question. Velamir looked away.

"Bring him before the target," Talon ordered Chishma Jyorm.

"What!" Jax sputtered.

Jyorm pulled Jax to the large target across from Velamir on the other end of the arena. Jax followed Jyorm's lead, although he protested the whole way. After telling Jax to stand in front of the target, Chishma Jyorm moved back.

Talon stepped beside Velamir, extending a bow. "Your final test. You must shoot the three red circles on the target."

The three red circles that happened to be very close to Jax's head.

"Sight," Velamir muttered.

Talon nodded. "Sight."

12

NATASSA
KARALIK EMPIRE
THE GRAND PALACE

NATASSA CLOSED HER eyes, enjoying how the brush felt against her hair. *You have beautiful hair, Natassa*, her mother would say as she combed it back. Krea rubbed oil into her gloved hands, and the scent permeated the air. Natassa inhaled as Krea massaged it into her hair. Kasdeya brought decorative hair ribbons over, placing them on the vanity.

"Your father sent a note with a servant this morning urging you to get a haircut," Kasdeya told her.

"A simple braid," she instructed Krea. And then she replied to Kasdeya, "He will likely chop it off himself soon."

She expected Kasdeya to laugh, but her handmaiden seemed somber. Krea finished the braid and pulled it forward so it fell over Natassa's shoulder, landing in the silken fold of her nightgown. Natassa fiddled with ends of her hair. It was not a popular style in the Empire. Women had shoulder-length cuts, and the men wore their hair short, shaved close to their head.

"I can't believe Prince Thorsten threw himself into that situation," Kasdeya said, shaking her head.

Natassa pressed her lips together. She had been trying to block the memory, but now she saw it again. The drunk man advancing on her, Thorsten pushing him.

"General Zenrelius saved the day," Krea said with a dreamy smile.

Kasdeya rolled her eyes. "And I thought Lady Flivane was the one in love with him."

Krea scoffed. "I was just stating a fact." She glanced into the mirror and saw the stricken look on Natassa's face. "We should have stopped him before Thorsten. I'm sorry."

"I want to be alone," Natassa said.

The twins exchanged troubled glances before bowing to her and entering the room attached to Natassa's chamber. Natassa released a heavy sigh and stood. She stepped onto her balcony and watched the setting sun. She attempted not to think about how her father would punish Thorsten. Emperor Malus told her she wasn't allowed to leave her chamber unless he called for her, but she found she couldn't stay still without knowing how her brother was.

She retreated into her chamber and changed into one of the twins' gray dresses, tucking her braid into the dress before pulling some hair out to rest at her shoulders in the impression of a short cut. She opened her chamber door and strode out. The guards didn't stop her, just as she hoped. Natassa moved through the halls, only spotting the occasional guard making their rounds. When she reached her father's chamber, she hesitated before the doors. Two of his personal guards stood before her, their faces expressionless. When she tried to walk in, they blocked the door. She lifted her chin and stared them down.

"I have something about the princess to report to the emperor."

They eyed her and traded a glance before allowing her through. She swept into the room, surprised they had permitted her in so easily. The moment the door closed, a piercing sting thudded in her head. Natassa grimaced and touched her temple, praying the headache would relieve soon.

The lounge room was empty. She eyed the two side doors and moved to the one on the right. As she came closer, she heard a raised voice.

"I told you many times! Many times!"

"She is my sister. I will protect her no matter the cost."

Natassa reached for the door handle, her fingers shaking with fear for Thorsten.

She heard a bitter laugh, and her father said, "There will be a cost. There's a cost for everything." A pause. "Don't think of Natassa as your sister. She is a pawn to be bartered. She will be gone soon, and hopefully, so will your lousy attempts at playing the chivalrous hero."

Natassa's heart cracked at her father's careless words. It did not matter that she already knew what he thought of her. Hearing him say it made it ten times worse.

"She deserves acknowledgment, just like the rest of us," Thorsten shot back, anger brimming his tone.

"Look what she caused today. She created a rift with General Zenrelius, an important figure in our Empire. I would rather be rid of her than the filthy uncooperative Savorians!"

"Have you no heart? She is your daughter."

"I have no daughter," the emperor replied.

A silent sob burst past Natassa's lips. She pulled away from the door, attempting to contain her emotions as she left the room. Natassa moved through the halls blindly until she entered a chamber, realizing through her numbness that it was Thorsten's. It was plain, as was his liking, with drab wooden furnishings. The only decorations were paintings of jousters that she had done for him and his extra jousting equipment. Natassa spotted the burning fireplace in the corner of the chamber and drew close to it, hoping to warm her cold-pricked heart. As she approached, she saw a stack of wood and an axe resting near it. Beside the wood was a basket filled with supplies: bandages, dried meat, clothes.

They were for the shelter. Everything Thorsten did was selfless. He was trying to make a difference, and he was being punished for it. Tears burned Natassa's eyes and slipped down her cheeks. She didn't even attempt to wipe them away. She was tired of this oppression. Through the blurriness of her vision, she made out the shape of the axe. She picked it up gingerly.

She is a pawn to be bartered.

Natassa's hands clenched around the handle, and her jaw tightened. Tears continued to trail down her face.

I would rather be rid of her than the filthy, uncooperative Saviorians.

Natassa lifted the axe and smashed it into the wood. It stuck deeply, wood chips flying. She struggled to pull it out.

I have no daughter.

Natassa released a cry of anguish and shoved the axe. She fell to her knees, wrapping her arms around herself, her body racking with sobs. An image of her father holding a blazing orange knife flashed through her mind. It was shortly after her mother had died.

You are not one of them, he'd said and placed the edge against her head. She had screamed as it burned her birthmark, searing her skin. The Cadellion held her arms so she couldn't escape.

You are not one of them, he'd repeated and threw the knife away.

They'd left her burned, shaking and alone. Natassa's trembling hand lifted to her forehead, touching the scarred skin. It was small, but the pain it brought her when she remembered it was agonizing.

She didn't know how long she sat there when the door opened. Thorsten entered, limping to his bed with a grimace. He didn't notice her as he sank onto the mattress, leaning his head against the bedpost. His breathing was ragged, and his jaw clenched as he tried to fight his obvious pain.

"Thorsten," she whispered, and his eyes jerked open.

"What are you doing here?" He struggled to pull himself off the bed and approached her.

She noticed the blood soaking his shirt.

"What did he do to you?" Natassa exclaimed as he sat in front of her.

"Nothing I'm not used to." His voice was bitter.

"Stop defending me, Thor. I can't stand seeing your pain." Fresh tears sprung in her eyes.

"And I can't stand seeing yours." He reached out, wiping a stray droplet.

"Please, I can take care of myself," Natassa begged him.

Thorsten shook his head. "Even if I stopped looking out for you, Father wouldn't be satisfied. He knows I am doing charity work but doesn't know who I'm helping. He threatened me, but I won't give in."

"The supplies." Natassa motioned to the basket. "When did you have time to collect them?"

"After you went to the library. Were you able to get the tonic to Graga?"

Natassa explained what had happened in the library and ended with, "I told Kasdeya to give the bag of tonics to her. She informed me she had done so. The rest lies in Graga's hands."

"I hope it reaches Aylis."

Thorsten winced, and she reached for linen from a basket and tore a piece. Natassa placed it against his wound. He attempted to wave her off.

"It's only a few pricks. I will be fine."

Natassa gave him a disapproving look. "You should see a True Manos."

"I cannot. Word of Father's *methods* cannot get out."

Natassa's lips twisted in disgust. "Did Father order that?"

Thorsten nodded weakly. "He doesn't want the people to know."

"They already know, and if they don't, they guess. He is feared, Thorsten, feared." She changed the topic. "I have jewelry. I want you to bring it to the shelter."

"Why don't you come with me?"

Natassa gave him a brittle laugh. "As if I could."

"I was planning to take you knife throwing tomorrow, but we can go to the shelter instead."

"Father will be livid if he finds out."

"He won't."

Natassa contemplated the idea. "What about Gavin?"

"What about him?"

"He will trail you as usual," Natassa reminded him.

"I will do what I always do." Thorsten grinned. "Lose him."

13

VELAMIR
TARIQI
KALEA FORTRESS
CHISHMAN ACADEMY

"HIT HIM AND you fail. Miss the target and you fail." Talon's words were blunt.

Velamir took the bow from Talon. Jax stared at him from his position in front of the large target. His blue eyes were wide, and his curly hair appeared damp.

"This is the first part of your test," Talon called to Jax. "If you move, you will fail, even if you think the arrow will hit you, you must not move."

Jax swallowed and nodded in acknowledgment.

"I've never used this bow before. I am not sure of its capability. I might hit him," Velamir explained to Talon.

"I'm not looking for excuses. If you can't do it, then say so."

Velamir gritted his teeth and lifted the bow, reaching for an arrow that Jyorm provided. He nocked the arrow onto the string and pulled back.

"Vel!" Jax called to him. "You heard the Chishma. I can't move, so make sure you don't kill me."

A thin, humorless smile pulled at Velamir's lips. "You know I never miss!" he called back. *Mostly*, he thought.

Velamir kept his stance wide and feet planted firmly. He released the arrow, and it smacked into the target half an inch beside Jax's cheek. Velamir could see Jax's throat bob as the arrow thudded beside him. Jax composed himself, though his face was pale.

Chishma Jyorm checked the target and nodded in affirmation. "He hit the red."

Talon turned to Velamir. "Next one."

Velamir waited for Jyorm to return and took another arrow from him. He aimed again, and Jax closed his eyes, unable to stare at the arrow pointed at him. Velamir released, and it struck the target. Jyorm checked it and nodded. Velamir held up his bow for the last time. He stared down the shaft of the arrow, staring at the point at the end. This was it. He just had to make this one. After a determined narrowing of the eyes, he let the arrow fly.

Jax's inhale was sharp as the arrow landed beside his head. Velamir placed the bow in Talon's waiting hand and strode to Jax, outpacing Jyorm. When he reached the target, he peered forward. Jax was grimacing, and for a second, Velamir thought the arrow had struck him. Jyorm brushed Jax's hair to the side, revealing the arrow buried a breath from his ear. A blond curl rested around the tip. Jyorm yanked the arrow out and called to Chishma Talon.

"He hit it."

Talon glanced at the Head Chishma before turning back to Velamir. "You can take a seat, Cadet Velamir. The Head Chishma will decide if you passed."

Velamir strode to the chairs, taking a seat as far from Lissa as he could. Heavy tension stretched between them. He soon found himself watching the final part of Jax's test. He was bound in a thick rope that Talon said was coated in something Frumgan had made. Jax smiled, and Velamir knew that he could easily get out of the knots. Talon told Jax to begin, nodding at Jyorm to count. They were timing him. Jax was out of the rope in seconds. He passed the Speed test. Jax made his way to the seats and took one beside Velamir, blocking Lissa from view.

"How was I?" Jax asked.

"Not bad."

Jax muttered, "They made it easy for me."

It was Quintus's turn. He did the first two parts of his test well, breezing through them.

Jax laughed. "It wasn't just me they made it easy for."

Velamir glanced at the Head Chishma and saw his hand clenched around his quill. If he held it any tighter, it would snap. It was obvious he didn't approve of Talon's testing methods.

A Handler came in, leading a young rumlok. As soon as the Handler dropped the leash, the rumlok was off, charging at Quintus with ferocious speed. Quintus avoided his snapping teeth, his fingers burying in the rumlok's thick coat, using the hairs to hold him back. Quintus wrapped his arms around the rumlok's neck. His muscles bulged and his face grew red as he struggled.

The rumlok stopped thrashing and fell over. Quintus rolled off and pumped his fists in the air, proud of his accomplishment. He walked around the arena, pounding his chest. He pointed at Velamir, then Jax, and made a thumbs-down sign, laughing. Everyone watched in horror as the rumlok got to his feet behind Quintus. It darted forward and bit into Quintus's leg, dragging him around by it. Quintus let out a piercing cry and kicked the rumlok's head with his other leg. The rumlok gave a pitiful whine and released his leg, setting sights on his arm. Quintus wrapped his arms around the rumlok's neck once again, but this time, he held on. He didn't let go until an audible snap echoed in the arena. Quintus collapsed, and the rumlok fell beside him.

After a moment of shocked silence, chaos erupted. Jax shot forward, and Velamir raced behind him. Chishmans gathered around Quintus. He was curled into a large ball, his hands gripping his leg. More Handlers rushed in, working together to take the rumlok's body out of the arena.

Jax dropped beside Quintus. "Give me my bag!"

Velamir retrieved the bag and handed it to Jax. Jax drew out a tonic and placed it to Quintus's mouth, tipping it up so he could drink. Everyone held their breath as Quintus spasmed. Eventually, he stopped, lying still. Jax leaned forward and checked his pulse. He cut Quintus's pant leg and poured water over the wound. Minutes later, Quintus's wound was cleaned and wrapped.

"He will be fine," Jax told them, and everyone exhaled in relief.

The Head Chishma exchanged a glance with the other mentors and then addressed Jax.

"Cadet Jaxon, we are pleased with how you responded to the situation. Your group is very lucky to have you."

"Group?" Velamir asked.

Talon smiled. "You all passed."

"We shall have the ceremony tonight," the Head Chishma informed them. "Let's give Quintus time to recover."

A few hours later, Velamir, Jax, Lissa, and Quintus stood in line before the Head Chishma. They were in the assembly room. Cadets and mentors were seated around them, watching the proceedings. The Head Chishma read from a scroll.

"For many years, Lord Prolus fought for the freedom of Tariqi. He destroyed the chains that held Tariqi and spread through the lands, saving more and more people from the Empire's cruel reign. To be Chishmans, you must be ready to sacrifice your desires for the good of Tariqi. A Chishma has no feelings, no emotions, they simply fight to save others." He paused and looked up at them. "Are you ready to be Chishma? Are you willing to sacrifice a life with a family and a home for the life of a soldier?"

"We are ready," Velamir replied, his voice blending with the others.

"Repeat after me," the Head Chishma ordered.

"I will fight to my last drop of blood and sacrifice my very soul."

They repeated the words, and he continued, "I will fight against the flood, to achieve Prolus's goal."

Velamir's throat was dry as he spoke.

The Head Chishma nodded in approval. "Pledge your oath. You are now brothers, life partners."

Velamir glanced at the others. Quintus stepped forward, his head high.

"For Tariqi." He slapped his palm across his forearm. "I swear to hold Jaxon, Velamir, and Lissa in trust, my weapon as my family, and my duty as my life."

The Head Chishma took a searing-hot branding iron from a bucket of coals Talon provided and held it out, urging Quintus closer. Quintus lifted his sleeve, and the Head Chishma placed the iron against his skin, branding the symbol of the Golden Crown into his arm. Quintus clenched his teeth, releasing a hiss of pain, sweat building at his hairline.

"Wisdom." The Head Chishma pulled the brand away, and Quintus's head lowered in relief. "Power," he whispered along with the Head Chishma. "Eternal."

Quintus stepped back, brandishing the new symbol with pride. Lissa went next, and although she swore to trust them, Velamir knew she couldn't possibly mean that.

Jax followed, the brand making its place next to his shadow mark. Velamir stepped forward soon after. Guilt pooled in his mind at the promise he would make, knowing it wasn't true. The first part, at least.

"I promise to hold Jaxon, Quintus, and Lissa in my trust, my weapon as my family, and my duty as my life."

The Head Chishma urged him nearer and took the branding iron from the flaming coals once again, positioning it above Velamir's arm. Velamir drew in a fortifying breath. The Head Chishma moved fast, searing it into Velamir's skin. Velamir's fists clenched along with his jaw, exhaling in relief when the Head Chishma finally pulled back and motioned behind him.

Chishman mentors neared, holding neatly folded uniforms.

The Head Chishma announced, "We have four new members for Tariqi. May they bring us strength. May they bring us victory."

The cadets and Chishmans watching clapped profusely and shouted, "For Tariqi!"

Velamir whispered, his voice lower than the rest, "For the better."

The applause came to a halt when the doors to the chamber flew open. Velamir froze at the sight that met his eyes. The Chishmans and cadets rose as one from their seats, placing their hands on their forearms.

Bear walked inside, but Velamir focused on the person behind him. Gleaming gray hair, tinged with brown, warm blue eyes, and a wide smile.

"We have taken the Borderlands!" Cheering flooded the halls once again, following General Winston's words.

14

THORSTEN
KARALIK EMPIRE
THE GRAND PALACE

"I T SMELLS HIDEOUS in here."

Thorsten smiled at the revulsion in Natassa's tone.

"Are we almost there?" Her voice was labored, the basket she carried weighing her down.

Thorsten shifted his own basket, holding his torch out farther, lighting their way. The tunnel was dark and wet. Thorsten remembered when he used to pinch his nose closed against the foul smell of refuse. Those days were long past. He'd taken this path too many times to count, and the stench hardly affected him.

"Nearly," he called back.

Natassa let out a yelp and screamed his name. Thorsten was at her side in a flash, placing the torch close to her face, trying to see what was wrong. Her hand gripped the handle of her basket so tightly her fingers turned white.

She gripped his arm with her other hand and squeaked, "There was a snake."

He chuckled. "Don't worry, the ones down here aren't poisonous."

She glanced up at him. "I don't care if they are poisonous or not. It slithered over my foot!"

He shook his head with amusement. "Stay close."

She kept hold of his arm as they trudged through the tunnel. Though he could have doubled his pace, he kept it minimal because she was struggling. Natassa wasn't used to this. She barely left the castle as it was. Thorsten was sure sneaking through filth-ridden tunnels was a new thing for her. Eventually, they stopped, and Thorsten reached out with the torch, the firelight revealing a staircase leading up. Thorsten handed his torch to Natassa and walked up the stairs. After setting his basket down, he lifted his arms up, pushing against the ceiling. It didn't move despite the amount of force he placed on it. He grimaced, the strain sending a shiver of pain through his whipped chest and back.

"It's not budging," he grunted and looked down at Natassa.

She appeared small, her eyes wide like a terrified child, and a shudder passed over her. Thorsten had to laugh at the pitiful picture she made.

Her eyes narrowed. "What?"

He shrugged. "Nothing, I thought I saw something behind you."

She peered over her shoulder, waving the torch

around as if the shadows would jump out at her. She turned back to face him, glaring when she saw the wide grin on his face.

"I should have gone to my lesson with Lady Flivane instead."

"Don't tell me you're a coward." Thorsten pushed against the ceiling again, and this time it rose with a groan of protest. Light, far brighter than the torch, shined over him. He lifted the hatch door up as far as he could and picked up his basket, setting it on the ground above him. He motioned Natassa to follow him, and when she reached him, he took the torch from her, snuffing it out before placing it on the top step.

Thorsten hoisted her up through the hatch and then pulled himself up. He inhaled the fresh air, a definite bonus compared to what they had been smelling for the past ten minutes. He closed the hatch door and picked up his basket, turning to see Natassa holding her arms out as the wind blew at her. Her eyes were closed, her face angled toward the sun. Thorsten felt almost guilty to interrupt her reverie, but he cleared his throat and her eyes snapped open.

"It's something, isn't it?"

She nodded, staring at the endless trees, the endless beauty around them. "How did you know about the tunnels?"

"Father told me. Apparently, it is tradition to tell one's heirs, even if you don't care for them."

"So, it's a secret, then?"

Thorsten nodded and gestured for her to continue forward. They moved in silence for a while.

"Thank you for showing me," Natassa said softly.

A few moments passed, and he didn't respond. The fact that she thought she should thank him for something she should have already been told saddened him. The trees grew fewer and farther apart. Thorsten could see one of the gates leading into the city ahead. Natassa moved closer to his side. He'd snuck into the city enough times that he was no longer nervous about facing the guards, but this would be her first time entering Hearcross without an escort.

"Lift your hood," Thorsten instructed as he placed his own over his head, darkening his peripheral.

She lifted the black wool over her braided hair and glanced at him. "Won't these cloaks draw attention?"

"Almost everyone wears them in the city. As if they are hiding from something, and perhaps they are. The soldiers have been storming through the houses, finding hideaway Savorians. Father is taking no chances."

Natassa scoffed. "He's that desperate to locate the crown?"

"He believes the tales of the crown giving eternal life and power over others. In my opinion, I think it's false. After all, no one has seen the crown with their own eyes. Some fool must have spouted the tale."

Natassa murmured in agreement and looked as though she wanted to speak, but they were approaching the gates, giving her no time to express her opinion. The guards sent them curious looks, perhaps wondering why they had come to the city from the less traversed forest side.

"What business do you have?" one of them barked.

Thorsten motioned to his basket. "Here to sell supplies at the market."

The other guard leaned closer, and Thorsten lowered his head, hoping Natassa would follow in his movements so the guards wouldn't see her profile.

"I've seen you before."

A chill rushed up Thorsten's spine, and he glanced up. The guard was peering at him, eyes narrowed.

"Who are you?" the other guard asked, hand dropping to his sword. "State your name."

Thorsten fumbled for words. "I'm Galva Vane's servant. He sent me here."

"Is that so? He sent a servant all the way from Ondalar?" The guard sneered. "And with the girl too?"

"She's a maid in his household."

"Let me see you, girl." The guard reached out for her hood.

Thorsten stepped in front of her, lowering his voice to a dangerous whisper, "Don't touch her."

"Mighty protective, aren't you?" the guard said and then his eyes widened. "I know you, you—"

Natassa pushed to the front. "He was lying to you. He's Vane's brother. He didn't want to draw attention and so wore the guise of a servant."

Thorsten held his breath. He hoped she knew what she was doing. Galva Vane was a respected noble in the Empire, a distant cousin of their mother's.

"He looks like him." The guard nodded, trying to peer under the hood.

The other guard wasn't so easily fooled. He crossed his arms. "And you are?"

"Vane's betrothed," Natassa said. "He won't appreciate you detaining me."

The guard was still hesitant, but then he nodded. "Yes. Yes, you are."

Thorsten glanced at Natassa. Her eyes gleamed as she held the guard's gaze.

"You may pass," the first guard told them.

Thorsten went without hesitation, walking past them. As soon as they were out of earshot, Thorsten smiled.

"I thought they would catch us for a moment."

They entered the city. It was bustling with people. Merchants roamed through the shops, and women beat rugs from their balconies. It seemed like a city full of prosperity. Except for the beggars lining the corners waiting for scraps of food and the lack of children. One of the Savorians his father recently tortured had screamed in agony, saying the Golden Crown was buried in the caverns just to escape further torment. Emperor Malus was desperate to chase after any lead, willingly making the Imperial children mine in the caverns.

Thorsten glanced back several times to ensure Natassa was following him. Her steps were slow. Thorsten would offer to carry her basket, but he knew his assistance would hurt her pride, especially since she was trying to prove herself capable of helping the cause. A while later, Thorsten stopped at the end of an alleyway. He glanced around to guarantee they were alone and pushed aside a large stone. He crouched down and opened the hatch beneath. He sensed Natassa's worry and knew she was considering what their father would do should he ever find out about the shelter. Thorsten knew the price would be high.

He jumped down, and after handing him her basket, Natassa dropped as well. She fell onto her knees, a cry slipping past her lips at the impact. Thorsten took her arm and hauled her to her feet. He sent her a concerned look.

"I'm fine," she said and retook her basket.

He guided them forward, his hand outstretched, feeling along the rock-solid walls. Before long, they reached a door at the end of the tunnel. He knocked, using the rhythm Aylis taught him. His heart raced, eager to see her and worried about the injury she sustained at the hands of the slavers. The door opened a crack, and a bright blue eye peered at them. The door swung open fully, and Aylis stood before them. Everything faded when he saw her.

Her eyes found his, and she gave him a small smile. "You came."

Her accent was strong, and though she worked hard to disguise it, there was no doubt she was from Savoria.

Thorsten nodded. "I'll always come." After a long pause, he said, "I brought supplies. I'm sorry it's not much."

"We should be fine." She took the basket from him, running her hand over the blankets folded inside. "The children will be thankful for these. The night chill is getting stronger."

Her blond hair was pulled back into a braid, and tired lines filled her face. Dust coated her brow and clothes from being underground, but to Thorsten, she appeared to be one of the most beautiful women he'd ever seen.

"Winter will be upon us soon. I need to supply you with more blankets, and I will try to bring wood, at least to stock up." Then he glanced at her arm. "Why are you guarding the door? You are wounded."

Aylis shook her head. "The tonics you sent were plenty of help. Besides, I need to take my shift as guard. Everyone has to put in their share."

"Stubborn, always stubborn," Thorsten muttered.

Her smile bloomed, and all traces of hardness disappeared, leaving no doubt that she was the most beautiful woman he'd ever seen. She far surpassed the spoiled princess of Ondalar and the noble women in Ayleth.

"You are the proudest person I know, and yet you tell me I'm the stubborn one," she said softly, and his gaze dropped to the long scar cutting across her lower lip, only adding to her allure.

Thorsten chuckled, leaning toward her, freezing when he heard Natassa clearing her throat. Aylis's eyes flew to her and widened. Thorsten's smile faltered, wondering why he'd thought it would be a great idea to bring Natassa along. He took her arm and pulled her forward, feeling guilty when she sent him a questioning look.

"Who is this?" All evidence of happiness was wiped from Aylis's face, and she stared at Natassa with distrust.

"His sister," Natassa remarked dryly.

Aylis ignored her and continued staring at him with brows lowered. "How could you bring someone here? I trusted you."

"She wouldn't tell anyone, Aylis." His voice cracked when he said her name, and he cursed his weakness.

Aylis ran a hand over her eyes in frustration. "She's a princess, Thorsten."

He glanced at Natassa, who raised her brows when Aylis called him by his name. How was he going to explain this to her when they left?

"She will tell her father, and he will torture us to death, one by one. Not everyone's like you."

Thorsten grimaced when Natassa crossed her arms, her lips pressed into a thin line. She was upset. But somehow, he was more distracted by Aylis's words.

Thorsten smiled. "You think I'm unique?"

She didn't reply, but the way she stared at him answered his question.

"I'm not. There are others who wish to change the corruption in the Empire." He motioned to Natassa. "My sister is one of them. Our father has trapped her in the palace, not allowing her to have free will. Will you take this moment from her? This chance to help?"

Aylis held her stiff posture and looked at Natassa, staring so deeply as if to see if she would betray her.

"She's the one who ensured you were receiving supplies while I was at the Borderlands."

Aylis hesitated, and Natassa said, "I will tell no one."

Aylis's posture slumped. "I believe you."

Natassa pulled a small sack from her belt and held it out for Aylis.

"What is this?"

"I thought it might help," Natassa told her.

Aylis opened the sack, and her eyes widened into

large spheres. She looked up at Natassa. "This is gold. Are you sure you want to give this to me?"

"That jewelry reminds me of a prison. Wearing them is like placing chains around my neck."

Aylis stared at her with a new light, and it relieved Thorsten that she was warming to her.

"Thank you," Aylis said.

Natassa smiled. "Thorsten told me there are some children in the shelter. I brought something for them."

Aylis moved from the doorway. "Please, come in."

They stepped inside. Thorsten glanced around, spotting the children hovering in the corner of the small space. Despite his many attempts to befriend them, they were still scared, and now that he had brought someone else with him, it only increased their fear.

"How many of you are here?" Natassa asked Aylis.

"We have room for forty as of now. We are planning on digging farther underground to create more space. There are ten men and one woman we rescued a week ago. She'd been left stranded in the street nearly beaten to death." Aylis's lip curled as she spoke of the torture inflicted.

She gestured to small cloths that lay in neat rows in the room. They were makeshift beds. On one of them lay a woman, her face covered in healing cuts and fading bruises and her eyes closed.

"The rest are children, from twelve years and younger," Aylis finished, motioning back to the group, who were watching Thorsten and Natassa with wariness.

Thorsten stepped forward, adding to the conversation and answering the question he knew Natassa had been about to ask. "The men are gone during the day, to find food and bring more of their kin."

"But what if they are seen or recognized as Savorian?" Natassa asked in a worried tone.

Aylis's lips lifted in her small smile. "They won't be. They cut their hair short, and they dye it with ashes or whatever they can find. No one sees them for more than a moment, so there isn't a chance to notice."

"You haven't cut your hair," Natassa pointed out.

Aylis shook her head, and her braid swayed with the movement. There was a determined gleam in her eyes. "I won't lose my heritage, no matter who attempts to force me. I am Savorian, and if I must die, I will die as one."

Thorsten gazed at her with awe, and Aylis shifted under his attention. Natassa smiled, newfound respect evident in her stare. She turned back to the children and approached them. Thorsten continued watching Aylis until she looked at him.

"I'm sorry I didn't trust your sister. It's clear that I'm wrong about many people." She searched his gaze, and Thorsten knew she was remembering the same thing he was.

Aylis had crashed into him a year ago, when she attempted to escape the palace. She'd thought she would be killed, since the punishment for running was death, so she had used her last moments to curse and scream at him. Thorsten had allowed her to do so as he'd felt like a useless wastrel, unable to do anything to change the worthless rule of his father. But that was when he realized maybe he could. Maybe one by one, person by person, he could save the Savorians. He'd helped Aylis escape that day.

Thorsten cleared his throat, breaking the moment between them, and glanced around before asking, "Why didn't one of the men stay?"

"I can defend the shelter alone."

Thorsten's brows lowered. "Are you insane? You are one person. If the shelter is found, there will be no chance you can fight against my father's guards."

"Because I'm a woman?" Aylis shot back.

Thorsten ran a hand across his short stubbled head. He glanced at Natassa and saw she had taken candy from her basket and was offering it to the children. There was a crease in her brow as she struggled to understand them. One of the young boys stepped forward, offering to translate for her.

"Come with me," Thorsten said, taking Aylis's hand and pulling her to the storage room.

She followed him without struggle, and soon they stood alone, surrounded by stacks of wood and a small amount of food.

"I don't want anything to happen to you, Aylis," Thorsten said, gazing at her.

"Why? There is nothing you can do to change the oppression happening."

"Why?" Thorsten repeated. "I care for you, more than I ever thought I could care for someone."

"I care for you too," she replied, "but it would never work."

"We can make it work. Run away with me." He reached for her hand. "We can leave the Empire. Hell, I will even live in the Savagelands if it means I can be with you."

"I won't leave my people," she said.

"Let's take as many as we can from here."

"I won't leave the enslaved Savorians in the palace."

"Then let's remain here, get married. I will change things." Thorsten was desperate.

"Your father will never let that happen." Aylis shook her head vehemently. "You are a prince, and I'm the one your Empire sees as a slave."

Thorsten closed the distance between them. "If he banishes me, so be it. I don't care about being a prince. I couldn't care for anything less. I love you." She turned away, but he pulled her back to him, holding her chin. "Look at me and tell me you don't love me, and I will walk away." Thorsten stared at Aylis, his emotions burning through his eyes.

Aylis planted her hands against Thorsten's chest and pushed him away firmly. She moved past him, but he reached out, snaring her wrist. She met his questioning gaze.

"No, Thorsten, I don't, and I never could."

Thorsten dropped her wrist as though it was fire, and hurt cracked through his chest. A lion's claws could have torn his heart open, and it wouldn't equal this agony. Aylis took another step and then froze. Thorsten followed her gaze and saw Natassa staring at them by the storage room entrance with parted lips. Aylis brushed out of the room, leaving Thorsten with his sister.

"I . . ." Natassa started.

"I don't want to talk about it." Thorsten's voice was gruff.

"But—"

"You heard her. She could never love me." He closed his eyes, jaw clenching. "It's over."

Natassa reached out, but he shook his head.

"Let's go."

Leaving the shelter was strained. Aylis refused to meet his gaze and shut the door behind them the moment they stepped out. Thorsten didn't say a word despite Natassa's attempts at conversing. They made their way through the city, back to the secret tunnel. The sun was setting, and Thorsten hoped no one had noticed their absence. They had been gone much longer than he planned. As soon as they reached the area where the hatch was, Thorsten froze, because standing before it was a cloaked figure. He pushed Natassa behind him and reached for his dagger.

"That won't be necessary."

Thorsten stiffened at the calm voice, his fingers grazing his dagger hilt. The person threw back their hood, revealing none other than Honzio.

15

VELAMIR
TARIQI
KALEA FORTRESS

VELAMIR WAITED IMPATIENTLY, his fingers tracing the scar at his wrist. He glanced down at his arm, lifting it to examine his new brand. The pain was fading thanks to a tonic Jax provided. He scanned the Head Chishma's office. Bear's arms were crossed, blocking the closed door with his bulk from the curious cadets who had followed them. Jax drummed his fingers against the windowsill, staying far from Lissa, who was arguing in low tones with Quintus. The Head Chishma waved his hands, praising Winston and offering him the seat behind his desk.

"You have brought us wonderful news. We will hold a grand feast for you. The Borderlands at last belong to us," the Head Chishma proclaimed.

"The Borderlands belong to Prolus," Winston corrected and declined the offer. "I'm afraid I must be going. I came to take my new team."

The Head Chishma sighed with disappointment. "Of course, of course. Here are the members of the group." He urged the others forward and listed off their names.

Winston smiled at each introduction. When his eyes fell on Velamir, he stopped. Velamir grinned, feeling like a child again. He strode toward his mentor, his savior, and for a moment just stood there before him. But then General Winston held out his arms, and Velamir fell into his fatherly embrace the same way he had been comforted from his childhood nightmares.

It's just a dream, lad, Winston would say.

And Velamir would respond, *I never want them to come true.*

Winston would look him straight in the eye, *Don't be afraid of what lies in the darkness, because sometimes, the things hidden in the dark are our greatest allies.*

"It's been too long, lad," Winston said, loosening his grip and pulling back to see Velamir's face. "You've grown strong."

"It's good to see you."

"And you, lad." He lifted his hand, placing it on Velamir's shoulder. "I know you have many questions. I will answer them as soon as we arrive at the manor."

"We are leaving now?"

Winston nodded and glanced at the others. "Pack whatever belongings you have."

Velamir was reluctant to leave Winston's presence so soon, but he did as ordered. Before long, they were mounted—Winston on his Ondalarian warhorse, Dauntess; Velamir on Vandal; and the others on academy horses.

"Vandal looks well," Bear said, edging beside him on his horse. He gripped the reins in a tight fist and struggled to keep a good seat in the saddle. Bear had never taken to riding.

Velamir chuckled, looking away.

"What's that face for?" Bear frowned.

"Maybe you should have stuck to ships," Velamir responded.

Bear swatted him, but Velamir pushed Vandal forward, avoiding it.

"You stuck up little—"

"Let's move," Winston called back to them.

Velamir glanced at the academy as they rode out, spotting the flag with Lord Prolus's symbol and colors. It drooped down, as there was no wind to carry it. This had been his life for the past seven years, and he was more than ready to put it behind him.

They rode for hours without stopping, passing by crumbled homes and barren land, destroyed by Shadow Manos creations. Velamir spotted the Qistool in the distance, a long wall that ran for miles, barricading what was once one of the strongest kingdoms in the Empire. The kingdom had been a tremendous obstacle in Tariqi's path. But when at Prolus's command the Shadow Manos invented a poison that spread sickness, it had infected the kingdom. No one could enter it now. It was a place that held demise, its gates locked shut. Velamir wondered if the people inside were dead or if any remained. When he was younger, the children at the academy used to tell horror stories of what would be unleashed if the gates of the Qistool were ever opened.

General Winston halted by a murky river and dismounted. Velamir followed his lead, watching Winston take a vial from his belt and pour it over the river. Dark water rose into the air, freezing into a large circle. A thick sheen formed over it.

"What is that?" Quintus asked, a tinge of fear in his voice.

Jax was awed. "Zamanin Sulari, waters of time. Frumgan told me about it, but he said no one could make one that worked."

Winston smiled. "You could say I have connections." He waved for Bear to step forward.

Bear grunted and lifted his axe, swinging it into the air. It broke through the frozen water, and cracks appeared along the circle. Bear took a second blow, and a large gap emerged, pieces flying back into a circulating portal. Bear jumped through without a word, disappearing. Winston slapped Dauntess's rump, and she trotted to the hole, rearing up and slamming her hooves against it. Because she was so large, the sheer size of her created a wider opening. Winston whistled, and she paused, inches from entering the opening. He beckoned Velamir to send Vandal. Velamir tried to bring Vandal close, but he neighed, shying away. Velamir rubbed his face.

"It's all right," he whispered until Vandal calmed.

Vandal allowed Velamir to lead him forward, and when he neared Dauntess, he followed her willingly and they jumped through the portal. Winston smacked the academy horses, and they trotted away.

"They will find their way back," he said and gestured to the others. "Come along."

"How long does it stay open?" Quintus asked.

"Strong ones last a few minutes."

"I'm assuming this is strong?" Quintus shifted uneasily.

"Stop being a baby," Lissa scoffed. "It's just a portal."

She stepped forward, her face as solid and cold as the water had been when Winston placed the concoction on it. She strode to the circle and took a leaping jump into it. Jax went after her without hesitation. Velamir approached the circle and stared into the swirling depths. He looked back at Quintus, seeing him frozen in place.

"Let's go, Quintus," he called. "We do this together."

Quintus's approach was cautious. Velamir glanced at Winston, who gave him an encouraging smile.

Velamir took a deep breath. He pulled Quintus by his arm and stepped into the portal. He flew forward, and air whooshed past him. His eyes stung, scenery rushing by in a blur, and soon his feet were racing across grass. He saw an opening before him and sailed through it, a thrum vibrating against his skin. He crashed into something solid, releasing a pent-up breath.

"Ow," he heard Jax grumble.

"Sorry." Velamir backed away.

Quintus smashed into him from behind, propelling him forward. Velamir's head thumped against Jax's. Velamir winced, lifting a hand to his throbbing skull.

Jax groaned. "I don't think I will recover from this."

"Nothing your tonics can't help," Lissa sneered, watching with arms crossed.

Velamir glanced around, recognizing where he was. Red Eagle Forest. Trees filled every part of the area, and soft wind blew by. The sun shone, its light touching everything. He had missed this. Winston's land was the only place in the Empire he would ever consider home.

Velamir spotted Bear heading to the barn, holding Vandal's and Dauntess's reins. Boots smacked the ground near Velamir, and he turned to see Winston arrive. It was obvious he had done this many times, because unlike the rest of them, his entrance was controlled and steady. The dark, swirling portal closed with a sudden snap. Sparks shot into the air where it had been.

"That was amazing!" Jax exclaimed, his experimental mind turning. "Do you have more?"

Winston smiled. "A few."

Quintus grumbled. "I don't get it. How does it work?"

"Whoever makes it must give it a direction, a place to go. This vial brought us here." Jax waved his hand around them. "I assume they used an element from the land the portal will take you to." He clapped his hands together. "I can't believe someone made it work."

He pulled his journal from his bag and scribbled something inside. Lissa rolled her eyes and pushed past them, storming after Winston, who was walking to the manor house in the distance. Winston glanced behind him and called.

"Follow me!"

Velamir walked forward, and Jax hurried to match his stride, waving his journal in the air so the ink would dry. When they reached the manor house, it was just as

Velamir recalled. Quiet and peaceful. Winston led them to his private chamber. Velamir had always wanted to see it when he was young, but he had never been allowed. He looked around with reverence now but found himself disappointed. It looked like a regular meeting chamber, with maps and parchments layered over a large center table and simple furnishings throughout.

Winston stood on the other side of the table, across from them, looking down at the parchments.

"You must be wondering why you are here," Winston began. "Every plan the Chishmans made to conquer a kingdom never worked as well as the Fye plan. Anyone know what that is?"

They nodded. Velamir remembered learning about the mastermind Chishma Ovus Fye back in the academy. He had single-handedly taken a kingdom by earning its leaders' trust before assassinating them one by one. By the time Prolus and his army had arrived and smashed through the gates, Fye had already been sitting on the throne with the dead king's crown in his hand. Everyone had thought Fye would claim the kingdom as his own, but he stepped away from the throne and handed the prize to Prolus, proving his loyalty.

"That is exactly what we are going to do," Winston said.

"How?" Quintus asked.

"I am an Imperial Galvasir, and I was a trusted warrior of Verin's king," Winston told them. "That was a long time ago, a time when I hadn't realized how evil the Empire was. Since then, I've only been to Verintown disguised, but I never returned to the castle. I withdrew from King Dale's army when I joined Prolus. The king assumed I retired and sought solitude. Because of that reasoning, my manor and lands have been left alone by Verin soldiers. But now . . . now I am going to return, not as Prolus's general, but as the man they knew all that time ago. They will believe me, and that will be their first mistake."

Winston drew a map of Verin over the rest of the parchments and placed his hands on either side of it. "Despite the Borderlands being in our hands, Verin will still host their yearly jousting tournament. Nothing will keep them from their entertainment, even when we are right at their door. The tournament is one of the largest in the Empire. It would make sense that we would want to participate, especially because the prize is high. Promotion to Galvasir status."

"You're going to compete in the tournament?" Velamir asked.

"No, you are." Winston smiled. "There's a reason I brought you to the best horse master when you were younger."

"Blayton," Velamir recalled.

"The tournament begins in two weeks. We are going under the guise of competing. That is our cover. But slowly, we will gain the leaders' trust. The king, his advisors, the *general*." There was a bite in his voice at the last word. "We won't kill them until the day of the feast, which is held after the tournament. It is Verin's grandest celebration, conducted in honor of the tournament's winner, the new Galvasir." Winston slammed a fist into the map. "We will kill them then, and when the people run in disarray, huddle into each other with confusion, we will open the gates for Lord Prolus." He gave them a satisfied nod. "Until then, we will pick off lesser people of influence with minor roles in Verin. The less support they have, the better."

"Won't they wonder why you've returned?" Jax pondered.

"They will be pleased. I was something like a hero when I lived there. The king, in particular, will be delighted."

"And you're going to kill him," Jax said. "Isn't it going to be hard for you to murder someone who knew you like a friend?"

Winston leaned closer to him. "What was your name again, lad?"

"Jaxon."

"Ah, the Shadow Manos, that's right. Listen, Jaxon, there is no time for feelings of pity. We do our job. That's the only reason we live. That is the reason we will thrive. Because we are changing the world."

"For the better," they repeated, except for Jax, whose expression was inscrutable.

"And besides, I'm not going to kill him. You are."

Jax's eyes grew wide. "What?"

Winston laughed. "Do you think you can simply walk up to the king and stab him? No, we must be discreet. Frumgan has taught you many poisons. You will kill the king," Winston repeated, and turned to Lissa. "You will kill the princess. She has been uplifting the soldiers' fighting spirit from what I hear, and we cannot have that."

Lissa nodded, her smirk lifting. "At your order, General."

"Good. As for you," he addressed Quintus. "You will kill Advisor Liston on one of his late-night trips to the taverns. If he's still the same as I knew him, he will probably be too drunk to notice."

Quintus cracked his knuckles. "Sounds like fun."

Restless, Velamir asked, "And what is my task?"

Winston glanced at him, his face dark and solemn. "The most important of all. You will kill General Boltrex."

16

NATASSA
KARALIK EMPIRE
WHISPERING FOREST

T HE KNIFE SAILED through the air and landed in the targeted tree. A satisfied smile slid across Natassa's face. Thorsten nodded in approval and retrieved the knife.

"Good throw," he said. "But watch your wrist. A rigid, unmoving throwing wrist is needed. The target is farther than the last time we practiced."

He returned her knife, and Natassa adjusted her grip, holding it lower down on the blade. She lifted her arm, preparing to throw. After a moment of concentration, Natassa released, allowing the knife to glide smoothly out of her hand. It hit the target with a thump in the spot she had been aiming for. Natassa grinned again and looked at her brother. He smiled back, although it wasn't as wide as normal. It faded fast, replaced by a troubled expression. Natassa knew what was on his mind.

"Do you think Honzio will tell Father?"

He ran a hand over his head and went to retrieve her knife once again. "It's been two days and still no word. If he meant to tell, he would have done so."

"Do you think he bought our excuse?"

Thorsten snorted. "Honzio is not that gullible to believe we went for a stroll in the city and nothing else."

Natassa winced. "And also, the fact that we used the hidden tunnels."

Thorsten nodded. "He was not happy that I told you."

"He inherited that trait from Father. Wanting to keep me in the dark and bereft of knowledge." She waited for Thorsten to defend Honzio, to tell her to give him time. When he didn't, she felt a raw ache inside. Thorsten was the positive one, the one who looked to the light. If even he had given up on their brother, Natassa knew there was no hope.

Thorsten gave her knife back. "You're going to need a new set soon."

"I want to keep these forever."

She slipped the knife into her belt to join its companions. Natassa was terrible at hand-to-hand combat, so she was glad she had at least one skill that could help her if she were in trouble. She had loved practicing throwing knives from the first day Thorsten had gifted her with them.

"Now, it is time for close combat." Thorsten smirked.

Natassa groaned and lazily positioned herself into

a fighting stance. Thorsten mirrored her and waited. Natassa didn't move. She never attacked first. Thorsten rolled his eyes and lunged toward her, throwing a punch. Natassa ducked and jumped back to put space between them.

"How are lessons with Lady Flivane?" Thorsten asked as they circled each other.

"Better than usual," Natassa replied. "She told me I had to learn a new language. You should have seen her face when I said I wanted to learn Savorian."

Thorsten feigned an attack, scowling. "Why Savorian?"

Natassa retreated farther, out of his reach. "I want to converse with them better. Most of those children could only speak their own language. If we want them to trust us, we need to understand them first."

"We are not going back there."

Natassa's mouth parted, and she dropped her stance. "Why not?"

Thorsten was adamant. "We just aren't! Besides, we were almost caught. It's too risky."

"I don't believe that's the reason."

Thorsten's jaw clenched. "Aylis doesn't want me there."

Natassa stared at him in disbelief. "Did you help those Savorians only because of her? Because you wanted to secure her affections?"

"Of course not!" Thorsten exclaimed. "I helped because they needed it."

"Are you going to stop now? Because they need you now more than ever." Natassa stared at him, willing him to meet her gaze. She lifted her hand where the thin bracelet encircled her wrist. "Be brave and never give up. Those were your words when you gave me this."

Thorsten's fists clenched, and he looked down.

"Is this the example you are giving me? To back away from difficulty? To run when things get hard?"

Thorsten glanced at her, a small smile forming. "You always knew how to make me feel guilty."

Natassa raised a brow. "What is your choice, Thor?"

He sighed. "You are right. Of course I cannot leave them to fend for themselves. I will return to help them."

"*We* will return," Natassa emphasized.

"We will return," Thorsten amended.

Natassa smiled and then winced.

"What is it?"

She touched her head for a second. "Nothing."

She shattered his concerned look by jumping at him, surprising him with a left hook. He ducked and caught his foot behind her legs, sweeping her off her feet. Natassa hit the ground, the wind knocked out of her.

"Always be on your guard," he admonished.

Natassa grumbled, pulling herself up. Thorsten narrowed his eyes, and she rolled hers before retaking her stance. Thorsten smiled, trying to goad her into an attack. When she didn't move, he advanced again. After a quick series of blows, which Natassa barely avoided, she found her back pinned against a tree. Thorsten had the advantage now.

"All right, that's enough. Let's start over," Natassa told him.

Thorsten usually agreed with her at this point in a

fight, but this time, he shook his head. "You need to learn what to do in a situation like this." He pointed at himself. "See how many vulnerable places I have? You can poke my eyes or throat, and that would cause enough damage for you to escape."

Natassa nodded, soaking in the information. Thorsten closed the remaining distance between them. "Turn around."

When she did as he said, he wrapped his arms around her from behind. "It is hard to defend against a hold like this. Escape is hardly possible. More so if your captor is strong. The best thing to do is go limp, as if you fainted. Then they will drop their guard."

Natassa nodded and turned around, facing Thorsten.

"Now, pretend I am going to choke you. What will you do?" He reached for her neck.

He had probably expected her to strike him in the eyes or throat, so Thorsten doubled over in surprise and pain when Natassa kneed him in the groin instead.

She placed a hand on his shoulder. "Thor, are you all right?"

"That will do the trick," he wheezed.

A piercing birdcall sounded from a tree. Natassa pulled her cowl over her head. "Someone is coming."

She ducked behind a cluster of bushes, watching Thorsten retrieve his sword and attempt practice drills. Hoofbeats thudded close, and seconds later, a rider on horseback appeared. The rider halted when he spotted Thorsten. Her brother dropped his sword tip to the ground, watching the rider dismount and approach.

"Gavin." Thorsten spoke with an air of boredom.

"Your Highness, I have been searching everywhere for you."

"I have been here." Thorsten motioned to the small clearing. "Practicing, as you can see."

"My apologies, but why not train at the barracks or in the courtyard? Why so far from the palace?"

"It is none of your business where I practice. I simply wanted privacy."

"It is my business, Your Highness. As your body-guard, I'm sworn to protect you wherever you are." Gavin was scowling.

From what Thorsten had told her, when Gavin hadn't been able to find him when they snuck out to the shelter, he had gone straight to Honzio, too scared to tell the emperor. That was how Honzio had realized they were gone. But how he figured out that they had used the tunnels, Natassa didn't know. He must keep closer tabs on them than they'd realized.

Thorsten waved his hand in the air. "All right, all right. I will finish my training at the palace tiltyard."

Natassa's heart squeezed. Thorsten was going to practice for the joust. She had hoped he wouldn't compete this time, but he already seemed determined.

"I will ride ahead to assess any danger." Gavin saluted and mounted his horse.

Thorsten nodded at him, and as soon as Gavin rode away, Natassa came out of hiding.

Thorsten saw the look on her face and spoke up. "I know you will tell me not to take part, but I must."

Natassa's eyes filled with tears. "You saw what it

did to Honzio. I don't want another of my brothers to be destroyed by it."

Thorsten put his hands on her shoulders. "I won't, trust me."

"You can't promise that. Jousting is dangerous."

"I have to," Thorsten repeated.

Kasdeya, the one who had alerted them of Gavin's approach, came down from her tree. "We should leave."

Thorsten smiled at Natassa and went to his horse, mounting up.

"When will we have our next lesson?" Natassa asked her brother.

"We have to attend Father's birthday celebration tonight, and I need to take a few days to practice for the joust. Then there's the betrothal ball." He looked irritated at the thought of the ball. "After the ball, then."

Natassa accepted the chosen practice day, and Thorsten rode off, leaving a trail of dust in his wake. Natassa watched until he disappeared. She couldn't help the sinking feeling that came over her. The feeling that they wouldn't have another lesson.

17

VELAMIR
KINGDOM OF VERIN
RAGA MANOR

VELAMIR DISMOUNTED, PATTING Vandal's sweat-lathered side, and glanced at Jax, who lay on the ground breathless from hours of training. Velamir's hair stuck to his face, and he pushed back the long strands. Trickles of sweat soaked his leather glove. He walked over to Jax and stared down at him. Jax opened his eyes, releasing a heavy sigh.

"Well, now I know the definition of the word *terrifying*," Jax muttered.

Velamir hauled him to his feet. "And what is that?"

"Terrifying is when a certain Chishma named Velamir charges at you from atop a fearsome beast"—he motioned at Vandal—"holding a long lance pointed at your chest."

Velamir laughed, glancing at said lance, which lay on the ground a short distance away. "It would have been terrifying if I actually hit you with it."

"No, that would have been horrifying," Jax replied with wide eyes.

Velamir had been practicing jousting for two days, for several hours each day. It pleased him that he remembered the movements well. Winston had taken Velamir to Verintown years ago to receive jousting lessons from a man he knew there. They'd gone in secret. Winston had warned Velamir not breathe a word of Prolus or Tariqi to anyone.

This is the land of our enemies, lad. Blayton's a good man, but he's Imperial, and Imperials cannot be trusted.

"Next round?" Velamir suggested.

Jax's head hung, and his curls fell over his face. He was weary. The last time Velamir charged him, Jax had fallen off. He'd fallen off even though he knew Velamir wouldn't hit him.

"Why don't you ask Quintus?" Jax gestured to the clearing a short distance away from them.

Quintus and Lissa were practicing there. Lissa was doing takedowns, swinging around Quintus, using her legs to bring him down.

"They have been avoiding us," Velamir said as they watched them practice.

"I mean, after your encounter with Lissa, it's understandable."

During one of their breaks while jousting, he had told Jax what Lissa said to him, about killing Kisto, about liking him, about threatening him.

"But Quintus? I'm surprised he isn't attempting to bully us," Velamir said.

"Bully me, you mean? He doesn't have his friends with him now, and he knows you can take him."

A rush of footsteps pulled Velamir's attention, and he turned to see the only maid at the manor walking toward them.

"The master requests your presence for dinner." Her eyes were on Velamir.

Velamir glanced at the darkening sky. "I didn't even notice the time. Let's go, Jax."

They paused when the maid held up a hand. "Only Master Velamir. The rest of you will take your meals in your chambers as usual."

Velamir sent Jax an apologetic glance and nodded at the maid. He soon found himself seated at the grand dining table across from Winston. Velamir took a bite of the delicious mutton Winston's cook had prepared. He chewed carefully, ensuring his table manners were immaculate. The cook, gardener, and maid were the only people he had seen employed in the manor. But Winston had always been like that. The fewer people to talk, the fewer secrets to be revealed. He was Prolus's general, living in the Empire. The threat to his life if anyone found out was immense.

The candles on the dining table flickered, highlighting Winston's graying hair. Winston lifted his glass of zat, a drink seldom available in Tariqi. Some of the Chishmans complained the brin fruit trees, from which zat was made, were too fragile to maintain and care for long enough to survive the tainted Tariqin air.

Winston took a large sip. "Ask me anything you like."

Surprise must have shown on Velamir's face, for Winston chuckled.

"It's been so long since we spoke. I want to know all that I missed. You have been practicing so much these past days to prepare for the mission that we haven't caught up. I'm sure you have questions for me, even if you simply want to ask about our mission."

Velamir cleared his throat. "You will go to the castle as Galvasir Winston. What about the rest of us? Who will I go as?"

Winston smiled, stroking the rim of his glass. "I spoke with the others as to their roles. Lissa will pose as my wife, Jax as our True Manos, Quintus as my guard. And you . . . your identity will be the only true one."

"Velamir the nameless," Velamir joked, stabbing a piece of the mutton as he mocked his lack of a surname.

"No," Winston said so seriously that Velamir looked up at him. "As Velamir . . . my son."

Velamir didn't respond for a few moments and finally said, attempting to jest, "Isn't Lissa a little young to be your wife?"

Winston chuckled. "They all know that my first wife has passed on. They will assume she's my second."

"But you didn't have children with your first wife, and I'm too old to be Lissa's child."

Winston took another sip of zat. "They won't care."

Understanding filled Velamir. "You will pass me off as illegitimate?"

Winston slammed the cup down, an intensity in his

gaze that Velamir had never seen before. "You are my son, Velamir. No one can say differently."

After a second of strained silence, they resumed eating. The clinking of silverware was the only sound until Velamir asked, "How did you become a Galvasir?"

"Most Galvasir prove their worth in battle, in tournaments, or through heroic action. I defended King Dale's nieces, and he honored me with the title."

Winston's face darkened, the same way it had when he mentioned Velamir's task was General Boltrex.

"Who was he to you, the general?"

Winston's eyes shot to him. They were rimmed with red.

"He was . . . a confidant. A trusted friend, loyal, honorable, selfless." He paused. "He was a betrayer, an enemy, treacherous, corrupted, selfish."

Velamir's brow knit, his confusion growing. How could someone be something and then the complete opposite? His words made little sense.

Winston's gaze bored past Velamir into the wall, his thoughts elsewhere. "He was one thing, then he changed. And yet he had the guts to tell me it was I who was different." He scoffed, and his attention turned back to Velamir. "He will be there, in the castle, and he will be just as hateful and jealous as I remember."

Velamir could hear the anguish in Winston's voice. He wanted to say something, to reach out with comforting words, but didn't know how. If Boltrex fought for the Empire and Winston for Tariqi, wasn't Winston a betrayer to him as well? But the general obviously didn't know that, or he would have attempted to kill

Winston years ago. Winston downed the rest of his zat and backed away from the table, putting an end to the meal and the conversation. Velamir stood and pushed his chair in.

"If you'll excuse me."

Winston nodded. "Send Bear here if you see him."

Velamir left the dining room. He was nearing his chamber when he saw Bear's form at the end of the hall near a large window. His shoulders appeared to be shaking. Velamir approached cautiously, unsure what to make of it. Bear turned, and the moonlight shining through the window highlighted his profile. Velamir could see a tear trailing down his cheek. Unease filled him at the sight. Bear had always been one solid rock, unbreakable. He was staring at something in his hands. A carving of a Savorian warrior wielding an axe. He had seen Bear looking at it before when he was younger and had felt compelled to ask him about it, but he hadn't wanted to delve into his privacy. Velamir stepped closer, ensuring his boots made noise against the wood floor.

Bear glanced up, startled. He wiped his face and tucked the carving away, giving Velamir a strained smile. "What is it, lad?"

"General Winston wanted to see you."

Bear's expression fell into a stiff mask. "I will be right there."

Velamir nodded in return and continued to his room. He entered his chamber and closed the door, resting his head against it. Weariness filled him to the core. There were secrets here, he could feel it. Things Bear and Winston weren't telling him. He tried to push aside all his mangled thoughts and moved away from the door. He undid his belt, tossing it onto his bed. His eyes caught on a wooden chest set on the window ledge. It had been there from the day he had come to live with Winston. Velamir crossed over to it, staring at the small chest. The name engraved on the top was fading. Velamir traced the letters. It spelled the name Cselnsor in Imperial. Beneath it were extravagant symbols, the same name written in Savorian.

Who's this for? he'd asked Winston.

Winston had been upset by the sight of it. Velamir still remembered the hurt that cracked through his features like it was yesterday.

It doesn't matter, lad. Everything in this room belongs to you now.

Velamir reached down into his boot, unsheathing the dagger Winston had given him all those years back. His finger traced the elaborate carvings on the hilt.

And this? he'd asked Winston, holding out the dagger.

It's yours, lad.

Velamir had never touched the chest since that day. He shrugged off his tunic and fell onto the mattress. He stared at the ceiling above him, wondering how he would accomplish this mission. Winston had too much faith in him. If Velamir botched the tournament, not only would his faith be misplaced, but it would also ruin Prolus's charge. Velamir tossed and turned, heaviness weighing on his eyes until he drifted off, dreaming of the dead and pained cries for help.

NATASSA
KARALIK EMPIRE
THE GRAND PALACE

PERFORMERS CARTWHEELED ABOUT the stage, cracking jokes and making bizarre expressions. Emperor Malus's booming laugh could be heard throughout the entertainment room, and Natassa winced. He'd downed more than his fair share of zat. Natassa opened the curtain wider from behind the rows of seats and peered at the crowd. Besides the stage, the rest of the room was dim, but she could make out the forms of her father, her brothers, and Draven in the highest seats, farthest from the stage and closest to where Natassa was positioned. She could hear Draven's voice. He was loud too, although not as boisterous as her father.

"The princess is very delicate," Draven said. From his tone, it sounded like an insult.

"She is easy to mold into what you want. Weak though she is, it shouldn't pose a problem against any childbearing," Emperor Malus replied.

Natassa flung the crimson curtain closed. She was sick of hearing people speaking this way about her. She took a deep breath, trying to calm herself.

"What's wrong?" Krea asked, stepping away from the wheeled cart she had been placing Natassa's canvases on.

"Nothing. Let's move to the back of the stage."

Krea nodded and propelled the cart forward. Natassa walked with her through the large circular corridor that ran around the entertainment room. It was built so the performers could move around without having to enter the performance area and interrupt the show. When they reached the back of the stage behind the humongous curtains, Natassa stopped. Entertainers were rushing back and forth, carrying equipment off the stage. A few of them stared at the cart as they hurried by, giving Natassa quick bows as they went. Everyone knew she was going to perform, but they didn't know what she was going to do.

Kasdeya hastened to them, her breaths fast. "The performance is almost over. It's nearly your turn."

Kasdeya and Krea spent the next minutes readying Natassa, adding layers of face paint to make her features pop. Butterflies swirled in Natassa's stomach. What she was about to do was dangerous enough to get her killed. It wasn't too late to back out, but she had come this far. She couldn't stop now.

The twins were dressed in their usual gray with a

few more embellishments. Their hair in the classic buns with some extra locks to hang down their backs, the same hairstyle Natassa had chosen. Her gown was plain as well but its color significant. Imperial red with the curved shape of a hand resting on her bodice, the symbol of a half heart, the same symbol that was on the Imperial flag. It was meant to show the people and remind the emperor that half his heart belonged to the people.

Natassa told Krea and Kasdeya in which order to reveal the paintings, and they nodded, although Krea looked worried.

"Natassa, this is . . ." Her voice trailed off.

"Dangerous," Natassa finished. "But I must do this. The nobles need to wake up. They need to see how we are failing as an Empire. I need to do something, and this seems like the only way I can make a difference."

"You can't blame yourself," Kasdeya told her. "Emperor Malus is the one who prevents you from doing anything."

Natassa shook her head. "The truth of the matter is the people in the Empire are suffering. I am their princess. If they suffer, I should be in anguish. If they are left out in the cold, I should freeze. If they must endure a wound, I should bleed. But what have I done?" She stared at her handmaidens, but they couldn't hold her gaze. "I've done nothing."

Applause broke through their conversation, and the curtains swung open. The performers rushed off the stage. Natassa peered past them where the second set of curtains were closed, blocking the crowd from view. Krea and Kasdeya helped bring the paintings on stage. Natassa stood at the center, her hands clasped in a tight grip.

I can do this, she thought over and over.

Kasdeya's worried looks weren't making it any easier. Krea set up the large easel, leaving it empty. The paintings were piled in order beside the easel, their faces turned down so as not to be seen by the crowd. The announcer asked if Natassa was ready, and she gave a resolute nod, her chin firm. Her decoys took up their positions behind her, with their profiles visible to the audience.

"Princess Natassa Hartinza!" the announcer cried out.

The curtains were swept aside, and Natassa was nearly blinded by the lights that fell upon her. The crowd clapped politely and stopped to hear her performance.

This is for you, Mama.

Natassa closed her eyes and sang.

> *One Empire, one emperor.*
>
> *One people, one rule.*
>
> *The shower of red, our victory.*
>
> *It belongs to him, the crown upon his head.*
>
> *He saved us, and he will again.*
>
> *One Empire, one emperor.*

Cheering rose at the start of the Empire's anthem. Natassa didn't need to open her eyes to see her father's proud smirk. He was so self-centered that he'd had the Empire's anthem changed so it revolved around him. Natassa heard the canvas transferred onto the easel behind her. The first painting was covered with smiling people and a prosperous city. Natassa continued, willing her voice to stay strong.

> *The people he was to keep fed, the army who trusted his rule.*
>
> *They lay starving, without a home, without a bed.*
>
> *Those soldiers are dying. They were fools.*
>
> *Because they believed him.*

The cheering died down, and the audience started glancing at each other in confusion. General Zenrelius sat near the front, and he stared at her with silent, assessing eyes. Natassa began walking as she sang, back and forth across the stage. The paintings transferred rapidly from a peaceful empire to one of ruin and destruction. The audience shifted uncomfortably. Natassa had added her own version to the anthem, a version they didn't know but was heartbreakingly true.

> *Kingdoms vanquished, families ruined,*
>
> *Warriors fallen, the Empire doomed,*
>
> *Shadow Manos cursed, their gift a tomb,*
>
> *The end is close, it's coming soon,*
>
> *Because they believed him.*
>
> *Saviors crushed, their aid unheeded,*
>
> *Heroes came, but he said unneeded,*

The enemy arrived, and the army was defeated,
Before the fight, they already conceded,
Because they believed him.

Natassa glanced behind her at the portrait of her father with a maniacal gleam in his eyes as he placed a golden crown upon his head. Fallen soldiers littered a battlefield around him. When she had painted it, tears had streamed from her eyes. How she wished he was different; how she wished it wasn't true. The crowd was quiet, stunned to silence. She knew her father would scream out at any moment. She was surprised he hadn't already. Natassa continued, her voice low, the pain in her tone unmistakable.

He called them a curse,
His own flesh and blood,
He said they were worse,
Than a Savorian flood,
They believed him.

She saw her father stand through the blurriness of her vision. He pointed at her and yelled at the guards posted at the entry door. A tear dripped off her bottom lashes, dragging down her cheek in a never-ending trail of pain. She felt every hurt deep inside and willed herself to continue, to finish what she had come to say. Her voice rose, stronger than before.

In the wake of terror,

A hero will rise,

A just and fairer

Ruler in everyone's eyes.

The painting shifted to the boy. She had completed him, and she could not help but use him as the hero in the verse. The muttering grew louder, and she heard her father call out to the guards again.

"Get her off the stage!"

Natassa continued singing.

A phoenix at his right,

Steel in his left,

He will bring the light,

That left them bereft.

The emperor's face was a deep red, his eyes jutting from his head as she continued. Thorsten was attempting to hold him back while Honzio watched with what looked like a crease of worry. Draven stared with visible confusion. And it was no wonder he was confused. Most of the audience was. Emperor Malus had banned the tome, the tome that contained the prophecy of the Empire's Hero. He had banned it, and when Natassa's mother hid a copy for her, he had burned it. He may have trampled it to ash, but he couldn't rip out what was already in Natassa's mind. Her father tried to kill the prophecy, but she wouldn't let it go. She believed this hero would come, that he would stop this oppression. Natassa saw the guards approaching and sang faster.

He will end the pain,

He will right the wrong,

Avenger of the slain,

The phoenix beside him,

Their reign will be long,

The Golden Crown of power,

Before him, the evil will cower,

His secrets revealed,

The phoenix his shield,

Against whispers spread,

Vitality healed,

Though unrest is rampant,

The hero will end it,

The rider in the field,

His destiny sealed.

Krea and Kasdeya pushed against the guards, attempting to hold them back. The crowd stared at her, transfixed. The constant throbbing in Natassa's head blazed through, and she nearly blacked out. She blinked to clear her vision. The crowd seemed to snap out of their daze as guards swarmed them, escorting them from the room. Natassa watched the chaos, the last word of the prophecy lingering on her tongue. General Zenrelius reached the exit door and paused, turning to lock eyes with her. He stared at her for an imperceptible moment before turning away, disappearing with the others.

The guards broke past her decoys and grabbed hold of her arms, dragging her off the stage. Natassa went numbly. They left. All of them left. None of them had listened. She had seen the fear on their faces when she recited the prophecy. They were happy as they were. Rich and without fear. They didn't want to change.

Her father marched behind the guards. He was furious, she could tell. But she was chilled to the core when she saw the Cadellion appear behind him. When they reached her chamber door, the guards opened it and shepherded her inside. The ones holding her arms couldn't meet her gaze. They held her lightly and stared at the ground.

"Get out," the emperor ordered, and as they left, Krea and Kasdeya rushed inside along with Thorsten.

The Cadellion took the guards' places and grabbed hold of Natassa's arms.

"Chain her to the bed." Malus's voice was emotionless.

"What are you doing?" Thorsten was horrified.

Emperor Malus waved his hand at the Cadellion, and two of them broke away from Natassa and approached Thorsten. They manhandled him to the door.

"Father! Leave her alone!" Thorsten's voice grew higher and panicked as they thrust him out the door and slammed it in his face.

Krea stepped forward, but Emperor Malus held up a hand. "If you want to stay in this room, I suggest you don't attempt another thing."

Kasdeya pulled her back, and they stood with faces white as sheets as the Cadellion placed chains around Natassa's wrists, securing her to the bedposts. Natassa tried to keep her breathing even as the expression-less faces of the Cadellion leaned forward, tightening her restraints.

Emperor Malus ordered them away and approached her. "If I weren't about to marry you off to Draven, I would have killed you. You are an embarrassment to the Hartinza name."

Natassa closed her eyes, her protective shield forming around her.

"Frankly, I am surprised he didn't call off the wedding after seeing your stupidity."

He bent over her, his foul breath fanning her cheeks. "Once you leave to Ayleth, I never want to see you again."

Her father lifted his hand, staring at the numer-ous rings adorning his fingers. Rings that had broken her skin countless times. He slid one off, the seal of the Golden Crown imprinted on it.

A wicked sneer curled the emperor's lips. "But I'm not heartless. I shall send you away with a wedding gift to remember your emperor by."

Natassa's heart pounded, and she thrashed against her bonds. Malus waved at one of the Cadel and handed him the ring. He brought it to the fire, extending it into the flames, not even flinching when the heat danced across his leather gloves.

Natassa shook her head, nausea growing. "Don't do this."

The emperor smiled, sliding a glove over his fingers. "You should have thought about that before you made a spectacle."

The Cadel returned to her father's side, holding out the ring. Malus accepted it with his gloved hand and approached her.

"No! No, don't do this," Natassa pleaded.

Malus ripped her dress, exposing her shoulder. Natassa jerked against her chains, struggling with all her might.

"Hold her steady."

The Cadellion pressed her down, and Malus thrust the ring against her skin. Natassa's agonized screams mixed with Krea's. Kasdeya held her sister back, keeping her arms around her.

The burn seared into the front of Natassa's shoulder, sizzling with the same anger in her father's eyes. He gave a satisfied nod and pulled back. Natassa sagged against her pillows, her breathing shallow and hoarse. She looked weakly at her shoulder. The brand of the crown stared back at her.

The emperor turned away, facing the twins. "Until the ball, she will stay in chains, without food or water. A thorough beating would have done her good, but we can't have the bride looking bruised, can we?"

Krea's fists were clenched, and Kasdeya was motionless.

"Is that understood?"

They remained silent.

"I said, is that understood!"

"Yes, Your Majesty." Kasdeya bowed her head.

Krea followed suit a moment later. The emperor stormed out with the Cadellion behind him, taking the keys to her chains with them. Krea rushed to Natassa's side, and the chains rattled as she sank onto the mattress. Tears dripped from her lashes.

"I'm so sorry, Natassa, I'm so sorry," she whispered, reaching out to brush away the wetness staining Natassa's cheeks.

Natassa watched Kasdeya approach. She looked weary and tired and baffled.

"Everything you did, was it worth it, was it worth *this?*"

Natassa thought of all those useless nobles who had left as quickly as they could. But then she remembered Zenrelius's piercing stare. They would remember her words, of that she was certain. Even if it changed just one of them, it meant everything. It could be the start of a different Empire. She held Kasdeya's gaze for a long second.

"Yes, it was worth it."

19

VELAMIR
KINGDOM OF VERIN
RAGA MANOR

"THE FIRST STEP in sailing is to let the wind guide you forward," Bear said as he escorted Velamir into the barn.

"Meaning?"

Bear smiled. "Meaning if you want to act like a pompous Imperial, you have to let yourself go."

Velamir glanced at Bear's hand, which was motioned toward a stool resting in the middle of the barn.

"By sitting?" he teased, knowing exactly what Bear wanted.

Bear huffed, a twinkle in his eye. "You make fun of my riding, my poetry. Anything else you want to say, lad?"

Velamir scratched his head. "Hmm, I can't

think of anything else you've done that could be considered a skill."

Bear unsheathed a dagger. "Take a seat."

The sound of sharp slicing emitted for the next few minutes as Velamir's hair drifted down around him. Jax came in to saddle up the horses, and each time he led a horse out, he would glance at them.

"Looking good," he called cheerfully as he led Winston's mare.

"It will be your turn after," Velamir replied.

Bear laughed, the movement making his dagger work jerky, causing him to nick the back of Velamir's neck. "Sorry, lad," he said. "Jax doesn't need a haircut. The True Manos wear their strange hoods."

Jax shot Velamir a smirk before heading out of the barn.

"All done," Bear said, and Velamir stood, brushing flyaway hairs.

He felt different. The tips of his hair no longer touched his shoulders, and there was nothing covering his ears. Bear motioned to Velamir's sword, and he unsheathed it, staring at himself within the blade. Dark green eyes stared back at him. His skin was darkened to a deep bronze from the past days practicing in the sun with Jax. His long scar caught his attention. It was normally hidden by his hair. It ran from behind his ear down the side of his neck. Velamir rubbed the area. Just looking at the scar made it itch.

"Any idea why Winston was talking to Lissa and Quintus for so long this morning?" Velamir asked, looking away from his reflection.

Bear shrugged and gave no answer. Velamir sheathed his sword and eyed Bear for a long second. He wondered why he had been crying the night before, what pain he held. What family he'd left behind in Savoria. He wanted to ask him. He wanted to know him better. But Bear wasn't one to spill his life story. He didn't like to speak, not when it came to painful wounds.

"Thank you," Velamir told him, gesturing up at his hair.

"Aye." Bear reached out and rubbed the top of his head the way he used to when Velamir was young.

"Why aren't you joining us? There wasn't a task for you on this mission?" Velamir asked.

"Someone has to look after the place," Bear joked. "Don't want something to be stolen."

"Make sure no one takes you," Velamir said with a serious expression that lasted a moment before a smile cracked across his face.

"Why you little." Bear glared in mock anger before giving him a rough hug.

"Take care."

"You too, lad," Bear told him. Velamir sensed uneasiness in his stance.

"Vel!" Jax called, poking his head in. "Could you grab the general's shield?"

Velamir nodded and made his way to the armor storage. He approached one of the side walls where the shields hung. After grabbing Winston's shield, he brought it outside to Dauntess, attaching it to her saddle. He examined the design on the shield, a heroic warrior astride a powerful horse. Velamir traced the pattern with his finger.

ISRAH AZIZI

"A cavalier," he whispered.

Someone who saved lives, who changed people for the better, who created second chances. A hero. Velamir had been striving to be like that all his life. To help the starving orphans, the children left alone to rot, people like him.

Someone brushed against him, and Velamir blinked, pulling out of his thoughts.

"Gonna stand around all day, zelont?" Quintus spat as he walked by, holding bundles of dried meat and fruits. "Or are you going to do some work?"

Velamir exchanged a glance with Jax, who rolled his eyes.

"I've done everything while you were in the manor speaking with the general for hours," Jax told Quintus, adjusting the saddlebags on his horse.

Quintus's jaw flexed, and Velamir tensed, waiting for the comeback, but none came. Jax seemed confused, as well, not to receive any lashing words. Their attention was diverted when they saw Lissa exiting the manor. Velamir stared in shock at the billowing dress she wore in place of the Chishman robes. Lissa ignored them and walked breezily to the horses.

"Which one?" she asked Jax.

Jax pointed, and she moved to mount the horse. It was a struggle, but she managed to climb on and sat sideways in the saddle.

Jax sidled next to Velamir. "That's why Winston told me to bring a side saddle."

"She's taking her role as his wife seriously," Velamir replied. "We are not even at the castle yet."

"She has to practice." Jax shrugged. "Nice haircut, by the way. It looks better than I thought it would."

Velamir smiled and shook his head. "You don't have to lie to me."

"I was being honest."

"*Mavaalin*," Bear called, standing in the barn's doorway.

It meant *wind in your sails*. It was a Savorian farewell wish for a quick and pleasant journey. Velamir lifted a hand in reply and turned back to the group. Quintus was now astride a horse. Only three horses remained with their saddles empty. Vandal, Dauntess, and the horse Jax was using.

Jax smiled. "There was a stunning suit of armor I packed at the general's order. I wonder who it's for."

Velamir gave him a questioning look. "What armor?"

"You will have to ask him."

"Where is Winston?"

"Saying goodbye," Jax said, motioning.

Velamir followed his movement and saw Winston in the distance, kneeling beside a gravestone. His wife's grave. Velamir swallowed a lump in his throat and walked forward. He stopped when he was a short distance away, not wanting to intrude on his privacy. Velamir knew little about Winston's wife because he never mentioned her.

The wind blew, carrying some of Winston's words to Velamir.

"I wish you were here with me. I wish things were different."

Velamir couldn't imagine how hard it was for

Winston. He knew the feeling of loss, the enormous pain that came with it, but he didn't even remember his parents. Winston had known his wife for years.

"I will fix this. I will keep the promise I made to you," Winston said in a determined voice before rising. He turned and paused when he saw Velamir.

"Is everything ready?"

Velamir nodded. "Yes, sir."

"Then let's get on the road."

VELAMIR
KINGDOM OF VERIN
PASS OF NAMAAR

T HEY TRAVELED FOR hours, until the sun lowered in the sky and darkness began to set. Velamir rode at the front of the group beside Winston.

"Why didn't we use the portal on the river by the manor to cut the traveling time?" Velamir asked.

Winston laughed. "That would be a fast route, but I only have one left for now." He drew his overcoat to the side, revealing a vial in the inside pocket. "And its destination is Castle Verin. We need supplies in Namaar."

Velamir nodded in understanding and drifted off into his thoughts.

"I know that look. Who's the girl?"

Velamir's vision was bleary as he blinked against a strong wind. He glanced at

Winston and took in the red rimming of his eyes and the heavy bags beneath them. They would have to spend the night in Namaar. Winston was smiling despite his exhaustion as he waited for Velamir's response. Velamir looked ahead, the corners of his lips lifting.

"There is no girl. There never will be," Velamir replied. The Chishman rules were strict. No family, no emotions, no ties.

Winston chuckled. "Once this mission is complete, you will be promoted and can have a place with me in Tariqi as one of Prolus's heads. The girls will fall for you even if you won't marry them."

Velamir's grip on the reins tightened. "I won't use women that way. If I had a relationship, I would want it to be a lasting one, a faithful one."

Winston's posture turned rigid. "There is only pain in that."

Velamir cursed himself. He had reminded Winston of his wife. Velamir remembered him kneeling by her grave, the agony in his voice and the tremor in his fingers as he brushed the stone. Velamir closed his eyes, trying to think of something else, but what came to his mind was worse. The nightmare he'd been having every night since arriving at the manor. The woman had been bound by ropes. Her lip bled and her hair fell loose around her, but it was her eyes that ensnared him, that had held him captive by their terrified depths.

Help me, she had pleaded.

Velamir's fingers tightened on his reins. "Jax told me about some armor he packed."

Winston nodded. "It's a fine set. Gifted to me by King Dale himself when I became a Galvasir."

"He thought highly of you."

"That he did."

"What made you choose Tariqi over the Empire? How did you decide the right path?"

Winston leaned forward, patting his horse. "I didn't like what the Empire did, and I grew uncomfortable in Verin."

"Because of the general?" Velamir said.

"Not only him. It was many things." Winston stared off into the distance.

They rode in silence until Velamir spoke.

"When Prolus comes to take Verin, what will happen to the people?"

"If they surrender, they shall be under his law."

"But if they don't?"

"This is war, lad, and from what I know, wars are not won peacefully. We are trying to avoid the most bloodshed. But we cannot control people. We cannot choose for them." Winston glanced at Velamir. "And about the armor . . . it's yours."

Velamir's head snapped toward him.

A ghost of a smile traced Winston's lips. "You will need it for the joust."

"Thank you." Velamir's expression was earnest.

"I sent word to Blayton that we're coming. He will offer us lodging in his home. We will tell him we are there for the tournament, the same story we will tell everyone."

"Blayton doesn't suspect anything, does he?" Velamir asked.

"If he does or doesn't, we should be on our guard. Remember, lad, trust no one."

Hooves clomped closer as Jax pulled nearer. "There's a town ahead."

Velamir squinted. Sure enough, a walled town came into view. They rode to the entrance of the town. Winston leaned forward in his saddle and rapped on the wooden doors. A tiny flap opened, and an old man with a pointy nose stuck his head out.

"No one allowed entrance at nightfall."

"But it isn't night yet," Winston replied.

The old man sniffed. "There are lots of bandits 'round these parts. Better to be safe than sorry."

Winston smiled and reached into his coin purse. "I assure you, we are not bandits. We simply need a place to stay the night, and we pay well."

Winston tossed a gold coin to him. The old man caught the coin nimbly. He beamed as he inspected the coin, revealing broken and missing teeth. The old man lifted the coin and tested its solidness against his remaining teeth. A piece of his tooth chipped off.

"Looks real fine," the old man said, his demeanor changing.

He closed the flap, and the wooden doors swung open. Winston and Velamir steered their horses inside. The clomping of the other horses followed. The old man came up alongside Dauntess.

"Name's Lil'Jimmy," he introduced himself, craning

his neck to look up at Winston. "I'll be around here if you need me."

Winston tossed the man another coin. "Where is a good place to stay in this town?"

Lil'Jimmy's eyes filled with greed. "The tavern called Bloody Fools has good grub. They also has rooms you can rent. They are mighty costly about the rooms. We have an inn nearby too." Lil'Jimmy leaned forward and whispered, "But no one knows when they changed the sheets last."

Winston gave a thin smile. "Bloody Fools it is."

Velamir watched the entire interaction with interest. Winston dismounted from Dauntess. "Where are the stables?"

Lil'Jimmy nodded. "Right by the tavern."

"Thank you." Winston began leading his horse.

Lil'Jimmy chuckled. "Anytime. Anytime."

Velamir dismounted as well and followed Winston. After a quick glance behind him, he noticed the others doing the same.

The town was quite small, making it easy to locate the tavern. Strange smells wafted around them, and Velamir covered his nose several times as they passed by unscrupulous people. Venders sold foods and goods in many areas.

After paying board for their horses at the stables, Winston turned to Velamir. "Go rent us two rooms."

"You aren't coming with?"

Winston jangled a coin purse and dropped it into Velamir's hand. "I am going to meet with an acquaintance who owns a shop around here. Quintus will go with you."

Quintus's mouth dropped open, and he appeared ready to protest but composed himself after Winston raised a brow.

"At your order, General."

Winston shook his head. "Remember, from now on you will refer to me as Galva Winston."

They nodded, and Winston motioned for Jax and Lissa to accompany him. Velamir watched them stride off toward the shops.

"Wonderful," he muttered, staring at the coin purse.

"Scared to be left behind, zelont?" Quintus sneered.

"More like annoyed that I have to look after you."

Velamir walked to the entrance of the tavern. When he reached the closed double doors, he heard raucous laughter from within. Velamir paused, bracing himself.

"How long are you going to stand there?" Quintus taunted.

Velamir released a heavy sigh. "As long as it takes for you to shut up. But then, that would take forever so . . ."

Without another word, he threw the doors open. They swung to the sides, one of them smacking into someone. He cursed at Velamir. The stench of vomit and body odor assaulted Velamir's senses. He had to blink a few times to adjust his eyes to the low light. The man coming at him smacked into Quintus and froze. Quintus hefted him by the collar and thrust him aside. He crashed onto a chair, and the wood split, leaving the man on the floor.

"You're welcome." Quintus smirked at Velamir.

A roar of protest rose as another man rushed at Quintus.

"No one gez away wit hitten me brother."

The man was heavyset and reeked strongly of zat, the smell growing stronger when he flew into Velamir who stepped in front of Quintus. The man smashed Velamir against the wall. Velamir gasped, the air knocked out of him.

"You will pay!" the man growled, lurching back and then forward, swinging a punch at Velamir.

Velamir had a moment to react. He ducked, and the punch sailed over his head, landing on the wall. The bulky man grunted and shook his fist before moving again to attack. His anger grew as he missed every blow. Velamir evaded them with ease, and as the heavyset man swung another punch at him, Velamir stepped aside. The bloke's momentum carried him past Velamir toward the doors. Velamir assisted his exit with a powerful kick to his backside. He dusted his hands off and glanced at Quintus.

Velamir smiled. "You're welcome."

Quintus sniffed and focused on the other brother, who stood from the crumbled chair pieces. The brother lifted his hands in surrender before dashing out the doors. The tavern had grown quiet to watch the fight, but now that it was over, the ruckus returned as everyone focused on their heated conversations and tankards of zat.

"What are you looking around for? Another fight?"

"Something to hit you with," Velamir shot at Quintus.

Quintus pursed his lips. "You could always use your fist, but I forgot, you have no power behind the punch."

Before Velamir could reply, he caught the eye of an old fellow sitting beside the door. His face and hair were just as disheveled as his worn clothes, and he was smoking a pipe like it was his last day in the world.

The man let out a puff of smoke. "You got some skills, son."

"You watched the fight?"

Quintus rolled his eyes. "The whole tavern was laughing when you crashed into the wall."

"Nothing gets past me." The old man nodded, raising his tankard high in salute. He spilled half his zat onto his body. "Oh, damn," he slurred through drool and fell over onto the dirty floor, fast asleep.

"Stop wasting time on fools, zelont," Quintus muttered and walked forward.

Velamir caught up and said, "Maybe you should stop accompanying me. Then I won't have any fools around to waste time on."

He didn't listen to Quintus's reply as he navigated to the counter. A man with a dirty apron looked them over. "You ain't from around here."

"Thank God for that," Velamir muttered.

The barkeeper leaned toward Velamir. "You say something?"

"I need three rooms for the night."

Quintus punched Velamir's shoulder and not gently. "The general said two."

Velamir returned his stare. "Lissa will need her own."

"Ah, has the zelont become a gentleman overnight,

or was he always a prissy? That's not your money to spend."

"And it's not your place to talk. Or have you forgotten we are on a mission?"

The tension was thick and hung around them when the barkeeper interrupted with a frown.

"Do ye have coin? I don't have time for homeless."

"Hey!" Quintus flexed his arm muscles and leaned over the counter.

Velamir yanked him back and growled in his ear, "For the love of Tariqi, would you shut up?"

Quintus clenched his jaw but thankfully remained silent. Velamir returned his attention to the barkeeper and shook the coin purse in imitation of Winston. The barkeeper's eyes grew wide and widened even farther as Velamir took out a few coins and dropped them onto the counter piece by piece. "I. Need. Good. Service."

The barkeeper smiled, sweeping the coins into his hand. "Care for a drink?" With a flourish, he flipped out a dirty rag that had been hidden somewhere in the dark recesses of his apron pocket. He grabbed an empty tankard and *cleaned* it with all the rag's unpleasantness.

Velamir shook his head. "Just the rooms."

The barkeeper seemed disappointed but called over his shoulder, "Stanley!"

A wiry young man around Velamir's age stumbled into view. "Yeah?"

"Bring him to our *best rooms*," the barkeeper instructed.

Stanley laughed and walked away. Velamir wasn't

sure if he should be wary or not but took that as a sign to follow him.

"I am sure there will be tip, won't there?" the barkeeper called after him.

Velamir ignored him and followed Stanley to the curtained back of the tavern. Stanley brushed the curtain aside and walked up a short staircase leading to the next level. As soon as they crested the top, Stanley turned toward them and handed Velamir a ring that held one key.

"Your rooms are there," Stanley said, pointing at the doors.

"We rented three," Velamir informed him. "Which ones are available?"

"We only gots three, and the same key opens all of 'em." Stanley laughed and hurried down the stairs, leaving Velamir and Quintus in the darkened hallway.

An uncomfortable shiver went down Velamir's spine. This whole town was shady.

"Since you rented the rooms, I will find Winston," Quintus said.

"We need to inspect the rooms first."

Quintus smirked. "Something you can do yourself."

He moved to the stairs without a backward glance. Velamir shook his head to himself and walked to the first door, inserting the key. The door swung open with a groan of protest. He inspected the inside of the room. It was simple with only a bed as furnishing and a sooty fireplace against one of the walls. He leaned forward, examining the bedsheets with a grimace.

"These are their best rooms?" Velamir muttered, brushing something off a pillow.

There was enough space for two others to put their bedrolls on the ground. Velamir continued his inspection, spotting a small window on one side of the room. He approached it, eyeing the dust coating the frame, and peered out, spotting the stables. People moved around the stables, coming for their horses or bringing more inside.

Velamir's eyes landed on a motionless figure. Since his back was facing the window, Velamir could only see the man's thick black hair tied back with a strip of leather. The man had a proud bearing about him. He held himself as if he were a prince or high advisor who was entitled to everything. Velamir leaned forward, his eyes narrowing when he saw he was conversing with someone. Velamir couldn't see the other person, for he was hidden from view by the towering height of the first man. The black-haired man looked toward the window, and Velamir froze.

His dark gaze examined the tavern's structure. There was something about his eyes that was unsettling, almost evil. When Velamir was sure the man hadn't seen him, he drew away from the window. After inspecting the other rooms and seeing they were identical to the first, Velamir went down the stairs and exited the rowdy tavern, only for more shouting and screaming to meet his ears. A crowd of people formed a line, pumping their fists in the air. He focused on the yells and realized what they were saying.

"Run! Run!" they shouted in unison.

Velamir walked past the line and saw a man sprinting straight at him. His eyes were wild and crazed. His hands were extended, trying to grasp at salvation. The man's body jolted as a crossbow bolt went through his chest, spraying blood everywhere. The bolt continued its trajectory, narrowly missing Velamir before burying itself into the soil. The man convulsed and collapsed facedown onto the ground, exposing the gaping hole in his back.

21

JAX
KINGDOM OF VERIN
TOWN OF NAMAAR

"THE TAILOR'S SHOP is near," General Winston said.

Jax walked behind Lissa, focused on the gloves hanging from her belt. Ten long talons formed the gloves' fingers. Jax had crafted them for her after their tests in Tariqi. They were as lethal and beautiful as her. His gaze lifted to her hair. The unevenness of it made her more alluring. She had cut it during one of their riding breaks. He was so focused on her that he startled when a rough hand wrapped around his arm. He was jerked to the side. A tough man wearing a shirt with sliced sleeves to show off his muscular arms faced him.

"What is a Savorian doing here?"

Jax restrained himself from touching his

hair. The blond curls and his pale skin and light eyes had always troubled him.

"Did you escape the slaver's cart?"

Jax didn't know how to respond, but then he didn't have to, because a second later, Lissa's elbow struck the man's windpipe. He choked, releasing Jax, and held his throat. Lissa grabbed Jax's arm and pulled him away. Winston waited in the doorway of the shop, and as soon as they entered, he closed the door behind them.

"We should have cut your hair too," Winston remarked casually.

Jax stayed silent, as did Lissa. He glanced around, noticing racks upon racks of dresses and coats, different-colored fabric. Capes, scarves, boots, numerous amounts of apparel.

"Hello, hello, welcome." The voice was airy.

A man stepped forward from behind a rack. Compared to all the surrounding colors, he looked dull. Brown coat, brown pants, brown hair, brown boots, brown eyes. But everything he wore was impeccably clean and crisp, including his mustache, which was trimmed neatly across his upper lip. Jax could only think, *What is this man doing in a town like Namaar?*

"How can I hel—" Mustache man's voice cut off when he saw them, and he leaned forward in a half bow. "You have arrived."

Winston nodded. "I trust you haven't been detected, Harold?"

Harold's smile was strained. "Do you not have trust in one of your own?"

One of your own.

Harold was Tariqin, and from this tailor act, he probably was a Chishman spy.

"It is no matter," Winston replied. "Now that we have arrived, you will surely be detected."

Harold smoothed his coat. "What?"

Winston glanced at the closed door and stepped closer to Harold. He spoke in a low voice. "Verin's general might have sent men after me. If they've seen me enter here, they will come to interrogate you."

Harold blew out a breath and smiled a perfect merchant's smile. "I was going to leave nonetheless. I hear there is more business in Verintown—and more gossip. News of importance that could be collected."

"We always have need of that."

Harold nodded and snapped to attention. "Well, what do you need?"

Ten minutes later, Jax sat beside Winston, True Manos robes in his arms. A wooden chest rested beside Winston, full of clothes for Quintus and Velamir. Winston took some things for himself after a lot of prodding from Harold. Jax rested his head in his palm, thinking of the man who had accosted him in the street. When would the day come when he could roam as a free man? Not a Shadow Manos, not a True Manos, not Savorian, Tariqin, or Imperial. Just him. Just Jax.

The sound of rustling brought his attention to the curtain. Lissa moved it aside and stepped forward. Jax's mouth slackened. He reached up and closed it before he made a fool of himself. She was stunning. Lissa wore a long blue dress that pooled at her feet like water. Jax could drown right there in awe. It was plain, without embellishments, but it looked so right on her. The color went well with her warm skin tone. The sleeves hung off her shoulders and fell in swoops. Harold had altered her hair as well, and it lay in a straight cut, ending just past her jaw.

"Well?" she asked.

Jax was mute, and Winston stroked his chin. Harold observed from where he stood against a rack.

"It's a little plain," Winston admitted. "But again, we don't want to draw too much attention."

Harold tapped his head. "I have just the thing."

He returned with two belts, one inlaid with dark blue gems and the other with violet.

"Which do you think?" Harold held them out.

Lissa raised a brow. "I doubt it matters."

Winston opened his mouth to reply when Jax blurted, "The violet!"

They turned to look at him, and he said weakly, "They match your eyes."

Lissa's long stare made Jax want to scratch at his burning neck.

"I don't think people will want to notice my eyes," Lissa said, reaching for the belt anyway.

"It's a rare color, and I would like for my wife to differ from the other ladies who will be present there," Winston said.

Though he was referencing their mission, that statement made Jax uncomfortable. Lissa placed the belt on and tightened it around her waist. Harold clapped his hands.

"Perfect! This one next?" He held out a gold gown in a different style.

Winston shook his head. "We have six gowns. That should be more than enough."

Lissa went back to the dressing room and returned in the clothes she had been wearing before they came to the tailor's shop. Winston shook hands with Harold.

"Thank you for your assistance."

"Of course. I might arrive at the castle before you. Perhaps I will see you there?"

Winston's brows lifted in amusement. "I doubt you will beat us there."

Jax knew what Winston found amusing. No one could beat them when they were using the Zamanin Sulari to travel. His hands itched for his journal. He wanted to review everything he knew about the traveling formula. Lissa took his robes from him and motioned for him to take the chest. Jax grabbed hold of the chest, and they stepped outside.

While they waited for Winston, Jax's attention caught on a cheering crowd. A table and bench were set up in the middle of the street. A man set one leg on the bench and leaned forward. He held a crossbow in his arms. A slaver's cart behind him was filled with panicked Savorians. The slaver shouted an order to his men, and they dragged out an older Savorian. He cried out, and his kinsmen attempted to hold on to him, but they fell back when the slaver's guards slashed them with their vicious whips. They dragged the slave to the man with the crossbow. Jax's heart raced as he watched the scene. The world darkened to a gray haze around him.

"Here, Lilly! Try it with this," Jax told his older cousin.

She frowned as she stared at the new contraption he had built. But her arms were so tired from kneading the dough that she relented.

"How do I use it?"

"Hold these two pieces together, and it will turn," Jax instructed.

She did as he said, and the lower part of the contraption whirled. Lilly startled, almost dropping it. After reclaiming her wits, she tried it again and brought it toward the dough. It turned the dough quickly, helping form its shape three times faster than she could have done. Lilly laughed in delight, and Jax smiled until he heard a creak in the doorway.

"What is this? Are you manipulating my daughter to accept your witchcraft?" Uncle Casr spat.

"No, I . . ."

Lilly set the contraption down. "He was just helping me, Father."

"Just helping you," Uncle Casr repeated, his face darkening with fury. "It seems you haven't learned your lesson."

He grabbed Jax's shirt and hauled him outside into the snow. They lived on the edge of Devorin, and the cold was biting. Lilly screamed for her father to stop, but he didn't listen. He shoved Jax to the chopping block, and Jax's heart chilled. Uncle Casr grabbed Jax's hand and pulled his pinky away from the other fingers before picking up the axe that rested nearby.

"Please," Jax whispered, his voice hoarse.

The cold air blew over him, racking him in shivers. His threadbare clothes hardly provided him with any warmth. Despite Jax's protests, Uncle Casr didn't listen. He lifted the axe, but Jax jerked away. Uncle Casr shoved him back and punched him. Jax's head snapped to the side, and his teeth bit into his lower lip, causing blood to burst forth. Jax shook his head, disoriented, and before he knew it Uncle Casr lifted the axe and brought it down on his hand, slicing off half his little finger. Jax screamed, even though he couldn't feel the pain. He was numb, frozen. He couldn't even register what happened.

Uncle Casr cursed him. "Don't you dare come into the house, Tana!"

He left Jax in the snow. For minutes, Jax lay there, shivering and bleeding. At that moment, he didn't care if he died. Lilly snuck out and bandaged his finger.

"Get up, Jax," she sobbed and helped him reach the barn. He crumpled against a block of hay inside.

Lilly placed a blanket over him and kissed his forehead. "I'm so sorry."

"Lilly!" Uncle Casr shouted, and she ran back to the house.

Jax clutched his midsection. He shook in pain and terror. Tears fell from his eyes, mixing with the blood on his chin and lip. Jax remained there for what felt like an eternity when a shadow fell over him. The torch Lilly had lit was snatched from its place and held over him. Jax blinked, staring up at a pair of menacing brown eyes. The man's lip lifted, and the firelight shined on a gold tooth.

"Hey, kid."

Jax kicked him and scrambled off the hay. He ran through the back door toward the house. A sound came from behind him, a sound that haunted him for years to come. A deep laugh of amusement. Jax tripped over the snow. His makeshift shoes couldn't keep out the snow, and his toes felt icy. He couldn't care less at that second, because when he glanced back, the man was there, walking toward him with confident strides.

"Uncle Casr!" Jax shouted. The fear in his voice sounded strange to his own ears.

Uncle Casr threw the door open as Jax reached it.

"I told you not to come!" He held a butcher knife in his hands.

Jax froze. If he went forward, his uncle would kill him. If he went back, he wasn't sure what was awaiting him.

Uncle Casr peered over Jax at the man. "Who are you? What do you want?"

"I'm Vykus," the man said, and Uncle Casr took a step back, his hand inching to the doorknob.

Jax's breath clouded the air before him. Vykus, the man who worked for Prolus, the mercenary king, the child stealer.

"You know what I want."

"You can have him. He's an extra mouth that I couldn't care less to feed."

Those words cut Jax deep, not because of what they said but what they meant. His uncle was giving him up, to be killed or taken to who knows where.

"Perfect." Vykus's lip pulled up.

The memory faded, and Jax stared at the man leaning over the bench. The mohawk that adorned his head. He yelled at the Savorian slave and held up the crossbow, aiming at his back. His lip curled, and the tooth flashed just as Jax remembered it. Vykus was here. Vykus was back.

NATASSA
KARALIK EMPIRE
THE GRAND PALACE

S WEAT ROLLED DOWN Natassa's brow, and a
rush of heat blazed through her head. She
jerked, throwing up into the pail Krea held
out for her. She sagged back against her pillows,
her throat raw and head aching. The skin around
her wrists throbbed from the chains.

"It's going to be okay," Krea told her, stroking
her hair. "Maybe it will help if I brush your hair."

She took Natassa's brush and rubbed ovaline
into her hair. The scent was overpowering, making
her feel worse. Her stomach revolted, and she
sputtered, the remaining food Krea had smuggled
to her climbing its way back up. Krea brought
the pail just in time, and Natassa retched. There
was nothing left inside her when she was finished. Natassa gripped Krea's hand.

"Should I call for a True Manos?"

"No, no, I'm fine." Natassa attempted to smile. "Just sit beside me."

Krea sat back on the stool, and they didn't speak for a while. Darkness closed in on her. Natassa didn't know why her body was reacting this way. She had always been weak, but never like this.

"Tell me a story of your village, where you used to live."

Krea cleared her throat. "You know everything about us."

Natassa closed her eyes. "So, tell me again, when you were girls."

"Deya was born first, a minute before me. She was forever the more serious one. When our mother got sick, she made Deya promise to take care of me, to make sure we would never beg in the streets like she did." Krea glanced down, and Natassa squeezed her hand. "Kasdeya heard the emperor was looking for decoys. She was the one who made sure we were found in our remote village. She sent a letter, and it fell into the right hands. The guards came and took us away."

She smiled at Natassa. "And then we had the pleasure of meeting you."

Natassa shook her head, wincing when a sharp pang danced across her vision. "How do you see the positive side of everything?"

"If we worry about things going wrong, we will always be worried. And that creates wrinkles." She pointed at her forehead and laughed. "Truly, Natassa, Deya and I are beyond lucky and proud to be your bodyguards."

They shared a smile that broke off when the door opened. Natassa saw the Cadellion first and then her father. He stopped a short distance from her and motioned for them to unlock her chains. Natassa held in her exhale of relief when the heavy metal dropped away. Her wrists ached, and she kept herself from rubbing at them.

"Stand up."

At the emperor's command, Krea helped Natassa rise. She grimaced at the darkness crossing her vision and leaned against her decoy. Malus stared with disgust.

"It's only been a few days and yet you look as if you haven't eaten for a century. You're just bones." He glared at Krea. "The joust begins soon. Ready her into some semblance of a princess."

Then he was gone.

Natassa turned to face the mirror, but Krea grabbed hold of her arm. "Don't look. Let me work on you first. Stay here, I will draw a bath."

She entered the door on the side of Natassa's chamber and readied the bath. Natassa's curiosity won over, and she turned toward the mirror. A stranger stared back at her, pale and haggard. The circles under her eyes were darker than ever before. Her nightgown hung on her, and when she pulled the fabric against her form, she winced at how thin she looked.

What is wrong with me?

She heard Krea returning and moved away from the mirror. Krea took Natassa's arm, escorting her to the bath. Natassa soon found herself in the steaming tub, staring at the wall across from her. Heat rose in the form of vapor wafting around her. Natassa dunked into the water and washed her hair. Krea came to assist her, applying soap and scrubbing her head. Natassa stepped out of the tub minutes later, rejuvenated. She sat on the chair before the vanity, noticing it was positioned away from the mirror. Krea worked on her face, smoothing creams and powders over and under her eyes. Rouge on her lips and cheeks. Natassa held still the whole while. They were interrupted once by a knock on the door. When Krea opened it, a servant stood in the doorway. He bowed and held out a package.

"A gift from His Royal Highness, Crown Prince Draven."

Krea took it and waved the servant away.

His cheeks flushed, and he peeked at Natassa. "Your Highness, ah . . ."

Krea raised a brow and glanced at Natassa, who spoke up. "What is it?"

"The emperor ordered me to inform you that you must wear the gift."

The servant darted away, clearly uncomfortable telling a princess what to do. Krea closed the door and paused a moment before glancing at the package.

Natassa nodded. "I suppose we better open it."

Krea couldn't contain her excitement as she tore through the package. Natassa wasn't sure why Krea was so thrilled to see Draven's gift. Inside the package was a gleaming silver gown. Krea gasped as she ran a hand across the soft fabric.

"It's stunning," she whispered, longing entering her gaze.

At that moment, Natassa wanted nothing more than to give her the dress. Krea shook through her daze and gave Natassa a smile, returning to her side to finish applying products to her skin. Then she brought the gown and helped Natassa dress. Natassa felt repulsed by each layer. The fact that Draven had her in mind while picking it out made Natassa want to throw it from the balcony and watch it fly away while imagining it was the prince. Kasdeya entered the room and assisted Krea with the final touches.

"Look in the mirror, Natassa," Krea told her.

Natassa turned slowly, afraid of what she would see. Her hair was half up, and the rest trailed in loose curls past her waist. The face powders hid the circles beneath her eyes and the strain between her brows. The gown hugged her shape. It would have been very unflattering if Krea had not filled in areas with extra padding to make her appear to have generous curves. Natassa winced as she stared at herself. It felt fake; she felt fake. This body that the dress showed wasn't hers; the face she wore wasn't hers. The crown upon her head wasn't really hers either, for she was powerless to stop what was happening in the Empire despite how much she had tried.

"You look beautiful," Kasdeya said, a hint of something in her voice.

Natassa turned to look at her. She didn't want to think it, but it sounded as if Kasdeya's voice was layered with a touch of jealousy.

"I don't feel it," Natassa replied.

Krea adjusted some of Natassa's hair from behind

her. "Your father sent word for you to cut your hair before leaving for Ayleth."

"Again?" Natassa sighed. "He knows I won't."

"He said it would be a shame on the Hartinza family if the princess didn't follow the customs," Krea said.

Natassa remembered Aylis's words about keeping her heritage strong by staying with her customs. A wry smile lifted her lips. Aylis was respecting her traditions by keeping her hair long, and Natassa was rebelling by doing the same thing.

"It would save us the trouble," Kasdeya grumbled, her voice so low Natassa barely heard it.

"I'm sorry," Natassa told them. She felt as though the only things she ever said to them were apologies.

"Don't apologize, Natassa," Krea said, giving her hand a gentle squeeze.

Natassa glanced at Kasdeya, noting her expression hadn't changed in the slightest. In fact, she looked agitated and impatient.

"What's wrong?" Natassa asked.

"The seamstress sent word an hour ago that your cloak is ready."

Natassa knew something else was on her mind but didn't want to press her. She turned to Krea. "Will you retrieve it?"

Krea nodded, and after she left, Natassa's thoughts returned to the ball. She smoothed over her skirts and set a hand on her stomach, trying to quell the sick feeling that erupted at the thought of seeing Prince Draven again. The worst part was that the ball would take place after the jousting. She was dreading every part of the joust. She hated it. She hated this whole day.

"Your father requested you be early, but I'm afraid we are going to be late if we wait for Krea," Kasdeya told her. "We should go. Krea will catch up to us."

Natassa pushed aside all her doubts and worries and straightened her shoulders. She lifted her chin, convincing herself that she could face the coming onslaught. Kasdeya followed her as she walked out of her chamber. The hall was empty. An eerie feeling went through her. The hairs on her neck raised. It was odd that the hall would be vacant. There usually was a guard posted on either end.

Natassa walked down the hall, stopping when she saw someone standing under one of the torches that lit the area. The person was dressed in black and stared straight at her. Natassa's heart pounded when the figure took a step in her direction. A hood was pulled low over his face. Natassa could tell it was a man by his build and height, and the thing that terrified her most was the disturbing smile pasted on his face. It was so wide it looked as if it would split his face in two.

He strode toward her, his hand reaching for the dagger in his belt. Natassa's eyes grew wide, and she turned, running back to her chamber. Pounding feet behind her made her heart race faster. Just as she reached the door to her chamber, brawny arms wrapped around her waist and flung her back. Natassa screamed as loud as she could. He covered her mouth with a gloved hand.

"Shut your mouth, girl," he growled in her ear with a heavy accent.

She tried to bite his hand, but the cloth he wore was too thick. She kept struggling, but he didn't release her. Instead, his hold on her strengthened. Trying to thwart her increasing panic, Natassa remembered Thorsten's words.

The best thing to do is go limp, as if you fainted.

Natassa stopped struggling and sagged against him. At first, the man seemed surprised and kept his iron grip on her. Then his arms slackened. Natassa dropped, twisting her upper body as she went down. He cursed in disbelief and reached out, trying to grab her. He caught onto her wrist, and Natassa grabbed a knife, ripping it out from her belt and stabbing it into his arm. He howled and released her. Natassa opened her chamber door, bursting inside. She saw Kasdeya rummaging through the chest on her vanity. At the commotion, Kasdeya turned, and shock crossed her face.

"Help me," Natassa gasped out.

The man barreled into the room and thrust the dagger at Natassa. She jumped to the side. The dagger sliced into part of her dress. Natassa stumbled and fell, letting out an oomph as she crashed onto the floor. She turned onto her back and clambered to the corner of her room. The assassin was approaching with his dagger held tightly in his hand. Natassa pulled another knife from her belt and threw it at his face. The blade sailed through the air, slicing along his left cheek. His mouth opened, revealing his pointed teeth in all their glory as he released an animalistic shout. Blood poured down his face and over his mouth. The assassin licked the blood from his lips and smiled, red staining his teeth. Natassa's heart pounded as she continued scrambling away from him. Her back smacked the chamber wall. There was nowhere to go.

He lurched forward, holding the dagger above her heart. Natassa caught sight of the exposed skin at his wrist. A tattoo covered the area. The curving S shape of a snake. The mark of a Savagelander. Natassa's eyes snapped to his face, and her look of horror was met with his menacing, bloody smile. Natassa closed her eyes and drew in a shuddering breath. The dagger came down.

VELAMIR
KINGDOM OF VERIN
TOWN OF NAMAAR

VELAMIR WIPED THE blood that had splattered onto his face. He looked up from the body, and his gaze landed on a man leaning over a table in the middle of the road. He guffawed and pointed at Velamir, finding his shock humorous. It was clear he had shot the man from the crossbow he held in his hand. It took Velamir a moment to realize who he was. Vykus, the man who brought orphans to the academy. But what was he doing here? And why did he kill this man? Velamir glanced at the person standing beside Vykus. He was a giant, muscles widely visible as he crossed his arms over his chest. Salvador, Vykus's number one henchman.

The crowd was motionless, watching the interaction. Velamir's hand edged to his sword. Vykus looked away from him and spoke to another man, handing him a small bag of coins.

"Pleasure doing business with you." The slaver pocketed the coins and motioned to the large cart holding Savorian men and women prisoners. "Which one?"

Vykus contemplated for a moment and pointed at a scrawny, pale-faced old man. "Him. we shouldn't waste the young ones."

Velamir moved to intercept the transaction, but someone grabbed his arm. "What are you doing?"

He turned to see Quintus glaring at him and shook his hand off. "What I have to."

"Are you trying to interfere with Vykus? Are you crazy?"

Velamir leaned closer and said in a biting tone, "Prolus conquered Savoria. Those people are part of Tariqi. I won't let him kill them."

"You have a death wish, zelont."

Velamir looked back at Vykus. The slave trader handed over the old man. Although they were a fair distance away, Velamir could hear Vykus's words perfectly.

"Now run. If you escape this"—Vykus held up one of his bolts—"then you're free."

Velamir gritted his teeth. What kind of game was this? How could Vykus toy with people's lives in this disgusting way?

"Run!" Vykus bellowed.

The poor slave did as he was told, running as fast as his bony legs could carry him. Vykus lifted his crossbow and aimed, his smile inching wider as he heard the people's chants urging the slave on. Velamir ignored

Quintus's shouts and leaped just as Vykus released. The bolt shot through air, twisting in the slight breeze. Velamir pushed the slave to the side, and the bolt ripped across his shoulder. He glanced down and saw a steady flow of warm blood. His sleeve was torn, and the blood-stained fabric clung to his skin. Velamir glared at Vykus. The crowd hushed, and Vykus scowled back.

"You're spoiling the fun, boy. That's my slave."

Velamir walked toward him, ignoring the mercenaries in his employ who stiffened and reached for their weapons. Velamir stopped when he was mere paces away and spoke in a low tone so the crowd wouldn't hear. "You should be thankful you are in Prolus's service."

Vykus's calculating brown eyes danced. "Or what?"

"Or your neck would need a new head."

Vykus laughed, but then his amusement faded. "And who are you?"

Before Velamir could answer, Winston was there, glowering at Vykus. "What are you doing here?"

"My job." Vykus lowered his voice. "Searching for recruits. Retrieving the Savorians that tried to run from their duty."

"You should look for the orphaned, homeless children, what you usually do," Velamir informed him.

Vykus exchanged a glance with Winston. "Put your pup on a leash so he doesn't get involved in things too big for him."

Velamir stiffened and stepped closer. Salvador did the same, reaching for the broadsword strapped to his back. Vykus held up a hand to stop his henchman, and Winston grabbed Velamir's shoulder in a firm grip. Velamir winced as it increased the pressure on his wound. Winston glanced at the blood, and worry turned his expression. He released Velamir and spoke to Vykus.

"This is no pup. He will soon be a face you take orders from."

Vykus scoffed, and Winston nodded.

"You should be careful with your words." He glanced at Velamir. "Go, lad. Let Jaxon handle your wound."

Velamir backed away from the mercenaries, not breaking eye contact with Vykus until he was forced to turn to see where he was going. Most of the crowd had left, seeing nothing of interest to incite them any longer. Velamir saw Quintus standing in the same place with his arms crossed. The slave Velamir had saved curled into himself on the ground. He kneeled beside the Savorian and touched his back.

"You are safe now," Velamir told him.

His features were haggard and eyes haunted. The white in his hair spoke of wisdom, but his face was younger than Velamir had thought. This man had endured much, too much. Through the grief and weariness, a new light shone in his face, and it took Velamir a moment to realize it was respect.

"You took that for me?" the man asked, glancing at his shoulder.

The way he stared, as if it was impossible for anyone to sacrifice anything for him, made Velamir think of himself when he was a boy. Newly arrived at the academy. Orphaned, alone, put down by the other children. The Head Chishma's words rang in his mind.

He just isn't good enough.

Velamir's fists clenched. Those days were gone. He would never believe those lies. Velamir looked back at the Savorian.

"Everyone deserves a chance. You don't always get the life you want, but you make the best of it." Velamir stood and offered him a hand.

The man stared at it for a long moment before clasping it. Velamir pulled him to his feet. He heard someone calling his name and turned to see Jax approaching with Lissa by his side.

"You are bleeding," Jax's eyes fastened on his arm.

Velamir was about to reply when he saw the old man walking back toward the cart. Velamir opened his mouth to tell him to stop, but he noticed the cart was open and all the Savorians were standing outside it. Winston was still speaking with Vykus, and the slaver appeared upset.

Jax waved a hand in front of his face, bringing his focus back. "Let's go to the tavern so I can patch you up."

Velamir grimaced and glanced at his sleeve. The material was soaked through, and blood ran down his hand, dripping in fast drops onto the ground. Jax grabbed hold of his good arm and gave Velamir a slight push.

"You are an idiot, Vel," Jax said, shaking his head as they walked toward the tavern. "The bravest idiot I've ever seen."

Velamir smiled, wrapping a hand around his arm to stem the bleeding. Lissa and Quintus followed them. They could hear yelling and laughter from the tavern before reaching the doors. Jax pushed them open and strolled to the bar counter with Velamir behind him.

Jax banged on the counter, catching the barkeeper's attention. "Send someone to start a fire in one of our rooms and be quick about it."

The innkeeper smiled. "Will do, but I need to be compensated."

Winston entered at that moment. "I will handle this."

The barkeeper called for Stanley who proceeded up the stairs. Velamir followed, the others close behind. Stanley took a duplicate key of the one Velamir had from his pocket and opened the first door in the hall. Stanley began the procedure of starting the fire. While waiting, Velamir shrugged his shirt off.

Stanley stood up from the fireplace and glanced over at them. His gaze landed on Velamir's wound. "Well, that sure ain't pretty."

Velamir bunched his shirt into a ball and pressed it to his wound. He winced when the cloth met his torn skin. Quintus scoffed.

"If he'd listened, he wouldn't be in this mess."

"Why don't you help for once?" Jax snapped.

"What do you need?" Lissa asked.

Her eyes lingered more on Velamir's chest than his wound, making him uncomfortable. Jax noticed and handed her a dagger. "Hold this into the fire. As soon as the blade turns red, hand it to me."

"Move aside," she told Stanley and crouched beside the fireplace.

"You are going to cauterize me?" Velamir asked.

Jax nodded. "The tonics only do so much, but I need to stop the bleeding before I use them." He sounded nervous. It was his first time without Frumgan as his guide.

"I need another dagger," Jax muttered.

Velamir pulled his own from the sheath in his boot. Jax told Velamir to sit on the bed, taking the dagger from him.

"Open your mouth," Jax commanded.

Velamir obeyed, and Jax placed the hilt of the dagger between his teeth. Velamir clamped his teeth onto it, holding it in place. Lissa appeared with the other dagger, which was now glowing orange. Jax took it carefully and nodded at Velamir.

"Ready, Vel?"

Velamir braced himself and nodded back, moving his shirt from the wound. Winston stepped inside the room at that moment and watched as Jax moved forward, placing the blade on Velamir's shoulder. The dagger hissed as it touched the wound. Smoky steam rose into the air, along with Velamir's roar of pain. He tried to hold it in, especially when he saw Winston's look of pity. His teeth felt as though they would shatter on the hilt between them. The pain continued to smolder until Jax finally pulled away. Velamir reached with his good arm to pull the hilt out of his mouth. His breath came out in gasps. Jax set his dagger aside, and Winston came closer, motioning for Stanley to leave. Stanley exited with an awestruck look.

Jax took a vial from his bag and popped the cork off. "Drink this."

Velamir gulped the stuff as fast as he could, not wanting to linger on the bitter taste. He wiped his mouth when he finished and felt the tingling sensation. He glanced at his shoulder, watching as the burn faded to a light pink.

"There will be a scar still," Jax said.

Velamir grinned. "A mark of honor."

"More like a mark of stupidity," Quintus grumbled.

Velamir ignored him and glanced at Winston. "What happened with Vykus?"

"He's taking the Savorians home."

"What?" Velamir rose, horrified.

Winston held out a hand. "Relax, lad, he will obey my command. Although Vykus may be a ruthless cut-throat from The Docks, he still has some sense in him. They will not be harmed. I've made sure of that."

"But—"

"We will leave early tomorrow, head to the stream near the town, and use the Zamanin Sulari to arrive in Verintown. Rest now," Winston said and addressed Jax. "Make certain to check on his wound."

Jax nodded and glanced at Velamir, who was removing his boots.

Winston smiled at Velamir. "You're a good lad. It was kind of you to help those Savorians today. Be careful not to be so generous at the castle. Our people aren't there, only our enemies. In the nest of snakes, you will be poisoned."

"Wise words," Velamir said. "I shall remember them."

After Winston and Lissa left, Quintus fought to have the bed, but Jax told him Velamir needed the rest to recover faster, so in the end Quintus grumbled and placed his bedroll on the floor beside Jax's. Velamir lay against the pillows on the bed, sleep dawning on him when he heard Quintus whisper.

"Why did you do it?"

"Do what?" Jax replied.

"At the academy, during the test, you saved my life. Why? I bullied you for years."

"Maybe I wanted you to change your mind about Shadow Manos."

Quintus didn't reply, and soon, their snores were the only sounds in the room. Velamir faded into a troubled sleep. He saw Vykus attacking the Savorians, hacking away their lives. He saw a set of gleaming hazel eyes peering at him.

Help me.

Velamir jerked awake and sat up. He swept off the bed and moved to the window. The cool night air wafted in, a welcome reprieve on his heated skin. He knew sleep was futile, so he grabbed his boots and dagger.

A loud thump came from the room beside Velamir's, and he paused in the middle of reaching for his sword belt. There was a movement that sounded like a scuffle. Velamir left his belt, unsheathing his dagger instead. He crept to the door and opened it, cringing when it made the creaking noise. As he stepped into the hall, a rapidly moving figure caught his attention. Velamir glimpsed the same black-haired man he had spotted from the window earlier rushing down the steps to the first floor of the tavern.

"What are you doing?"

Velamir turned and saw Quintus standing in the doorway. Velamir motioned to the fleeing man. "Follow him. He looks suspicious."

"I don't take orders from you, zelont," Quintus scoffed.

"Do it."

Something in Velamir's voice must have convinced him of the seriousness of the situation, because without another word, he took off toward the stairs. Velamir moved to the next door and knew something was wrong when he saw it was wide open. He rushed inside, releasing a strangled gasp when he found Winston lying in a heap on the floor. Velamir rushed over, falling to the ground beside him.

"What happened?" Velamir asked, checking Winston for wounds.

Winston's breathing was heavy. His chest rising and falling unnaturally fast. "It was . . . Boltrex."

Velamir struggled to understand. "Boltrex? What did he do?"

Winston's eyes clouded over. "He had me killed just as he killed your . . . parents. Take my . . . revenge. Finish the . . . mission, lad."

"No." Velamir shook his head. "You aren't dying!"

Foam spurted from Winston's mouth. Velamir remembered Jax telling him foam was a sign of poisoning.

"I will get help!" Velamir said with a crazed look.

He started to rise, but Winston grabbed his arm in an iron grip. Winston struggled to speak. He convulsed as Velamir wiped the foam from his mouth. Winston's eyes were glazed, and he stopped moving. His hand dropped from Velamir's arm.

"No, no, no, no, no," Velamir repeated over and over. He fisted his hand in his short hair and sat in shock for a while next to Winston's motionless form.

Finally, he stood and searched the room for the

source of poisoning, his eyes blurry with tears. There was nothing except for an empty glass. Velamir looked at the pitcher beside it and noticed that it was full to the top with water. He took the glass in his shaking hand. This couldn't be the source. The man he had seen must have been Boltrex's hired assassin, and if he had any brains, he took the poisoned evidence with him.

Velamir dropped to his knees beside Winston's limp form. A single tear dropped from his lashes. His eyes darkened with hatred as he swore over his mentor's body. "I will avenge you. I promise."

The glass shattered in his clenched fist, the sharp pieces cutting into his skin, sealing his vow in blood.

24

NATASSA
KARALIK EMPIRE
THE GRAND PALACE

NATASSA LAY WITH her eyes closed, waiting for the brutal blow. Instead of the dagger piercing her, the assassin crashed on top of her. Fearing the worst, Natassa screamed and shoved him off with all her might. He landed on his stomach, a dagger shoved deep into his back. Natassa looked up. Kasdeya stood in the place the assassin had been moments before, her eyes wide and a dagger sheath empty. Kasdeya dropped beside Natassa.

"Are you all right?"

Natassa was shaken but managed to nod. She saw Krea standing in the doorway, covering her mouth.

"Natassa!" She rushed forward, falling to her knees next to her. "What happened?"

"He attacked me." Natassa stared at the body. She looked back at Kasdeya. "Why didn't you come with me?"

"I remembered the necklace Prince Draven sent to your room when you fainted. The one he tried to give you in the sitting room. I hurried back to retrieve it." Kasdeya's head lowered. "It was an unforgivable mistake."

Krea seemed ashamed as well. "I should have come sooner. I didn't think it would take so long to acquire this."

Natassa saw the long cloak flung across Krea's shoulder.

"This was planned," Natassa whispered. "Where were the guards? No one was in the hall. This man had connections in the palace."

Krea nodded. "What are you going to do?"

Natassa rose. "First, we must attend the jousting tournament. I will make my move after."

Krea draped the cloak around her shoulders. "We don't want anyone to see your gown until the ball."

Natassa grimaced. "About that . . ." She moved the cloak aside so they could see the tear in her dress.

The twins entered their chamber to retrieve their sewing essentials, leaving Natassa alone. It was a strange moment, isolated with merely a dead man for company. A while passed, and still the twins didn't return. Natassa walked to their door, and when she neared, she heard agitated voices.

"I will tell her, and I don't agree to this."

The twins' voices were as identical as they were, making it impossible for Natassa to tell who was speaking.

"What you are proposing is treason."

Their voices grew lower until Natassa couldn't hear them any longer. Footsteps neared the door, and she spun away, retreating to the spot she had been standing before. They reentered the room, both wearing strained smiles.

Krea made quick work sewing the dress closed while Kasdeya looked at the man on the floor and checked his pulse to ensure he was dead.

"What should we do with him?" Krea asked.

"We must dispose of him," Kasdeya hastened to say.

"No," Natassa cut in. "I need to show my father."

Honzio probably hadn't mentioned anything about overhearing Draven's conversation with the Chishma, and if he had, Emperor Malus had done nothing about it. Draven was still a guest in the palace, able to move freely. If she showed her father the body and told him it was Draven's man, he might finally realize that a marriage between them wouldn't work. If Natassa played her cards right, her father might call off the wedding. Natassa smiled at that thought. Her handmaidens surveyed her expression curiously.

Her smile died as she remembered the tattoo on her attacker's wrist. He couldn't be Draven's man, unless Draven worked with Savagelanders now.

After Krea fastened the cloak in place over her dress, Natassa motioned them forward. "We have a joust to get to."

When they reached the royal box overlooking the tiltyard, Emperor Malus turned his disapproving glare on Natassa. She kept her face blank, knowing he wanted to see her broken and obedient, results of his wedding gift. Natassa analyzed the nobles near them, nodding with a tilt of her chin, and sat in the seat designated for her. Her handmaidens stood behind her chair, ready to assist.

"Where were you?" the emperor hissed from the corner of his mouth. "You have missed two matches."

"Has Thorsten gone yet?"

"No," her father muttered. "You should ask if Prince Draven, your intended, has jousted."

Natassa bit back a retort, glancing at the seat beside him, meant for Honzio. She wasn't surprised to see that he wasn't present. He stayed far away from anything that reminded him of his past. The herald stole her attention as he announced the next jousters.

"The Invincible Dragon, Prince Draven Valent of Ayleth, and His Royal Highness, Prince Thorsten Hartinza!"

The crowd seated around the tiltyard erupted in cheers. Natassa gripped her cloak as the two men rode up to the royal box. The emperor paused for a few dramatic moments and then nodded at the men and the herald. Thorsten and Prince Draven took their positions on opposite sides of the list. Their armor clanked as their horses shifted. They seemed to eye each other's weaknesses through the narrow slits of their helmets. They lifted their lances to show they were ready, and the herald blew his horn. Natassa held her breath as they charged at each other. The first pass was over in a flash. No damage or unhorsing was done. Natassa sighed in relief but couldn't help thinking Draven was toying with her brother.

The second pass was far worse. Draven drove his lance into Thorsten's shield. Thorsten barely stayed on his horse. His lance shattered against Draven, but it didn't affect the prince at all. Natassa was leaning on the edge of her seat by the third pass. The horses galloped, dirt flying from their hooves. The crowd's chants pierced Natassa's ears. Both men had their lances aimed at each other. But one had better aim. Draven's lance struck true, and Thorsten went flying off his horse and crashing into the dirt, unmoving. The crowd hushed.

"No," Natassa whispered. Fear swirled around her heart and gripped it like a cold hand.

Natassa pushed off her seat and ran down from the gallery, ignoring her father's angry shouts. She rushed into the tiltyard, falling to her knees beside her brother. Tears streamed down her face. Draven had dismounted by then and removed his helmet. His normally slick blond hair lay damp and limp on his forehead.

"Princess, you shouldn't have come."

Natassa snapped, "Help me remove his helmet."

Draven muttered under his breath and crouched beside her. They pulled Thorsten's helmet off. Natassa gasped when she saw his condition. His face was ashen, and his forehead dripped with blood from a crack in his head. Natassa covered her mouth, holding back a sob. True Manos crowded them, assessing Thorsten's state.

"Excuse us," one of the True Manos said.

Natassa backed away, feeling Draven's looming presence behind her. The Head True Manos pressed a cloth to Thorsten's head to stem the bleeding while other healers removed his armor. Natassa's chest shook with sobs.

The Head True Manos's brow was creased.

Natassa stepped closer. "Tell me he will be all right."

"The prince's situation is dire. If I cannot stop the bleeding, he may die."

Natassa crumpled to the ground. That was the last thing she wanted to hear. The True Manos brought a wooden board, and they lifted Thorsten onto it.

"Careful, don't jostle him," the Head True Manos said and instructed them to take Thorsten to the healing quarters.

Gavin appeared distraught and lost as he retrieved the fallen armor. The True Manos carried Thorsten away. Natassa remained on the ground, silent sobs bursting from her chest. Draven kneeled before her and placed his hands on her shoulders.

"Princess, this is neither the place nor the time. We have an audience," he said in a low voice, nodding his chin toward the crowds of people.

Natassa got to her feet and jerked away from him. "Don't touch me!" She seethed. "This is what you wanted, isn't it? This was your entire plan!"

People near enough to hear her shouts gasped and spread her words to their friends. Draven's gray eyes turned stormy.

"I know you are in pain, but there is no reason to accuse me. This is a joust. Your brother was too weak and shouldn't have competed."

"How dare you!" Natassa shouted. "You wanted this. You want my whole family dead!"

Draven's jaw twitched. "It *was* you in the library."

Natassa's heart beat in rapid thumps. All she could

feel was the burning fire building within her chest, and the flames wouldn't be doused until she made him pay for hurting her family. Her fingers darted within her cloak, to her knives, and she stepped forward.

Draven glanced at her hand, and his eyes made a trail back to her face. A smile pulled at his lips, and he closed the distance between them. "Are you truly trying to stab me before all these witnesses?"

His heated breath brushed her nose. Natassa fought the impulse to look away. She clenched her teeth, hand closing around her knife.

"That is enough!" the emperor boomed, leaning over the gallery railing. "Apologize to Prince Draven!"

Natassa jutted her chin. "Never."

She ran from the tiltyard and didn't stop until she reached her chamber. She slammed the door shut and collapsed onto her bed, weeping into her pillows. Her door opened, and Natassa heard the bar being placed over it. She sat up, seeing Kasdeya shaking with agitation and fear. Kasdeya rushed forward and took Natassa's hands.

"I'm so sorry."

"What am I going to do without Thorsten?" Natassa murmured. "I have no one left."

"I don't want to make matters worse, but there's something I have to tell you." Tears welled in Kasdeya's eyes.

"What is it?" Natassa asked, worry building.

"It's—" Kasdeya's voice broke, and she swallowed. "It's Krea."

"What about her?"

Kasdeya glanced to the ground, and Natassa followed her gaze and stiffened. The body was gone.

Kasdeya bit her lip. "She's my sister, Natassa. She made a stupid choice. I'm begging you."

"What is going on?"

"She . . . she was working with him. The man who tried to kill you." Kasdeya closed her eyes, and a tear slipped from her lashes. "She tried to convince me to join her, but I refused."

Natassa's heart dropped to the pit of her stomach. "Why would she do this?"

"She said she wanted to be free of the torment of serving you."

"So she wanted to have me killed?" Natassa said incredulously. "If I had known she carried this much dislike, I would have found a way. Even if my father disapproved, I wouldn't care."

"That's not all," Kasdeya whispered. "She was poisoning you every day."

Natassa released a shocked breath. "What?"

"Ovaline is toxic, Natassa, and she was brushing your hair with it for months."

"That's why I was ill," Natassa realized, the pieces falling together.

"You should be dead," Kasdeya said bitterly. "That was her goal."

There was a knock at the door.

"It's her," Kasdeya said, wiping her tears. "Please, Natassa, go easy on her."

Kasdeya opened the door, and Krea glanced at her with a frown before turning to Natassa. Natassa felt hurt and angry and frustrated.

"Why?" she whispered.

Krea seemed confused. "Natassa, I need to tell you someth—"

Natassa held up a hand. "I've heard everything I need to hear."

Krea's lips parted. "What?"

"Krealyn Vosta, I release you from your duty."

"Natassa! You are making a mistake." Krea's eyes were wide and panicked. "Let me explain."

"Leave," Natassa ordered, and when Krea didn't move, she raised her voice. "Get out!"

A tear slid down Krea's cheek. "You always were my princess, Natassa, and you always will be." She lifted a hand over her chest in the half heart symbol and bowed her head.

Then she was gone. Natassa crumpled and cried more tears than she ever had before. Her brother was at death's door, and the person she saw as a sister had betrayed her. Her heart was torn in two, and she didn't think she could stitch it back together again.

25

VELAMIR
KINGDOM OF VERIN
TOWN OF NAMAAR

"J AX!" VELAMIR CALLED.

He hoped that Jax could do something, anything, to change what lay before him. Velamir was frozen, overcome by the loss of his mentor. He couldn't believe it. It drove him insane every time he looked at Winston lying there on the floor. There had been a moment when he thought Winston stirred, his imagination getting the best of him. He could wish all he wanted for his mentor to return, but he had to accept the truth. Winston was dead, and he wasn't coming back.

"Velamir?" Lissa whispered.

Velamir snapped out of his daze and looked up at her. She peered at Winston's body.

"What happened?"

"He was killed," Velamir's voice cracked. "They poisoned him."

Where was Quintus? He hadn't returned since chasing after that man. Velamir stood when Lissa came close.

"The Imperials," Lissa said, disgusted.

"It was Boltrex." Velamir ran a hand over his hair and felt wetness trail across his forehead. He looked down and realized it was blood from his hand. He took a strip of the bedsheet to wrap around the wound. Blood filled the cloth in moments, dying it crimson.

"What's going on?" Jax burst into the room. "What is that?"

He dropped beside Lissa, his gaze fixated on the object in her hand. Velamir came closer and realized it was a vial. She shook her head.

"I found it near his body."

Jax leaned over Winston's chest and pressed his ear to it, checking for a heartbeat. Velamir watched tensely as Jax pulled away, his face distraught. He checked for a pulse at Winston's neck.

"I feel nothing." He glanced up. "I'm sorry, Velamir, he's gone."

Velamir's fists clenched at his sides.

"Can you tell me what happened?"

When Velamir didn't speak, Lissa said, "Velamir told me he was poisoned."

Velamir retreated to the window and opened it, leaning out. Desperate to inhale the fresh air and dispel the sharp ache swirling through him.

"Maybe the poison was in the vial," Jax suggested as

he and Lissa continued speaking behind Velamir. "Can I see it?"

Velamir heard a light thump and shattering glass. He turned to see the vial in broken pieces. Jax winced, and Lissa's lips twisted into a grimace.

"It slipped from my hand," she said.

Jax ran his thumb over his last finger, deep in thought. The sound of footsteps neared, and Quintus entered. He shook his head, swearing.

"He got away."

Velamir couldn't contain his anger. "How could you let him go? You're a Chishma, for Tariqi's sake!"

"Keep your voice down," Lissa said, brushing past him to close the window.

"He's not an average man, zelont," Quintus growled. "I would like to see you chase after him."

"Who are we speaking of?" Jax asked.

Velamir relayed to him what had happened, and then Lissa asked Quintus, "Did he see you?"

Quintus hesitated. "Yes."

Lissa shook her head. "If he works for the general, he will be at the castle. If he sees you there, the plan won't work."

Velamir scoffed. "The plan? What plan? We don't have a plan anymore."

Jax stared at the ground. Lissa and Quintus exchanged glances.

"You don't even care that Winston was killed. How can you speak of the mission?" Disgust rolled off Velamir in waves.

Jax spoke first. "Vel, I can't imagine how hard this is for you, but—"

Lissa interrupted, "In two weeks, at the end of the jousting celebration, Prolus will ride through Verin, expecting it to be crumbling on the inside. We have to finish this."

"If you want to stay behind, that's your choice." Quintus sneered at Velamir.

Velamir's fists clenched, and more blood poured through his thin bandage, sliding between his fingers until it dripped onto his boot. "I have to bury him."

"Quintus will do it," Lissa said. "He can take the body to the manor."

Quintus didn't argue, to Velamir's surprise, but he didn't like the idea of Quintus burying Winston.

"I want to do it," Velamir said, his voice hoarse. "I have to. At least in my final act to him, I must be the one to place him in the ground."

Lissa stepped closer to him. "Your final act will be avenging him. Killing Boltrex will put him to rest. That man saw Quintus. He cannot come with us."

Velamir gritted his teeth, breaking away from her dark purple eyes. Winston's last words floated through Velamir's thoughts.

Finish the . . . mission, lad.

"Fine," Velamir said, glancing at Quintus. "I have one request."

"What is it?"

"Bury him beside his wife."

"Done," Quintus agreed.

Lissa nodded and cleared her throat. "We better get moving before the body starts decomposing."

Jax lifted another vial from Winston's coat. "I found the Zamanin Sulari. As soon as we arrive at the stream, we can use it to reach the castle."

Quintus and Velamir carried Winston's body from the room. It was dark outside. The tavern was closed, so they encountered no one on the trip to the stables. They found an abandoned cart and placed Winston's body in it. Velamir helped Quintus hitch the cart to his horse. Velamir heard a nicker and saw Dauntess lifting her head. He ran a hand over her coat in silent apology.

They readied fast, saddling the horses and retrieving whatever belongings remained in their rented rooms. Soon, they were all mounted and riding through the town. The cart slowed their pace. Velamir trotted beside Quintus, ponying Dauntess, who carried all the armor and extra clothes. Lissa and Jax rode in front. Lil' Jimmy, the gatekeeper, grinned when he saw them. His eyes landed on Winston's motionless form.

"Want to know where the undertaker is? I just need one coin, son." Seeing Velamir's spearing glance, Lil' Jimmy's head hung. "Or not."

After leaving the town, they came across a split in the road where they would go in opposite directions. Velamir reined in Vandal and looked up at the dark sky. A sprinkling of stars found its way in the darkness overhead. The moon's soft glow stared down at them. It was a shame such a beautiful night was fated to be sorrowful.

"Prolus needs to be alerted to Winston's death,"

Velamir said. "Send word to Chishma Talon after you bury him."

"I will," Quintus said. "Make sure you don't blow this mission. I like it here."

Jax laughed, and Velamir found his lips curving of their own accord, which surprised him. He would have never believed he would consider Quintus a friend. He wasn't even sure if he did now, but he wasn't an enemy.

Quintus gave them a nod. "For Tariqi."

"For the better," they answered and watched him set off with the cart.

After Quintus faded from view, Velamir urged the group on. They traveled for hours. Velamir pushed Jax and Lissa on through the day, not stopping for rest until darkness blanketed them once again. Velamir caught sight of the stream Winston had been speaking of in the distance. The water sparkled under the moonlight.

"There it is," Jax said.

They dismounted beside it and untacked the horses. Dauntess's coat was lathered in sweat from carrying so many things. Velamir gave her a good rubdown and did the same for Vandal and the other horses while Lissa and Jax set up camp.

"We will rest here and come up with a new plan." Velamir joined them by the fire. Jax handed him dried meat. "I will go as Winston's son like planned. Jax will be our True Manos."

Lissa started, "I will be your—"

"Sister," Velamir cut her off. "We don't have Quintus, so someone will have to take his target. Lissa?"

She took a bite of meat. "Why not? What's one more?"

"Winston won't be there to guide our way. We need to be careful and communicate with each other."

"Try not to kill the general right when we get there and mess up the plan." Lissa smiled at him.

"Out of everyone here, I want this to succeed," Velamir replied.

Jax glanced between them, fidgeting. "I, for one, am not looking forward to the True Manos robes."

"No one asked," Lissa said, keeping her eyes on Velamir.

"I will take first watch," Velamir said. "Get some rest."

They moved away from him, unfolding their bedrolls. The wind blew in soft breaths and grew cooler as the night progressed. Velamir leaned back against the trunk. Memories of Winston flitted through his mind. He stood, the sharp ache returning to his chest. He walked over to Vandal, running a hand along his coat. He would see the castle in the morning. After many years he would return to Verintown. He wondered if it would look different to him now that he was grown, or if it would seem more treacherous now that he knew of Boltrex living safely behind the castle walls.

Velamir thought of Blayton, his jousting mentor. Winston had said he'd contacted him. Velamir pondered if the renowned lance master would want to assist him now that Winston was gone. He remembered him as a kind man, sometimes praising Velamir's riding ability over Latimus, his own son. And the day they had left

Verintown, Blayton had even gifted Velamir with the choice of a horse from his stables.

"Well, son, go on."

Velamir passed the stalls, walking past all the prized colts until he reached the far end of the stable. Blayton followed, and even Latimus accompanied them.

"I want him," Velamir said.

Blayton's brows shot up, and he exchanged a glance with Winston, who had joined them.

"Son, he's a fierce one. Since he was born, no one has connected with him. He's good as wild." Blayton tsked. "Which is certainly a shame. I expected great things for him."

Velamir didn't respond as he stared at the two-year-old colt. At all the attention, the horse grew skittish, digging his hooves into the ground. Velamir opened the stall door despite Blayton's warnings and went inside. The horse stared at him, his pawing growing faster as Velamir neared. Velamir reached out, and his fingers grazed the colt's coat. The horse stiffened, and Velamir stepped beside him, his head level with the horse's eye. After a moment of hesitation, Velamir placed his palm flat against the horse's back. The horse lifted halfway into the air in an angry rear.

"Get out, son!" Blayton called to Velamir.

Velamir saw Latimus's gaze, already burning with jealously, become determined, and he reached out, slamming the stall door in supposed terror, closing Velamir in. But Velamir wasn't afraid. He stroked the horse's coat until he calmed under his touch. Velamir stepped closer, whispering soothing words into his ear.

"It's all right. They cast you aside, but I won't," Velamir told him. "You will be fearless, and you will be free."

It was a bold promise for a boy of ten years. General Winston watched him with a soft gleam in his eye. The horse dipped his head over Velamir's shoulder and let out a friendly nicker. Blayton's mouth dropped open.

"Four kingdoms!" he exclaimed.

Winston smiled. "We will take him."

Velamir pressed his head to Vandal's. His horse snorted softly as if conveying his sympathies. Velamir could still see Winston's smile, proud and pleased. He wouldn't have gotten anywhere without him. Velamir owed Winston the world. He reached into his well-worn boot and unsheathed his dagger.

"Thank you . . . for everything," Velamir whispered, looking at the dagger's sharp edge as a tear rolled down his face.

26

NATASSA
KARALIK EMPIRE
THE GRAND PALACE

NATASSA PEEKED INTO the chamber. It was Oslavit Day, a celebration in remembrance of the massive battle that had taken place over a hundred years ago. When the Karalik Empire had defeated the Savagelanders. Natassa watched her father shower Hesten and Honzio with gifts. A niggle of jealousy found its way to her heart. She hadn't been invited to join.

She blinked back tears and turned to leave but bumped into someone.

"Whoa!" Thorsten grasped her arms to steady her.

"Sorry, Thor, I didn't see you." Natassa continued looking down so he wouldn't notice her tears.

"Hey," he said, lifting her chin.

"You should go inside. Father has gifts for you." She hated the way her voice cracked, but there was no way for her to control it.

"I have something for you," Thorsten told her.

"Really?"

"Really." Thorsten smiled and reached into his belt. He pulled out a bracelet. It was thin and plain, with a small black pearl resting in the center.

"I love it!" Natassa exclaimed, throwing her arms around her brother.

Thorsten pretended to stumble from her weight, and Natassa laughed. After she pulled away, Thorsten placed the bracelet around her wrist. *"The man I bought this from said it was a special bracelet and could only fit a very special person."*

Her chin wobbled when she noticed it was too big. *"It doesn't fit."*

Thorsten shook his head. *"That's because you're too small yet. It will fit fine in a couple of years. Besides, that was not what the man meant. He told me it is rare to find a black pearl. Natassa, you are one of a kind."* Thorsten took her small hand in his. *"And whenever you look at this bracelet, I want you to remember that and be brave. Never give up Natassa, you are so much stronger than you think, and you can face anything."*

Natassa sat on the edge of her bed, playing with the bracelet encircling her wrist. Her fingers brushed over the pearl.

"I'm trying to be brave, Thor," she whispered.

She had attempted to see Thorsten in the healing chambers several times. The True Manos had prevented her, telling her his situation was critical. There was a sudden banging on her chamber door. Natassa stood as her father stormed in.

"Why aren't you at the ball?" he demanded.

"You didn't postpone it?"

The emperor growled. "First, you embarrassed me with that ridiculous so-called prophecy, then you shamed me by arguing with Prince Draven in front of crowds of witnesses. You defied me by removing your handmaiden from the palace." He nodded, sneering. "And now you are going to make a late entrance to your own betrothal ball."

"I didn't think you would be that unfeeling toward your own son and still host the ball."

The emperor slapped her across the face. Natassa winced and covered her stinging cheek. Her head spun, her sickness from earlier hadn't faded. In fact, it had worsened.

"That . . . was a warning. Watch your tongue with me, girl, or I might see fit to cut it out." The emperor glanced at Kasdeya. "Fix this mess."

He left as quickly as he came. Natassa ran a hand over her belt, feeling the comforting knives placed within. She unsheathed one and gripped it. Sometimes she felt like stabbing him, or even herself. It was better to be done with it.

Half an hour later, Natassa waited outside the doors of the ballroom for her name to be announced. She felt Kasdeya's precise hands smoothing out the layers of her ballgown behind her. Nerves quaked in her stomach at the thought of seeing Prince Draven again. Who knew how he would act after her accusations?

Footsteps echoed down the hall, and Natassa turned to see Honzio approaching with his guards and decoy, Bronus. Honzio's face was gaunt and eyes bloodshot. He was attired in finery, and despite his ill appearance, it seemed he was going to the ball as well.

The herald motioned for them to enter. After exchanging glances, Natassa hooked her arm in Honzio's good one, and they proceeded forward, leaving their protectors behind.

"His Royal Highness, Crown Prince Honzio Hartinza, and Her Royal Highness, Princess Natassa Hartinza!"

The doors opened. Natassa glided in, managing to keep up with Honzio's long stride. The pressure of hundreds of eyes probed her. Natassa stared ahead, keeping her shoulders squared. Whispers flittered around the ballroom as the people gossiped to each other.

As they continued walking forward, Natassa whispered, "What's wrong?"

"Thorsten has been injured in the tournament, surely that is enough wrong."

She looked up at him. "You are upset for Thorsten?"

"I'm not unfeeling."

"All those times you never came to the tournaments, I thought it was because it bothered you to remember."

His jaw flexed, and he didn't reply.

"But it was because you didn't want to watch Thor get hurt." It wasn't a question. Natassa knew in her heart that was the true reason.

She returned her attention forward. They were almost at the raised platform. Prince Draven sat on a chair near the emperor's dais, where her father reclined on his grand throne. Honzio stiffened, and Natassa followed his gaze. The emperor was motioning for him to sit beside him.

Prince Draven stood and strode toward her. Honzio glanced at him and then down at Natassa. There was hesitation in his gaze that Natassa had never seen before. She gave him a small nod and withdrew her arm. His face turned to stone once again, and he walked forward till he reached their father's side. Natassa's attention returned to Draven, who was drawing near. The whispers hushed as everyone waited to see their interaction.

Draven stopped a foot from her. Natassa almost took a step back to put room between them but didn't want to give him the upper hand. She waited for him to say something or do something to show his anger. After a few moments of building suspense, he bowed and took her hand, placing a kiss on it. Natassa knew her face must have shown her astonishment, and she composed herself.

"Your Highness," Prince Draven said as he lifted himself from his bow.

"Prince Draven." Natassa curtsied.

"You need not tell me the apology you have no doubt thought of. I will spare you," Prince Draven said, louder than necessary.

People started tittering.

Natassa's brows drew together. "You don't have to spare me as I haven't even—"

"Princess, I forgive you," Draven interrupted, narrowing his eyes.

Prince Draven nodded at the group of minstrels in the corner, and they started playing a slow song. Draven closed the remaining distance between them, wrapping an arm around Natassa's waist. She tried to pull away, but he tugged her closer and grabbed her hand.

"What are you doing?" she hissed.

Draven gave her a wolfish grin. "It's our ball, isn't it? We must have the first dance."

She leaned away from Draven's tight hold, but he pulled her back, his arm locking behind her like a band of steel.

"You are hurting me," Natassa said through clenched teeth.

Draven leaned closer so their faces were mere inches apart. He laughed, sending a shower of his breath onto her face. "Did you say something?"

He seemed to enjoy watching her discomfort. Natassa tilted her head to the side.

"Don't look away," Draven said. "I am leaving tomorrow, and I want to take the memory of your beauty with me."

Good riddance, Natassa thought. Hoping he was going so far that she wouldn't see him anytime soon, she asked, "Where are you heading?"

"Ah, so you will miss me?"

"Why would I?"

Draven's face darkened, and he whispered in her ear, "I have tolerated your disrespect so far. But once we are married, I will have none of it." He paused. "I know you listened to my conversation in the library, but I'm still willing to marry you."

The unspoken words hovered in the air. *Marry you and not kill you.*

"Don't even try to speak to your father about this. He will not heed your words. Your best chance at living a longer life is choosing me."

Natassa chilled at his words. He was threatening her. He would kill her if she didn't go along with him. Anger followed the rush of fear, and all Natassa wanted to do was stab a knife into his gut.

She scowled at him. "Do not speak to me in that manner if you wish to keep the betrothal intact. I am the emperor's daughter, and you are a mere prince."

Draven tilted his head and chuckled as if she had said something humorous.

"Arrogance does not become you, Natassa."

She lifted her chin and met his iron gaze. "I did not give you leave to use my name."

Draven twirled her under his arm and sent her spinning back into his hold. His piercing stare leveled on her face, the lanterns setting his eyes alight as they traveled over her form. His smile was dangerous and cunning, eager to play.

"Whatever you say . . . *princess.*"

27

VELAMIR
KINGDOM OF VERIN
VERINTOWN

VELAMIR WAITED FOR the others by the stream. The sun peeked into view, casting its first rays onto the water. He heard clomping hooves behind him. Lissa and Jax approached with their horses. Velamir edged closer to the water, gripping Vandal's reins. Vandal shied away, as if sensing what was coming.

"Easy boy," he whispered.

Velamir gave Jax the go-ahead, and he took the vial from his pocket, pouring it over the stream. The liquid spread across a portion of the water, and it sprung into the air, crackling as it froze over.

"Would you do the honors?" Jax asked.

Velamir stepped forward, unsheathing his sword. He drove it into the portal, piercing through the frozen water. A burst of shock coursed over the blade, all the way to his fingertips. Velamir flew backward, landing in the grass with a thump.

"Vel!"

Velamir sat up gingerly, spotting his sword a few inches from his hand.

"What in Tariqi was that?" Jax exclaimed.

Velamir stood, snagging his sword from the ground. "I don't know, maybe the vial was faulty."

Lissa mounted her horse and called to them, "It looks big enough to ride through. I'm going in."

Her horse reared, and without a backward glance, she galloped forward, jumping into the portal. Velamir's jaw slackened when he saw how wide the void was. At least twice as large as the opening Bear had made the first time they used the Zamanin Sulari.

"We don't know how much time we have until it closes. We should go," Jax suggested, mounting his horse.

Velamir slapped Dauntess's rump, and she trotted through without further prodding. He mounted Vandal and urged him in after Jax. Velamir was flying, the air rushing at him, whipping Vandal's mane into his face. Velamir's stomach turned, but somehow, it wasn't as terrifying as the first time had been. In fact, it was sort of fun. Vandal shot out of the portal, hooves kicking up the grass. Velamir regrouped with the others and glanced at his surroundings. They were on a high hill. He rode to the edge, spotting the castle in the distance. It was a formidable-looking place with its high towers and walls. A large town encircled it. It was highly unlikely that an army could penetrate the castle walls. It was possible, but it would mean many casualties. That was what made Velamir's mission so important. They had to finish the battle before it could start. What were a few lives in place of hundreds?

Velamir's skin itched under his fine clothes. They had changed into their disguises early that morning. Jax rode up beside him, his True Manos hood pulled over his head, covering his blond hair and casting his pale skin in shadow. Jax's eyes traveled down, landing on Velamir's hand, where a large ring fit around his forefinger. The cavalier symbol caught in the sunlight, and Velamir's hand flexed, uncomfortable with the new weight and the burden it reminded him of.

"I found it in Winston's pack," Velamir told Jax. "I might need to show it to the guards."

As they neared the town, Velamir could see smoke rising from the tops of houses and shops. Farmers were out in the fields harvesting crops. The castle keep was visible, rising high above its fortifying walls. The cool breeze blew against Velamir's face as he urged Vandal down the hill to the entrance of the town. He held the reins in one hand and Dauntess's lead rope in the other. People looked up at them as they rode in. Some waved in greeting, and others stared with suspicion. There was a blacksmith and livery, bread stalls and a tavern. Velamir nodded at the people who stared and gave them a friendly smile.

They reached the drawbridge that crossed to the castle's gatehouse. A deep moat surrounded the castle, and accessibility would have been impossible if not for the bridge. Velamir took in the six armored guards posted at the gate. The head guard signaled with his finger, and two of the others stepped forward to search their bags. They left Jax's bag alone, trusting him because of his True Manos appearance. Lissa stiffened, but she didn't stop them as they glanced through her saddlebags. Luckily, they didn't pry under the dresses where he knew her gloves were concealed.

"Thorough gate security these days," Velamir commented.

"Tough times. We are instructed to trust no one," the head guard explained. "With Prolus's dogs prowling the area and the Borderlands overtaken, it's only a matter of time before the Tariqins come."

"Dogs?" Velamir asked, although he knew the man meant rumloks.

"They've been lurking around, spying perhaps, or waiting for their moment, who knows." He cleared his throat. "Your purpose here?"

"We came for the tournament."

"Your names and crest please," the guard commanded, the red plume atop his helmet swaying as he looked down at a parchment in his hands.

Velamir held out his hand so the guard could examine the ring and then introduced the others. "My sister, Lissa Raga, my True Manos, and I am—"

Before he could introduce himself, the guard's eyes widened. He glanced at the parchment again and then up at Velamir.

"Winston Raga? *The* Winston Raga?" Surprise coated his voice. "Please forgive our scrutiny. You may enter freely, Galva."

"I, uh—" Velamir was cut off by the other guards.

"The Cavalier?" one of them said in astonishment.

"Call for an escort." There was more whispering between the guards, and one of them took off toward the castle entrance.

"Open the gate!" the head guard called and smiled at Velamir, saluting him with a half heart. "Good luck in the tournament, Galva Winston."

"Thank you, but I'm afraid you have mistaken me. Galva Winston is my father. I'm Velamir Raga."

The head guard's smile dimmed, and he stumbled for words. "My sincerest apologies, sir. I didn't intend to mistake your identity."

Velamir smiled. "Truly, I'm not offended. I find it the highest of compliments to be mistaken for my father."

"Well then, Velamir Raga, I wish you the best of luck."

"Thank you." Velamir glanced back at Lissa and Jax and motioned with his head for them to follow him.

They walked their horses through the entryway. A royal escort greeted them as they passed into the courtyard. He informed them of their upgraded accommodations in the castle and led them to the royal stables, where they were to keep their horses and gear. All provided free of charge by King Dale. Once the horses were settled, the escort led them to the tavern for a meal and refreshments. After the escort left, they placed their order with a server.

Jax raised his brows at Velamir from across the table. "It's clear those guards have never met the gene— Galva Winston."

"But they know of his reputation," Lissa added while glancing over the tavern occupants.

They were situated in the corner of the tavern, which granted them some privacy. Velamir looked at the other two.

"I could've pulled it off."

Jax frowned. "What?"

"They believed I was Winston. Imagine how many others would too."

Lissa shook her head. "You would have been caught. The general knows what Winston looks like and so does the king."

"Besides," Jax started, "if Boltrex heard Winston was still alive, he would be after you. This time to ensure the job is done."

Velamir's lips lifted in a grim smile. "I would count on it."

"Didn't you say just yesterday that we should communicate with each other and not ruin the plan?" Jax said.

"What are we doing right now?" Velamir replied.

Lissa sighed in frustration.

Velamir glanced over their shoulders. "The server is returning."

They sat in silence as plates of well-prepared meats were placed before them. The server set three glasses of water on the table and left them to their meal.

"What is this?" Jax asked, picking up a thick hunk of juicy meat.

Lissa took a bite. "Rumlok."

Jax dropped it back on the plate, disgusted.

Lissa chuckled. "You are so easy to play. It's lamb."

Velamir took a sip of water and watched a man walking near their table. He paused and turned to look at them. Velamir stared back. He seemed familiar, his narrow eyes calculating and sizing them up. His hair was light brown and cut short, thinning by his hairline.

"Can I help you?" Velamir asked.

The man smiled and slid down on the bench beside Lissa. She paused mid-bite to examine the new addition to their table.

"You're a little young to be in your fifties," the stranger commented with a sneer.

Velamir stiffened, his guard lifting. "I don't understand."

"Don't worry, I'll keep your little secret." He gave them a patronizing smile.

"What secret?" Velamir asked.

Lissa pushed her plate aside and reached for the table knife.

"You can't fool everyone, boy," said the man, acting like he was twice his age, although he could not be much older than Velamir.

"And who are you?" Lissa whispered near the man's ear, her voice slithery like a snake as she placed the knife's tip onto his thigh.

"Relax, I'm a friend," he told them. Velamir noticed his throat bob as Lissa increased the knife's pressure.

"I have no friends." Velamir said.

"I'm hurt you don't remember me, Velamir. I'm the captain of the king's royal lancers and son of the lance master who trained you."

Velamir startled when he heard the man call him by his name.

"Latimus? Commander Blayton's son?" Velamir realized that was why he'd looked so familiar to him. He remembered Latimus, but as a much younger, arrogant, and rude boy. It seemed not much had changed. "How did you find me?"

Lissa removed the knife and placed it back on top of the table. Latimus winced when he saw blood staining the tip.

"We are a well-connected people, us lancers. Word of Galva Winston's arrival spread like wildfire. Mind if I join you?"

"You already have." Jax slid his plate down to Latimus and glanced at Lissa as he said, "It's lamb."

Latimus eyed the meat and then focused on Velamir again. "If you wish, you can stay at my home for the night. I believe my father offered Galva Winston accommodations. My father is staying in the castle for a few days to help organize some matters. I can show you around the town and castle in his stead, if you so desire. I also have information about the competitors who are most likely to enter the tournament."

Velamir exchanged a glance with the others. Jax nodded at him, approving of the plan, but Lissa shook her head. He knew she wanted to get straight to the castle and build their web of deceit, but Winston had wanted them to stay with the Blaytons. Perhaps it would be more beneficial if they were better prepared before entering the viper's nest.

"We would appreciate that."

A smile spread across Latimus's face. "Excellent. As soon as we are finished here, I will show you the way to my home."

"And hopefully not a trap," Lissa snapped.

Latimus smiled, reaching for her hand. "And why would I trap a lovely lady like you?" He brushed his lips over her fingers.

Jax choked on his water. His fingers gripped the glass as he watched the interaction.

"That's my sister you are touching, Latimus," Velamir warned.

Lissa snatched her hand out of Latimus's just as he held his up in apology. "I didn't know you had a sister." He peered at Jax. "Is he your brother too? Winston has a lot more family along with a younger face."

"Shut it, Latimus. Winston is dead."

28

GENERAL BOLTREX
KINGDOM OF VERIN
VERINTOWN

GENERAL BOLTREX VAZ was many things—
a murderer, selfish, controlling—but not
a coward. The dungeon was cold. Almost
as cold as the mornings in Devorin, and it was only
heated by the anger emanating from Boltrex's eyes.

"What did you say?" he whispered as he leaned
over the chained man.

Prolus's phantom coughed blood as he laughed.
"If you weren't a coward, you could have stopped
us. But the Empire has no place for courage."

Boltrex slammed his fist into the Chishma's
gut, and he grunted from the impact.

"Where are the hostages? We said we would
exchange for them."

"There are no hostages," the Chishma

wheezed. "Before your men captured me, I was honored to witness their death."

Boltrex stepped back. Galvasir Jevin, Captain Fortin, Captain Kalex. They were gone, and he would have to announce their deaths to their families. Boltrex stepped out of the cell and snarled.

"Kill him and make it slow."

The guard waiting by the cell nodded.

"Prolus is coming!" the Chishma screamed. "He will end you!"

His laughter echoed behind Boltrex as he walked up the stairs out of the dungeons. Boltrex strode down the hall to his chambers. His eyes landed on a guard rushing past him.

"Stop," Boltrex boomed, his deep voice as dark as his hair.

The guard froze. Boltrex had a reputation in the castle. Not only about his brilliant combat strategies but also his ability to make one fear for their life.

"Yes, General?"

"Any news of importance?"

"General, I am to report to the king," the guard mumbled.

Boltrex's emerald eyes darkened with rage. "You will report to me first."

The guard's hands trembled. "Of course, General."

"What. News. Do. You. Bring." Boltrex bit out every word. His hand dropped to the large broadsword resting by his hip.

The guard's face was pale when he responded. "Galvasir Winston!"

Boltrex drew back as though slapped. "What about him?"

"He is here."

Boltrex towered over him, and the guard cowered, unable to meet his gaze. "Winston is here?"

"I saw him at the gate and was sent to inform King Dale."

"You may leave." Boltrex waved him away like he was a fly hovering over his food.

The guard raced down the hall. Boltrex entered his chambers, approaching his table of maps. He lifted a large hand and touched the scar running down his cheek. It was red and angry despite the years of healing. He slammed a fist onto the table, scattering papers.

"Mordon," he growled.

A knock on the door startled him. "Enter."

"General," the voice was unsteady. "We received a gift for the king, but as per your wishes we brought it for you to inspect first."

Boltrex beckoned the guard to approach. He nodded behind him. Two other guards entered, carrying a chest between them. They approached Boltrex with caution, the chest swinging as they moved. Boltrex threw open the lid. His nose was greeted with a smell so rancid, he nearly flinched. Three decapitated heads met his eyes, proving that the Chishma's words were true. They had killed them. Boltrex snapped the lid closed and glanced at the guards. Their faces were pale. Boltrex scoffed at their queasiness.

"Send word to King Dale that I wish to meet with him," Boltrex ordered. "You are dismissed."

They hurried from the room, and Boltrex was left alone once again. He felt vacant, almost as if even his hardened heart of stone had disappeared from his chest as well. Boltrex moved to the back of the chamber, opening his closet and reaching inside. He pressed his fingers against the secret wall. It slid open, revealing a small chest. Boltrex brought it to the table, setting it over the maps. The parchments crinkled at the movement. Boltrex's hands shook as he held them over the chest. He pulled out the chain that rested beneath his thick overcoat. A small key dangled at the end. Boltrex brought the key forward and paused. He knew what was inside. He knew it was the only thing that reminded him of who he was, or rather, who he used to be. That man was long gone, and no one could bring him back. Boltrex cursed and returned the case to the closet. He flipped through the maps, not even looking at them. The gears in his mind whirred as he contemplated his next course of action.

A loud knock pulled him from his thoughts. Mordon entered, pausing in the doorway. His head almost touched the top of the frame. Boltrex looked at him with disappointment. Mordon faltered in his step but regained his confidence and strode closer.

"Father, I have good news." Mordon wore a proud grin.

"I'm sure it can't be any better than finding out Winston is here."

Mordon frowned. "How is that possible?"

"You know how much of a threat Winston is to us! Once again, you have failed a mission. And not just any mission, but the most important one of all."

"I haven't failed you, Father. I killed him myself. I know he is dead." Mordon was adamant.

"Then what is this nonsense I am hearing?"

"I am not certain myself, but I aim to find out."

"You had better, Mordon," Boltrex told him. "If Winston is alive, you will never have the chance to be king."

Mordon nodded and turned to leave.

Boltrex called after him, "Do not fail me again."

Mordon turned. A dozen emotions crossed his face until it settled on one. Determination.

"I will not."

29

VELAMIR
KINGDOM OF VERIN
VERINTOWN

L ATIMUS LED THEM through the busy streets, informing them with an apologetic smile that they were in the poorer section of the town. People stared at Velamir hopefully, begging for a coin or two. Velamir attempted to stop several times, but Latimus ushered them through the town, not giving him a chance.

"These people don't deserve your pity, Velamir. Their bad choices led them to the streets," Latimus advised him.

"Children are begging, and it's their fault?"

"If you are born in the main town in Verin and you are begging for scraps in the street, then yes. It is your fault," Latimus replied without mercy. "King Dale is generous. He gives charity to those who ask. There should be no poor."

Just as Latimus said those words, Velamir caught sight of the darkened figures hiding in the corners of buildings they passed. Their greed-filled eyes were alight as they searched for victims.

"There is more crime rampant than the supposed help King Dale gives," Velamir shot back. "These people are being robbed."

Latimus glanced around to see if anyone had heard, and said, "King Dale is a just ruler, but even he has to obey Emperor Malus. If he doesn't collect the yearly taxes from the people, he will be stripped of his kingship. He offers the people protection if they pay the taxes, and if they don't, he doesn't harm them, but he doesn't help them either."

"Why doesn't he just pay the taxes himself? It seems his coffers are deep."

Latimus chuckled. "Ah, Velamir, you don't understand the way this works. Verin will be destroyed if King Dale empties the treasury to pay the taxes. The people need to give a portion of what they make from farming or selling other products, or else they will become too rich and overthrow the nobility. A civil war is the last thing we need."

"And apparently, so is a little humanity," Velamir muttered.

Latimus pretended not to hear him. "One more street before the next section." He sounded relieved to be leaving the desperate beggars behind.

Lissa and Jax had stayed quiet the whole while, Jax's face furrowed with concern and Lissa trying to hold back her annoyance. Velamir was thankful that soon, with Prolus's arrival, the people of Verin would receive the help they needed.

As they continued, Velamir's attention landed on a woman with her back to him. She wore a black cloak that dragged on the dusty ground. She didn't seem to mind that as she leaned forward and handed a pouch to some of the poor. They cheered and praised her. The woman moved, and Velamir glimpsed a small smile on her face. She had to be noble, or at least the daughter of a captain. The material of the cloak was fine for a commoner, and she looked too clean to be from this part of town.

A cry rang out, and Velamir tore his attention from the lady. A woman in a plain work dress and head covered with a kerchief was screaming and pointing behind her where a muscular man was running off.

"My son! He took my son!"

Velamir didn't waste a second and chased after the man.

"Velamir!"

He ignored the shout and continued pursuing the kidnapper until he reached the end of the alleyway where the ruffian slowed to a stop. Once Velamir caught up, he saw what was blocking the kidnapper's path.

The cloaked woman from earlier.

The kidnapper grimaced when he realized he was cornered. A child of eight or nine years struggled in his arms. Tears ran down the boy's cheeks. The kidnapper turned to face the woman rather than Velamir.

"Give me the child." She spoke with authority.

The kidnapper unsheathed his blade, revealing a long, jagged sword. He lunged forward and brought the blade down toward the woman. Velamir rushed to protect her. She dodged with ease, and with dangerous precision, took a dagger from her belt and sliced through the kidnapper's wrist. He howled as his hand smacked the dirty ground. Velamir stared with an open mouth, watching blood pulse out where the hand had been. The kidnapper dropped the boy, and the child crumpled to the ground. Velamir took his arm and hauled the boy behind him, keeping a firm grip on him.

The kidnapper whimpered, and the woman stepped closer. She leaned over, placing her dagger beneath his chin, and lifted his face toward hers.

She nicked his skin and said in a severe whisper, "If I ever see you again, there will be more than a hand missing. Tell Vykus to get lost from these lands or his head will be next."

Velamir froze when he heard her say *Vykus*. A memory of the slave came to his mind, the hole in his back and the blood that pooled around him. The kidnapper backed away from the dagger, moaning pitifully as he crawled to escape them.

"Don't forget your hand," the woman called after him.

Her hood had fallen back during the interaction. Velamir studied her. Thick plaited hair fell to her mid-back. The inky braids complemented her tan skin. She was tall and moved with a strong gracefulness that showed her confidence.

"Thank you for your help." Her dark eyes examined him. "You are braver than most."

Velamir replied in truth, "I did nothing." He nodded

to where the kidnapper disappeared. "You spoke of Vykus. This man works for him?"

"Nearly every mercenary in the Empire is in Vykus's pocket. He came from The Docks and brought all the filth with him." Her lip curled. "What he does is disgusting. Kidnapping children for Prolus to train as killers for his army."

Velamir stiffened at the mention of Prolus and processed what she had said.

"I thought he only took the orphan children."

She laughed. Her teeth shining white against her skin. "He takes anything he can. I wouldn't put it past him to carve a child from its mother's womb. But you can rest assured, he will be caught sooner or later."

Velamir felt the boy struggle against his grip and looked down.

"Let us return him to his mother," the woman told him. "She must be worried."

Velamir nodded in agreement. "You are safe now," he said to the boy. "What is your name?"

"Derolos," he mumbled.

"That's a nice name." Velamir struggled to think of something else to say. "You live with your parents?"

It was a dumb question, but Velamir wanted to find a reason the bandit would take a boy who had a mother. Maybe his father was dead, and the bandit had seen how hard it was for the mother to support her child. It would be a painful separation, but both sides would emerge better. At least, that's what Velamir told himself. He didn't want to imagine that the mercenaries were kidnapping children no matter their situation in life.

"My father is on a mission." The boy spoke louder this time, and his face lit up. "I will be like him when I'm older."

Velamir smiled. "I'm sure you will." He glanced over at the woman as they continued walking. "And I'm afraid I didn't catch your name."

She continued facing forward. Lifting her hood over her head. "You may call me Cora."

They exited the alley. A crowd was gathered around the distraught mother. Latimus, Jax, and Lissa were there as well. Although they stayed farther away. When the people saw Velamir and the boy, they cheered. The mother ran to them, crying tears of joy. She took the boy from Velamir and wrapped him in a crushing hug.

"How can I ever repay you?" she asked Velamir.

"I did nothing. It was . . ." Velamir turned to give the glory to Cora, but she was gone.

"What is your name, young man?" the poor woman asked him.

Before he could answer, a man in the crowd called out, "I know him! I saw him cross the drawbridge this morning and overheard the guards talking. He's the Cavalier!"

A low gasp flittered through the group. Everyone focused on Velamir with a new light. Jax wore the same grimace Velamir was sure mirrored his own.

"Actual—"

Loud drums cut him off. The crowd parted for a messenger declaring, "General Boltrex has an announcement to make."

Velamir's blood chilled and then boiled at the cursed

name. He held in his rage as a small platform was set up and guards surrounded it. A muscular man stepped onto the platform. His hair was dark and short, and a scar ran down his face. That was the most Velamir could make out from the distance. But it didn't matter. He knew who he was. Boltrex, the murderer of Winston and his family. Velamir could kill him now, finish him and receive the peace he craved.

Before he could move, Jax met his gaze and shook his head.

Not now, he mouthed.

Velamir inhaled sharply and tried to slow the burning anger smoldering through his veins.

"I have some unfortunate news," the general began, his voice loud and clear. "I regret to inform you that one of our Galvasirs and two of our captains have died at the hands of the Tariqins."

The people murmured, and Velamir exchanged a glance with Lissa and Jax.

"My sincerest apologies to the families of the dead. We have shelter for them in the castle, and they may stay for a month. They will be provided with the last earnings of the deceased, whose names are as follows . . ." He cleared his throat.

A strangled hush fell upon the people.

"Captain Fortin, Captain Kalex, and Galva Jevin Loster."

Velamir's heart froze at the same time a woman screamed, "No!"

It was the same woman whose son Cora had rescued. She held her boy tightly, her face pale and head shaking in refusal to believe. All Velamir heard was Talon's voice echoing:

He's Galva Jevin Loster.

Galva Jevin Loster.

Jevin Loster.

"No. Jevin's alive. He cannot be dead." She continued crying as the other people stared at her with pity.

General Boltrex met her gaze. "I'm afraid so. We received his head in a chest."

Velamir drew in a stuttered breath.

Imagine King Dale's rage when he sees the head of one of his best soldiers.

Chishma Talon had laughed when he'd said that. There had been no remorse for the actions about to be done.

"No," the woman cried, falling to her knees. Her son was confused and scared, feelings Velamir knew too well.

He wanted to say something, to comfort them, but he didn't, he couldn't. Velamir watched the moment the boy realized what happened to his father. The moment he realized the man he wanted to grow up like was gone, and a curtain of hate shadowed his face. Velamir backed away. He'd done this. Instead of creating peace, he'd created another monster.

Because he killed Jevin Loster. A husband, a father, a human. He'd done it for the sake of a future world where peace reigned, and he regretted every moment.

30

NATASSA
KARALIK EMPIRE
THE GRAND PALACE

NATASSA'S POSTURE WAS rigid as she stood at the bottom of the steps leading up to the palace's front entrance. Well-kept flowers of every kind were planted in straight lines in the courtyard, expensive stone boxing them in. Her father conversed with Draven by the sparkling fountain. He had enough common sense to be wary of Draven, keeping space between them. The Cadellion were heartbeats away from him.

The prince looked up at that moment, catching Natassa's watchful stare. He sent her a wink and one of his wolfish grins. Natassa's expression remained cold, her muscles frozen in place. Emperor Malus glanced back and gestured for her to join them. A palace guard accompanied her. Ever since she had dismissed Krea,

Kasdeya had been out of sorts, too distracted to do the simplest tasks and disappearing for long hours. Natassa's guilt was immense because she was the cause. She was the one who separated the sisters. She'd wanted to let Kasdeya go but knew her father would lash out. He wouldn't tolerate anything else from her.

Natassa moved forward, her steps appearing light as she walked toward her father and Prince Draven. To her, it felt as though bricks were lodged on the bottoms of her soles, each step a painful lead to her fate.

"Prince Draven is leaving to joust in Verin's tournament. Wish your betrothed luck," her father told her, a warning in his tone. After those words, he walked away with the Cadellion behind him.

"So, you are going to Verin," Natassa said. "How long is the tournament?"

"It shall be over in time for me to return to Ayleth for our wedding," Draven said, running his finger along her arm. "I picked a wedding dress that will look divine on you."

Natassa's fists clenched as she shrugged off his touch. "I hope you don't fall off your horse during the tournament. Or that an opponent knocks his lance into your helmet. Or for a knife to twist in between the open spaces in your armor."

Draven chuckled. "Why do I have a feeling that you want all those things to happen to me?"

Natassa's smile was thin. "I won't marry you, Draven. You can rest assured I will stop this wedding."

He leaned closer. "Your father won't care what

you want. He told me as much. He will see this marriage through."

A sting of pain flew through Natassa. She hated that her father's heartlessness still affected her. Natassa straightened her shoulders, lifting her chin to stare into his cold gray eyes.

"Then you might as well call this farewell our last, because I will be dead before that happens."

Draven's eyes roamed over her face, and for a moment, they softened. "You remind me of my mother," he whispered. "She fought just like you, but eventually the fire inside her died and she surrendered to my father." His gaze dropped to her lips. "You will too."

He brought his head down, and Natassa lowered hers so that his lips pressed into her hair. He laughed as though that was what he had intended and wrapped his arms around her in an awkward embrace. Natassa crossed her arms over her chest like a shield. Her posture stiff.

"My lady." The guard stepped close to them, her hand at her sword.

Natassa struggled against Draven's hold, and he released her without a fight. His lips lifted in a smirk.

"I'm fine," Natassa said, holding his gaze.

"No one lays a hand on the princess." The guard's voice was razor sharp.

"Not even her intended?" Draven looked amused. "Don't miss me too much."

He tapped her chin with a finger, and before she could react, he was mounting his horse. He reared high and saluted her with his hand curled in a half heart over his chest.

Natassa turned away from the prince, not waiting to watch him and his procession leave. She startled when she saw Kasdeya rushing toward her, a folded note in her hand.

"What is it?" Natassa asked.

Kasdeya's face was pale, her voice shaky. "Thorsten, he—"

Natassa moved past her, running up the palace steps. Her eyes blurred as she raced through the halls. Her breaths came out sharply, her body still weak from the poison Krea had given her.

"Please," she whispered, dread filling her.

She rushed into the healing quarters and scanned the room, spotting Thorsten in the corner of the chamber on a soft mattress.

"How is he?" she asked the True Manos examining Thorsten's head. Natassa grimaced when she caught sight of the gruesome stitches they had sewn there.

The True Manos glanced at her. "I am sorry, Princess. We have done all we can."

Natassa sank to her knees beside the mattress. Her head spun, and she blinked. The wall in front of her appeared to move as she stared at it. The True Manos turned and disappeared into the storeroom. Natassa rested her head on the edge of Thorsten's mattress, her hands covering her face. Tears slid into her palms as she remembered her childhood memories with Thorsten. Soon, he would be a memory as well. She gripped the mattress, clenching the linen within her fist. Natassa startled when something warm fell upon her hand. Her head snapped up, and her lips trembled when she saw Thorsten's hand rested over hers. His eyes remained closed.

"Thorsten?" Natassa whispered.

His lashes fluttered as he opened his eyes. He turned to look at her, wincing at the movement.

"Lie still," Natassa told him.

"I know . . . my time is up," Thorsten groaned.

"Don't say that." She swallowed a sob.

Natassa turned in the direction the healer had gone. Thorsten's grip on her hand tightened. "There . . . is nothing more he can do . . . for me."

"Shh, save your strength." Tears slipped down her cheeks.

"No matter . . . what . . . get away from Draven." Thorsten started coughing. Blood spurted from his mouth and dribbled down the side of his face.

"I will, I will," Natassa said, trying to reassure him as she cleaned the blood away. "Don't exert yourself. You need to gather your strength. For Aylis and the children."

He heaved another cough, more blood splattering. "Aylis," he said weakly. "Natassa, promise me . . . promise me." He wheezed, and his chest rose and fell with harsh breaths. "Promise me you will look out for them."

She nodded, biting her lip to keep from crying. "I promise."

Thorsten's fingers brushed her bracelet. "Be brave, Natassa . . . Never give up."

Natassa sniffled, tears rolling down her face, gathering at her chin, and falling in drops onto the linen sheet. "I will."

Thorsten stared at something behind her. "Take care of her."

Natassa turned and saw Honzio standing there. His face was expressionless as usual. Thorsten gasped and released a weak breath before falling still.

"NO! No, no, speak to me!" Natassa screamed and held his limp hand. "He's not dead, he's not."

Honzio touched her arm, and she stared up at him in denial. "He's not dead."

Honzio wrapped his arm around her. Natassa was too devastated to notice how unusual that was for him. A stray tear dropped from Honzio's eyes.

"He's gone," he whispered.

Natassa pulled away and slumped beside the bed again, gripping Thorsten's hand. "Come back to me, Thor."

Her brother, the only one who had cared, was gone. Just like her mother, just like Krea, just like anyone she cared about. They always left. The tears in her eyes were bitter, and the ache in her heart worsened. She felt a coldness sweeping through her and fought against it. *It's the sickness*, she realized. *The sickness that has been poisoning me.*

She heard her mother's voice.

Face your fears, Natassa.

And her father's voice.

She's not one of them.

Then the power came, flashing brilliant gold.

31

VELAMIR
KINGDOM OF VERIN
VERINTOWN

L ATIMUS'S HOME WAS spacious and grand, almost
as large as Winston's manor. After depositing
their belongings in the guest rooms Latimus
provided, Velamir and the others were led through
the manor. Latimus motioned to different relics and
family heirlooms as he gave them a tour. Velamir's
interest waned when Latimus began speaking
about his ancestor from a century ago and how
he fought in the war against the Savagelanders.
Velamir couldn't focus. He'd felt numb ever since
the general's announcement. He'd thought he
would only face the consequences of his actions
in his dreams, but his nightmares had become
reality, and no matter how far he ran, they
would always be faster.

Latimus led them to a small library

and waved at the seats situated around a coffee table. After everyone settled, Latimus focused on Lissa.

"I understand if you want to rest. Evening is drawing close."

She smirked. "I'm fine."

Latimus didn't bother asking the others and pulled out a sheet of paper from a hidden drawer in the table. "You are lucky Winston sent word before you came, or else I wouldn't have been able to prepare this list for you."

Velamir stiffened at the mention of Winston. "I thought you said he informed your father."

"My father is too busy to be concerned with trivial matters such as a tournament. And as I said before, he's been staying in the castle. King Dale has need of him."

"But you have time for trivial matters?" Velamir couldn't help the jab.

"I don't, actually." Latimus's reply was stiff. "But my father wishes for me to help you, and so I will. You should appreciate the time I am taking."

"Get on with it, then," Lissa snapped, and the others glanced at her with surprise.

"I mean," she corrected herself in a soft voice, batting her lashes, "so we don't waste too much of your time."

Velamir almost laughed. Her demure lady act needed work. Latimus cleared his throat and placed the sheet on the table.

"These are names of people who have already placed a bid on who they think will win the tournament." He ran a finger down the list. "They are high individuals with much coin to spend. Most of them aren't even from Verin but came just for the tournament."

"But they aren't the people I will be up against," Velamir said.

"No," Latimus confirmed. "But they will show us who your strongest opponent is. Most of the competitors haven't declared their interest to compete yet. The official entry day is in about two weeks."

Velamir's brow furrowed. "But the tournament is in two weeks."

Latimus chuckled. "You didn't know?"

Velamir and Jax shared a confused glance.

"The tournament has been delayed by Prince Draven Valent. He sent a letter to King Dale that he means to participate."

"The tournament will be postponed for one man?"

Latimus shook his head. "Not just any man. *Prince Draven*. He's rumored to be the best jouster in the Empire, although I've never seen him compete myself."

"And he is from which kingdom?"

Latimus laughed. "He is one of the most popular men in the Empire. Do you truly not know who he is?"

Velamir stared at him. "I've never heard of him before you mentioned his name."

"Have you been that sheltered in your life?"

The words stung, and Velamir gritted his teeth to keep from snapping at Latimus.

"Everyone knows him. I bet your *sister* does, too. The ladies are falling for him the moment he comes within their sight." Lissa sniffed but said nothing. "He is betrothed to Princess Natassa, daughter of Emperor Malus. You have heard of the emperor, I'm sure?"

"I'm not an idiot," Velamir managed to say in a calm voice.

Latimus was still grinning as he looked him over. "Good, I was just making sure."

Jax cut in, "So we know Prince Draven will be there. Who else?"

Latimus spent the next hour telling them about the most competent competitors and some of the wealthy investors. Velamir tried to process all the information, but it felt as if his brain would explode.

"And last but not least is Galva Mordon Vaz." The way he said the name was bitter. "He is one to watch for."

"If he is already a Galvasir, why is he competing?" Jax asked.

"For the fame. To keep up his reputation. Prince Draven is a Galvasir as well. It's all a big show. Everyone thought you were Winston when you came." He addressed Velamir. "They thought you were coming to show how good you were, and they all know Winston is a Galvasir."

They nodded, and Latimus said, "Most of the votes are for Galva Mordon and Prince Draven. But now that you're here and rumors are spreading that you are Winston, that might change."

"Do you have information on high officials?" Velamir asked him.

Latimus frowned. "And what would you do with that knowledge?"

"Convince them to spread my name."

Latimus sighed. "You really are arrogant, aren't you?"

"Do you have it or not?"

Latimus flicked out a clean sheet of paper and produced a quill. "One thing you should know, Velamir, a Blayton is never lacking for knowledge."

A few minutes later, he handed the parchment to Velamir. "Careful, it's still wet."

Velamir scanned the list, pausing on a name. "Advisor Liston."

His eyes locked with Lissa's and Jax's. It was the advisor Winston had told them about.

Latimus nodded. "He is very vocal about the tournaments and has wagered on the correct winner three times in a row. If anyone holds sway, it's him."

"Thank you for this. It's very helpful."

Latimus stood. "I will retire for the day. In the morning, I will introduce you to my mother, if you find that acceptable?"

Velamir nodded, and Latimus moved to leave, pausing by the door. "I have a feeling you are up to something, Velamir." He turned. "Don't do anything reckless, because I won't be able to clean up your mess, and I won't have you drag my father's name in the dirt."

Velamir said, "I can't promise anything."

"Don't look for Winston's killer here, because I can promise you the person who did it must have worked for Prolus. Winston is—was famous. A hero of sorts. Prolus must have wanted to remove him before his attack."

"You know nothing about me or my plans," Velamir said, his expression hardening.

"Trust me," Latimus scoffed. "I don't want to."

He closed the library door behind him. There was a moment of silence before Lissa said, "It's clear what the next course of action is."

"What?" Jax asked.

"Advisor Liston," Lissa began. "As Winston said, he handles the treasury and records. And he goes to the tavern late at night. We should start with him."

Jax frowned. "I don't like this. We just got here. We should settle in first, learn more before moving along with the plan."

Lissa rolled her eyes. "We don't have time to waste. Either way, we will have to kill people. Stop being a baby."

"I think Jax is right," Velamir said.

She stood and glared at them. "Then you two can wait. But I will do what I came to do."

"Lissa!" Jax called, but she stormed out of the library.

Jax lowered his head into his hands. They sat in silence. Velamir stared at the candles flickering around the library.

"They are taking children from their families, Jax," Velamir said in a quiet voice. "Not only orphans."

Jax looked up at him. "Vykus doesn't care who he takes. As long as he gets paid for it."

"Maybe Prolus doesn't know. Maybe Winston didn't."

"You figured it out, Vel, and you think they wouldn't?"

Velamir leaned back. "I killed that boy's father. The one I helped save."

"I know."

"Do you ever feel like . . ." Velamir paused. "We're doing the wrong thing?"

Jax laughed. It sounded empty and hollow. "All the time. But I never really had a choice."

"We are saving the Empire. We are changing it. We are bringing harmony," Velamir told himself as well as Jax. "We are doing the right thing. We have to be."

There was a shadow dimming Jax's eyes, and Velamir knew what he was thinking. He didn't believe in this mission, not the way Velamir did, the way Velamir *had*. Velamir shook his head. He couldn't doubt this path. It was the only one he'd ever known. If it wasn't the right one, it meant he was lost, and Velamir didn't want to believe that. Because it would mean everything he believed in was false.

32

NATASSA
KARALIK EMPIRE
THE GRAND PALACE

NATASSA OPENED HER eyes, staring at the canopy above her. The rich fabric was embroidered with swirls of color. She was in her room. Natassa rose into a half-sitting position and glanced around. The long curtains hanging by the balcony door were draped aside, revealing the dark, starless night outside. She shifted, moving her legs off the bed, and soft silk rubbed against her skin. Did Kasdeya change her outfit? She stood, freezing when she saw herself in her vanity mirror.

It was like looking at a different person. The sick girl was gone, and so were the dark circles that always lingered beneath her eyes. Her nightdress didn't hang over her body like it usually did, appearing as though it only contained her bones. She took a step closer and studied herself, overcome by the change. The feeling of absence and cold seeping into her skin wasn't there. For the first time in years, she felt alive.

Natassa's fingers trembled as they lifted to her forehead. She touched the soft skin that had been coarse and scarred for so long. The effects of the burn had disappeared, leaving in its place a golden phoenix.

How had this happened? Her father had burned it beyond repair to hide her true lineage, to hide who his ancestors had been. And yet, even as Natassa kept repeating to herself that it was impossible, she felt something running through her veins. Something new and strange, but at the same time, it felt as if she had known it all her life.

A brisk knock startled her. She reached for the robe draped atop a chair, slipping it over her shoulders.

"Come in."

Her chamber door opened and Honzio entered. His face drawn and shuttered. His shirt rumpled and hung untucked. Natassa watched him for a moment, a flood of images washing over her. Thorsten gasping for breath, blood dribbling down his face. Honzio's broken whisper. *He's gone.* Natassa shook her head. It had to be some sort of terrible dream. If she stepped out of this chamber, she would see her brother. She would see Thorsten. His soft smile, his kind brown eyes. A tear slipped down her cheek as Honzio approached her. He gripped her shoulder.

"He's in a better place now," he mumbled. "His pain is no longer, his glory remembered."

She shook her head again, more tears springing into her eyes. "No."

A pulsing sensation filled her. She felt as though she could set the world ablaze. Her brother was gone. Natassa covered her mouth, and her chin wobbled. Honzio gripped her arm to steady her. He motioned behind him. "Someone is here to see you."

He released her and bade the person forward. Natassa blinked back tears, hoping to keep herself together.

"Manos Xeni?"

The old True Manos from her childhood stood by the closed door. His eyes were pools of white just as she remembered. Her father had banished him from the palace when she was ten years old.

"How?"

"I thought he could help with . . ." Honzio waved a hand at her. "Your ability."

The True Manos neared, his hand extended. "My dear princess."

She led him to the cushioned seat off the side of her room and sat beside him. "But you were banished."

"He returned because of you," Honzio said, standing beside her vanity.

"Me?"

"Father wanted to kill him when he realized he was Shadow Manos. I helped him escape before that could happen. I told him to never return. Father had to keep up the act and pretended he had banished him. Just an hour ago, Xeni requested to see me under the guise of a tailor. Imagine my shock when I saw him."

"But why did he come for me?"

"He's a Seer," Honzio told her. "He saw a vision of you."

"Dear girl, from the moment I first saw you, I sensed the presence of a shadow around you," Manos Xeni began. "But it wasn't the usual domineering spirit. At first, I thought it was because you were young, too weak to contain its power. I know now that I was wrong."

Natassa's fingers clenched against a cushion. "What did you see?"

"I will answer as soon as you sate my curiosity." Xeni leaned closer, his long white ponytail flopping over his shoulder. "Did you know you were Shadow Manos?"

Natassa shrugged. "I thought about it a few times, but there is nothing special about me. I can't craft and don't have enhanced abilities."

"Those are the basic traits of a Doer. But tell me, have you had any visions?"

"No." She shook her head. "I don't think so."

"A vision doesn't only mean of the future. It can be of the past, the present."

"Yes, I've had memories of my past."

"And have you ever found someone falling under your command too soon to be natural? Can you order or persuade anyone to do anything?"

Natassa remembered Thorsten telling her how quickly everyone listened to her words. A pang rushed through her at the thought of him.

"I've been told so."

Manos Xeni's eyes seemed to glow in the darkness of the chamber. "You aren't a normal Shadow Manos, girl. Even now I can see them."

"See who?"

"The shadows around you. They listen to you, follow your orders, and you never even realized. You are a Lure and a Seer. I have never seen the like."

"I don't understand . . . What is wrong with me?"

"You're different. You've always been different." Honzio let a small laugh loose. "But I guess the Hartinza family has stood out in our own ways." He looked at his arm.

Manos Xeni spoke. "In time, you may be able to control more than two shadows. Who knows how strong you will become. You will be a threat to anyone who sees you as an enemy."

"What was your vision?"

"I saw the Empire crumbling. Hearcross trampled to dust. The palace gates opened and faceless men pouring in. On the throne sat a masked man. My vison flickered at that point. My shadow was afraid of him. A light pierced through the throne room, and I saw you."

"What does that mean?"

"A future that may come to pass. To save the Empire, you must leave the castle. There's a secret order. They call themselves the Elders. They are located near Devorin and have devoted themselves to the Hero's cause. They are waiting for the prophecy to come true. For the hero. For the phoenix." He glanced at her mark.

She brushed her fingers against it. "You think it's me."

Xeni peered at her. "I know it is."

All her life, Natassa had wanted the prophecy to come true, but now she was afraid. How could she help save the Empire when she couldn't even save herself? After a few more words of wisdom, Manos Xeni left with Honzio. Natassa sat alone, thinking about her predicament. Xeni said she controlled the shadows, but how? Natassa closed her eyes, searching for some sort of contact. Her head tingled, and a brush of power swashed by.

Natassa, a voice murmured.

"Show me," she whispered.

She was thrust forward, falling onto her arms. She groaned and turned onto her back into a position that struck her with a sense of déjà vu. Her heart pounded with incessant thumps when she saw the man leaning over her. A snake curled around his wrist and knife poised over her chest. Her fear faded to confusion at the sound of booming horns.

Violent shaking rang over her head like claps of thunder. The ceiling gave way, and the walls crumbled around her, revealing a high hill in the distance. Natassa found herself there, a cavalry riding toward her at a fearsome pace. Their yellow flags wafting in the wind. They were charging to battle. At the head was General Zenrelius. He peered at her, his eyes probing for her secrets. Natassa backed away from the approaching horses and rolled down the hill. Her landing was soft, into a bed of flowers. Natassa glanced around, trying to find a way through the mass. The overpowering smell of ovaline flooded her nose, and she wheezed, coughing hoarse gasps. Thunderous echoes came toward her, and she scrambled away. Instead of being trampled by horses, she saw a pair of gleaming red eyes peering at her from between the stems. It rose high and mighty, its claws outstretched. The creature pounced, and she screamed, covering her ears.

"Natassa!"

A hand jerked her back, and her eyes flew open. She stared into Honzio's concerned face. She swallowed, inhaling deep breaths to remove the cloying scent of ovaline.

"It was as if I was there, Honzio."

He didn't ask where, he just gripped her shoulder tighter. "You're safe now."

"A man attacked me on the day of the joust." Natassa spoke before he could ask more questions. "Kasdeya killed him. He was marked with a Savagelander tattoo."

Honzio gritted his teeth. "He must have been smuggled in. What was his tattoo?"

"A snake," Natassa told him.

"He was part of the spies." Honzio's disfigured arm pulled tighter against his stomach, and his fingers dug into his twisted hand.

"Spies?"

Honzio nodded. "Savagelanders are tattooed from a young age. There is meaning behind the markings. The leaders with ferocious beasts such as lions or wolves. Snakes stand for spies, and rats for the lowest in ranking, such as slaves and expendable soldiers."

"What should we do?"

"All you need to worry about is getting away," Honzio told her. He reached out and touched her mark. "You need to cover this."

Natassa pulled her hair forward. She looked back at

Honzio, staring at his earnest face, and wondered why he was helping her after all the neglect.

"I gave Thorsten my word to protect you," he said as though reading her thoughts.

"I made him a promise as well," she began. "There is a shelter for Savorians. You must take care of them when I'm gone."

He searched her face for an imperceptible moment before nodding. Her chamber door opened and Kasdeya entered, her face sorrowful. "The emperor orders you set off for Ayleth in the morning."

Natassa let out a stuttering breath. "What about Thorsten's funeral?"

Kasdeya looked down. "He said if you remained for another day, there would be two funerals."

Natassa laughed. It was humorless. "Ayleth or remaining here. Either way, I'm as good as dead. My pain no longer, my glory remembered."

33

LISSA
KINGDOM OF VERIN
VERINTOWN

CURSING JAX AND Velamir didn't improve her mood. In fact, it made it worse. Lissa navigated through the alleys, the long cloak she had *borrowed* from Latimus's manor concealing her. She reached the tavern and dragged her hood down farther before entering. No one paid her any mind as she took a seat close to the bar top. She glanced around the candlelit area. Men played cards and downed zat at almost every table. The few women there wore revealing dresses and swayed their hips beyond what Lissa thought was possible. She eyed one woman walking past her and studied the movement to put to use later if needed.

Lissa's hands flexed within her cloak, reaching into the inside pocket for her secret weapons. She strapped on the thick gloves that contained claws, ensuring to keep them hidden in the folds of her cloak. They were lethal and long, taken from the rumlok Quintus had killed in Tariqi. Lissa had carved the claws from its body and paid Jax to make her a weapon from them. He hadn't charged her much now that she thought of it. She rolled her eyes. Him and his ridiculous infatuation. She sheathed and unsheathed the claws, the slow hissing sound they emitted strangely comforting. A laugh, lively and bright, drew her gaze. Her thumping heart returned to its cold state when she saw an older woman in the corner of the tavern flirting with a nobleman. For a single moment, she'd thought she'd heard her mother. Her fists clenched.

That's not possible, Lissa. She's a prisoner, and you won't see her until you . . .

Lissa's eyes caught on a tall man speaking with the barkeeper near her, mostly because of the generous number of muscles that stretched his shirt but also because he looked familiar.

"A man . . . named Winston . . ."

She strained her ears to make out more.

He was a good-looking man. Dark hair, chiseled features. Who was he? A boisterous voice grabbed her attention, and she turned.

"Calm down, Liston. You're going to take all my coin before the night is gone."

The speaker was sitting at a table with three others. The man he'd addressed flicked a card into the air.

"You know my hand always wins," Liston replied. "They call me Aces around these parts."

He was far into his cups. Lissa smiled as she focused on their conversation. It didn't take long to figure out that this was the advisor she was after. She couldn't believe a king would trust his treasury in the hands of this man.

"I bid on Prince Draven. The dragon will emerge victorious, I have no doubt," one man said.

The advisor laughed. "He doesn't stand a chance!"

"What about Galva Mordon? I've seen him joust. I'd say he's got a fair shot."

Liston snorted. "The Cavalier will crush them both. Mordon will get what's coming to him, arrogant brat, just like his father."

They were the wrong words to say, especially because the muscled man approached and halted behind him. His arms were crossed, and his shirt appeared as if it would rip off at any moment. Lissa appreciated the effect.

"Keep it down!" someone told the advisor. But it was too late.

"It's been too long since we've had a chat." The muscled man lifted the goblet of zat and poured it over the advisor's head before giving it a quick rub. "Wouldn't you agree?"

A hush fell over the tavern. The advisor grew an odd shade of green, and apologies fell from his mouth faster than his companions edged away from the table. Lissa scoffed. That was why she didn't believe in friendships.

"Galva Mordon! You misheard, I—"

Mordon slammed him onto the table, shattering glass and causing cards to go flying.

"It's too late!" Mordon growled. "You're lucky I

don't kill you right now. Very lucky. Because that's what happens to those who slander my name. No one disrespects my family."

"I'm sorry, I'm sorry." The advisor's lips flapped like a dying fish.

Mordon shoved him one last time and stormed out of the tavern. After quivering like a coward for a few minutes, the advisor left as well. Lissa took her cue. She followed him, keeping a good distance between them. Two guards stayed at his back, their gazes focused before them. A mistake. Lissa buried her claws into their necks in the span of a heartbeat. They dropped. The advisor turned, holding his arms out as if that would protect him.

"You are one of them." He trembled. "Prolus's phantoms."

They were his last words. Lissa's claws smashed into either side of his skull with a note of shredded finality. He smacked onto the ground, his brains leaking into the dirty water spilling through the alley. Lissa left, but not before she painted the dry ground near the bodies with blood.

No One Disrespects My Family
She smiled. Mission accomplished.

KARALIK EMPIRE
NEAR THE BORDERLANDS
PROLUS'S ADVANCING CAMP

Wind blew through the dark gloom of the forest, rustling the wilting leaves. The leaves fell every so often, wafting over to a large clearing. Hundreds of tents filled the area. Deedans draped in black-and-red uniforms moved with precision, following their commanders' orders. Some lit fires and cooked meals, while others trained tirelessly, readying for war.

A massive tent stood in the middle of the mass. An emblem of a masked face encased the animal-skin tent. It was painted black to show its distinction from the other tents. A Chishma slipped unnoticed through the camp. His hood was pulled low over his face, and his hand gripped his longbow with ease. The Chishma approached the large tent and nodded at the guards posted there. They saluted him and allowed him entrance. The Chishma walked inside and kneeled, his gaze on the floor.

"Rise, old friend." A grated voice resonated through-out the tent.

The Chishma stood and looked toward his master. The Dark Lord Prolus was dressed in black. The color of death. On his face, a mask hid him from view. Some say it was because of battle scars, while others say it was because he was a demon. The truth would never be known since no one saw him without the mask and lived. The mask was intricate, with masterful designs drawn around the eyepieces. The corners of the mask went up in the shape of devil horns, the bottom crafted into smiling lips. The purpose was to strike fear into the hearts of enemies. For how would you know your fate if you could not see death's face?

The Chishma spoke. "You summoned me, my lord?"

"With the death of Winston. The first part of our plan is complete," Lord Prolus said, his voice low and hoarse. "Winston's heart was too good. He felt mercy and would have been an obstacle in our path. Do you disagree?"

The Chishma opened his mouth, then hesitated. He hated to answer questions. More so ones he did not know the answers to. "My lord, you know best."

Prolus's lips stretched beneath his mask. "Our time is coming. I can feel it. Before long, I will be lord over these lands, and the only one sitting on Karalik Empire's throne will be . . . me." He chuckled. "But for now, I have a mission for you."

"Whatever you say is my command, Lord Prolus," the Chishma responded with undying fealty.

34

VELAMIR
KINGDOM OF VERIN
VERINTOWN

AFTER A RESTLESS night's sleep, Velamir
was relieved to be astride Vandal. He rode
through the large field. Latimus had given
him leave to practice on his land. There was a long
jousting list set up on one side of the field. Velamir
halted near the list, staring at it. He didn't have to
do well in the competition. It was for show, after
all. The real event didn't begin until the party
after, when he had to kill Boltrex. But he wanted
to win. Simply to prove to himself that he could.
At the sound of hooves thudding against the
grass, Velamir looked up. Latimus neared. He
was astride a beautiful chestnut and held out a
wooden training lance.

"Care to practice?"

"You would risk injuring yourself to help me?"

Latimus scoffed. "Who said *I* am the one that would get injured?"

A smile crept onto Velamir's face. He reached out, taking the lance. "No helmets?"

Latimus nodded. "Unless you are afraid."

Velamir huffed a laugh. "That wouldn't be me."

Latimus rode to the other side of the list and waited until Velamir lifted his lance. Velamir let out a piercing whistle, and they charged at each other. It felt different, without his long hair or any armor besides the thin leather padding over his chest. It was different and yet the same. Vandal's hooves made divots in the ground, and grass shot into the air. Velamir focused on his target, angling the lance at Latimus's shoulder. It all happened in moments, his lance crashing against Latimus's steel armor. He didn't even feel pain as Latimus's lance struck alongside his arm.

Latimus landed in a heap. Velamir dismounted, hurrying to check on him.

"Are you all right?"

Latimus groaned. "Why do I feel like a child again?"

Velamir smiled. "Jousting like old times."

Latimus sat up and grumbled under his breath. "You still have that horse."

Velamir nodded, although he wasn't sure it was a question.

"He's amazing. It's a pity he didn't take to my father's handling. He would have made a good horse for one of King Dale's Galvasirs."

"He still is," Velamir replied.

The corner of Latimus's lip lowered. "That's not funny. You aren't Winston. Being mistaken as a Galvasir isn't the same as being one."

"But I will be. Once I win the tournament."

Latimus's laugh was coated with sarcasm.

"If you don't believe in me, why did you offer to help me?"

Latimus stared up at him. "Everything I did, everything I do, is for my family. I did this for my father."

The same things he had said last night. It infuriated Velamir when the only things he received from Latimus were efforts to bring him down.

"You can tell him I don't need your help."

"Velamir," Latimus said. There was a smile on his face. "Let's go again."

Velamir's brow crinkled. "I don't understand you."

"It takes brains to understand me." Latimus pulled himself to his feet.

Velamir shook his head and remounted Vandal. They continued practicing for hours until the sun was high in the sky, and they were drenched in sweat and covered in bruises. Latimus called for a stop.

"They will serve brunch soon. My mother is expecting me."

Velamir nodded, and they returned their horses to the stables. After washing the grime off, Velamir changed into one of the outfits Winston had procured. A long white tunic that fit well and thick trousers. He made his way to the dining hall, hesitating a moment before entering.

Latimus was greeting a middle-aged woman when

Velamir came in. She sat at the front of a grand table covered with food.

"Mother." Latimus bowed his head in respect and leaned down to kiss her cheek.

The woman smiled at Latimus, reaching up to pat his face. "How are you today, my dear boy?"

"Very well, especially now that we have company." He motioned toward Velamir and at Jax, who Velamir noticed was already sitting with a loaded plate.

Lady Blayton's deep brown eyes settled on Velamir, assessing him. Latimus noticed her attention and said, "This is my mother, Lady Blayton. Mother, this is Velamir. The lad Galvasir Winston took in when the poor boy was destitute."

Velamir nodded at Lady Blayton and held back the scowl that he wanted to shoot at Latimus.

"You poor child!" Lady Blayton exclaimed. "It hurts my heart to hear of children who've had to endure so much. My son, Latimus, is the epitome of kindness. He learned much from his father. Always helping the poor."

Velamir's smile thinned as he strained to keep it in place. "Your son is quite a different sort."

Latimus frowned, wondering what to make of that.

"Brother." A voice carried into the dining hall.

Footsteps approached, and a young man stepped inside. His eyes widened when he saw Jax and Velamir. As he walked closer, Velamir noticed he looked like a miniature version of Latimus, with minor differences. His hair was brown and thick, falling over his ears. Both their eyes were brown and their faces narrow, although the boy still had roundness to his cheeks that spoke of youth.

"Lore!" Latimus said, meeting his brother halfway to the table. He threw an arm around the boy's shoulders and pushed him forward. "Velamir, meet my brother. Lore, this is Velamir."

Lore stepped forward and held out a hand. "Pleasure to meet you, Velamir." He paused. "Or is it Captain Velamir?"

Velamir smiled and shook his hand. *Finally*, he thought, *someone with respect*. Velamir opened his mouth to reply when Latimus cut in, "Oh, Velamir is just an apprentice. But I'm sure he will earn a title soon enough."

Velamir's jaw clenched. Lady Blayton clapped her hands together. "Dear Latimus! How magnanimous of you to say. I adore the faith you have in everyone."

"Sure . . . *magnanimous*," Velamir muttered, pulling out a chair with a sharp screech. Jax coughed, overhearing Velamir's comment.

The others glanced at him, and Jax cleared his throat. "Lissa is late."

It was then that Velamir realized Lissa wasn't there. Latimus and Lore took their seats.

"She sent her apologies with a maid. She wasn't feeling well," Latimus told them.

Velamir doubted she was sick. What was she up to?

"We have another guest, dear?" Lady Blayton asked.

"Velamir's *sister*." Latimus grinned.

"How lovely! Is she blood related or another child Winston adopted?"

Before Latimus could say anything, Velamir spoke.

"Blood related. In fact, I refer to Winston as my biological father. It's easier that way, and I prefer it since that was what he was to me."

"Ah, I see." Lady Blayton nodded. "I shall not make the mistake of referring to you as adopted."

Velamir nodded his thanks and started eating. The clinking of glass and silverware were the only noises until Lore glanced around.

"Have you heard the news?"

They looked at him curiously, and he said in a low tone, "Advisor Liston was killed last night."

"How horrible!" Lady Blayton exclaimed.

Velamir froze, and Jax choked on his food. He clutched his throat.

"Oh my!" Lady Blayton stood and pounded his back.

Jax gulped water from the glass by his plate, and his coughing eased. "I'm all right." He grimaced.

He exchanged a glance with Velamir, who knew exactly what he was thinking. Lissa. She must have done this. Latimus wore a befuddled expression as he stared at them and returned his attention to Lore.

"What happened to the advisor?"

"I went to see Father today. That's all everyone was talking about in the castle." Lore seemed excited as he spoke. "He was found with his guards in an alley near the tavern."

Latimus took a bite of bread. "And do they know who did it?"

Lore looked down. "That's the strange part. There was something written in blood on the ground. Something people overheard Galva Mordon say the night before."

Galva Mordon. One of the men Latimus had told them about. Velamir soaked in the information and continued listening.

"Everyone thinks it's him. But they are too scared to confront him."

If anyone would kill and write on the ground in blood, it would be Lissa. Of that, Velamir had no doubt. He forced himself to take a slice of bread from the large plate in the middle of the table and place it onto his platter. Lady Blayton motioned for him to try other items, and soon Velamir had sample portions of three different jams and a few well-cooked eggs decorating his dish.

He had just taken a bite when Lady Blayton spoke up. "I was sorry to hear about Winston. Latimus informed me of his passing. He was a good man." She glanced at her son with mournful eyes and patted his arm.

Whatever remained of Velamir's appetite fled for three reasons. First, at the mention of Winston's demise; second, at the knowledge that Latimus could keep nothing to himself; and third, because of the disturbing love-filled expression Lady Blayton showered upon her son. Something tightened in Velamir's chest every time she complimented and praised Latimus. He was sure the feeling inside him was jealousy, and it disgusted him.

He could not help the thoughts that fluttered through his head. The thoughts that made him wish he had a mother beside him to care and worry about him. Velamir's fist clenched beneath the tablecloth. Perhaps his mother would have been loving and kind, but he would never know. Boltrex had stolen that from him.

Winston's dying words raced through his mind. *He had me killed just as he killed your . . . parents.*

Latimus cleared his throat, snapping Velamir out of his dark thoughts. Lady Blayton was staring at him expectantly, and after a quick glance around, so were the rest of them.

Velamir returned his attention to Lady Blayton and answered, "Thank you. Although he has passed on, I know he does not rest in peace. Justice needs to be served, and I aim to find the people behind his murder."

Lady Blayton shook her head. "It is best to let it go, my boy. Or the thirst for revenge will never fade. Even after you've caught the men, it will eat you up inside and you will never be happy."

"You are wise, Lady Blayton, and I'm sure your words would be best in most situations. But this is different. I cannot allow these killers to roam free. Not when they can hurt more people," Velamir said, and before she could protest his words, he continued, "I hope you will keep this conversation in confidence." He narrowed his eyes at Latimus, who shifted in his seat.

An awkward silence ensued until the door attendant stepped into the room. "Captain Latimus," he addressed Latimus. "A messenger arrived from the castle. King Dale requests to see Galva Winston."

Latimus shrugged, glancing at Velamir. "It seems the king hasn't been informed of who you are."

"We better tell him." Velamir stood, pushing his chair in.

He gave Lady Blayton a polite nod before heading to the door. Jax and Latimus accompanied him to the castle.

A servant escorted them through the grand halls until they reached the throne room doors, where they were told to wait. Velamir examined the gilded engraving on the doors. The carvings stretched into the shape of an eagle. Velamir had seen the symbol on the flags rising from the parapets. A heart held in the eagle's talons, the thick cloth dyed green. Velamir paced the hall as he waited. He examined the paintings lining the wall, stopping on one in the middle. Four armies faced each other, their flags billowing in the illusional air.

"The four kingdoms." Latimus stepped beside him.

Velamir nodded, and Latimus traced the flags in the painting. "Verin. Ondalar." His finger touched a yellow flag, a rearing horse in the center with a heart resting between its forelegs. "Ayleth." He paused on a purple flag with a dragon head, a heart clenched in its jaws. "And Devorin."

The final flag was dark blue with a crown split in two. A heart held the two pieces intact.

"We would have fallen to Prolus long ago," Latimus said, "but an Imperial's heart doesn't give in. Even when all the odds are against us."

"Is it strong enough to withstand a civil war?" Velamir motioned to the painting, to the armies charging at each other.

Latimus stepped to the next painting. "Strong enough to stand together despite our differences."

It showed the armies gathered in battle formation behind a man on a horse. A crown gleamed on his head, and he raised a flag high into the air. A red flag with a half heart. They faced an army of shadows. Velamir assumed these to be Prolus's army.

Latimus stepped back, returning to his position by the doors. Jax pushed off the wall he had been leaning on and approached Velamir.

"Did you want to stay in the castle instead of the manor?" He spoke in a low voice.

Velamir shook his head. "It's easier to practice in the manor, and besides, if we are in the castle, who knows what Lissa will bring down upon it."

Jax lowered his tone to a whisper. "It was her, wasn't it?"

Velamir nodded. "Who else could it be?"

"What should we do?"

"Pray that she covered her tracks well or we will be caught before we even start."

The doors swung wide open, and a servant called to them, "You may proceed!"

Velamir exchanged a look with Jax and strode forward. Latimus walked beside him, his posture rigid. They entered the throne room, and Velamir fought the urge to look around in awe. Spears and lances and swords of every type decorated the walls. A large circular, crystal-inlaid object hung from the ceiling. Hundreds of candles were positioned on it, showering the throne room in an orange glow. Men dressed in thick garments observed from both sides of the room. They wore green robes with silver circlets. Velamir assumed they were part of the king's council. He focused ahead of him.

King Dale sat on a plain wooden throne. His tunic and trousers seemed the same style as Velamir's, if not a lesser kind. He didn't even wear a crown on his thinning gray hair. For a second, Velamir wondered if an imposter sat on the throne. But then Latimus halted, pinching the back of Velamir's shirt. Velamir stopped as well, copying Latimus's movements as he bowed his head and saluted the king with a hand curled over his chest. Velamir hoped Jax was doing the same behind them.

The king stared for a long moment, confusion warring in his brown eyes. Dark circles rested beneath his lids, competing with the other aging lines to dominate his features.

"At ease," he finally said.

Velamir straightened to his full height. Something moved in his peripheral, and he glanced to his right. A man watched him with narrowed eyes. He seemed to shoot fire through his gaze. A thick scar cut down his cheek. General Boltrex. Fury grew inside Velamir at the sight of him.

"I was expecting Winston," King Dale spoke.

Latimus cleared his throat. "Your Majesty, may I present Velamir Raga, son of Winston Raga."

"Son?"

Velamir nodded. "Yes, Your Majesty."

"I didn't realize Galva Winston remarried."

Latimus shot Velamir a glance and continued, "Velamir recently arrived with his sister. He plans to compete in the tournament."

"And where is his so-called father?" The deep voice pierced through the room. Boltrex stepped beside the throne. "He disappears for years and, after all this time, sends his son to compete?"

"General." King Dale waved a calming hand at him.

"He was killed," Velamir spat.

Dale's eyes widened. "Killed? By whom?"

"I'm still figuring that out," Velamir said, resting his gaze on Boltrex. "But I have a feeling they are closer than we think."

"And how can we trust you are his son and not someone trying to gain from his reputation?" the general questioned, eyes flashing.

Latimus seemed offended. "I introduced him to you. Surely that is enough proof. Or does the Blayton name not carry the same weight it used to?"

Dale motioned Latimus to calm down. "Of course it does, son."

A man stepped from behind the green-robed councilmen. "I trained Velamir to joust when he was just a boy."

Velamir smiled. "Commander Blayton."

Blayton strode forward, enveloping Velamir in a hug in the middle of the throne room.

"It's actually Galva Blayton now," Latimus said.

Blayton pulled back. "Never mind that." His features softened. "I'm sorry to hear about Winston. He was a dear friend." Blayton turned to the king. "Your Majesty, I can say without a doubt this is Winston's son."

Rage raced across Boltrex's features when King Dale nodded, a smile gracing his face. "Welcome home, Velamir. I hope you intend to stay a long time."

Boltrex sputtered, and King Dale turned to him. "Did you find Advisor Liston's killers, General?"

Boltrex scowled. "Not yet. They are highly trained,

leaving no lead behind and even trying to throw my son under the light. But rest assured, I will find them."

He stormed past Velamir, out of the throne room. King Dale focused on Velamir. "Winston was a good man and an admirable Galvasir. I am grieved deeply by his loss."

"As we all are," Blayton agreed.

"His pain is no longer, his glory remembered." King Dale paused with expectance.

Velamir's panic rose. This was some sort of custom, but he did not know how to respond. Blayton placed a hand on his shoulder and filled in for him.

"His name stronger, his honor forever."

King Dale nodded and said, "Let me introduce you to some of my councilmembers. These men are the brightest in Verin. They plan many of our defense strategies."

Velamir nodded at each introduction. Many of them were names Velamir recognized from Latimus's list. He heard a crinkle of pages behind him and knew Jax was writing in his journal. After a while of small talk, Velamir took his leave. Latimus stayed behind, saying he wanted to speak with his father. Velamir left the castle with Jax trailing him, making scribbles in his journal.

"You're writing their names?" Velamir asked.

Jax showed him the page, and Velamir's brows rose. Lifelike sketches of the councilmen filled it.

"How did you do this so fast?"

Velamir looked up at Jax, noticing his eyes were brown. The color slowly faded back into blue. "My shadow helped."

His shoulders sagged as he closed the journal. He

seemed drained. Velamir had always hated seeing him like this.

"Let's return to the manor." Velamir paused, hearing clanging noises.

"What is it?" Jax asked.

Velamir glanced toward the sounds. "The Imperials are training. We should watch them."

Jax nodded, and they entered the barracks. Velamir spotted three open doors and entered the closest one. He walked into a spacious room filled with armored men. They were sparring, holding nothing back, their swords swiping in aggressive slashes. One of the soldiers approached him and removed his helmet.

Velamir's eyes widened. "Cora?"

She smiled. "Nice to see you again."

35

MORDON
KINGDOM OF VERIN
VERINTOWN

MORDON TOOK A swig of water, watching Coralie over his flask. She approached a young man standing in the doorway with a True Manos. They spoke for a few moments, and Mordon's heart thumped with jealous beats when she smiled at the man. He wiped excess water from his mouth and slipped his flask into his belt. He strode forward, coming to a stop behind Coralie. Mordon stared at the man over her head, straightening his shoulders and lowering his brows to frighten him.

"Coralie," Mordon rumbled. "Who is this?"

The man locked eyes with Mordon and instead of seeming daunted, his expression darkened, and his green eyes burned. *Strange.* He didn't usually earn looks like that.

Coralie glanced back, her inky braids flinging toward him, carrying her scent. Fresh mint with a hint of lilies. He didn't know how someone could smell so good after training for hours. Mordon stopped breathing for a moment, afraid he would bury his nose in her hair and ruin the whole intimidation thing.

"This is the brave man I told you about. The one who helped me save the child," Coralie told him.

Ah yes. That fool she has been going on about.

Mordon smirked. "Brave? I only believe what I see . . ." He made a show of looking him over. "And I don't see much."

Coralie glared. "Mordon."

She always looked prettier when she was upset, but that was usually when he teased her. He didn't like that she was so attached to this random stranger. He tugged one of her braids. The silky texture brushed his skin.

"Why do you care for him?" He stared at the man, hoping the challenge in his eyes was clear. If he tried to claim Coralie, he would have to go through him first.

Coralie flicked her braid out of his grasp. "Enough."

"Would you rather he touched you?"

The man stepped forward. "Have some respect for the lady. If you have a problem, I'm right here before you."

Mordon was taken aback by his directness but forced a smile. "Who are you again?"

"This is the Cavalier," the True Manos said.

Mordon had forgotten he was there. He raised his brow. "The Cavalier? The man I have been hearing so much about. Then your real name must be Galva-sir Winston."

"I'm Winston's son, Velamir Raga."

"How nice. You must be truly pathetic to use your father's name instead of building one for yourself."

"I came for him, to honor him by upholding his reputation in the tournament and fulfilling his last request. So no, I'm not trying to make a new name for myself but to make his everlasting."

"Then you will need a lot of luck, because you will be against me." Mordon straightened to his full height, using it to look down on Velamir. "You came running to the castle when you heard Prolus was advancing, didn't you? Using the tournament as an excuse. Hiding behind stone walls. You are not worthy enough to compete in your father's name."

"As a captain or whatever you are," Velamir began, "it gives you the opportunity to act like a fool without consequences. But watch your words, because if you keep talking like an entitled noble, the last face you will see is mine, and the last sound you will hear is the whisper of my sword unsheathing."

Mordon's hand curled into a fist. "How dare you threaten me?"

He lifted his arm, but Coralie grabbed it. "That's enough, Mordon!"

A soldier burst into the barracks, almost crashing into Velamir and the True Manos. He looked around with horrified haste.

"One of the creatures is in the town! It's attacking the civilians."

Mordon stiffened and traded a glance with Coralie. He drew his sword and looked back at the soldiers, motioning to some of them.

"You, with me." As they moved toward him, Mordon ordered Coralie, "stay here."

She drew her sword as well. "Like hell I am."

Mordon grumbled under his breath and shoved past Velamir. He heard Coralie and the other soldiers set off behind him. As soon as he exited the barracks, distant screaming met his ears. The screams grew louder when he crossed the drawbridge. Mordon pushed through the people rushing past him seeking safety in the castle. He stopped in the middle of the dusty road, sword high and stance strong. Coralie took a stance beside him.

A roar echoed through the empty road that stood between the shops and homes. The creature came into view. Mordon stared at it with unease. It was the size of a bear with the face of a lion, its hair blowing in a ferocious mane. It felt as though the ground shook with each approaching step.

"Four kingdoms," one of the men said in horrified awe.

"Steady," Mordon told them.

The creature was coming closer, its pace slow and predatory, nose lifted, sniffing the air. *Sniffing the air?*

"It's missing an eye," Coralie said.

Mordon grimaced when he noticed one eyeball hanging out from the socket, dangling by a strand of tissue.

"I can't do this," one of the soldiers said, voice stricken. "I can't!" He ran to the nearest shop, seeking refuge.

The beast was after him in seconds, galloping on all fours at a blinding pace. He ripped the soldier to shreds with his claws. Coralie rushed forward, attempting to save the man.

"Coralie!" Mordon yelled and threw himself into the fight as well.

He sliced the beast's legs, but that only enraged it further, and it tossed the mutilated soldier aside, thrusting its paws onto Mordon, flattening him to the ground. Mordon gasped, the breath knocked from him. Coralie yelled and hacked into the beast, but it didn't move, except to lean its face down to Mordon's, sniffing, searching. Although for what, Mordon couldn't tell. Mordon closed his eyes. The creature's hot breath fanned his face. Sharp claws rested on his chest, dangerous enough to end his life in a heartbeat. The hiss of an arrow sounded, and Mordon's eyes flew open to see an arrow embed itself into the creature's socket, severing the remaining strand of tissue. The eyeball dropped onto Mordon's lips, and he twisted his head, spitting in revulsion. The beast reared back with a roar of pain.

Mordon scrambled to his feet, looking back to see the imposter who claimed to be Winston's son at the start of the roadway near the drawbridge, his hands curled around a bow that he had taken from the slack-jawed castle guard standing beside him.

"You almost shot me!" Mordon yelled.

"It was tempting," Velamir called back.

The creature growled, and Mordon returned his attention to the fight.

"Help us!" Coralie screamed at the other soldiers,

and they reluctantly joined in, slashing at the beast. After Coralie gave it a particularly sharp jab, the creature reared and landed on top of her. Panic consumed Mordon, and he didn't think. He reacted, jumping onto the animal and clutching its mane.

He yelled, and the creature froze beneath him. Unmoving as Mordon sat on top of it, as if awaiting a command. Mordon slid off, his primary concern seeing to Coralie. He shoved at the creature, and with help from the other soldiers, it crashed on its side. It was then that Mordon saw the sword thrusted into its belly. Coralie's sword. Mordon dropped to his knees beside her. One of her braids had come undone, and her hair splayed across the ground. Her eyes were closed. He brushed his fingers across the crescent birthmark on her neck and pressed against her skin, feeling for a pulse.

"Coralie?" His voice was urgent.

Her eyes fluttered, and relief cascaded onto him in waves. She stared at him in confusion before a small smile lifted her lips. Mordon's heart stuttered.

"I never thought you would be happy to see me survive something like this," she told him.

Mordon realized he had been grinning like a fool and wiped it from his face. "I'm only glad I don't have to explain your death to your uncle."

"That would have been terrible work, wouldn't it?" she whispered, and for some reason, his heart began to race.

He didn't reply, he didn't tell her the answer that lay hidden in his mind. That he couldn't bear to lose her.

She sat up gingerly, and Mordon reached out to help

her. Touching her was almost as painful as the thought of her getting hurt.

"I killed it," Coralie stated with disbelief.

"You did."

"Are you all right?" The imposter asked, and Mordon jolted. He hadn't heard him approach.

Coralie nodded. "Better than all right." She grabbed Mordon's arm, and he hauled her to her feet. She approached the dead creature. "The first beast I've killed."

"An accomplishment to be proud of," the imposter praised, and Coralie's face lit up.

Mordon felt a trail of envy curl its way through him. The boy was just as aggravating as his father. If only he could get more poison. That would finish the job.

One of the younger soldiers prodded the dead animal with his foot, his face pale. "What in the Empire is it?"

Mordon's eyes narrowed, catching onto something. He kneeled beside the animal, moving aside the matted fur to reveal a mark. Prolus's mask branded onto its shoulder.

He glanced up at the others, his face grim. "One of Prolus's experiments. A warning to tell us he is coming."

The blue-eyed True Manos stood near the imposter. He frowned and spoke to him in a low tone. "Rumlok."

"And what does a mere True Manos know of rumloks?" Mordon asked, suspicion forming.

The True Manos answered, "Rumloks are like cats to Savorians. Every family has one in Savoria."

"That was when they were harmless, the size of a

wolf. Now they are monsters, what Prolus's damage has made them," Mordon spat.

Coralie nodded. "Everything he tampers with becomes one."

Mordon looked down at the dead animal. "He had a trainer. We need to send someone to search the forest."

"He will be long gone," Velamir told him. "Don't waste your time."

Mordon glared. "Don't tell me what to do."

The townspeople were creeping back, and at the sight of the dead rumlok, a wave of cheers rose.

"The beast slayer, Galva Mordon!" one of them shouted.

A roar of approval went around, and soon they were chanting his name. Mordon glanced at Coralie and opened his mouth to speak, but she shook her head.

"I would rather my uncle didn't know."

Mordon frowned, but a messenger rushed to him before he could respond. "Galva, King Dale requests your presence."

Mordon nodded. "I will be there shortly."

"The soldiers who fought alongside you as well."

Mordon watched Coralie disappear into the crowd. He glanced at where Velamir had been moments before. His eyes darted over the space twice, but there was no trace of him. It was like he had never been there.

NATASSA
KARALIK EMPIRE
HEARCROSS

NATASSA RAPPED ON the carriage ceiling, and it slowed to a stop. The door opened, and one of her new guards looked at her, a scowl on his face for the inconvenience. A niggle of doubt wormed its way through her. She should have asked Honzio to choose the guards himself, instead of entrusting his personal guard to do so.

"The princess has business in this street," Kasdeya informed the guard.

He looked away from them, perhaps toward Captain Thander, who was riding in front of the carriage. The guard returned his gaze to them, scratching his beard.

"The emperor said we had to reach Ayleth fast."

His directness took Natassa aback. It was frank disobedience not to comply with a royal's wish.

"I will be quick," she told him.

With a grunt, he moved out of her way. Captain Thander had dismounted and approached the door to assist her. Natassa took his hand and alighted onto the gravel roadway.

"What are you doing, Princess?"

Natassa motioned Kasdeya to follow her. "I need to retrieve something from the shops," she told the captain.

"I can send one of the men."

Natassa lowered her tone. "It's a personal matter."

"I see," he replied, although he clearly didn't.

"Kasdeya will accompany me."

Captain Thander didn't look convinced, but he agreed. Natassa set off, walking in the direction of the shops. Once they were out of view, Natassa changed direction, weaving through the narrow alleys. She stopped in front of a large rock, enlisting Kasdeya's help to move it. She crouched by the hatch, hand resting on the handle. Natassa glanced up at Kasdeya.

"Stay here."

She wrenched the hatch open and dropped down. This time, she miraculously landed on her feet. Kasdeya closed the hatch above her, and Natassa walked down the passageway. The surrounding darkness seemed to curl closer, trapping her in a confining circle. She inhaled, trying to push away her nerves as she approached the door. She rapped lightly, attempting to imitate how Thorsten had knocked.

It swung open, and Aylis stood before her, axe lifted in a tight grip and mouth curled down.

"What do you want?"

Natassa was startled by the venom in her voice. "I came to tell you I was leaving."

"Like everyone else." Aylis released a rough, humorless laugh. "I'm not surprised."

"I am being forced to marry against my will. I have no choice."

"But you will have a warm place to stay, riches, a crown, safety." Each word was spoken harshly.

"I—" Natassa stopped before she began an argument trying to defend herself. "Honzio will help you."

Aylis gritted her teeth. "You told him about us? You said you would keep our hideout a secret." She clenched the axe and stepped closer. "How dare you?"

Natassa held out a sack. "I came to give you this as well."

Aylis's arm shot out, and she smacked the sack out of Natassa's hand. Gold coins spilled along the floor. "I don't want your charity."

Seeing her up close, with the light in the room behind her, Natassa could see her biting anger. *She's in pain*, Natassa realized.

She touched Aylis's arm. "I miss him too."

Aylis flinched, and her hard facade broke. Her red-rimmed eyes filled with tears. "I wish I told him," she whispered, regret pooling across her features. "I wish I told him I loved him."

Tears welled in Natassa's eyes. "I think he knew."

Aylis's breath hitched as she tried containing a sob. "He didn't. I told him I didn't."

The hatch opened behind Natassa, and Kasdeya called out.

"We need to go."

Aylis's face contorted, anger replacing the sadness. "Who did you bring?"

"It's just my handmaiden."

"You will tell everyone before long," Aylis said. "It would be best if you don't return. Honor your brother's word, because the only way you can help us is by staying away."

She stepped back, slamming the door between them. Natassa stood frozen for a moment, hurt by Aylis's cold dismissal. But then again, the Savorian was right. She'd never seemed to help them in the way they needed.

MORDON
KINGDOM OF VERIN
CASTLE VERIN

Mordon entered his father's chamber. A day had passed since the death of the beast. Boltrex hadn't been present when King Dale had spoken to him, and he hadn't attended the funeral of the soldier who had been ripped apart by the creature. It wasn't like his father to avoid such matters. Mordon wondered if he had stayed away so he wouldn't chance a meeting with Winston. Mordon smiled. He had good news if that was the case. Boltrex was examining maps and seemed determined to ignore him. Mordon cleared his throat.

Silence.

"Father," he said.

Boltrex glanced up. "What is it?"

"I'm sure you heard of the disturbance in the town. There was a beast, they say it was a rumlok. A Savorian animal."

Boltrex stared at a parchment. "You solved the problem, didn't you?"

"The rumlok is dead." A hopeful smile fastened onto Mordon's face. "King Dale informed me he might give me a promotion in the castle."

Boltrex scoffed. "*Might*." He threw his hands into the air. "*Might!* I want the facts. Once you're promoted, notify me then."

Mordon's jaw flexed. He needed to give him something. "Winston is dead. He is not here. A man arrived, disguising himself as Winston, and now he claims to be Winston's son."

Boltrex sneered. "I've already met him and seen his impossible claims firsthand. I shouldn't have to be doing your work, but I always seem to. Your name is covered in dirt!" Boltrex crumpled the parchment in his fist. "Because you could not control your anger, you are the chief suspect for Advisor Liston's death."

Mordon looked down, swallowing the lump in his throat.

"Now I have to fix this mess." Boltrex strode to the window overlooking the courtyard. "Any other news?"

"No, I . . ." Mordon wanted to hear words of encouragement from his father. He hungered for the praise he never received.

"Then leave. If you ever want to be king, work on wooing the princess."

Mordon took a step back, hardening himself like he had countless other times. No matter how hard he tried to win his father's approval, it never seemed to work. He was starting to understand that he never would, and it made him furious. He turned, leaving the room quietly, and made his way to the barracks. Neglect from years past flitted through his mind, giving him the urge to destroy something. He stormed into the barracks and tried to focus, but a red haze crept into the edges of his vision. He spotted one of the soldiers warming up on his own and started toward him, unsheathing his sword as he went. The soldier grew alarmed when he saw Mordon approaching.

"Draw your sword!" Mordon shouted. "NOW!"

The soldier drew his sword and placed his helmet over his head. Mordon wasn't wearing any armor, but that didn't stop him. He lunged forward, striking blow after blow. Anger coursed through his veins. He could hardly see what he was doing. The soldier crashed onto the hard floor, his helmet sliding off. He raised his sword in a weak attempt to deflect Mordon's attack. Mordon smashed his sword so hard onto the soldier's weapon that the man lost his grip and it clattered beside his head.

Mordon heard someone shrieking at him, and others were shouting, but he was blind to it all. He lifted his arm in the air and brought his sword down. Someone jumped in front of him, screaming.

"Mordon! Don't do this!"

It took him a moment to realize it was Coralie. She stood in the way of his sword, her arms outstretched. Horror written in every feature of her face. Mordon stood there with his sword hanging in the air. Something inside him awakened when he saw a tear slip down Coralie's face. Mordon swallowed hard when he realized something. Somewhere along the years of knowing her, he had fallen for her. And now she had stopped him from making a terrible mistake. He cared for her. He cared for her far more than he should. And that would ruin him. His father had engrained the strict rules he must follow. Loving Coralie was not on that list. The goal was the crown. The kingdom. No attachments.

If you ever want to be king, work on wooing the princess.

Mordon shouted and lifted a wooden side table. He flung it at the wall, and it splintered into jagged pieces. Mordon breathed heavily as he stared at the fragments of wood. They reminded him of himself: broken and useless. He stormed out of the barracks.

CHISHMA
KINGDOM OF VERIN
TOWN OF NAMAAR

RAIN PATTERED ON the shabby rooftops and empty shopping stalls. A cloaked man walked down the muddy roads and entered the tavern named Bloody Fools. He made his way through the raucous group of drunk men and took a seat in the far back of the tavern. The barkeeper brought a tankard of zat, and the man finished it in a few swigs. His keen eyes took everything in and watched the doorway most of all. The doors to the tavern opened, and another man walked in. He was average-sized but carried himself with importance and power. He had scars running down his arms, and his lips were curled into a sneaky grin. The scarred man spotted him and approached, sitting across from him.

"Vykus, welcome," the Chishma said.

Vykus scoffed. "The only way I feel welcome is with a purse full of gold."

The Chishma leaned forward. The dim light fell on his black beard, the only part of his face showing. "What would you say about chests filled with gold?"

Vykus grinned, showing off his gold tooth. "I would feel *very* welcomed."

"Lord Prolus has another mission for you," the Chishma said. "Princess Natassa."

"What about her?"

"Lord Prolus wishes you to capture her."

Vykus barked a laugh. "Capture the emperor's daughter?" Vykus laughed again but sobered when the Chishma stayed silent. "Of course I could accomplish this task. But you must be joking?"

"I never joke."

"How does Lord Prolus expect me to break into the palace?"

"Not the palace. Princess Natassa is traveling to the Kingdom of Ayleth. She does not have a big escort. Easy job."

Vykus stroked his stubbled chin with a roughened hand. "Where am I supposed to deliver her?"

"We will inform you once you have gotten the princess. Send us word." The Chishma leaned back in his chair.

"I better receive those chests," Vykus warned as he stood.

"When has Lord Prolus failed to keep his word?"

An evil smile spread across Vykus's face. "So far, never."

The Chishma returned the smile.

As Vykus turned to leave, the Chishma called after him. "We also received news about a shelter housing Savorians in the capital. Once you're done with this job, I will inform you of the exact location."

Vykus's lips curled into a wicked grin. "Perfect. See you around, Talon."

Talon dragged his hood lower and pulled himself farther into the shadows.

NATASSA
KARALIK EMPIRE
WALLINGTON

"I will separate from the group tonight," Natassa said.

Kasdeya shifted on her seat in the carriage across from her. "Are you sure?"

"I have to do this. I cannot marry Draven, and this is the only way I can escape. I want you to come with me or run away with the captain." When Kasdeya sent her a startled look, Natassa nodded. "I know you like Thander. You and Kre—" She cleared her throat. "You and Krea always argued because of him."

"Isn't it selfish?" Kasdeya said. "If you don't marry Draven, your father's deal will go to shreds and your brother will suffer the consequences." Kasdeya's arms were folded across her chest, and Natassa feared the frown on her face would become permanent.

Unfathomable guilt swirled inside Natassa. "It is selfish," she whispered. "It is."

"There is a way to solve this," Kasdeya said. "If I take your place."

"I cannot ask that of you. I won't."

"You're not asking, I'm offering. This will fix everything. You will be free to live how you want."

"At your expense," Natassa replied. "And that is too high a price."

"One I'm willing to pay." Kasdeya's posture was determined, her chin lifted in a way Natassa's always was. Her mannerisms had become engrained into her.

Natassa turned to stare out the carriage window. They had set out from Hearcross days ago and had just arrived in Wallington.

The carriage slowed to a halt, and a moment later, the door was opened. Captain Thander helped them down and signaled to the guards to take care of the horses.

He motioned her forward. "The inn is this way, Your Highness." Natassa followed him inside. Thander stopped by the entryway and announced, "Clear the inn for Princess Natassa Hartinza, daughter of His Royal Majesty, Emperor Malus Hartinza, ruler of the four kingdoms!"

The innkeeper ushered his other patrons from the inn and turned all his attention to them. "We have as many rooms as you need, Your Highness." He bowed low. "We can prepare a meal and are ready to assist your every need."

Natassa dipped her head in acknowledgment. "Thank you. My handmaiden will inform you of my needs."

"Splendid. My serving girl will show you to your room."

A young girl appeared from behind him and bobbed Natassa a quick curtsy. "Right this way, Your Highness."

Natassa followed her to the stairs. She paused at the foot of the steps and glanced back. Kasdeya was speaking with Thander in the entryway. Their faces were grim, and Thander moved his hands in animated gestures. They glanced her way and stared. Natassa smiled, but neither returned the gesture. She felt a strange shiver go down her spine.

"Your Highness?" The serving girl waited at the top of the stairs.

Natassa nodded with a strained smile. After the girl had shown her to her room, Natassa settled inside. She sat at a small table, looking into a hand mirror. She thought over Kasdeya's words for a long while. When Kasdeya entered the room, Natassa spoke.

"I agree to your plan, if you still wish to pose as me."

Kasdeya held her dagger. She closed the door behind her and set the weapon on the table. She smiled.

"I'm glad you changed your mind."

"But I want you to consider what you're getting into," Natassa started. "You will go to Ayleth to marry Draven. If he finds out or my father realizes you are not me . . ."

"I will handle that when the time comes. We should change places now."

Natassa nodded. She helped Kasdeya dress into one of her gowns and placed a necklace around her neck. She gave her the royal signet ring and added the finishing touch, a crown. Kasdeya examined herself in the mirror, taking in every angle. She peered at Natassa through the glass.

"You've been covering your forehead."

Natassa shrugged. "I like how it looks. You will not add extensions?"

Kasdeya smirked. "Maybe it's time Natassa got a haircut."

Natassa frowned but brushed aside her uneasy feeling. "I will pack my things to prepare for tonight, then."

Kasdeya moved in a flash. She lifted her dagger from the table and placed it below Natassa's chin. "Ah, Natassa. You are so naïve."

The steel bit into Natassa's neck. She winced, leaning back. Kasdeya stared at her with cold eyes, bitter and vengeful. Natassa had suspected her of something, but not this, not this far.

"Kasdeya," Natassa warned, lifting her hands to show she was unarmed. She attempted to reach out to her shadows. Xeni said she controlled them. Maybe they could help her.

Kasdeya gritted her teeth, reaching out to grab Natassa's hair. She took a firm grip of her bun, wrenching her head back. Natassa flinched as the dagger grazed her neck. A trickle of blood made its way over her skin, reminding her how close she was to death.

"Kasdeya," she tried again. "You aren't doing the right thing."

Kasdeya laughed. It was full of scorn. "I'm doing what I should have done years ago. Removing the biggest thorn in my life." She yanked Natassa's hair. "You don't know how many times I've tried to kill you. That time when we went for a walk in the garden and I pushed you into the poisonous weeds, it wasn't an accident."

The pain in Natassa's heart grew until it was too much to bear. She could still remember Kasdeya's panicked expression when Natassa had fallen into the pile. The weeds had been reserved for one of her father's prisoners.

"But you've always somehow been immune to poison. I figured that out very well."

A tear slid down Natassa's cheek. "Krea had nothing to do with this."

Kasdeya scoffed. "Krea was a fool. I could have made her something if she'd stayed at my side, but she chose you. She chose you over me."

"If you wanted to pretend to be me, why didn't you let me run away? You could have taken over without me in the way."

Kasdeya stared down at Natassa with a grim smile on her lips. "Until you are dead, you will always be in my way."

She continued pulling at Natassa's hair, gathering it in one hand. She lifted the dagger from Natassa's neck and slashed at the hair.

"Stop!" Natassa screamed, thrashing against her.

Kasdeya shoved her against the wall, staring into Natassa's eyes as the last strand of hair fell.

"I've wanted to do that for so long."

She placed the dagger against Natassa's throat once again. Natassa was numb. She lowered her head, her hair shielded her face, falling in jagged cuts to her shoulders. Kasdeya pressed the dagger closer.

"Any last words?"

Natassa lifted her head, trying to reach her shadows once more. She peered into Kasdeya's eyes. "It's not too late. You can stop this."

Kasdeya faltered, the grip on her dagger loosening. But in a moment, she returned to her vicious manner. "It is too late . . . for you."

Natassa focused on her eyes, attempting to communicate with her. "You need me, at least until we reach Ayleth. They will look down on you if you don't have a handmaiden."

Kasdeya's cheek flexed, and she hesitated.

"You want Draven to fall for your ruse, don't you?"

Kasdeya's nod was slow. "Yes."

Natassa felt a thrum of power. The headache that she now knew came with the use of her power was gone. Instead, she felt rejuvenated. The shadows were pleased.

"Fine." Kasdeya shoved her. "Only until we reach Ayleth."

Natassa knew she shouldn't speak to her further but couldn't help asking. "Why? Why did you do this?"

"Why?" Kasdeya repeated. "You're a selfish, spoiled brat. You were given the world, but you threw it away."

Natassa was startled by the venom in Kasdeya's voice.

"You are the emperor's daughter, but you would rather be a servant." Kasdeya leaned forward. "You should thank me. I granted your wish. Once we reach Ayleth, you will join your brother . . . in the afterlife."

Jax

Kingdom of Verin
Verintown

A FEW DAYS HAD passed since the rumlok attack, and Jax was restless. Why did Prolus send a rumlok? The soldiers' routines had gotten stricter, their training more rigid. Was he tiring them out before the attack, or was he trying to get a message to his spies? To him and Velamir. Jax watched Velamir and Latimus train through the grand window in the main living area in the manor. Velamir was more distant these days, his emotions hidden.

Jax grew tired of watching Latimus being knocked off his horse and turned away from the window. He focused on Lissa, who was demurely sipping tea, or attempting to. She held the cup with a rigid hand, her expression irritated. She set the cup down with a clang.

"I don't understand why Velamir is angry. He should applaud me for kill—for removing one of the targets."

Jax shrugged. "I think he's right. The advisor was supposed to be one of the last targets. We don't want to alert people to us before Prolus is closer. We need to act wisely."

Lissa rolled her eyes. "Whatever. How will I act like a proper *lady* when I don't even know the Imperials' way of dancing?"

"Well . . ." He scratched his head. The True Manos hood was beginning to irritate him on a personal level.

"Did I hear something about dancing?" Lady Blayton floated into the room, a pleasant smile on her face.

Lissa and Jax exchanged a swift glance. How much had she heard?

"Yes. I never had much practice, you see." Lissa's smile came across as a grimace.

Lady Blayton tsked and sat beside her. "Poor dear, it's completely understandable. You never had a woman to see to your needs. Winston was an admirable man, but when his wife passed on, he lost a part of who he was. I can see why he would forget to ensure your full tutelage."

Lissa nodded, ready to agree with her assumptions.

"But that changes now. I will hire a dancing instructor, and my son, Latimus, can sing while you dance."

Jax snorted at the thought of Latimus singing. Lady Blayton glanced at him, and he cleared his throat. "Excuse me."

An hour later, they waited for the dancing instructor to arrive. Lady Blayton led them to a large sitting room with plenty of space. Jax rested against the wall, watching Lissa cross her arms in the middle of the room.

"What did I get myself into?" She sighed.

Latimus entered along with his mother, who had left to see if the instructor had arrived. Lady Blayton shook her head. Her mouth turned down.

"It seems the instructor was unable to make an appearance today. Such a shame. Latimus is here ready to sing, and Lissa dear was anticipating it so eagerly."

"Shame indeed." Lissa's sarcasm wasn't noted by Lady Blayton.

Latimus smiled, relieved. "Well, since you don't need me, perhaps I will go visit Father."

"Where's Velamir?" Jax asked.

"Taking another tour of the castle. I don't know why he is so obsessed with that." He looked back at Lady Blayton. "By your leave, Mother."

He was halfway to the door when Jax said, "Wait."

Everyone looked at him.

"I know the dance."

Jax didn't know who looked the most shocked out of the three. But when his gaze focused on Lissa, it lingered there. Even with her mouth hanging open, she was stunning.

"How?" Latimus was skeptical.

"I wasn't always a True Manos. I helped my cousin when I was a child."

Lady Blayton clapped. "Fantastic! Shall we begin?"

Latimus's smile was strained as he took a seat, opening the case he'd brought with him and taking out a small lute. Lady Blayton nodded at her son, and he cleared his throat. Jax realized he was waiting for him and moved forward. He tried to appear determined as he walked toward Lissa. She stared at him as he approached, unfazed when he stopped a breath away. He flushed. His heart pounded in his chest, and he wondered if she could hear it.

"Now what?" she whispered, and Jax's perusal trailed from her dark brows and violet gaze to her lips.

He forced his attention back to her eyes. "Take my hands."

Latimus hummed a pleasant tune, his fingers strumming along the lute strings. Jax recognized the song because he'd heard it a million times. Homesickness rushed through him like a powerful wave crashing over a ship. Lissa's face changed to Lilly's, and he heard her childish voice. He had been much shorter than her back then. They'd laughed about the dance as they struggled to figure out the moves. Lilly had wanted to go to the town dance that week and needed someone to practice with. Jax had offered to help, and Lilly taught him the song, which they hummed together as they navigated the moves. Jax wondered what happened to Lilly. He hoped she was safe, that she was happy.

"Are you okay?" Lissa asked, and Lilly's face faded from view.

Jax nodded. "Twirl under my arm. I'll pick you up."

Lissa moved without the hesitation or alarm that Jax felt as he pondered if he could actually lift her. He wasn't what one would call very muscular. Lissa twirled, and Jax placed his free hand on her lower back, bending her backward. He released her hand and placed his arm under her knees, lifting her off the ground and spinning in a circle. It wasn't easy, but seeing her face take on an expression of delight was worth every moment.

Latimus stopped humming and started singing the lyrics.

> *I spotted you, and I knew it was fate,*
>
> *The sparkle in your eyes, the wind in your hair,*
>
> *The way you didn't hesitate,*
>
> *You faced the strongest of storms,*
>
> *With the strength of a thousand hearts,*
>
> *The biggest obstacles,*
>
> *Overcoming them not knowing how,*
>
> *You tore me apart,*
>
> *Because you had me from the start,*
>
> *Oh, Imperial girl, don't you see?*
>
> *How you will be the end of me.*

Jax instructed, and they created a rhythm. Lissa moved fast. Twirling and spinning. Learning the movements as quickly as she had learned to use daggers. Each spin as deadly and precise as herself. They repeated the dance several times. It was the most common Imperial dance. Latimus restarted the song every time, but Jax barely noticed. He wanted to memorize the moment with Lissa. The way her lips tilted up in a smile that, for once, wasn't filled with sarcasm. The way her hair spilled over her ear, falling into her face. He wanted to push it back so he could see the violet in her eyes. He wanted this moment to last forever.

They neared the end of the song, and Jax lifted her in the air. His hands gripping her waist. In the dance, the lady was supposed to be lifted very high. Jax managed a slight lift, his arms shaking. She gripped his shoulders and returned to the ground, executing the next twirl without direction from Jax. They swayed as Latimus sang the last lyrics.

Because you had me from the start,

Oh, Imperial girl, don't you see?

Jax leaned closer to Lissa and whispered, "How you will be the end of me."

He regretted it as soon as he said it, but he couldn't help himself. It was hard for him, struggling against his feelings. She pulled back, searching his gaze. Shrill clapping jerked them apart.

"Wonderful! Wonderful! Are you sure you haven't done this dance before, Lissa dear?" Lady Blayton exclaimed.

Lissa looked away from Jax. She appeared perfectly put together. As if the dance had meant nothing to her, when it had meant so much to Jax. "This is the first time."

"It must have been Latimus's musical voice that allowed you to learn so quickly."

Lissa glanced back at Jax. "I had an excellent teacher."

Heat rushed up Jax's neck, and he fought the urge to rub it.

"Latimus is a good singer," Jax admitted, attempting to throw the attention off himself.

Latimus took a bow and strode to his mother. "If you will excuse me, Mother?"

Lady Blayton nodded, and as soon as he left, she escorted Lissa from the room, telling her they had to look over her dresses and see if they were suitable enough for the castle. Jax was left alone. His embarrassment floated away, and he felt cold, lonely. Feelings he was well acquainted with. He wanted to dance with Lissa again. To feel the exhilaration of having her in his arms, so close to him, yet so far. His feelings were tormenting him, dragging him to the edge of a cliff. And if he didn't rein himself back, he would fall, and she really would be the end of him.

Karalik Empire
Near the Borderlands
Prolus's Encampment

Rumloks couldn't act for themselves. Even when they lived in harmony in Savoria, they still had an owner. The Handler knew this very well. Which was why he trembled before Lord Prolus's throne. Because he couldn't explain what he'd witnessed.

Prolus leaned against one side of the throne, his mask hiding his expression. The way he sat made him appear bored, but he could very well be in a murderous mood. The Handler's eyes darted around the murky corners of the tent, but everywhere he looked he saw the horns and the demon face. He couldn't evade the symbol.

"I'm asking you again. What happened?"

The voice was low and drove chills through the Handler's heart. He glanced at the two Chishmans standing on either side of Lord Prolus. They were still as statues, sentries awaiting orders.

The Handler licked his dry lips. "I don't know. I was controlling him as I normally did, and he attacked the town as planned but—"

"But what?" The question was sharp despite the lowness of tone.

"The vial we used must have been expired, or the concoction wasn't right," the Handler babbled.

Lord Prolus stood from his throne so swiftly the Handler retreated a step. "I won't ask you again."

"He . . . he stopped following the commands I sent." The Handler swallowed. "He just froze and allowed them to kill him."

"Who killed him?"

"I couldn't make out from the distance, but I believe it was a Galvasir. I could feel the rumlok. He was hungry for blood. One instant close to his prey, and the next, waiting. I know this is insane."

Prolus held up a hand, silencing him. He motioned to the Chishmans. "Hang him by his feet for two nights. If he survives that, drown him, slowly."

They nodded and strode forward in such horrifyingly identical movements that they seemed lifeless. Almost as if they were being controlled like the rumloks.

"Please!" he cried out. "Spare me, my lord. I answered your questions."

"You failed to do well in the only task you had. I have no use for you." Prolus redirected his attention to the Chishmans. "Spread word to the other Handlers. This is what happens when they try to go off on their own."

"But I wasn't!" The Handler's pleading cries were dragged out of the tent with him.

Prolus returned to his seat. His mask could hide his emotions from others. No one would know there was fear filtering through him. He knew this was no accident. Rumloks were raised a certain way. If they were obeying someone else, especially someone from Verin, it would mean doom for Prolus's domination.

39

VELAMIR
KINGDOM OF VERIN
VERINTOWN

TIME FLEW PAST, and Velamir's knowledge about the castle inhabitants grew along with it. Most of the councilmembers liked to take tea together in the late evenings, and it so happened that one of Jax's concoctions ended up in their porcelain cups. The mixture could make a person incapacitated with a strong feverish sickness for up to two weeks. Lissa had suggested they use poison, but Velamir knew that not only was that unnecessary, it would draw too much attention. The goal was to get them out of the way and ruin Verin's defense system.

Velamir had also learned that Advisor Covskin, a close friend of the general's, spent his afternoons taking a stroll in the castle gardens. Lissa had asked him for assistance, acting

like a helpless young lady, while Jax and Velamir waited
by one of the archways. As soon as she led him through
it in search of her lost kitten, Jax thrust a cloth over his
mouth and Velamir attempted to bind his arms. Jax had
inlaid the cloth with a serum that could knock someone
into a coma. The advisor held out against the serum.
He twisted his head and spat, thrashing and shouting at
the top of his lungs. Out of fear of being caught, Lissa
had silenced him with her claws, much to Velamir's disapproval. They worked efficiently to bring his lifeless
body into a garden shed, sealing him into a box that
resembled a coffin.

Since then, they had laid low. Too many incidents at
once were sure to cast suspicions. Jax had stayed in his
guest room, crafting and experimenting, only coming out
to help Lissa with her dancing sessions. Prince Draven
arrived the night before with a large entourage. With the
number of servants he had brought, it seemed as if he
was moving into the castle and not staying a few days
for a tournament.

Velamir strode forward, taking in his surroundings
as he approached the tiltyard with Latimus. A line of men
formed to register at a booth. Everyone who wanted to
compete was told to gather there. Velamir noticed after
the men spoke to the scribe at the booth, they were led
to a raised platform near the middle of the tiltyard. A
throng of people gathered around the platform.

"What's with the crowd?" Velamir questioned,
glancing at Latimus.

"Young, naïve Velamir." He smirked, pausing to let
his words sink in. "You weren't aware? People make

their fortunes betting on jousting matches. Verin's yearly joust is the most anticipated in the Empire. It's even better than the Karalik Joust that the emperor himself hosts."

Velamir's lip curled. He was getting sick of Latimus's cutting comments. "It's a good thing you aren't competing. Nobody would bet on you."

Latimus's face froze in a surprised expression. He forced his lips into a stiff smile. "Tournaments aren't worth my time. I have far more important duties to attend to."

They joined the line, and Velamir realized that even though it appeared long, it moved rather fast.

"I went up to the castle to see my father," Latimus started. "We decided to pay your entry fees for the tournament."

Velamir shook his head. "There is no need for that."

"While I would agree with you, my father insisted." He gave Velamir a look. "You should be grateful. Not everyone receives this much attention from the Blayton family." Latimus chuckled. "It's almost as if we are sponsoring you."

"The name Winston is well-known throughout Verin," Velamir replied. "I don't need a sponsor."

Latimus scoffed. "Count it as charity then. Like Winston showed you when he took you in."

That snapped a cord within Velamir. He grabbed hold of Latimus's collar, not caring that the men in line turned to stare. Velamir's breaths came out sharply as he tried to contain his anger.

"You don't understand me, Latimus. I grew up without the love of parents, knowing that my family was murdered. I was trained to kill, and I'm here for revenge, not charity. Watch yourself, or you might end up on my list," Velamir whispered so only Latimus could hear.

Latimus's eyes grew wide, and Velamir could have sworn he saw fear in them. Hearing murmurs from the other participants, Velamir released him. Latimus brushed off his clothes.

"You are lucky, Velamir. You've never had to prove yourself to your parents. You've never had to show that you were worthy. Every little thing you do is not being evaluated. You think your life is hard and mine is easy and full of happiness, but you have no right to judge. Not when you don't know my life at all."

They glared at each other for a few moments more, and then Latimus reached into his belt, pulling out a coin purse. He grabbed Velamir's hand, shoving the purse into it. "That's from my father, not me. If you want to refuse it, that would be an insult to him."

Velamir's jaw clenched, and he placed the purse into his belt. "Give him my thanks."

"He also instructed me to assist you during the joust, and though that is the last thing either of us wants, I will do it."

Velamir knew it was hard for Latimus to say those words, and so he nodded in return. They moved up the line. The men kept glancing at them with curiosity. Velamir watched as each man was led to the tiltyard. The crowd stared at the competitors with greedy eyes, looking them up and down as they calculated their worth. Velamir craned his neck, trying to see past the throng. Unable to get a good look, he turned to Latimus.

"Where is the guard taking the men?"

"To the Joust Master. You will see him soon," Latimus said.

"Next!" the scribe called.

Velamir took a step forward. The conversations taking place around him died off, and Velamir turned to see what caught the people's attention. Mordon joined the back of the line. He stood tall and stared straight ahead. After a long second of silence, the men fell back into their conversations. Velamir overheard the discussion of the men nearest to him.

"I heard Galva Mordon almost killed a man in the barracks," one said.

"I'm not surprised," another replied.

"He takes after his father." The first one snickered.

"Don't let his father hear that. General Boltrex will have you rotting in the dungeons for the rest of your existence," the second one warned.

That was something else Velamir had recently learned. Mordon was Boltrex's son. They had both worked together to kill Winston, and Velamir would take them down together too. The sound of music pulled him from his thoughts, and he glanced at the source. A band of minstrels made their way past them and through the rowdy crowd.

Latimus laughed at Velamir's confused expression. "Courtesy of the Joust Master. He likes to put on a show."

"Next!" the scribe called out.

Velamir realized the scribe was staring at him with impatience.

"Title?" the scribe asked, his quill poised over parchment.

"The Cavalier," Velamir replied, pulling out the coin purse from Blayton and placing it onto the stand.

The scribe wrote that down before looking up again. "Name?"

An abrupt shove from behind sent Velamir staggering to the side.

"Out of the way, peasant," ordered a distinguished voice.

Velamir turned to see who had pushed him. A man stood in front of the scribe. His blond hair was long and slicked back in straight lines. Close-trimmed sideburns covered his cheeks. He appeared strong despite his fashionable appearance. Velamir noticed the men behind him looked disgruntled. They were upset that this man just placed himself in the front without having to wait like the rest of them. But none of them seemed willing to do anything about it. Velamir stepped forward. Latimus grabbed his shoulder in a firm grip, shaking his head.

"Crown Prince Draven Valent of Ayleth," the man said in a haughty voice.

The scribe scribbled, and a dose of anger coursed through Velamir. Just because this man was a prince didn't mean he could barge in.

"I haven't finished." Velamir shrugged off Latimus's hand.

Prince Draven didn't spare him a glance, and neither did the scribe.

"My title, as I am sure everyone knows by now, is the Invincible Dragon."

"I said I haven't finished," Velamir repeated in a louder voice.

"*Velamir*," Latimus growled under his breath.

"You are done here, Cavalier," the scribe barked.

"Fetch me some blasted water! I am parched," Prince Draven called to his servants.

One of them rushed forward. Just as he was about to reach Prince Draven, Mordon stuck his foot out and tripped the servant. The jug of water flew into the air, smacking Prince Draven in the chest. Water drenched his clothing, and Prince Draven yelled. Another servant hurried to assist. She held out a cloth and attempted to dry him off. Draven wrenched her wrist, causing her to cry out and drop the cloth.

"Foolish wretch!" Prince Draven shouted, lifting his hand to slap her.

The servant closed her eyes, bracing herself for the pain. Velamir caught Draven's arm before it could land. Gasps rang out. The prince's eyes flashed with fury.

"Is this how you treat your subjects?" Velamir snarled, thrusting Draven's arm away with disgust.

The servant opened her eyes, staring with shock before moving away.

Prince Draven's lip curled. "And who do you think you are?"

"Someone who will never bow to cruelty," Velamir replied.

Draven barked a laugh. "This is why I don't mingle with peasants. They think they know everything, but they are scum."

Latimus stepped between them. "Leave it for the joust."

The guard escorting the men to the platform appeared next to Velamir. Velamir looked past Latimus and locked eyes with Prince Draven's steely ones.

"C'mon," Latimus muttered, motioning Velamir to follow the guard.

Velamir ignored the stares of the people as he walked past them. As soon as he passed the crowd, Velamir spotted chairs positioned beside the platform. The guard pointed at one of the empty seats, and Velamir went to sit. Latimus tried to follow, but the guard held out a hand.

"Competitors only," the guard said.

Velamir's attention caught on the platform. Court jesters juggled daggers to entertain the crowd. He looked away from the spectacle and noticed some men in colorful outfits setting up a betting table. Velamir assessed the other competitors sitting around him. Most of them looked rough and strong.

Prince Draven appeared, and the crowd grew wild when they saw him. Velamir frowned. The way they screamed and shouted, it sounded as if the emperor himself had arrived. Although, from what Velamir had heard, the people in the Empire didn't seem to care much about him. Draven waved and flashed them a blinding grin. He snapped his fingers, and his servants approached, carrying a cushioned lounging chair. They set it in front of the other chairs in accordance with the prince's wishes. Velamir scoffed. Of course Draven would pick the front. He wanted to ensure all eyes were on him. The prince reclined on his seat and grabbed a glass of something his servants brought, presumably zat.

The minstrel band went to work on an impressive tune. A man walked onto the platform, stealing everyone's attention, and the cheering started up again. Velamir blinked twice to ensure his eyes weren't deceiving him. The man was dressed in red leather with a white tunic underneath that plumed at the neck and wrists. He removed a feather-embellished puffy purple hat as he took a grand bow. His raven-black hair was spiked at the top and braided on the sides, ending with dyed red leather strips. He had enthusiastic energy and an alluring smile.

"Welcome, welcome," he announced in a congenial voice. "As you know, I am Koseer-ja." He gave another bow as the audience roared with praise.

Koseer-ja was not a name people used in the Karalik Empire or in Tariqi. In fact, Velamir was sure it was a Savagelander custom to end names in ja. The real question was how this man was here if he was a Savagelander. Velamir continued listening, noticing he didn't have an accent when he spoke.

"Today, I will interview all of our contestants." He waggled his brows. "And then we can get down to betting on our favorites."

That was accompanied by hoots, loud cheers, and more applause. This was getting ridiculous.

"You, young man." Koseer-ja pointed. "Come on up and introduce yourself."

The man stood from his chair and jogged up the stairs onto the platform. His smile seemed nerve-racked, and he tried not to look at the crowd.

"Let's play a game," Koseer-ja suggested. "Tell me

your title, and I shall see if I am as good at remembering names as I think I am."

The man gulped. "Uh, Prey Wing, sir."

"Such formality! Please, call me Koseer-ja." He tapped his chin. "Aha, I remember your father. He spoke of you a few years ago. How proud he was! You must be Lorgont Cavenshaw."

Lorgont nodded. "Yes, si— I mean, yes, that is correct."

Koseer-ja smiled. "I got the first one, ladies and gentlemen!"

The crowd cheered, and when they quieted, Koseer-ja continued, "Lorgont, do you think you have what it takes to win the tournament?"

Lorgont frowned. "I am not sure, sir. There are a lot of experienced men competing."

Koseer-ja nodded in approval. "We have a humble one, don't we?" he said to the crowd.

They murmured in assent. The interviews went on like this. Usually the men Koseer-ja interviewed were sure of their victory and said so. They also didn't seem to want to talk too much, but Koseer-ja was ambitious. He kept the energy flowing through each interview.

Finally, Prince Draven walked onto the stage. He waved to the crowd with an arrogant grin plastered across his face.

"There is no need for guessing or titles, is there?" Koseer-ja chuckled and bowed. "The one and only Prince Draven."

The crowd went wild, and the bidding table was occupied with eager investors.

Prince Draven nodded, smirking. "You are right. I only come in a one-of-a-kind package. Specifically, for the ladies." The prince winked at the audience.

Koseer-ja laughed right on cue, and the audience followed his lead, although none of them were as boisterous as him.

"Which has caught your fancy this week?" Koseer-ja asked, as if Draven had a new lady every week, and for all Velamir knew, he probably did.

"My last conquest was a lovely lady from Hearcross. But most recently . . . I believe it was just this morning that I spotted a beautiful lady here in Verintown. In fact"—Draven paused, his eyes roving the crowd—"she might be among you."

The ladies in the crowd swooned. Velamir shook his head in disbelief and glanced at Latimus, who rolled his eyes.

"Ooh," Koseer-ja said. "Ooh," he said again, motioning with his hands for the crowd to join him. Soon all the people were saying it along with him. Draven chuckled, and the interview continued with the prince boasting about how amazing he was.

Velamir was called up after Draven's interview. Koseer-ja looked him over. "We have a lot of younger men this year. And what title do you go by?"

"I am referred to as the Cavalier."

Koseer-ja exchanged a look with the crowd. "We all know who the Cavalier is . . . the renowned Galvasir Winston! From what I heard about you, I expected someone much older."

"I'm not Winston," Velamir started, and the crowd

hushed, eager to hear his words. "My name is Velamir. Winston is my father."

Koseer-ja nodded, pursing his lips. "And where is your legendary father?"

Velamir glanced at the ground, hiding the real pain in his eyes. "He was killed on our journey here."

The crowd was silent as a graveyard.

Velamir looked up, meeting Koseer-ja's grave look. "But he's in a better place now, and I know he is watching me from above. I came here to honor his memory. This is what he would want me to do."

The crowd clapped, and Koseer-ja slapped his hands together a few times. "That is very admirable, Velamir. I wish you success in your endeavor."

"Thank you."

Koseer-ja cleared his throat. "Of course, of course. Now I don't mean to seem rude considering what you just disclosed to us, but what do you believe are your chances of winning?"

"My father taught me something when I was younger, something I won't ever forget. He crafted a bow for me to use and stood behind me as I practiced my first shots." Velamir chuckled at the memory. "I missed every single one. I was angry at myself and tossed the bow aside. Even though I was foolish, he kneeled before me, hands on my shoulders. I complained to him, said I was a failure, but he shook his head."

Velamir paused, his voice vibrating with emotion. "He told me every shot was a victory. Each time I missed, it didn't mean I lost. It meant I was closer to getting it right. All I had to do was not give up." Velamir returned his stare to Koseer-ja. "So you see, every outcome will be a win for me."

Cheers rose louder than Velamir had heard any of the times before, and as he stared at the faces in the crowd, he saw respect, awe, adoration. The bidding table filled, and Koseer-ja beamed.

"Brilliant words from a wise man! Give it up for the Cavalier."

The audience continued clapping until Velamir reached his seat. Latimus caught his eyes and mouthed, *Great acting*. Velamir looked away. Latimus thought everything was a game to him. But he didn't realize his words about Winston were ones he kept inside his heart, the biggest truth he carried. Because they were a way of life.

Velamir felt someone's gaze on him and searched for the source. Draven turned in his seat, leveling a ferocious glare at him. Velamir held his gaze until Draven looked away. A deep chuckle rumbled behind him, and Velamir turned around to see Mordon's face crinkled in amusement.

"Be careful who you make friends with . . . *Velamir*." Mordon's voice was layered with sarcasm as he stood up, heading toward the platform for his interview.

40

CORALIE
KINGDOM OF VERIN
CASTLE VERIN

S WEAT RAN DOWN Coralie's brow. The clash of
swords echoed within the barracks. She raised
her sword and parried her opponent's blow.
After a few more strikes, Coralie gained the upper
hand, and the edge of her blade rested against her
opponent's neck. He lifted his hands in defeat and
dropped his sword.

Coralie moved her sword and rested the tip
on the ground. She removed her helmet, pulling
off the coif underneath. Her braids fell, brushing
and clinging to the sticky perspiration against her
neck. Coralie walked to one of the side tables,
grabbing a kerchief to wipe the sweat.

The soldier she had just faced spoke. "I
don't think you have ever suffered a defeat."

"Oh, I've lost plenty," she responded.

It was true. At first, she had lost every time. Every bout had left her sore and exhausted, but over time, she had gotten stronger. She had never given up, and now she rarely lost. Only to Mordon. Coralie scanned the area, searching for him. She sighed when she couldn't spot him. A wave of disappointment crashed over her. He hadn't returned since the incident with the soldier, and she was sad to say she missed him.

I don't miss him. I miss sparring with him.

No one else would help her improve.

"Good match," Coralie told the soldier she had sparred.

"Good match," he repeated and strode away to find another bout.

Coralie looked around, wondering who she should face next, when one of her uncle's messengers rushed inside. His eyes landed on her, and he jogged over.

"Princess Coralie!" the messenger said, stopping in front of her.

Coralie grimaced when she heard her title. Years ago, she had loved it. Loved being a princess with her own castle and her servants to do her bidding. Loved having caring, wonderful parents who granted her every desire. But then Prolus came and took that all away. He had killed her parents while she had been visiting her uncle, King Dale. He had taken their castle, adding it to his growing list of conquests. How she wished she could have died with her parents. Because then she wouldn't have to live with this bitter feeling of hate. It was the one thing that kept her going. She had sworn after the news of her parents' death that she would not die until she avenged them.

"Princess?" The messenger waved a hand in front of her face, pulling her out of her wretched thoughts.

"What?" she snapped.

The messenger jumped back when he heard the harshness of her voice.

Coralie sighed and asked again in a gentler tone. "What is it?"

"King Dale wishes to see you."

Coralie was grateful to her uncle. After her parents' death, King Dale had taken her in. He'd lost his own son and had no successor. He treated her like a daughter and made her his heir. Whoever married her would inherit the Kingdom of Verin. There lay the problem. She didn't want to be married off. She sought vengeance.

"Let's go." Coralie motioned the messenger.

He led her to the War Room, where King Dale usually pored over maps and had discussions with General Boltrex and Advisor Welix.

"Princess Coralie," the messenger announced and took his leave.

King Dale stood alone in the middle of the room. He was looking at a map, and as Coralie walked closer, she saw it was a depiction of Prolus's ever-expanding territories. Her uncle looked up, and his tired face broke into a smile. Coralie smiled back, but it was a little hesitant. Her uncle was looking ill these past days. The stress was getting to him, and with Prolus on the border of their kingdom, he had every right to be concerned. They would be the next target. The rumlok Prolus had sent confirmed that fact.

King Dale's hair was gray with black sprinkled throughout. Wrinkles lined his forehead, and his dark brown eyes were filled with wisdom and experience.

"Coralie," he said, noting her armor. "Training again?"

"Of course," Coralie responded. "We must be ready for the war."

One reason she admired her uncle was because he encouraged her to train. He wanted her to be strong. When she first told him of her desire to wield a sword, he employed the most capable of swordsmen to train her.

King Dale nodded. "Prolus is about to advance. My scouts have informed me he will attack Namaar any day now. I have sent reinforcements, but I know it will be no use." Her uncle shook his head. "His army is too strong."

Coralie laid a hand on her uncle's arm. "Do not fear. We will not lose this kingdom."

"We might not, with the help of another kingdom," he said, sitting in one of the chairs that surrounded the table.

"What's on your mind?"

"I was pondering the idea of allying with King Joster. He has a fearsome reputation and could be of great help."

Coralie frowned. She didn't know if that was the best idea. They barely knew him, or his son, Draven.

"I think we should be further acquainted with him before making agreements."

King Dale smiled. "I knew you would be sensible. I

have invited his son, Prince Draven, to the banquet we are hosting tonight. We shall see if he will make a good ally or not."

"You have thought well, uncle."

"I want your opinion on him, of course."

"I will be sure to watch for him," Coralie reassured him, although she detested gatherings, balls, and any party in general.

"I thought Galvasir Winston arrived in town, but it was his son who had come."

The new topic surprised Coralie. "You spoke to his son?"

King Dale laughed. "Yes, he seems like a good man, but it shocked me when I learned Winston remarried after Saphira." A shadow of hurt crossed his face.

"Perhaps she helped him through the pain. It's not a choice to fall in love, it just sort of happens."

King Dale's grief was chased away by a smile that creased his eyes. "And when did my beautiful niece become so well versed in love? Should I be worried? Is the future King Consort lurking around?" He made a show of peering around the room.

Coralie laughed. "Don't be silly."

Unbidden, an image of Mordon raced through her mind, accompanied by a memory.

The barracks were lit by a dozen or so candles. Coralie lifted the sword, staring at it with determination. She swung it through the air, smiling at the swoosh it made. She continued thrusting and slashing, her arms growing weaker with every move. She was so focused she didn't hear the footsteps.

"Your sword isn't a worthy enough opponent."

Coralie spun, pointing her sword in the direction of the voice. One of her braids fell over her ear, brushing her cheek. Mordon's arms were crossed, his hair short and his side smirk a contrast against the darkness in his eyes. He didn't seem fazed despite the fact that her sword point was almost touching his throat.

Mordon unsheathed his sword before Coralie could blink. One moment she was holding her sword, and the next it was flying through the air. It made a clanging noise as it clattered across the floor.

She scoffed. "That's not fair."

"Rule number one. There is no fairness in combat, just skill."

Coralie leaned over, picking up the sword. "My instructors wait until I'm ready before beginning."

Mordon chuckled. "That makes you weak. You will never be prepared in a real battle. You better get used to that."

He circled her, and she turned with him, keeping him in sight.

"They aren't teaching you right at all."

"It's been one week. How can you judge so soon?"

"I have an uncanny talent of perception."

She rolled her eyes. "And an uncanny talent of making people uncomfortable."

His brows drew together, and she took that moment, bursting forward. He lifted his sword and blocked her blow. She staggered back at his strength.

"What do you mean?" he asked.

"You think I didn't see you watching me train with

the instructor? You aren't exactly invisible." She waved her sword at him.

"I can't watch?"

"It's unsettling."

"I was observing to make sure he was training you right, and that is when I saw he wasn't."

"It's not your place to do so. You aren't my father," she shot at him and swung for his head.

He ducked and thrust for her midsection. She twisted her body, and his sword point smashed the wall. Her sword flew at startling speed, and her heart froze. I'm going to cut his neck, *she thought.* Then his hand was there, gripping hers, stopping the blade an inch away.

He pushed her back, moving with her until she stumbled against the wall. Her eyes were frozen on the edge of her sword. It was positioned a breath from his neck. She could have killed him. It took her a moment to realize how hard she was breathing, and when she did, she noticed Mordon's chest heaving just as heavily. She looked up past his neck and chin, her gaze trailing his face, taking in the beads of sweat dripping down his brow and the harshness of his jaw. When her eyes met his, she was overcome by their intensity.

He was staring at her as if he could read her secrets all the way to her soul. He was peering into her as if he could remove the shield she carried around herself. Somehow, during the meeting of their eyes, she had dropped her sword, but neither of them noticed. An ugly-looking bruise stood out on his cheekbone. Coralie's hand lifted, and her fingers brushed the skin, gently, carefully. His lids closed as she moved her fingers up closer to them. His lashes brushed her skin as she continued tracing the bruise. She stopped moving when a lump rose in her throat. Who hurt him?

His eyes opened, and the fierce darkness in them had faded into something lighter, something vulnerable. He stared at her like she could save him. Like she was his light at the end of the tunnel.

"Mordon." Her voice came out breathy.

His gaze shifted down, and butterflies danced in her stomach. She forced herself to focus on her question, not their proximity.

"Who did this to you?"

And just like that, all the vulnerability was gone and the constant anger and arrogance returned, something she was understanding he used as a cover for his true feelings. He pulled away from her, and the sudden coldness she felt overwhelmed her. He left the barracks, leaving her in confusion.

"Coralie? Coralie!" King Dale's voice snapped her back to the present.

She shook her head. "I should go . . . get ready for the banquet."

"Hmm." King Dale peered at her through narrowed eyes before waving her away.

Coralie forced her thoughts from Mordon. *He doesn't care. I don't care.* She repeated those words over and over.

JAX
KINGDOM OF VERIN
VERINTOWN

"Your serum works this time, doesn't it?" Lissa joked as she eyed Jax.

"The last one was slow acting, but I fixed the problem. And instead of a coma, it will induce a heart attack." He held out a vial that she accepted.

"How many left?" Velamir questioned.

Jax opened his journal, flipping to his sketch. An X crossed through many of the figures. "Four councilmen."

"We can't give them all a heart attack," Velamir said.

Jax held out another vial to Lissa. "This looks and smells like a tonic, but if one drinks it, they will start seeing visions of their worst nightmares. It fades after a week, but that's long enough for them to be locked away under the guise of insanity."

Velamir's eyes grew wide at the description. "I wouldn't wish that on anyone."

"Frumgan experimented on me once, but his wasn't fully developed, so it only lasted a day." Jax shook in revulsion. "That was enough for a lifetime."

He heard a creak by the sitting room archway and froze. They were keeping their voices low, but at any moment, someone could come into the sitting room and overhear a vital part of their mission. Jax put a finger over his lips. Lissa opened her mouth, but Jax covered it. "Someone's coming."

He lowered his hand from her lips just as Latimus

entered, looking smart in a fitted coat and flowing green cape that hung off of one shoulder. "Ready to leave?"

Velamir nodded. "Yes. Lissa?" He raised his brows at her.

She smiled the fakest smile Jax had ever seen. "I will be ready in a moment, *brother*."

Latimus laughed. "I'm going with my mother in the first carriage. You two can take the second one. I will not arrive late on your account."

"We will go with you," Velamir said and brushed past them out of the living room.

Latimus gave them a lingering look and took a parting shot at Lissa. "Don't waste too much time. I'm sure the True Manos has tasks."

When he left them alone, Lissa let out an aggravated sigh. "Latimus is poking his nose in our business at every opportunity. We should use the nightmare tonic on him."

"Don't worry about him. Focus on your job, charm, impress, gain information."

"It shouldn't be too hard. All the noblemen are stuck-up fools."

"And the fact that you look gorgeous should help as well," Jax said without thinking.

Her eyes snapped to his face, and his cheeks reddened.

"I meant gorgeous for the act." He let out an awkward chuckle.

She was wearing the dress from Harold's shop. The one with the belt that matched her violet eyes. A knot tightened his chest at the thought of other men dancing with her.

"Do you remember the dances we learned?"

She nodded. "I don't forget things, ever. What about you? Can't you come to the party? Linger in the back or something?"

"True Manos aren't invited. It's offensive to the seriousness of their work."

"What if someone has a heart attack?" Lissa winked.

He smiled. "Well, I guess that's it, then."

Besides, he didn't want to torture himself by watching her flirt with countless nobles.

"Lissa!"

It was Velamir calling.

"I better go." Lissa sighed in irritation.

She moved to leave, but Jax grabbed her wrist. "Wait."

She turned back, and he pulled a ring from his pocket. He demonstrated how to squeeze a small lever on the side, and a tiny knife emerged. "I made this the other day. There's powerful poison on the tip. If anyone harasses you, use this."

He closed it and slipped it onto her finger. She locked her hand around it and nodded a wordless thanks.

"Be careful, Lis."

She seemed stunned but cleared her expression so quickly Jax figured he'd imagined it. Velamir called her name again, and she hurried away, leaving Jax alone with his thoughts.

CORALIE
KINGDOM OF VERIN
CASTLE VERIN

ORALIE WATCHED THE guests mingle throughout the Great Hall. King Dale sat on his throne, but Coralie knew in a short while he would rise and socialize with his guests. She spoke with a noblewoman from Ayleth, one of the ladies in Prince Draven's entourage. The woman babbled incessantly, and Coralie was beginning to have a headache. Her eyes caught on the entrance of the Great Hall, where Velamir and a young lady were called in, along with Latimus Blayton and his mother. Coralie watched Velamir, noticing his hesitance as he glanced at the young woman with him. Was he married? For some reason, the thought made her uncomfortable.

"Princess?"

Coralie looked back at the noblewoman she had been speaking to, or rather listening to. Coralie gave her a strained smile. She wasn't the best conversationalist.

"Excuse me."

She walked toward the entrance, but when she neared, Velamir was no longer there. She glanced around.

"Searching for someone?"

She turned and smiled. "Good evening."

Velamir nodded in return. Coralie noticed he was looking quite handsome tonight, with his dark brows and deep green eyes. His height was a bonus as well, although he was not as tall as Mordon. Coralie found herself comparing the two men in her mind and brushed it aside, focusing on the present. There was something about Velamir that struck her as odd. His smile seemed off.

"Thank you for coming."

"Of course. Who in their right mind wouldn't attend an invitation from King Dale? But if I had known you would be here, that would have been tempting enough."

Coralie had been flattered enough times to be immune to it. But somehow, coming from Velamir, it was almost believable.

"The party is actually much smaller than it should have been," she told him. "The king was forced to rescind some invitations on account of the spreading illness."

"I heard something about it," Velamir said, "but I didn't realize how serious it was."

She nodded. "The councilmembers and their families remained home to keep the sickness in check."

"So none of them are here?" He looked disappointed.

"Not that I know of." She frowned. "Where you planning on meeting with one of them?"

He shook his head. "No, I was just concerned for their health."

"Won't you introduce me to your wife?"

Velamir appeared stunned, and then his expression cleared. "Oh, her. She's my sister, Lissa."

Coralie remembered how her uncle had looked at the thought of Winston remarrying. It seemed he had more than one child with this woman.

"Any other siblings?"

Velamir eyed her for a moment, as if she were a puzzle he couldn't figure out. "No, just us."

"And your mother?"

He laughed, low and strained. "Why so inquisitive?"

"I thought we were getting to know each other," she replied.

"You know much about me, but I don't have the slightest idea who you are besides a beast slayer."

Coralie laughed at the praise. He was very good at turning conversations around. Coralie's attention was stolen for a second when she noticed Koseer-ja making an organized entrance with some of his elite support-ers and fans. He made his way past them, nodding at Velamir and bowing at her with a flash of his signature grin. Coralie smiled when she noticed how puffed out his hairstyle was. Velamir's eyes flickered to Koseer-ja's wrist, and Coralie saw the exact moment he spotted the snakelike tattoo. Coralie had noticed the tattoo after years of living in the castle. Koseer-ja did a fantastic job of keeping it concealed. The fact that Velamir spotted it within moments proved he was no average man.

"So, who are you?"

"What?" Coralie had lost track of the conversation.

"We were getting to know each other, remember?"

"King Dale is my uncle."

She waited for him to stumble and bow and say something strange. Surely, he would at least mention how his father used to be friends with King Dale. But the only change was his eyes widening the slightest bit.

"I had no idea. You are very talented, Cora."

Coralie's eyebrows went up. "How so?"

"Not only are you a princess but a fearsome warrior as well."

"Thank you," she replied and changed the subject. "My uncle says he knows your father well."

Velamir fidgeted and looked away from her. A sure sign he was hiding something.

"Was your mother Saphira?"

Velamir's face was blank. It was strange that he didn't even recognize the name. He cleared his throat.

"Why are you so interested in my mother?"

"Then her name wasn't Saphira?"

He looked uncomfortable. "Wasn't?"

"Winston's wife is dead. You would know that if you were his son."

"I know nothing about his first wife," Velamir replied.

"Or maybe you know nothing about him at all."

His eyes snapped to hers, and the air crackled between them. Coralie knew she was onto something.

"Why would you say that?" Velamir reached

up, tracing a scar on his neck that Coralie hadn't noticed before.

She gave him a half smile. "Just a feeling."

"I'm not comfortable speaking about my parents since they are both deceased."

"Both?"

Velamir nodded. "My father was killed on the way here."

"I'm so sorry." Coralie felt remorseful about her interrogation.

"Thank you. I apologize if I seem strange, but I'm not used to being questioned like this."

"No. This was completely my fault and inexcusable behavior. Do you forgive me?"

"There's nothing to forgive."

She looked past him and glimpsed her uncle speaking with a blond-haired man. Her uncle pointed toward her, and the man turned, sauntering in her direction. *This must be the prince.*

Velamir turned to see what caught her attention, and his lips thinned into a grim line. It was obvious to Coralie that he bore no love for the prince. Velamir glanced over her shoulder and nodded at someone.

"If you'll excuse me, Cora. There's an urgent matter I must see to." After her nod of consent, he walked past her.

Coralie stared after him and smiled when she realized he had addressed her with her name, not her title. Something in her heart fluttered.

"Princess Coralie," said a smooth voice.

Coralie took her attention from Velamir's retreating

back and focused on the prince before her. He reached for her hand, brushing a kiss across her knuckles.

"I am Crown Prince Draven Valent of Ayleth."

Coralie curtsied. "And you are already familiar with my name."

"Would you give me the pleasure of your company for a dance?"

She had barely said yes when he pulled her onto the floor. He twirled and spun her far faster than necessary and glanced at the elaborate fold of fabric covering her chest more than once. Coralie ignored his strange attitude and attempted to pull him into a conversation.

"How fares your father?"

He dipped her backward. "As well as an old man can be, I suppose."

"You suppose?"

They navigated between other couples, continuing the dance. Coralie had to admit Draven was good at dancing, if not conversing.

"I remember seeing you in the Grand Palace before. I didn't approach because you didn't . . . suit my taste. But now . . . you've filled out." His eyes raked over her. "Yes, very much. There is simply one word to describe you . . . stunning." He raised his eyebrow in a way he must have thought made him look handsome.

"That wasn't a compliment," Coralie replied, wondering how scandalous it would be to leave him in the middle of the dance floor.

"Don't play coy with me." He leaned closer. "You should know, if there's a game, I always win."

"Aren't you betrothed?"

He laughed. "It's still in the process."

He swung her off the dance floor. "Perhaps we should take a walk in the garden for fresh air." But the look on his face spoke of his true intent.

Coralie wrenched away, but he grabbed her arm in a tight grasp.

"I'm warning you to release me," Coralie said through gritted teeth.

"Threats are my favorite part of courting." Draven smiled.

Coralie's attempts to escape his hold without drawing notice were futile.

"Unhand her at once," commanded a deep voice.

VELAMIR
KINGDOM OF VERIN
CASTLE VERIN

Lissa dragged Velamir behind one of the pillars holding up the grand ceiling of the Great Hall. She glanced over her shoulder, eyeing the guests.

"What is it?" Velamir asked.

Lissa's voice was low. "I danced with the general."

"What are you doing? Are you trying to get us caught?"

Lissa rolled her eyes. "Stop being dramatic."

She placed something in his hand. It was a long chain holding a small key.

"What is this?"

She shrugged. "He was wearing it. It seems important."

"So you took it?" Velamir was incredulous. "He's going to notice."

Lissa nodded. "And he just left the Great Hall. You need to follow him and make it look like he dropped it or something."

Sometimes, Velamir wondered if Lissa was compromising their mission on purpose.

"I learned none of the councilmembers are here. But keep your eyes open in case."

She winked. "Of course."

Velamir moved past her and exited the Great Hall into a side corridor. When he looked down the hall, he saw the general's broad shoulders as he disappeared into a chamber at the very end. Velamir inhaled steadily through his nose and made his way down. It was empty, but many doors lined the hall on either side. Anyone could walk out. Once he reached the end of the corridor, he pressed close to the door. How could he enter without Boltrex noticing him?

Velamir took a chance and pushed the door. It opened and he tensed, waiting for a telltale creak, but the door moved without a sound. He pushed it farther and waited. He heard paper rustling and footsteps move farther away. Once the door was open wide enough, Velamir slid through, staying against the wall of the chamber. Slowly, he closed the door, keeping his gaze focused ahead of him. The general's back was to him. His hands flipped through parchment. Velamir continued sliding along the wall, ensuring to keep hidden in the darkness.

He startled when Boltrex let out a grunt of frustration and threw the parchment off the table. Boltrex walked around the table and sat on the chair behind it, burying his face in his hands. If he looked up, he would see Velamir. Velamir grew befuddled when Boltrex's shoulders shook. Was he . . . crying? Velamir inched farther back, his bafflement building, and all the hate he had for this man evaporated for a moment. He still had a heart, but how could he? He killed a young boy's parents, he killed a family, he killed a father, a mother, and who knows how many others.

Velamir fought to control his emotions as pain circled in him. He could take this moment; he could kill him. Get it over with. And yet, as his hand reached down for his dagger, his fingers paused over the top of his boot. Boltrex whispered in a low voice.

"I miss you."

Who was he speaking to? The general stood and walked to a closet in the corner of the room. He reached inside the closet, sliding a secret door open. Boltrex retrieved a small chest and placed it on the table. He draped his hands over it, his head bent low. Boltrex stayed like that for endless minutes. Velamir's heart began to race when Boltrex's hand went up, reaching for his neck. *He's trying to get the key.* Velamir unsheathed his dagger, holding it in a death grip.

A sudden knock made Boltrex pause.

"General, King Dale requests your presence, urgently." The voice was panicked. "It's your son."

Boltrex growled, "I will be right there."

He left the chamber directly, not even putting the chest away. Velamir slid from his hiding spot and moved to the table. His intention was to place the key beside the chest, but as soon as he neared it, his curiosity got the better of him. *For the mission*, he thought, *it might have vital importance.*

Velamir slid the key into the lock and turned it until it made a satisfying click. He opened it and saw a folded parchment and scroll. He took the scroll first, unrolling it. It was a sketch of a woman. Her hair was long, and she wore a flowing dress. Who was this? Maybe Boltrex's wife or someone important to him. Velamir rolled it back into place and reached for the parchment. A few sentences were scribbled across. Words that made Velamir's blood chill.

You were right about him. Winston works for the Dark Lord. He will make a move to destroy you. Act quickly.

Boltrex knows. Boltrex knows about Winston. Why had he done nothing to the manor or his land all these years? And who sent this to him? The paper was yellowed, and the ink faded. Velamir resisted the urge to take the parchment with him and placed it back into the chest, along with the scroll. After locking the chest, he placed the key beside it and left the chamber. The hall was as empty as before. Velamir made his way down the corridor and reentered the Great Hall. He was expecting to see dancing and merriment or something of that nature, but instead, the first thing he saw was Mordon beating the life out of Prince Draven.

42

MORDON
KINGDOM OF VERIN
CASTLE VERIN

A T THE START of the banquet, Mordon had stayed in the background, watching the proceedings. Then Coralie arrived, wearing an emerald gown that spilled to the floor, her expression was regal as her gaze passed over the room, making everyone feel as though she had seen them. Truly seen them and appreciated their presence. Mordon had nearly walked to her and kneeled before her. There was something about her that made a person want to follow her lead. She was queen material, Mordon had no doubt about that.

He had resisted the impulse to greet her, watching from a distance as she garnered attention from everyone. She commanded the room with a single raise of her brows. Mordon laughed at his thoughts. When had he become so poetic?

His father wanted him to court her, but he couldn't do so without endangering his heart. The first rule Boltrex taught him was not to fall in love. *Fall in love and be destroyed* were his exact words. From the feelings Mordon was experiencing around Coralie, he knew he couldn't allow them to drag farther and throw him into a pit he couldn't escape from. So, he had stayed away from her. At least, he tried to stay away.

His resolve almost broke when that Velamir fellow strolled over to her with that alarming grin. The way Coralie kept smiling at him made Mordon think the man was flirting. And that did not sit well with him.

Mordon focused on a tray of pastries on the table near him, trying to keep himself busy. He sampled the treats, but the sweetness only increased the queasiness in his stomach. Still, he held one of the flaky pastries close to his mouth to dissuade anyone from speaking to him. The musicale King Dale had hired struck up a song, and couples floated across the floor. It was hard to keep track of Coralie when so many people blocked her from view. The dance ended, and another started. Mordon caught a glimpse of Velamir. He was still standing with Coralie. Mordon's frustration made him squash the pastry in his fist.

"A glass of zat, sir?" a servant asked, holding a tray filled with goblets.

"Get it out of my sight." Mordon slapped his crumbled pastry onto the edge of the tray.

The servant's eyes grew wide, realizing who he had

addressed, and disappeared in a flash. Mordon wiped his hand on the tablecloth. He heard a tinkling laugh and glanced toward the sound. For one hopeful moment, he thought it was Coralie. But much to his disappointment, it was a girl he didn't recall seeing before.

"I was looking for a dance partner, and I ended up here by the pastries. It seems it was fate." She giggled, the sound so high Mordon cringed.

She played with her hair and shot him a flirtatious smile.

"I never knew pastries could dance. Good luck with that venture."

She placed a hand on his arm. "You've been staring at her for a long time."

"It's none of your business."

She blinked large eyes. The purple color made him uneasy. "She is not worth torturing yourself over. See, she doesn't even care about you." She motioned to Coralie, who was now speaking with Prince Draven. "At least you should dance with me to show her she doesn't affect you."

It was a tempting enough offer that Mordon accepted. He escorted her to the dance floor, attempting to concentrate on her instead of where his eyes wanted to go.

"So, you will compete in the tournament?" She asked it like a question when the answer was obvious.

Mordon nodded. "I am. Are you attending?"

She fluttered her lashes. "I wouldn't miss it for the world."

"And I assume you are rooting for Prince Draven." Mordon's voice was full of sarcasm.

His eyes flicked to the side, and he noticed the prince in question dancing nearby with Coralie.

"I'm rooting for my brother. But if he doesn't make it, of course you would be my next option."

"And who is your brother?"

"Velamir Raga."

Mordon tightened his hand on hers as he twirled her under his arm. "Is that so?"

She nodded. "But enough about me. Tell me about yourself. How is life as a Galvasir and son of a general?"

Mordon took that moment to look at Coralie again. All rationale vanished when he saw the prince holding her against him, his fingers clasped around her forearm. Mordon left the girl in the middle of the dance floor and advanced in their direction. He reached them in a few strides.

"Unhand her at once!"

Coralie's head jerked toward him, and Prince Draven slowly turned his way. "Are you the serving boy? I need frosted carrot cakes. Fetch me some, will you? And bring the lady chocolate petits fours. Only a small amount, or it will damage her dulcet waistline." He finished that last sentence while eyeing said waist.

When Mordon didn't move, Prince Draven waved him away like he was a dog. "Hurry! I would like to give my lady a kiss with a semblance of privacy."

Coralie shoved him away, and he grabbed her other arm. "You are disgusting!" she spat.

Mordon took a threatening step forward and glared down at the prince. "I said, Let. Her. Go," he bit out through gritted teeth.

Draven's smile faded as he noted Mordon's fine clothing. Realizing Mordon wasn't the serving boy he'd thought, Prince Draven released Coralie's arm with reluctance. "Relax, I didn't know she was your woman."

Coralie gasped in outrage. "I am no one's woman, thank you very much."

Draven gave her a lecherous glance. "You could be mine, at least for a short while."

Mordon couldn't control what happened next. One instant he was standing still, and the next he was pummeling the life out of Draven. Blow after blow connected with his face, eyes, jaw. Mordon couldn't stop. He couldn't rein in his anger. People were gathering and murmuring. Hands grabbed hold of him, and soon he was pulled away from Draven.

"What do you think you are doing?" King Dale shouted.

Mordon's breath came out in gasps. Draven's guards were holding the prince up. The prince's face was bloody, his eyes bruising. His lips were cracked and bleeding, and hate spewed from every part of him.

"Kill him," Draven growled through his split lips.

The guards wasted no time unsheathing their swords and approaching Mordon. Mordon heard King Dale's voice ordering them to stop. The sound of his father calling their own guards came to him vaguely. But he was focused on the guard in front of him. He concentrated on the sword coming down at him. Mordon ducked to the side, and the sword smashed onto the floor. He kneed the man in the ribs and reached to twist his arm. Out of the corner of his eye, he saw the other guard thrusting to stab him and knew he wouldn't be able to move out of the way in time. He braced himself for the pain, but it didn't come.

Velamir appeared from nowhere, deflecting the guard's sword and slamming his dagger onto the guard's wrist. The guard dropped his sword with a cry, and Velamir got behind him. He pulled the guard by his hair and placed his dagger's edge at the man's throat.

Mordon twisted the arm of the guard facing him and brought him to his knees, holding the man's own sword to his heart.

Draven shouted in rage, and more of his guards came forward. Boltrex motioned his hand to the castle guards, and they advanced to intercept them.

"That is enough!" King Dale shouted.

The guards halted in their tracks. The crowd that gathered went silent. Koseer-ja watched, holding a parchment and quill as his eyes scrambled for details.

"Mordon. Explain yourself," commanded King Dale.

Mordon didn't remove the sword from where it rested at the guard's heart. "Prince Draven was molesting Princess Coralie."

Draven sputtered. "I did no such thing. Tell them, Princess."

"Mordon was trying to defend me. Something I could have done myself." She gave Mordon a pointed glance. "I am not a helpless female."

That stung a little. It hurt him that she didn't think she needed him.

King Dale was angry. "Is it true? Was Prince Draven making advances toward you, Coralie?"

"Yes," Coralie said.

Prince Draven huffed. "What a lie. She told me to kiss her!"

She grabbed a fallen knife and moved toward him. "How dare you!"

"Coralie!" King Dale stopped her.

"Arrest Prince Draven," Boltrex ordered.

Prince Draven retreated a pace. "Over my dead body."

"Precisely what I was thinking," Mordon said.

Draven wiped a dribble of blood from his face. "You cannot arrest me. I'm a prince."

King Dale sighed. "He is right. We cannot arrest him without bringing war on all of us."

Boltrex spoke up. "There is one thing left to settle the matter. At the jousting tournament. My son will put him to shame."

Pride soaked into Mordon. His father believed in him.

Draven growled in acceptance. "At the tournament."

He spun and stormed out of the Great Hall. Velamir released the guard's head, and the guard scurried after the prince. Mordon did the same with the guard he had pinned down, tossing his sword at him. The man caught it at an awkward slant and ran.

Mordon stared at Velamir, asking the question that had been bothering him. "Why did you help me?"

"It had nothing to do with you. I don't like that man," Velamir replied. "Don't think I am your ally because I aided you this once."

"I would never think of you as an ally," Mordon shot back.

"Good," Velamir said.

They stared at each other for a long second before Velamir bowed to the king and left. The girl who introduced herself as Velamir's sister brushed past Mordon, shooting him a glare. *Oh, yes*, he had deserted her in the middle of their dance.

Coralie scowled at Mordon. "I had it under control."

His father shook his head. Mordon didn't understand where he had gone wrong. He had defended the innocent, but all he received was disapproval. The tournament was on the morrow, and he planned on changing that negative to a positive.

LISSA
KINGDOM OF VERIN
CASTLE VERIN

Lissa paused as they were about to leave the castle. Velamir glanced back at her.

"I forgot something," she told him and rushed back.

She didn't listen to his calls of exasperation as she navigated the halls. When she heard cursing, she knew she was nearing her target. Draven stood in the hall, holding a wet rag over his face. His guards enclosed him in a defensive position.

"Prince Draven!" she called.

"Don't come near," one of the guards warned.

"I have a gift for the prince."

"Let her come," Draven said. "She's just a woman. It's not as if she can harm me."

Lissa almost laughed but caught herself in time.

The guards parted for her, and she pressed close to the prince, taking his hand in hers.

"I'm sorry this happened to you. It's disgraceful."

"Isn't it?" he muttered.

"You will win tomorrow. I have faith in you," she told him.

He peered at her through swollen eyes. "I haven't had the pleasure of seeing you before."

She curtsied. "Consider me an angel coming to your rescue."

He pressed the rag onto his cheekbone. "And pray tell, why do I need to be rescued?"

"You will win tomorrow, but only with my help."

"And how will you help me?"

"I know you hate Mordon and you want to defeat him, but that will not happen if you don't do as I suggest."

Lissa was almost as annoyed with Mordon as Draven was. He had been extremely rude to her.

"I'm listening," the prince said.

Lissa slipped her ring from her finger, extending it to Draven. "There is a small blade in it. Tipped with poison."

He started to smile, then winced when it pulled at the rip in his upper lip. He took it from her, eyeing it with caution.

"Good luck, Your Highness," she whispered and walked away.

Velamir frowned when she entered the carriage, sliding in beside him. Lady Blayton and Latimus sat across from them. She could tell by Velamir's expression that he wanted to know what she was up to, but he was forced to remain silent because of their audience. Lissa smiled as she thought about what she had done. Mordon would die, and Draven would be caught and killed as well. Two birds with one stone. *I must be the best Chishma Prolus has.* Jax's voice came to her.

Be careful, Lis.

A twinge of unease filled her, making her think she might have made a mistake.

43

VELAMIR
KINGDOM OF VERIN
VERINTOWN

THE DAY OF the tournament arrived. Excitement filled the air as the rules were announced. Koseer-ja, the Joust Master, stood on a large platform dressed in an outrageous orange-and-yellow embroidered tunic with flared out matching trousers. On his head was a strange pointy hat adorned with peacock feathers. If his goal had been for all eyes to be on him, Velamir would say the goal was achieved.

First, the competitors would joust, and if both were unhorsed, they would continue to combat each other on the ground with melee weapons. Ten points for unhorsing, five for shattering a lance, and one for hitting the small shield on the opponent's chest plate. Velamir watched from outside the jousting tent bearing

Winston's crest as the first competitors trotted to their positions. The tents were located along the edge of the tiltyard, across from the grandstands, to remain in sight of the spectators, and Koseer-Ja, of course.

"Opening, we have the Flying Eagle, Captain Tarin, and the Rock of Flame, Captain Honder!" Koseer-ja announced.

The betting table was situated in one corner of the tiltyard. The new treasury advisor was going through parchments and eyeing the stacks of gold coins he had acquired from the wagers. Velamir shook his head, remembering how the people had surveyed him like a piece of meat. He was not a person to them, but a way for them to fill their pockets.

In the ladies' gallery, a noblewoman leaned over the railing, waving and showing off Captain Tarin's crest. Many other ladies were dressed in competitor colors or had given their scarves to their favorite contestant. Several had tried to give their scarves to Velamir, but he had refused. He might have hurt a few feelings, but then again, he was only popular because of Winston's reputation.

Sweat dripped down his forehead. He was fully armored except for his helm, which was tucked under his arm. The sun bore down on the tiltyard. Velamir shifted, and his armor clanked. He was ready to begin. That is, if Jax would finish up with Vandal.

"How are you faring?" Velamir called.

Jax emerged from the side of the tent, leading Vandal.

"He's spooking," he said, stroking Vandal's neck, trying to calm him.

"He must have taken one look at your True Manos robes and went all jittery." Velamir chuckled.

Jax froze mid-stride, and Velamir tried to contain his laughter. Jax was a mess. Sweat contoured his cheekbones, and his bloodshot eyes were narrowed on Velamir.

"Hilarious," he deadpanned.

Velamir held his hands out in apology. "This is Vandal's first tournament. All the noise and so many people are new to him."

Together, they dressed Vandal into his bard. Jax buckled the connecting straps while Velamir retrieved Vandal's chanfron. Vandal shook his head, protesting when Velamir put it on.

"Be a good boy, Vandal. We don't have all day to dress you up."

Velamir kept an eye on the competitors. The Flying Eagle, Captain Tarin, won the first match, and Commander Evinshore won the next by knocking his opponent clean off his horse. He scored ten points, putting him in the lead. Velamir was itching to joust, but the other matches never seemed to end. Just then, Latimus came running up to them.

"I heard rumors that one of Verin's Galvas will compete next."

Velamir cracked his knuckles. "Mordon?"

"It's a probability."

Latimus reached over and scratched Vandal under his throatlatch. Vandal shied away, and Latimus retracted his hand with a grimace.

"Advisor Covskin's body was discovered this morning," he shared with them.

Velamir exchanged a glance with Jax.

"He was dead. The same marks found on his body that had marked Advisor Liston and his men. The general says they are connected." Latimus watched them, waiting for a reaction.

Velamir widened his eyes. "Shocking."

Latimus nodded. "General Boltrex commanded a search of all the homes in Verintown. Including mine, if you can believe it."

Jax appeared panicked. Many of his new projects were stored in the room he was staying in. Velamir gestured for him to calm down.

Koseer-ja's announcement grabbed their attention. "Next, we have the Red Wolf, Captain Keelo!"

The people cheered, but not as much as they had for other competitors. Velamir looked toward the center of the tiltyard. Captain Keelo was trotting to the start of the tilt. He waved his arms up and down, urging the crowd to cheer louder.

"And the Cavalier . . ." Koseer-ja shouted.

Velamir's heart raced. He placed his helmet over his head, keeping the visor lifted.

"The Cavalier, Velamir Raga!"

Velamir mounted Vandal and rode in. Cheers pierced his ears. Latimus ran ahead of him, holding a flag bearing Winston's crest. Jax jogged behind, breathing labored breaths as he held Velamir's spare lances.

Velamir reached his side of the tilt and adjusted himself in the saddle. He had a clear view of the king's gallery. King Dale was sitting in the highest chair. Coralie sat on a smaller chair beside him. Velamir had to admit she looked beautiful. She was wearing an exquisite gown of silk and a circlet of silver around her head. It had stuck with Velamir for hours after she told him she was the princess. She was one of their targets. Boltrex sat on King Dale's other side. He stared at Velamir, his brows drawn together in contempt. The light of day made the red scar on his face more apparent.

Jax appeared by Velamir's side and lifted his lance. Velamir took it and dropped his visor in place. Koseer-ja turned to the king, waiting for permission to start the match. Velamir and Captain Keelo held their impatient horses still. King Dale nodded, and Koseer-ja signaled to his helper, gesturing for him to blow the trumpet.

Hearing the loud blare, Velamir urged Vandal forward. Vandal exploded off his hindquarters, eager to charge. Velamir didn't hold him back. They practiced this so much it was like Vandal could read his mind. Together, they knew the next move that led to the exact point of contact. Velamir focused on the shield protecting Captain Keelo's shoulder. He moved his lance off target, attempting to outsmart his opponent.

Time seemed to slow the closer they came. Velamir breathed evenly, and at the last second repositioned his aim. His lance shattered against Keelo, and the strength of the impact sent the captain flying off his horse. Keelo's own lance had completely missed Velamir. The crowd cheered, won over. The ladies threw their handkerchiefs at him. Velamir dismounted and walked over to Keelo, who was rising with difficulty. He took the hand Velamir offered.

Keelo removed his helmet and gave Velamir a weak smile. "You are a skilled jouster."

Velamir nodded his thanks.

"The winner is: the Cavalier!" Koseer-ja announced, and the crowd went wild.

"I would like to see you against Prince Draven," Keelo said. "I hear he's the best around."

Velamir didn't respond, but in his mind, he agreed. He wanted to go against Draven, but he wanted to joust Mordon even more. Velamir looked back at the king's gallery. Boltrex was staring at him with cold hate. It seemed he wanted a fight as well. Velamir's smile was grim. He was certainly about to get one.

44

VELAMIR
KINGDOM OF VERIN
VERINTOWN

AFTER SEVERAL MATCHES, Koseer-ja made an announcement.

"I would like the Unstoppable, Galva Mordon; the Invincible Dragon, Prince Draven; Commander Evinshore of Wallington; and the Cavalier, Velamir Raga, to come to the center of the tiltyard!"

Velamir walked over to the tiltyard, wondering what was planned for them. Koseer-ja smiled as they grouped together. Commander Evinshore shifted his feet, a sign of nerves. Mordon looked stoic and didn't move a muscle. Draven attempted one of his signature grins, only to wince when it pulled at his split lip. He sent a scowl at Mordon instead. Velamir waited. His Chishma training made him at ease standing still for long stretches.

Koseer-ja looked each of them in the eye and spoke in a loud voice so the crowd could hear and pass his words on to their farther-away friends. "The highest bets were placed on you four. So we have decided to spice things up!"

"Each of you will perform a special talent for us. You can do whatever you would like. Anything you request will be brought to the tiltyard. You have five minutes to plan your show, and then you must perform. You will do so individually and in the order in which you were called here. Good luck! Everyone, give a hand for these courageous jousters!"

Applause spread like wildfire and got louder each moment. Velamir walked back to Jax and Latimus in bemusement. What in the world was he going to do? Since he would be last to perform, he had plenty of time to think. Velamir watched as Mordon ordered some servants to bring out a large humanlike figure and set it in the middle of the tiltyard. The figure was made from pure rock, or at least, that was what Velamir heard some people near him saying. Mordon walked up to the figure and planned his attack with the mace he was holding. The crowd hushed in anticipation. Mordon gave a roar and swung his mace, using both hands. He lopped the head of the figure clean off, and it landed on the ground with a thump. The cheers were deafening. Mordon gave an arrogant grin to the crowd and walked off to his tent.

Next came Commander Evinshore. He was holding a javelin and stood a fair distance from a few large rings suspended from a high beam his servants had set up for him. He lifted his arm, and after taking a moment to aim, he released it. The javelin sailed, passing through the rings. The applause was loud, but not as much as it had been for Mordon.

A chuckle escaped Velamir when he saw Prince Draven saunter his way to the middle of the tiltyard. The crowd applauded, and ladies squealed when he waved at them. Draven's servants rushed to him and handed him a glass of zat. The prince raised it to the crowd and drank. Velamir raised a brow. This was his show? Not very impressive. Velamir could not understand why the people fawned over him. Especially now that his face was almost unrecognizable. Draven waved a hand, and another servant brought him a bow and arrow. They set up a target at the far end of the tiltyard. Draven lifted the bow and closed one eye as he took aim. He released the arrow, and it hit the center of the target. Latimus clapped along with the crowd.

He turned to Velamir. "I would like to see you top those performances. With any luck, you won't do anything too embarrassing."

Velamir mounted Vandal. "Hand me my bow."

Latimus frowned as he gave it over. "What are you doing?"

Jax handed Velamir his quiver, which he attached so it hung beside his sword. Koseer-ja announced his name, indicating his turn.

Velamir urged Vandal into motion and called back to Latimus, "Watch me. Maybe you'll learn something."

He did not wait for a reply and burst forward on Vandal. The servants waiting to assist him watched him race past with their jaws hanging open. Velamir unsheathed his sword and swung his arm up, holding the blade skyward. He slashed down as Mordon's rock figure approached. His sword sliced through the rock with ease, and the top half of the figure fell off. Velamir was astonished that the sword Frumgan had given him was so efficient. It had felt like slicing through butter. Velamir continued running Vandal down the length of the tiltyard.

Pulling the reins to slow their pace, Velamir shifted Vandal's weight onto his hindquarters and pivoted so they faced the opposite direction. Velamir now had full view of the tiltyard. He spied the rings Commander Evinshore used and encouraged Vandal toward the beam. Vandal advanced, his powerful muscles pumping in time with Velamir's heart. Velamir eyed the three rings hanging from the beam as they approached. Standing in his saddle, Velamir pointed his sword at the rings. He raced by and captured all three rings on his blade. With one fluid motion, Velamir sent the rings flying toward the crowd. They cheered and fought each other to grab them.

Velamir sheathed his sword and galloped around the tiltyard until he was as far from Draven's target as possible. He pulled Vandal to a halt and grabbed his bow, nocking an arrow. As he drew back, Vandal reared and let out an awe-inspiring whinny. Velamir released, and the arrow slammed into the center, splitting Draven's in half.

There was dead silence until someone chanted, "Cavalier! Cavalier! Cavalier!"

Velamir looked for the source and saw Jax punching his fist in the air in time with Velamir's title. Latimus took up the chant, and so did the people nearest to him. Before long, the entire group of spectators were saying it together.

"Cavalier! Cavalier! Cavalier!"

Pride soaked through Velamir's bones. He noticed most of the other competitors leveling him with a glare, but none of them could master the ferocious glower Boltrex bestowed upon him. Velamir ignored them and dismounted. Jax approached to take Vandal to the tent. Velamir moved to join him when Koseer-ja blocked his path.

"Well, Velamir. You put on quite a show for us." He smiled. "Your sword was something else. I had to see it up close. Do you mind?"

Velamir's hand dropped to his blade, and Koseer-ja's eyes followed his movement, narrowing when they saw the sword. His eyes lifted and locked with Velamir's. Koseer-ja attempted a smile, but the seriousness of his expression broke through.

"That is a gorgeous sword. The way it cut so cleanly into the rock was amazing," Koseer-ja said, a threatening note in his voice.

Velamir remembered when Frumgan told him about the sword being forged by Savagelanders. Koseer-ja recognized it.

"That is a nice tattoo," Velamir replied, his eyes dropping to Koseer-ja's hand, where the snake coiled around his wrist.

Koseer-ja said nothing. The crowd muttered in boredom. Koseer-ja nodded at Velamir, giving him a lingering look before returning to his stage to entertain. Velamir walked back to his tent.

"He is a strange one," Latimus said, nodding his head at Koseer-ja. "From the Savagelands."

"He doesn't have the accent," Jax said.

"Well, he has lived in Karalik Empire most of his life. He knows our customs. The accent bit was a piece of cake for him."

Velamir spoke up. "Why is he accepted here if he is a Savagelander? I thought the Empire was at war with them."

Latimus chuckled. It grated against Velamir's ears, the sound he heard every time Latimus tried to be superior. "Don't you know, Velamir? Savagelanders have been sneaking into the Empire since the dawn of time. They trade with us in the black market. They supply us with a good amount of our weapons. Koseer-ja took it a step further by befriending us. No one sees him as a threat."

"That may be what he wants. They don't see him as a threat today, but tomorrow he could come leading a Savagelander army."

Latimus laughed again. "You have your head in the clouds, Velamir. Keep it down here. Look, they just announced the jousts to resume."

Velamir ignored him, his thoughts mangled. He worried all this effort to change the Empire and improve it would go to waste. Because even if Tariqi conquered the Empire, a Savagelander army may come bursting in, stealing the very peace they fought for.

45

NATASSA
KARALIK EMPIRE
FLONDIN WOODS

NATASSA COLLAPSED ON the log in relief.
She didn't know how many days had
gone by, but she knew they couldn't be
anywhere near Ayleth. Kasdeya had put extreme
pressure on her, forcing Natassa to wait on her hand
and foot. After she attempted to escape during one
of the breaks, Kasdeya told all the guards Natassa
was a traitor and would be hung in Ayleth. The
guards had been confused, except for Thander,
and Natassa realized he had been in on Kasdeya's
plan from the very beginning.

Ropes bound Natassa's wrists, almost
cutting off her circulation. Kasdeya had forced
Natassa to walk alongside the carriage as
everyone else rode, slowing their progress even
further. Kasdeya didn't seem to mind. She

shot Natassa malicious grins every time she ducked her head out of the carriage.

Natassa looked down at her shoes and grimaced. Her slippers were worn through, and her feet ached from the twigs and stones she had stepped on. A trickle of warmth slid into her palm. Natassa glanced at her hands to see the skin of her wrists ripped open.

"It's only a short break. Don't get comfortable," Thander muttered as he passed by. He took a moment to toss her an apple.

It rolled along the long grass and nestled between her feet. The mere sight of it made her stomach growl. She reached down, wincing when the rope rubbed against her raw skin. She took the apple and brought it to her lips. Footsteps stole her attention, and Natassa looked up to see Kasdeya exiting the carriage. She attempted to sweep past but stumbled a few times over her stolen dress.

Although Kasdeya was adorned in beautiful attire and wore stunning accessories, there would always be something missing about her. Compassion. Natassa remembered her own father. The one thing Emperor Malus lacked most was compassion. Maybe that was why he was a terrible ruler. He ruled with fear, not love. The very thing her mother had warned her about.

To be a princess doesn't mean a fancy dress or crown or beauty. You may rule a people one day, but that means nothing. If they fear you, they won't hesitate to choose your enemy over you. But if they love you, they will do anything for you. For them to love, you must do everything for them first. Earn their loyalty.

Kasdeya reached Thander's side and smiled flirtatiously. "Walk with me?"

"Of course, my princess." Thander offered his arm, and they strolled into the small woods that led off the road.

Natassa stood, dropping the apple into the pocket at the front of her work dress, and followed them. A guard blocked her path. "Where do ya think ya going, traitor?"

"I need to . . ." She cleared her throat. "You know?"

The guard scratched his neck. "Fine, but be quick about it."

She hurried past him. She didn't see Kasdeya or Thander as she walked through the trees. She tried to be silent, but it seemed every fallen branch and twig was against her. Natassa froze, hearing a sound. A woman's voice rose, loud and angry.

"You can't fool me, Thander. I saw you speaking with the men, and I saw you marked Verin on the map. You have been leading us in the wrong direction this entire time."

Thander protested, "This is our chance. I know a way out of the Empire. There is a hidden pass in Verin. We can sneak out through there. We can finally live our lives as we wanted."

Natassa peeked between the trees, making out their figures. Thander's hands were on Kasdeya's shoulders.

"Do you think I want to live as a fugitive? The whole reason I wanted to go to Ayleth was to claim Draven's riches so we can live a comfortable life."

"He will marry you."

"He won't. We will be gone before that happens."

"Do you promise?" There was uncertainty in his voice.

"I promise," Kasdeya replied.

Natassa easily read the lie. Kasdeya had played them all, even her so-called lover. She only cared about gaining riches and a title. She would marry a murderer of innocents without hesitation. Thander leaned forward and embraced Kasdeya. Natassa backed away. She was close to Verin from what she had overheard. What if she attempted another getaway? Even with her hands bound, she might have a chance.

Someone thrashed through the trees near her. "Where are ya?" The man was irritated.

Natassa looked right and left. Which way should she go? Before she could decide, the guard came into view.

"There ya are. I'm not paid to be a nanny. Move along."

He snatched her arm, hauling her forward. They were almost to the carriage when Natassa heard a piercing scream behind her. The guard paled.

"What in the hell?" he muttered.

Thick boots thudded from what seemed like every direction, and the screaming continued until it abruptly stopped. The guard moved faster, practically dragging her.

"There's someone out there. They might have attacked the princess," he told the other guards when they reached them.

The men unsheathed their swords, readying for a fight. Within moments, animalistic-looking men charged from the trees, hooting and yelling as they surrounded the guards. Some held bows and arrows while others had rough axes and wooden clubs that they swung around dangerously. One of them, a very tall bald man with tattoos crisscrossing his skull, walked forward, dragging a person with him. Natassa retreated a few paces. She wanted to be as far from these men as she could. The giant bald man threw the person, and the body landed with a thump before him. Natassa tensed when she realized it was Thander.

"Well done, Salvador," said a smooth voice.

Someone stepped from behind the giant. The man was rugged and bandit-like, except he was much cleaner than the rest of the crew. From the way he stood and the way his calculating brown eyes took everyone in, Natassa guessed he was the leader of the group. He drew someone from behind him.

"Release me!" Kasdeya shouted, trying to pull her wrist out of his firm grip.

He spoke up. "The name is Vykus." Immediate murmuring erupted between Thander's guards. "I see my reputation precedes me." He gave them a wide smile that made him look downright frightening.

The guards shifted, glancing between Thander's body and Kasdeya, not knowing their next move.

"Oh, the princess and I have already met." Vykus winked. "We've come to an agreement. Obedience in exchange for keeping her head on her shoulders."

Sensing their inner turmoil, Kasdeya spoke. "I will pay you double what Thander promised! Just get me away from this man!"

The guards tensed, their grips on their weapons tightening. Sensing their resolve and realizing it was not in his favor, Vykus pulled Kasdeya closer and whipped a dagger against her throat. Kasdeya let out a strangled gasp, and the guards hesitated.

"Let's not be hasty, or your princess will die," Vykus told them.

"She ain't our princess," one guard said.

One of Vykus's eyebrows went up.

"We ain't even real guards," said another man.

Vykus's other eyebrow joined its companion. "So what are you, then?"

Natassa watched in astonishment at the guard's revelation. She had assumed they hadn't had proper training, not that they weren't palace guards at all. Kasdeya glared at them, no doubt hoping they would keep their mouths shut.

"We are hired mercenaries. That man over there employed us," said one guard, pointing at Thander.

"That man over there . . . is dead," Vykus said. "It seems to me you need employment."

"They work for me!" Kasdeya said, trying to convince the mercenaries.

Kasdeya released a choked breath when Vykus pressed his dagger closer to her neck. Natassa winced as a dribble of blood ran down Kasdeya's skin.

"If you know what is good for you, you will be silent." Vykus was firm. He looked back at the mercenaries. "What say you work for me?"

They glanced at each other and nodded. "As long as we get good coin."

Vykus smiled. "That's my kind of men. Don't worry, there will be plenty of coin."

The mercenaries walked forward and joined Vykus. In a terrifying moment, Natassa realized nothing stood between her and the bandits now. She turned and ran, eyes glazing in panic. She tripped over the log she had been sitting on before. Natassa struggled to get up because of her bound hands. Deep chuckles vibrated the area.

"Why don't we give her a hand, boys," Vykus said.

Booming steps approached, and the grinning face of Salvador leered down at her.

46

MORDON
KINGDOM OF VERIN
VERINTOWN

ORDON STOOD STILL as Derolos finished adjusting his greaves and vambraces. After jousting several times and performing the show with the rock figure, Mordon was prepared to vanquish the rest of his opponents. He was tied for first with Prince Draven. Velamir was in third, and Evinshore right behind in fourth. Mordon rolled his neck to release some of the building tension.

"Let us resume the joust!" Koseer-ja shouted. His voice could be heard through the open flap of Mordon's tent.

Mordon inhaled. He was going next. His father arranged with Koseer-ja for him to joust Prince Draven. Mordon was eager to show the prince who was in charge around these parts. Derolos moved to the back of the tent to retrieve Mordon's helm. The boy was quiet. Mordon hadn't heard him speak more than two words these past two weeks. After the news of his father's death, Derolos's mother had begged King Dale to take in her son, as she lacked the means to provide for him. King Dale handed the charge off to Mordon's father, and the general told Mordon to train the boy.

He will become a soldier, like his father before him, Boltrex had said.

Besides what needed to be said, Mordon hadn't spoken to the boy at all. Mordon realized he was becoming more and more like his father. Not caring for the emotions of others, just using people for his own benefit. A twinge of guilt shot through him when Derolos handed him his helmet and turned to leave.

"Derolos," Mordon called.

Derolos turned, surprised. "Yes, Galva?"

Mordon gave him a small smile. "Thank you, boy. You have done well for me."

Derolos's eyes grew wide, and his lips split into a happy grin. "Thank you, Galva!"

Mordon nodded, and Derolos jogged out of the tent with a bounce in his steps.

"Next, we have the Unstoppable, Galva Mordon!"

The crowd grew wild over Mordon's name, and a smile crossed his face. Mordon could not shake off his arrogance as he strode out of his tent. Aslo, one of the stable hands, promptly approached, leading Mordon's lancer horse, Renegade. Derolos stood near the tent, and Mordon handed him his helmet while he mounted his horse. He wanted everyone to see his face as he rode in. Mordon rode to the center of the tiltyard, basking in the attention.

As he reached the tilt, he looked up at the king's gallery and bowed his head in respect to King Dale. The king nodded at him, and Mordon's gaze fell away from him, landing on Coralie. She was frowning, and Mordon knew she had been watching him preen at the crowd's attention. Embarrassment trickled in, surprising him. He covered the shame by throwing a savvy wink in her direction. She turned, but not before Mordon noticed the smile creeping onto her face. Mordon's grin stretched wider, and his gaze settled on his father. Boltrex shook his head, disapproving of his courting methods. Mordon scoffed. *What does he know of courting? Nothing.*

"And the Invincible Dragon, Prince Draven!" Koseer-ja finished announcing.

The cheers grew louder. Mordon focused on his approaching opponent. Prince Draven was fully armored except for his helmet, which a servant carried. Even from the opposite side of the tilt, Mordon could see the bruises covering Draven's face. He smirked in appreciation as he continued examining his appearance. Draven's eyes were swollen. Mordon wondered how he would be able to see through the narrow slits of his helmet. Draven's lip was curled, and he stared at Mordon with hatred.

Mordon looked back at the king's gallery. Coralie held Mordon's crest. Pride flowed through him. She stared at him and nodded. He returned her nod. He wouldn't fail her. Mordon glanced at Derolos, who was lifting his helmet up to him. Mordon placed his helm over his head and reached for his lance. Draven was prepared as well, although his horse moved uneasily, betraying his rider's calm facade. The tension stretched farther than the two of them. It spread into the audience, and everyone held their breath, waiting for it to begin.

King Dale nodded at Koseer-ja, who signaled with his hands. A helper blew the trumpet. Mordon shot forward on Renegade. Blood rushed in his head, and his heartbeat thudded against his chest. Mordon kept his lance straight and true, aimed at Draven's chest plate. Renegade's hooves pounded into the ground, and Mordon twisted in the saddle to get better aim. His lance crashed into Draven's chest, and Mordon felt a powerful impact on his own torso. He kept himself on Renegade only by the pure strength in his legs and stomach. Once he was steady in the saddle, Mordon looked back at Draven and saw that he appeared relaxed and focused on his horse. Mordon muttered a curse.

Koseer-ja afforded them both five points for their shattered lances. They positioned themselves at the tilt again for the next run. The trumpet blew, and Mordon pushed his spurs into Renegade, urging him faster than before. Draven was coming his way, matching him for speed. Mordon held his lance in the same position as before. The two lances struck true. Mordon grunted at the impact and fell back. He struggled to hold himself on Renegade, but he couldn't keep himself in the saddle. Disappointment and anger coursed through him. He had failed. It was over.

He hit the ground hard. Mordon pushed himself to his feet, cursing as he did. His eyes widened when he saw

Draven pulling himself off the ground as well. One look at Koseer-ja confirmed Mordon's thoughts. Koseer-ja was signaling them to continue the match with a melee fight. Mordon tossed his helmet aside and shot a glance at Derolos. The boy sprinted to him, handing Mordon his weapon of choice. A war hammer capable of crushing bones. Mordon wrapped his gloved fingers around it and advanced on Prince Draven.

"You're finished!" Mordon shouted.

Prince Draven snatched his own helmet off and unsheathed his sword, screaming, "You're a coward!" He spat blond hair from where it had been sticking by his mouth.

Mordon released an enraged yell and rushed at Draven, driving his hammer toward his shoulder. Draven ducked out of reach and thrust his sword at Mordon's midsection. Mordon slammed Draven's blade down with his hammer, and on his counter-swing aimed for his head. Draven bent backward, the hammer skimming the air above his nose. Mordon smiled at the flash of fear in Draven's eyes. They continued battling each other until Mordon tripped Draven. Mordon raised his hammer to strike a bloody finishing blow to his skull. Draven grabbed a handful of dirt and threw it. Mordon gasped and stumbled back, wiping a gloved hand over his eyes. Draven moved forward, punching Mordon in an open spot near his greaves. Fierce pain shot through him, and warm blood trickled down his leg. Mordon reached out, smacking at Draven's hand. His vision cleared enough to see, and he parried the rest of Draven's advances.

"*You're* done now." Draven smirked.

Mordon stared at Draven's bloodless blade while circling him. What did he stab him with? Mordon's breaths were labored until he found it difficult to keep moving steadily. Draven lunged, bringing his sword down on Mordon. Mordon stepped out of reach and reposted with a hammer strike to Draven's sword. The sword broke in half, and the tipped edge fell into the ground. Draven stared with his jaw dropped at his once beautiful sword. Mordon advanced, giving Draven a sharp jab in the face. Draven stuttered back, and Mordon grabbed him by the hair. He pushed him to the ground, wrapping an arm around his throat. Guards separated them before Mordon could break Draven's neck.

"The winner is the Unstoppable, Galva Mordon!" Koseer-ja declared.

Mordon scarcely heard the cheers that echoed around the tiltyard. The victory roses thrown his way appeared hazy. The only thing he could make out was his own heavy breathing and his heartbeat in his ears. He managed to look to the king's gallery at Coralie. She wore a beautiful smile. Mordon's heart stuttered. He grinned back at her because he knew her smile was for him and him alone. Mordon picked up one of the perfect red roses and walked to the gallery. He held it up to her.

"For you," he said.

Coralie accepted it. The truth was, this joust had been for her. He did it for her honor. He had promised to defeat Draven, and he kept his word.

"Are you all right?" Coralie asked.

He looked into her deep brown eyes. They radiated concern. Hope thrived within him. If she cared about his well-being, surely that meant she liked him. He wrapped his hand around hers.

"I am now," he answered.

Mordon pulled away and walked back to his tent. As soon as he entered, he dropped his head into his hands. His mind hurt too much to concentrate or even think. Derolos stared at him with worry. Mordon knew there was something wrong with him. He couldn't breathe, and he couldn't stop sweating. His tent flap moved, and his father entered.

"You did well enough, but now you must do better," Boltrex was saying.

Mordon's head spun, and his words slurred when he spoke. "What do you mean?"

Boltrex didn't notice. "I have arranged for you to fight that Velamir fool next. Do not fail me. You must kill him."

Boltrex left just as Mordon heard Koseer-ja announce the next match. He stumbled out of the tent and would have fallen if Aslo had not put his shoulder under his arm.

Derolos stepped before them. "Galva, are you all right?"

Mordon blinked a few times. His vision was getting hazy. "Yes."

The single word echoed in his mind and increased the sharp ache ten times over. Mordon mounted Renegade and made it to the tilt. Everyone was watching with anticipation, and Velamir stared at him from across the tilt. Mordon leaned forward on his horse, unable to keep himself upright. The trumpet blew, and Mordon struggled to get a good pace going. He was slipping from the saddle. He didn't have any strength left. He crashed onto the ground, and searing black crossed his vision.

Do not fail me. His father's words echoed in his head as he lost consciousness.

47

CORALIE
KINGDOM OF VERIN
VERINTOWN

"GET AWAY FROM my son," General Boltrex growled at Velamir, pushing him away from Mordon's limp body.

Coralie watched the True Manos gather around, hefting Mordon onto a wooden board. She observed them carrying him away. She was twelve years old again, her hands clutched around the letter that contained news of her parents' passing. The pain was pure agony. They died. He couldn't go too.

A tear slid from her eye, falling to the corner of her lips. She tasted the bitterness of the salt in her tear and stepped forward, each movement painful. Her boot hit something, smacking the object along the sandy tournament grounds. Coralie crouched and, through the blurriness of her vision, made out the gleam of metal. She lifted it, willing her hands to be steady as they always were. It was a ring. A small blood-covered knife protruded from it. As Coralie moved it in her palm, the sunlight shone, and it flashed silver. She racked her memory, picturing Mordon slamming his hammer at Draven. She remembered Draven hitting Mordon's leg, and as Mordon slapped his hand away, a silver light flashed. He dropped the ring, she realized. Suspicion built, and she rushed to the healing chambers.

"Bring me my sword," she told a maid who stopped to curtsy to her.

If Draven was behind this, if he was the reason Mordon was in dire condition, she would kill him. She reached the chamber and entered without knocking despite several nobles attempting to stop her. Boltrex's head swung to her, worry lines marking his face. The True Manos paid her no mind, their attention focused on Mordon as they covered him in cool cloths and tried to determine what was wrong.

Coralie strode to the general. "I found this."

He took the ring from her. "Is this supposed to mean something to me?"

Coralie explained everything, and he said, "You think it's poisoned?"

"I hope that is not the case, but if it is . . ."

Boltrex called one of the True Manos over. "I want you to test this for poison."

The True Manos worked competently, rummaging through his things, and returned with a vial of clear liquid. "If there is poison, the blade will turn green."

Coralie held her breath as he dribbled some of the liquid onto the blade. She felt eyes probing into her back and turned to see the other True Manos staring at them. He couldn't see what they were doing because their bodies were covering the ring, but he seemed concerned. Coralie frowned. Who was he? He looked familiar.

When he saw her staring at him, he looked away, returning his focus to Mordon. A sharp inhale from Boltrex brought her attention back to the ring. A moldy green was spreading across the metal until it covered the entire piece. Coralie shared a look with Boltrex.

A knock on the door was followed by a young soldier entering. He saluted Boltrex and handed him a vial. "We searched Galva Blayton's home as you requested, and we found this inside the guest room the True Manos was staying in. There were other gadgets as well, but we weren't sure if it was safe to touch anything."

"Good work," Boltrex said and turned the vial over to the True Manos, who had tested the ring. "Figure out what this is."

The True Manos placed gloves on his hands and got to work. A maid entered next and handed Coralie her sword and belt. Coralie strapped it around her waist.

The True Manos's voice was hesitant as he spoke. "General, this is the same poison that was on the ring."

Boltrex whipped around. "Are you sure?"

The True Manos nodded. Boltrex walked over to Mordon's bed and addressed the True Manos there. His voice had an edge. "How is he?"

The True Manos shook his head. "He is not well, General."

Coralie wondered if she should hold Boltrex back. It appeared as if he wanted to throttle the man.

"What is wrong with him?"

Coralie frowned. Why was he asking? He already knew Mordon was poisoned.

There were a few seconds of silence, and then Boltrex shouted, "Bloody spit it out!"

"I am afraid he has been poisoned."

"You know very well he has been poisoned," Boltrex told him.

"I don't understand."

Boltrex took the vial. "Was this not in your room?"

The True Manos's eyes widened.

Boltrex laughed. It was a terrifying laugh. He held up the ring. "Can you explain this?"

Something happened when the True Manos saw the ring. The shock and pain in his eyes were so real, Coralie could feel it. She could almost describe it. Like his heart had been cleaved in two.

His reaction was enough for Boltrex. "Let's call in your fellow traitor friends. Find Velamir and his so-called sister and bring them here," he told one of the guards.

After the guard left, the general addressed the other guards. "Hold him in place."

The True Manos backed away, but the guards grabbed hold of him. He thrashed against them. Boltrex stepped close to him and shoved his sleeve back, revealing a brand. He was Chishma. Coralie's lips curled in disgust. Boltrex pushed the sleeve back farther, and a purple birthmark came into view.

"Just what I thought."

Boltrex motioned for the guards to continue holding the man and stepped back. Coralie turned to face the window. Velamir worked with this man. She had known he was up to something from the moment she met him. But still . . . she had hoped he was as he appeared—kind, charming, rescuer of children. It seemed all of that was a ruse. If there was one thing Coralie knew as a princess, it was to never fall for the games.

After minutes of endless waiting, Velamir was brought in. He glanced around, his eyes landing on the True Manos. They exchanged a wordless glance, and Velamir's face fell.

Coralie nodded, sarcasm dripping from her tone. "You thought you would get away with it?"

He shook his head. "Get away with what?"

"DO NOT!" Boltrex shouted. He inhaled a heavy breath. "Do not lie."

The door opened again, and the sister was brought in. Coralie was startled at the blood soaking her skirts. The guard holding the woman's arm saluted the general.

"We found her as she emerged from a jouster's tent. Commander Tolsfin was found dead inside."

Coralie saw Velamir shake his head.

"I was so horrified to see it, I—" Lissa began, but the guard spoke over her.

"She said she saw the killer and described him exactly like Galva Mordon."

The general fumed. "Is this what he looked like?" He motioned to Mordon's immobile body.

Coralie looked away, unable to bear the sight. She watched the sister take him in. Regret and anger warred for dominance in her features. The sister glanced at the True Manos. Coralie watched the silent battle they fought, their expressions changing so fast.

The sister cleared her throat. "After I heard rumors of him killing men by the tavern, I assumed."

The general held up a hand. "You can stop there. Mordon wasn't the one to kill them."

"You don't have proof of that," she shot back.

He smiled, cold and conniving. "Actually, I do." He nodded at the guard. "Bring him in."

Coralie examined their alarmed faces. They waited in painful silence until the door swung open. The guard reappeared, followed by Latimus.

48

VELAMIR
KINGDOM OF VERIN
CASTLE VERIN

VELAMIR KNEW LATIMUS didn't like him, but he hadn't expected him to betray them like this. Latimus's chin was lifted, and his face bore no regrets. Boltrex waved a hand at him.

"Tell them what you told me."

"The day they arrived, I offered them shelter in my home out of kindness and because I knew Velamir in the past. He asked me for information on members of the council and high officials. I thought it was strange, but I complied.

"That night, Velamir's sister, who he had never mentioned before, snuck out of the manor. She took one of my cloaks. I thought nothing of it, thinking she had gone for an evening stroll. In the morning, I found the cloak, and after scrutinizing it, I noticed there was blood on it. Then I heard the news about Advisor Liston's death. It clicked in my mind that they must be related."

Velamir scoffed. "You have no proof of this except your word, which is not trustworthy in the least."

"Silence," Boltrex snapped. "Please, continue."

Latimus nodded. "They continued plotting together. Soon after, a sickness began spreading among the councilmen, people whose names I had written for Velamir. When Advisor Covskin was killed the same way Liston was, I searched Lissa's room and found this just this morning." Latimus tossed a sack forward.

Boltrex motioned to a guard, and he pulled the string, taking out clawed gloves. Velamir winced. They were done for.

"Well, well," Boltrex said. "What do we have here?"

"He is framing me!" But Lissa knew her argument was weak.

"There is one way to know," Boltrex said. "Lift your sleeve and prove you aren't marked."

Lissa's eyes darted desperately, and she lunged forward. The guard was so surprised he forgot to keep a strong hold on her. She didn't jump at Boltrex as Velamir thought she would, but instead she pulled a knife from her sleeve and flew at Coralie.

Coralie ducked under the knife and retreated, her back pressed against the window. Lissa moved fast, but Coralie was faster. She grabbed Lissa's hand and brought it down on her knee, hard. Lissa screamed, a cry of agony as the bone in her wrist snapped. The knife fell from her fingers into Coralie's waiting hand. Coralie pressed Lissa to the wall and held the knife against her throat. They both heaved heavy breaths.

"Good work, Princess," Boltrex said. "Her attack proved Latimus right. We have all the evidence we need, but just in case . . ."

He walked up to Lissa and yanked the sleeve of her good arm. She spit fire at him through her eyes. He lifted her forearm, and the crown brand was clear.

Boltrex chuckled. "And he is not a True Manos, either."

Jax stiffened at the mention.

Boltrex nodded. "So we have a Chishma, a Chishman Shadow Manos, and who are you, Velamir Raga?"

Velamir's jaw was rigid. There was nothing he could say or do to refute Boltrex's words.

"Winston orchestrated a marvelous plan. I wish I could have seen him choking on the poison." Boltrex's voice was wistful.

Velamir could not restrain himself. He lunged and grabbed Boltrex by his collar. "Don't you dare speak about him."

A guard hauled Velamir back, gripping his arms behind him.

Boltrex stared him down. "I can't believe he made you care for him."

"He was my father," Velamir seethed.

"Don't play games with me. Your show is over. I have the proof I need. As general, my job is to protect Verin. And I am very interested in the fact that Savagelanders decided to ally with Prolus. Although, I'm not surprised.

The Savagelander overlord would do anything for that sword." Boltrex motioned to Velamir's belt.

Confusion mounted, and the guards and True Manos seemed bewildered as well. Coralie turned her head to listen but still held her position against Lissa.

"I do not know what you are talking about."

Boltrex chuckled. "You cannot fool me, boy. You know who you are. You know who you work with."

Velamir didn't reply.

Boltrex said, "No matter. I will figure that out soon enough. For now, I need my son healed."

The True Manos shook his head. "This is too powerful a poison. We do not know how to make the antidote."

"Then the one who made it will fix him." Boltrex leveled his burning gaze at Jax.

Jax smiled. "You don't have the materials. I bought it off a passing merchant in Namaar. Ovaline is powerful, especially the one used in this poison."

"You will heal him," Boltrex repeated. "I will send someone to retrieve it."

"The ovaline I need is in the Karakan's lair. It's a death wish."

"It's a good thing Velamir came here with a death wish." Boltrex smirked, glancing at him. "You will retrieve the ovaline. Latimus will accompany you."

Latimus gulped. "What?"

"It's time to see if you can redeem your father for his mistake of siding with Velamir."

Latimus cleared his expression and nodded. "Of course, General. It would be an honor."

"I warn you, Velamir. If you do not return with the ovaline, I will kill your friends."

The threat behind the words was clear. Lissa pressed against Coralie's hold, and a thin trail of blood ran along the knife.

"Velamir doesn't care what you do with us. He will never listen to you!" she screamed at Boltrex.

Boltrex moved quickly, unsheathing his sword and swinging it at Jax's neck, all while keeping his eyes on Velamir. Velamir tried to keep his face impassive, but he couldn't help but flinch. The sword paused an inch from Jax's neck, and a slow, satisfied smile crossed Boltrex's face.

"Just as I suspected."

Velamir's teeth clenched, and his hands fisted.

"Now go. Make haste and return with the ovaline."

Velamir didn't move. Boltrex deserved this for his vile actions. Mordon dying slowly and painfully would mean Winston would be avenged. But Velamir couldn't allow Jax, or even Lissa, to pay the price. He released a heavy breath.

"I will do it."

Lissa screamed in frustration, struggling to free herself from Coralie's hold.

"That was never in question," Boltrex replied.

Latimus walked to the door, and Velamir followed him, staring at the back of his head with disgust. He shouldn't have trusted him. He shouldn't have stayed in his home. Velamir dug his own grave.

Boltrex called after them, "Take Finnean with you."

Latimus cursed under his breath, making Velamir

wonder who Finnean was. They stepped into the hall, and all the nobles waiting turned to stare at them. Before any of them could ask questions, a messenger rushed into the corridor. He bowed to King Dale and held out a scroll.

At King Dale's nod, he unwrapped it and read its contents before everyone. "My King, Namaar is overrun with the dark forces. Prolus will come to the castle next. I could not stop him. I sent this message in the hands of one of my trusted scouts. Your loyal Galvasir, Nildon."

The following silence was strained. It was interrupted only by the sound of the scout refolding the scroll. He bowed again and left at King Dale's command.

"Well, this changes things," Latimus said.

"Nothing changes for you two," Boltrex said, and Velamir turned to see he had followed them into the hall.

"I hope Ondalar won't use this to wage an attack on us as well," one noble said in a worried tone. "Then we would be cornered on both sides."

"General Zenrelius is honor bound. He wouldn't attack another kingdom while it is at war," someone else replied.

"Zenrelius is just a general. He is not the king of Ondalar," Commander Evinshore said with a sniff. "Whatever his king commands will be fulfilled."

Boltrex interrupted. "Let us speak on the matter at hand. My son's life is at stake. I am not in the least interested in what the other kingdoms and their generals are doing. Velamir, Latimus, and Finnean Colleda will retrieve an important ingredient to make the antidote for my son."

Commander Evinshore frowned. "I'm not sure Finnean is ready for a mission."

"Since Tariqi took the Borderlands, he has mourned alone. This will draw him out of his grief."

"I wish you luck, young men," King Dale said.

"Thank you," Latimus replied.

"Take any provisions you need before setting off," King Dale ordered.

Velamir wondered when Boltrex would tell the king what happened in the healing chamber. The worst part was that Prolus had taken Namaar and was nearing the castle, thinking victory would await him. But instead of completing the mission, Velamir was on his way to save his enemy's life.

49

VELAMIR
KINGDOM OF VERIN

THEY RODE FOR half a day until Finnean
called for a halt to water the horses. Velamir
found it humorous how Latimus tried to be
in command at the start of their journey and how
quickly he backed down. Finnean was not what
Velamir had expected. He was a smaller man, dark-
haired with a full beard. There was a gloominess
about him that made Velamir wary. He had no
choice on the matter though. He had to endure the
journey and return to the castle to save the others
and Mordon. Velamir closed his eyes against the
thought of saving his mentor's murderer.

Vandal drank the cool water in the rapidly
moving stream. Velamir searched the saddlebags and found some dried meat. He took a bite
and stared over the saddle at Finnean, who was
glancing at the sky, gauging the weather.

"Out of anyone to retrieve the ovaline, Finnean would be last on my list." Latimus's voice was grating against Velamir's ear.

He ignored him instead of shouting the buildup of words that threatened to slip out. He couldn't let Latimus see how much his treachery had affected him.

"He used to live near the Karakan's lair. His younger brother thought it would be fun to adventure there. He assumed the Karakan was a myth to scare him away. You can guess what happened next."

Velamir remained silent, although it wasn't hard to picture the rumlok claws ripping into flesh. He had seen it many times before.

"Finnean was good at everything. His sword skills impeccable, his actions immaculate, his status rising fast. At the time, it was even rumored King Dale would make him a Galvasir." Latimus laughed. "I will admit, I was jealous. It was hard not to be when my family compared me with him."

Velamir paused mid-bite, the dried meat tasting sweet and smoky. It was difficult to believe Latimus would admit to inferiority.

"But then his brother was killed. The one person he couldn't save. He became a drunkard and volunteered to fight at the Borderlands. I heard it was because he wanted to die. But he returned when his service was over, alive and well. In body but not spirit."

Velamir turned to face Latimus. "Why are you telling me this? Why are you even speaking to me?"

Latimus raised a brow. "I want you to know the stakes. You can't trust him. He will want to kill the rumlok. We are there to retrieve the ovaline and leave. He will do something rash. I don't know why Boltrex chose him, but this won't end well."

"Trust." Velamir chuckled. "I don't think you have the right to use that word."

Latimus's brows were drawn together. "You must know I put my family and the Empire before everyone and everything."

"Even before your honor?"

"I preserved my family's honor by telling the general your plans. I've known you since you were a child, Velamir. You can still make the right choice. When we bring the ovaline back, side with us. It's your only option for survival."

"I won't side with an Empire that imprisons and tortures people."

"And you think Prolus is different? He sends Chishma here to assassinate, to kill. He hires mercenaries to bring in slaves to use them in war or sell them. You would rather fight for that man?"

Velamir faltered. An image of Vykus heartlessly shooting Savorians ran through his mind. But Prolus was different. He was building a peaceful state. Velamir recalled Jax's words from weeks ago.

You figured it out, Vel, and you think they wouldn't?

Velamir shook his head, clenching his jaw. He turned to face Vandal, curling his fingers into his mane.

"You must realize I'm right," Latimus probed.

"If Prolus is trying to conquer and enslave everyone for his own gain, it doesn't mean the emperor's way is correct, either. Both sides are wrong." He looked at Latimus. "What's left is to choose the side that is less corrupt."

Latimus stared with horror. "Do you hear what you are saying?"

"Either that or create a new order. But that would be impossible."

"The Empire is good, Velamir. We have hope that once Malus is gone, Prince Honzio will change things."

"You can pray, Latimus, but first someone has to remove Malus, and I don't see anyone except Prolus trying."

"So you choose him? The man who sends these murderous rumloks to kill innocent civilians."

Velamir gritted his teeth. "If Verin surrendered, there would be peace."

"We need to leave." Finnean's voice was so unexpected that they both jumped. "Galva Mordon's life rests in our hands."

If it truly did, Mordon would be dead, Velamir thought.

JAX
KINGDOM OF VERIN
CASTLE VERIN

Jax waved a bowl of crushed herbs under Mordon's nose. It was one of the many things he had been preparing to ease his pain and prolong his life. He knew it wouldn't help much in the long run, but he had to show he was useful or else he might be tortured or tossed off the highest tower. At least, that was what he told himself, because he didn't want to admit to the truth. That he wanted to help. He wanted to help save General Winston's killer, Vel's enemy. He couldn't explain the reason. Maybe it was because he saw Frumgan's suffering in Mordon. Frumgan had gone through this exact pain. He had endured most of it alone, and Jax didn't want Mordon to be alone.

Or maybe it was because of the princess and the way she gripped Mordon's stiff hand. It might've been because of the way she stared at him, as if her whole world would collapse if something happened to him. Jax wished someone would look at him that way. He had wished for someone to love him his whole life, but everyone turned away. Sure, maybe Velamir and Lissa cared, but Velamir cared for him as a friend, a brother, and Lissa . . . he used to hope something would grow.

He set the bowl on a side table and glanced at her. Lissa was seated on a wooden bench a short distance away. Her hands were chained. Jax winced at the strain on her face as she tried to contain the pain her broken wrist gave her.

His heart ached for her despite her betrayal. He had given her the ring for her safety, and she had thrown their mission in the gutter with her terrible choice. A knock stole his attention.

"Enter," the princess said.

The door swung open, and a guard poked his head inside. "A man is here to see you, Your Highness."

"Let him in."

The door opened wider, and a man dressed in a plain

suit coat entered, spectacles perched on the bridge of his nose. Jax straightened and his eyes widened. Harold winked at him. It was barely perceptible, but Jax saw it. He had forgotten about the tailor Chishma.

"Your Highness, I came by King Dale's request. He said you needed new gowns?"

Coralie laughed. "At a time like this, the only thing I need is my wits and my sword, and thankfully I have both." She patted her sword where it was sheathed at her waist.

Harold's brow puckered. "The king was mistaken, then?"

Coralie didn't look at him. Her gaze focused on Mordon, her hand still wrapped around his.

Harold took the hint. "I shall be on my way, in that case." He tapped his hand against his forearm, the Chishman signal. It was a bold move, one that only Jax saw.

Jax shook his head, attempting to tell the man to be more discreet. Harold smiled and lifted two fingers. *Two days*, he mouthed before leaving the room.

Jax translated it to mean two days till Prolus arrived. It was also two days that would end Mordon's life, two days when the princess's heart would be crushed, two days in which they wouldn't complete their mission, and two days full of misery and failure.

Mordon shifted and Coralie swept closer, leaning over him.

"Mordon?" she whispered, hopeful.

He didn't respond, just as Jax knew he wouldn't. In the morning, the nightmares would start, and his movements would be wild, then he would lie motionless again, still as a corpse. By evening of the second day, he *would* be a corpse. Jax had contemplated whipping up the antidote Frumgan used, but that would need to be made on a regular basis, and once used, no other antidote would work. Jax wiped sweat off Mordon's face and placed a cool cloth on his head.

A groan of pain brought his attention to Lissa. She grimaced and straightened her expression.

Jax stood and spoke to the princess. "Allow me to set her wrist."

"You heard the general. Until Velamir returns, she will suffer."

"That is no way to treat someone. Will you prove how cruel the Empire is by leaving her in anguish?" Jax's frustration built.

Something in Coralie's gaze shifted, and she finally nodded. "Just her wrist. Don't try anything else."

Jax took his bag and approached Lissa. She stared at him as he lifted the metal cuff as far as it would go to assess the damage.

She whispered, "I'm sorry, Jax."

"Why did you do it?"

"I was trying to accomplish what we set out to do." She tried to reason with him, to prove that she was right. "I had to."

"Lissa, I think we were wrong," Jax said. "About it all."

"What do you mean?"

"We were children when we were forced into the academy. We didn't have a choice in what we became."

"What can we do about that now? It's too late for us to change paths."

Jax glanced at Coralie and back at Lissa. "I think there's still a chance."

"They will never forgive us. We've already done too much."

"They might." Jax stared at her earnestly and called to the princess, "I need to remove her chains in order to put a splint on her wrist."

The princess narrowed her eyes and walked over to them. Her kindness won over, and she handed a key to him. He opened Lissa's chains. The princess took a step back but kept watch over them. Lissa stopped Jax's hand with her good arm when he reached for her wrist.

"I have to go back to Tariqi," she said softly.

"Why?"

"He has my mother." Her eyes were pleading. "Prolus has her."

"What?"

Suddenly, his operating knife was at his neck. Lissa moved so fast his head jerked back and his throat bobbed.

"What are you doing?"

"I need to go, Jax. You can't stop me." She flicked her head. "Stand."

He rose, holding his hands up. The princess stared, her expression dark.

"Let him go."

"You will let me leave. You need him. I will kill him if you try to stop me."

A war waged on the princess's features. "You are tricking me."

"I will release him if you let me pass."

The princess glanced at Mordon and back at them. After a long moment, she nodded. Her fear of his death was the only fuel driving her to accept Lissa's terms. She opened the door and called to the guards. "Let them pass."

Lissa dragged Jax out. He knew her wrist must be paining her, but there was no hesitation in her steps. He could break out of her hold if he wanted to, but he didn't want to fight her. He didn't want to hurt her. The castle guards were wide-eyed as they walked past them. A crowd of spectators and guards gathered as they crossed the gatehouse. Coralie had followed them but stayed back. She warned everyone to keep their distance. Lissa's guard lightened once they crossed the bridge.

"I'm going to let you go," she told him.

She stood behind him, holding the knife at his throat while he faced the onlookers.

"But before I do, I ask you to come with me." There was pain in her voice.

It was then that Jax knew what they had was real, and now that he knew, he didn't want to let her go. She was returning to a place, back to something he didn't believe in any longer.

"When this is all over, I will find you." His voice broke, and his eyes welled.

Lissa's laugh vibrated in his ear. "You will likely find my grave."

Jax refused to picture her dead, so he repeated, "I will find you."

He heard the smile in her voice when she spoke. "Goodbye, Jaxon Tana."

The pressure on his neck was gone, and when he turned, so was she. Soldiers and guards rushed past him, searching for her. Jax stood there, feeling like he had lost a part of himself.

50

NATASSA
FLONDIN WOODS

SALVADOR HAULED NATASSA to her feet. She stumbled forward, and he grabbed hold of the rope binding her wrists to keep her up. Natassa looked past him, her gaze landing on Vykus, who was still smiling. He approached them, pulling Kasdeya with him. He stopped before them, handing Kasdeya over to Salvador to hold in place. Vykus examined Natassa, bursting into laughter when he saw the ropes.

"Figured it out, have you?" Vykus chuckled, directing his question to Kasdeya.

Kasdeya struggled against Salvador's firm grip. "I don't know what you mean."

"You must be Kasdeya," he told Natassa.

Natassa refused to answer, lifting her chin. Vykus took a step closer to her. "I finally get to meet the famed spy in the palace."

What is he talking about?

"Don't pretend to be clueless." Vykus chuckled. "I respect you. In fact, all Prolus's intelligence group respects you. The work you have done . . . has come in handy."

Shock filtered through Natassa as his words sank in. Kasdeya had betrayed them to Prolus. The Empire's worst threat and enemy besides those in the Savagelands. The sound of a weapon unsheathing snapped Natassa from her thoughts. Vykus leaned over her, holding a dagger. He lifted the weapon, and Natassa closed her eyes, bracing herself for the oncoming pain. Air brushed Natassa's face as the dagger came down. The tightness around her wrists eased. Natassa opened her eyes and stared in disbelief at the severed rope lying at her feet.

He exploded with laughter. "Come now, Kasdeya. You are too clever to think I would kill you just like that."

Natassa's heart beat with ceaseless thumps.

"You are too important to kill off. We may yet have use of you."

Kasdeya shot Natassa a fear-inducing glare. She probably wished Vykus had killed her. Vykus set up camp in the small area. It was Kasdeya's turn to have her hands bound. Vykus's group set off for Namaar, and Natassa was forced to share the carriage with Kasdeya.

Hours later, they stopped for another rest. Vykus placed a large map on the ground, speaking with Salvador. No one seemed to pay her any mind. The mercenaries were focused on Kasdeya, ensuring she didn't escape. Natassa found it funny how Kasdeya's entire plan had turned on her. She had stolen Natassa's identity and saved her by doing so.

"Natassa!" said a sharp whisper.

She glanced over her shoulder at the trees. She made out a figure and a hand beckoning her. Natassa looked back at the mercenaries and then closed the distance between herself and the mysterious person. It was a woman, her face shadowed beneath her hood. When Natassa reached her, the woman took her hand and propelled her into the trees.

"We must go." Her words were tense, but her voice was familiar.

Natassa moved along with her, and soon they were far into the woods, and she was gasping for breath.

"Let's stop here for a moment," the woman said.

Natassa heaved grateful breaths. "Who are you?"

The woman hesitated and reached up, throwing back her hood. It was Kasdeya. Natassa gasped and retreated a pace. She had been duped. How could she have fallen for this?

But then she noticed the glimmer of tears in her eyes, the tremble in her smile, and the kindness in her face that Kasdeya never had. No, this wasn't Kasdeya.

"Krea!" Natassa cried.

Krea enveloped her in a hug, and they sobbed together.

"I'm so sorry," Natassa said through her tears. "I'm so sorry."

"I'm sorry too."

Natassa pulled back. "What are you doing here?"

"I've been following you since you left Hearcross."

"What?" Natassa couldn't explain the emotions she felt.

"I would never leave my princess alone."

"Oh, Krea." Natassa hugged her again. "I should have believed in you."

"No, Natassa. Don't blame yourself, you were going through so much."

"She can't be far!"

They stiffened at the shout and exchanged a glance. Krea handed her a knife. "Take this." She gripped Natassa's shoulders. "We will get through this, Natassa."

Natassa nodded firmly in reply, and Krea said, "No matter what happens, I will protect you, Princess. Or die trying." The grim words darkened the dampened mood further.

The shouts grew closer. Natassa gripped Krea's hand as they set off. Heavy boots thundered behind them, and Natassa knew they had been spotted. They ran as fast as they could, but their pursuers were gaining on them. They sprinted into a large, empty clearing. Natassa chanced a glance over her shoulder and saw Salvador a horse's length behind them. He snarled and lunged forward, barely missing her shoulder. Natassa screamed and stumbled, falling and pulling Krea down with her.

Salvador grinned and reached for them, but Krea was too fast. In a flash, she kicked him in the groin and thrust a finger into his throat. Salvador gagged, hunching over them. Krea punched him between the eyes, and he fell to his knees, his eyes rolling in a dazed expression. Natassa got to her feet, searching for a way out. She heard a smack and looked back to see Salvador pull Krea on top of him.

"Krea!" Natassa rushed forward, but two bandits blocked her path.

Natassa held Krea's knife in her trembling hand. One

bandit advanced, and she slashed it before him, forcing him to keep his distance. The other circled around, approaching from behind. He grabbed hold of her arm and she spun, stabbing the knife into his shoulder. He roared as she jerked it out. The first bandit wrapped an arm around her waist, dragging her back. The man she had stabbed flung his hand at her face. Natassa kicked out, catching him in the stomach. She flipped the knife in her hand and sliced it into the bandit who held her. It pierced his side, and he screamed in agony, dropping her. Natassa backed away, putting distance between them. The other bandit growled and rushed at her, aiming a fist. She swung to the side, evading the blow, and brought her blade up, slicing his wrist. He howled and clutched his wound, holding back the explosion of blood.

The first bandit struggled, holding his bleeding side as he advanced on her once again. He held a dagger in his other hand. Natassa breathed deeply. *Stay calm, stay calm.*

He swung the dagger at her throat. She ducked, and it sailed over her head. Natassa kneed him between the legs, and his face contorted. He dropped his dagger, and she thrust her knife, impaling his empty hand. He screamed and fell to his knees, staring at his hand in horror. After a few moments, he sneered and pulled himself together. He yanked her knife loose. His blood spilled across the ground in a shower of red. Natassa kicked him in the chest, and he collapsed. The second attacker lunged at her, grabbing her hand and twisting it as he pulled her toward him. Natassa cried in anguish.

"Natassa!" Krea yelled and rushed to her. Salvador grabbed her around the waist, stopping her in her tracks.

Krea thrashed and tried to elbow him, but Salvador positioned himself so that her attacks would never hit.

A tear went down Natassa's cheek. She thought her wrist might be sprained. The bandit grabbed her neck. His fingers closed around her throat, blocking her airway, a maniacal gleam in his eyes. Natassa slapped at his hands, to no avail. Warm blood trickled along her neck from his bleeding wrist. She wheezed, desperate for air as darkness crept into the edges of her vision.

Velamir
Kingdom of Verin

"The lair is near," Finnean said in his usual monotone voice, slowing his horse.

"We should pause for a moment," Latimus suggested. "Gather our bearings."

Velamir could sense his fear, his attempt to put more time between them and the Karakan.

"That would mean losing more time," Finnean told him. "And losing more time means losing Galva Mordon. And losing Galva Mordon means failure to accomplish our duty."

Velamir nodded. "He's right. We need to finish this."

Latimus grumbled and waved them forward. "Well, lead the way, then."

Velamir flicked his reins, and Vandal hadn't even moved a step when the screaming began. Long terrified screams. Velamir glanced at the other two.

"Someone needs help."

Finnean shook his head. "We don't have time to waste."

"Where is your sense of chivalry?" Latimus shot at him.

Velamir was relieved to have Latimus agree with him for once, even though he was only doing so for his own gain. Indecision filtered across Finnean's face, but his thinking was wasting time, and the screams were only growing louder. Velamir urged Vandal into a trot and shot forward without looking back. They could follow if they wanted, but he wasn't about to leave someone who needed help.

Wind rushed past Velamir and blew Vandal's mane back like the flaps of a flag. Velamir reached for his bow, which he'd left strung. There was no knowing where danger would come from. It was better to be ready for it. He lifted the bow from his saddlebag, and his fingers twitched to his quiver. He heard hoofbeats behind him, and a smile grew on his face. They had followed. A wide clearing came into view, and burning rage shot through Velamir's chest when he saw the scene before him.

Two women were being held against their will. The one nearest to him was thrashing her legs as a man lifted her, his hands wrapped around her throat. Velamir raised his bow and nocked an arrow, releasing without hesitation. The arrow buried itself into the man's chest, and he released her. Velamir snatched another arrow, taking out the next aggressor. He focused on the other woman, but she had freed herself and ran to her companion. A large, bald man rushed after her. Velamir trained his aim on him.

"One more step and this arrow will be in your heart."

51

VELAMIR
KINGDOM OF VERIN
NEAR THE KARAKAN'S LAIR

VELAMIR HEARD A sharp gasp and glanced down at the women. One of them was staring up at him. Her lips were parted, and her short hair blew against her face, but what drew him was her eyes. Hazel and very familiar. Then he realized why, and his heart beat a little faster. It was her, the girl from his dreams.

Velamir tore his gaze from hers and dismounted. He kept an eye on the bald man, realizing with a start that it was Salvador. And where Salvador was, Vykus couldn't be far behind. Velamir motioned to Latimus and stepped closer to the women. Latimus drew his sword, watching Salvador, relieving Velamir of the job. Velamir lowered his bow and glanced at the women, staring at the one he had saved.

"Are you all right?"

She held his gaze, her cheeks turning bright pink. "Yes."

"Velamir," Latimus warned.

He glanced at him, and Latimus nodded his chin at the open clearing behind Salvador. Only, the clearing was no longer so empty. Bandits rushed in, shouting and scanning the area with wild eyes. They swung their weapons, focusing on the women. Vykus came to the front, dragging a screaming girl with him. He smiled as he placed a dagger on her throat.

"I see we have more friends," Vykus said with ice in his voice.

Velamir stepped forward, blocking the women from view, Latimus and Finnean on either side of him. Salvador was trying to inch closer, but Latimus kept him in his sights.

"Give her back," Vykus shouted.

Velamir stared him down from across the clearing. "You're welcome to try to get them."

Vykus smirked. His bandits spread around, creeping closer to them. Vykus chuckled, and a thin sliver of alarm raced through Velamir.

"Well, well, well, look who it is," Vykus spat. "You know, these men you just killed. They cost me a pretty coin. We're both on the same side. Give me the girl. I'm delivering her to Prolus."

"What does Prolus need with her?" Velamir questioned.

Vykus shrugged. "Hell if I know. But this one's a princess." He pressed the dagger against the woman's throat, and she leaned back. "He must have some use for her."

"So you are not only kidnapping small children but also women?"

Vykus laughed. "It's all part of the deal. Don't tell me you don't approve of the actions of your lord?"

"The Savorians in Namaar. What did you do with them?"

"Brought them to be rehabilitated in Tariqi. It was their last chance to join Prolus's army. The disobedient ones . . . I killed." There was a gleam in his eyes that told Velamir how much he had enjoyed it.

It was at that moment when clarity struck Velamir. Most of his life, he had been training to be a killer for Prolus. He had been taught to follow the rules, to not think for himself. To be a soldier and nothing else.

Vykus watched him. "Your place is beside me, Velamir. I can see you don't want to follow Prolus. I could use a man like you."

"That's the thing. I'm tired of being used," Velamir told him. "By Prolus or anyone else."

"Finally," he heard Latimus murmur.

Vykus shook his head. "These leaders . . . they don't hold any power. There is only the rich man. The richest man owns everything. Right now, that's Prolus. Tomorrow, the emperor. Next week, the Savagelander overlord. It is all a point of view."

Velamir wondered where he was going with this speech.

"I always work for the richest man," Vykus said. "You want fame, Velamir, recognition. I understand that. I could give you that. I see your worth."

"I want peace. That's all I've ever wanted."

Vykus sneered. "We both know you want more. At the very least, you crave revenge."

Velamir stiffened. Of course, that was something he had wanted. But seeing Mordon poisoned and suffering hadn't made him feel better. It changed nothing. The pain was still there. No one's death would bring Winston back. Velamir could kill Boltrex and Mordon and every single man in Verin, but it wouldn't change a thing. His mindset had been wrong from the beginning. Instead of coming to kill, he should have been thinking of saving lives. He had to change the Imperials' minds. He had to convince King Dale to surrender, or the bloodshed would fill an ocean, because Prolus wouldn't stop.

Velamir's attention fell on the girl Vykus held pinned in his arms, his dagger close to her major artery. Velamir lifted his bow. "Let her go."

He spotted Salvador from the corner of his eye, sneaking closer to them with his large sword. Velamir turned to face him, releasing the bowstring. The arrow pierced Salvador's arm. He cursed and dropped his sword. The mercenaries ran at them, roaring as they came. Velamir stayed calm, nocking arrows and shooting. He picked off at least seven men before the bandits were too close to shoot. Salvador retrieved his sword with his uninjured arm and swung at them. Latimus appeared in front of him and blocked the sword with his own. He counterattacked, hitting Salvador in his wounded arm. Salvador hollered as his blood splattered across the grass.

Velamir dropped his bow and unsheathed his sword. Finnean pulled out the short swords strapped to his back. Together, they fought the bandits. Slicing and slashing through them. Velamir was astounded by Finnean's agility. He spun, twirled, ducked, and stabbed with such efficient grace Velamir hoped they would never face each other on the battlefield. Vykus quickly realized this was not a fight his men could win.

"Retreat!" Vykus called. "Retreat!"

The princess took the momentary distraction to her advantage. She bit Vykus's hand and elbowed him in the stomach. Velamir was unsure how she managed that feat quite so successfully, since her hands were bound. Vykus howled and released her. The princess ran as fast as she could toward them. The bandits rushed back into the woods to regroup. Vykus stared at Velamir with menace.

"This isn't over!" he called. "Prolus will hear about what you have done." And with a determined spin, he joined his men in the woods.

The princess was standing with the other girls. Velamir was struck by how similar they looked. It was unnerving. The princess conversed with them in a low voice. She obviously didn't want Velamir and the others to know what she was saying, and by the look of anger on the other girls' faces, they didn't like what she was telling them. Velamir stepped forward to speak with them, but Finnean blocked his path.

"What are we going to do with them? Look at the mess we are in now."

"You would have ignored them?" Velamir shot back.

Finnean's jaw clenched, and he didn't reply. His answer was clear from his silence.

"It is obvious what we must do." Latimus joined them. He flicked blood off his blade with his leather glove. "We protect them, and we bring them back to the castle with us."

"Do you know what kingdom this princess is from?" Velamir asked him.

"She looks familiar, but it's hard to tell with all the grime," Latimus admitted. "The girls must be her bodyguards."

"They don't fight well," Finnean said. "Their princess was more skilled with her hands tied."

Velamir spoke up. "We didn't exactly see their fighting skills."

Latimus smirked. "Of course you would defend them. I saw how you stared at the one girl."

Velamir scowled at him and glanced at Finnean to see that even he cracked a smile. Someone cleared their throat, and all six eyes swung to the noise. The princess stood there with her so-called bodyguards behind her. Velamir wondered how much of their conversation they had heard. He met the stare of the woman he had rescued, but she looked down as soon as their eyes locked, a thick strand of hair spilling over her face.

"I wanted to thank you for rescuing me," the princess said. "As you must know, I am Princess Natassa Hartinza." She introduced herself in a haughty voice.

Velamir froze. They were in a mess, a huge mess. They hadn't rescued just any princess. They'd rescued Emperor Malus's daughter.

52

NATASSA
KINGDOM OF VERIN
NEAR THE KARAKAN'S LAIR

N O ONE SPOKE for a long moment. The three
men were exchanging glances. Why, oh
why, had Kasdeya said that? They might
be worse than Vykus. After all, they had been
speaking about working for Prolus. Still, Natassa
couldn't see her rescuer bringing them to the Dark
Lord for gold or whatever Prolus promised in
return. Despite her best effort, her eyes strayed
to him.

He wore a long green cloak. Leather armor
covered his arms and chest. He was olive-skinned
and his nose bent, showing signs it had been
broken in the past. He glanced at her at that
moment with his piercing emerald gaze. Her
portrait of him didn't do him justice. Natassa
looked away, a dark blush infusing her

cheeks. He had caught her staring. She peeked and noticed he was still watching her.

His lips parted, and he spoke, his voice deep and a little hoarse. "I'm Velamir." He introduced the other men. "This is Finnean."

Natassa tore her gaze to the others. Finnean had hollow blue eyes and a thick beard. His armor was light, like Velamir's.

"And this is Lati—"

The brown-haired man brushed past Velamir and took Kasdeya's hand. He bowed over it and placed a kiss on her fingers. "Captain Latimus Blayton, at your service, Your Highness."

Natassa glanced at Kasdeya, watching her attempt to nod regally at each introduction.

"These are my handmaidens." She motioned to them. "Krea, and the other is *Kasdeya*."

Natassa ducked her head, and more hair spilled across her face. She hoped her mark was covered securely and no one noticed the way Kasdeya emphasized her false name.

"They are twins," Kasdeya clarified.

"Pleasure to meet you," Krea said.

Kasdeya cleared her throat. "As I was saying, I was on my way to Ayleth to wed my betrothed, Prince Draven." Natassa noticed how Velamir and his friends grimaced when Kasdeya mentioned Draven's name. It seemed they were acquainted with him. Kasdeya continued, "We were attacked by those mercenaries. My betrothed must be sick with worry."

"Prince Draven is in Castle Verin," the man named Latimus said.

Kasdeya stuttered, "But isn't the tournament over?"

Velamir shot Latimus a look. Natassa could see he was telling him to keep quiet about something. "He might have left by now," Velamir told her.

"You are going to Castle Verin, aren't you?" Kasdeya pressed.

"The general sent us to retrieve something. But yes, as soon as we finish, we will head to the castle."

"You will accompany us, then?"

"Certainly," Latimus said.

"I assume you know how to ride?" Velamir asked Kasdeya, but his gaze shifted back to Natassa.

Kasdeya sniffed. "Of course."

The black-bearded man, Finnean, let out a disapproving sigh. "We only have three horses."

Latimus puffed his chest and suggested, "Why don't we follow that bandit fellow, Vykus, and ambush him? We can take his horses."

Natassa had to admit the idea had merit.

"No," Kasdeya snapped. "I want to arrive at the castle in one piece, and I don't want to waste any time chasing after bandits."

Velamir glanced at his companions. "They will have to ride with us."

Kasdeya ignored him and moved to the nearest horse, swinging onto the saddle with effortless prowess. A niggle of jealousy wormed through Natassa. She had never been very good at riding.

Latimus stepped forward. "I am afraid you will have to ride with me, Your Highness."

Kasdeya looked down on him while somehow sticking her nose in the air. "Why?"

Natassa rolled her eyes. Kasdeya's snotty behavior was as different from hers as could be. How would she trick people who had actually met Natassa?

An awkward smile crossed Latimus's face. "That is my horse you are seated on, Princess."

"You can walk," Kasdeya said with a dismissive flick of her wrist. She signaled the horse forward.

Latimus sent Velamir a desperate look. Natassa watched Velamir grab the horse's reins, bringing him to a halt. The horse snorted and shook his head. Velamir looked up at Kasdeya.

"You may be a princess, but here, right now, you are in our charge. If you want to make it back to your *prince* safely and securely, then you will have to trust our judgment."

Kasdeya huffed and stared at the trees. Natassa approached the horse and glanced up at her. "Listen to him," she said and tried to communicate how things would go wrong if she didn't.

They had made a deal. Natassa would allow Kasdeya to continue pretending to be princess as long as she left Natassa alone. Kasdeya paled at her words. Natassa felt Velamir's gaze on her but refused to look at him.

"Fine," Kasdeya muttered.

Latimus heaved a heavy sigh of relief and mounted behind her. She leaned forward in the saddle as if he were a detestable plague. Natassa stepped back. Was she making the right choice allowing Kasdeya to continue her charade? She made a promise to Thorsten. That she would get away from Draven, and she told Honzio she would go to the Elders. If she revealed she was the true princess, she would be in danger again. This was better, safer.

She glanced at Krea and saw her mounted on Finnean's horse. "Let's move!" Finnean urged.

That left one horse. Velamir stepped closer to Natassa, and she felt his overwhelming presence. She glanced at him after a long moment. He was staring down at her, a question in his eyes. He was so close she sucked in a breath. She craned her neck to hold his gaze. Not for the first time, Natassa lamented her short height. She thought of his name. It suited him so well. Velamir meant courage in Savorian. She was glad she had taken lessons on the language. Velamir's gaze dropped, and his expression became frightening, almost as if he wanted to rip something apart. He reached out, fingers inches from touching her.

"What are you doing?"

"You have a bruise on your neck." His voice was rough.

Natassa remembered the bandit's vile grip around her throat and touched her skin, feeling self-conscious. When she glanced at her hand, dried blood coated her fingers.

"I'm fine."

He struggled for words and cleared his throat. "Ride with me?"

It wasn't like she had much choice. "I suppose."

His brows rose at her answer, but he turned, leading the way to his horse. "Do you need assistance?" he asked, cupping his hands for her to step in.

She ignored his hands and placed her foot in the stirrup, but the horse was too large for her to mount with ease. After a long moment of struggling, she turned to Velamir. Heat flooded her cheeks.

"I would appreciate some help."

Velamir cupped his hands again, and she set her worn-slipper-encased foot in them. He threw her up with ease, and as soon as she landed in the saddle, he reached up to steady her by taking hold of her wrist. Natassa gasped at the contact, and he sent her a questioning look. Natassa blushed, feeling foolish. He mounted behind her, locking her in place. She stiffened when he reached around her for the reins. Finnean rode past them, calling for them to hurry. Velamir clicked his tongue, urging his horse into motion. Natassa jerked against his chest. As they rode, Natassa's mark burned. Her shadow was trying to break through. Images flickered in her head, and Natassa pushed back against the vision. Nothing in her life went as planned, but at least in her mind, she still held control.

53

CORALIE
KINGDOM OF VERIN
CASTLE VERIN

CORALIE LOOKED OVER at Mordon for what
felt like the thousandth time that day. The
sun was setting. She could make out the
pink line on the horizon from the window. He had
one more day, just one. She wanted to scream and
swing her sword in the barracks, but she couldn't
leave him. Not for one second.

Boltrex had been furious when he learned the
Chishma girl had gotten away, but there wasn't
much he could do. Coralie had told him to arrest
Draven, no matter that he was a prince. He
had committed a crime when he used the ring.
Boltrex had shaken his head.

"King Dale will be devastated if I reveal
what has happened. You know his health
is waning."

Coralie knew exactly how shattered her uncle would be to know the man he once trusted, Galva Winston, had been working with Prolus all these years. It would be too much for him to learn the Chishma infiltrated and killed many of his men. No. They couldn't tell him, but they couldn't let justice go unanswered either. Draven needed to be taught a lesson. Coralie just had to figure out how.

The chamber door swung open after a brisk knock, and Coralie's maid entered. She curtsied and handed her a note.

"Prince Draven left the castle minutes ago, after reading this."

Coralie opened it, scanning the words.

Retreat to your castle or you won't be shown mercy when we arrive.

It wasn't signed, but it wasn't hard for her to figure out who it was from.

"Prolus," she whispered. "Where did you find this?"

Her maid had a sly look in her eyes. She darted a glance to the corner of the room where the Shadow Manos was mixing herbs. "I was spying on the prince as you ordered. I saw him read the note and rip it and toss it into the waste bucket. After he left the room with his men, I pieced the strips together and copied the words onto another parchment."

Coralie smiled. "Brilliant."

The young maid blushed. "He left with his personal guards. The rest of his entourage is preparing to leave as we speak."

Coralie nodded. He wasn't wasting any time, not even to ensure the safety of his own people.

"Do you have another task for me?" her maid asked.

"No, you may leave."

After the door closed, Coralie crumpled the parchment in her fist. Draven was corrupted. He had chosen his side. Ayleth was in Prolus's grasp. Devorin, the mountainous Kingdom of Snow, was rumored to work with Prolus as well. That left one kingdom, Ondalar. Coralie buried her face in her hands. The last kingdom that would help Verin was Ondalar. Verin was alone, all alone. Prolus would crush them.

Coralie lifted her head and stared at Mordon, at the trickle of sweat that rolled down his face. She took one of the wet cloths and placed it on his forehead. Coralie grasped his hand in hers and lifted it to her lips. She smiled, tears filling her eyes. She imagined his shock if he woke and saw her kissing his hand. As she continued looking at him, she couldn't make out the rise or fall of his chest. She panicked. Was he dead already? Coralie stood over him, dropping his hand. It thudded against the linen. She glanced desperately at the Shadow Manos. What was his name?

"Jax!" she called.

He hurried over. "What's wrong?"

"I-I don't think he's breathing," Coralie said, her voice breaking.

She almost slapped herself. She wasn't a weak maiden. She was strong, stronger than many men. She would not succumb to useless emotions. She took a deep breath and watched Jax check Mordon's pulse.

He looked up. "He is alive, but weaker. He won't last much longer."

"What should I do?"

Jax's blue gaze was sympathetic. "Pray."

She retook her seat, pulling the chair closer so she could rest her head beside Mordon's. Her eyes started to feel heavy, and she blinked more and more often. She stared at his jaw, where his beard was growing thicker. She wondered how it would feel but resisted reaching out, especially with Jax nearby. She closed her eyes and sensed a dream of a treasured memory invading her sleep.

Mordon circled his horse around her. Coralie held her reins in tight fists. The wind whipped their hair around.

"Why are you upset?"

"My uncle sent you after me, didn't he?" Coralie shot at him.

She glanced behind her at the distant castle.

"I came myself."

She shook her head. "I don't have to answer to you."

"You were sulking the whole time at the celebration."

"I wasn't sulking."

He smiled. "You were. And as soon as I confronted you, you took off."

She didn't answer him.

"Is it because the party was held in my honor instead of yours like every celebration is?"

He was trying to make her angry, but she just felt hurt. The sting of tears only made it worse. She couldn't let him see her cry.

"You are a complete idiot, Mordon," she snapped and nudged her horse's sides, taking off.

"Coralie!" The wind carried his voice past her.

She rode faster, propelling her horse through the trees. Coralie stopped after minutes of riding and pulled her horse to a halt. She was waiting to hear hoofbeats signaling Mordon's arrival, but they never came. She turned back, riding slowly now. Coralie almost didn't notice the saddleless horse until she was upon it.

"Renegade?" She gasped.

It was Mordon's horse. She dismounted and rushed to him. She stepped over a giant log, holding Renegade's reins. The reins slipped from her fingers when she spotted Mordon's motionless body a short distance away. He must have fallen off while riding. She ran to him, falling to her knees.

"Mordon!" She shook him, but he didn't move a muscle. "Wake up."

She slapped his cheeks, pinched his arms. This was her fault. She shouldn't have run off. She shouldn't have thought only about herself. A tear fell from her lashes, dropping onto Mordon's face. Her head thumped against his chest.

"Wake up, you big idiot."

She felt a rumble against her face. Was he laughing? She sat up and saw his eyes were open.

She stood. "What is this?"

"I wanted to see what you would do."

"You did this on purpose?" She was growing more and more disgusted.

He rose, but the image of him lying motionless didn't fade from Coralie's mind.

"Don't go," she told him.

He stepped closer. "Why should I stay?"

The tension built between them as he searched for an answer.

"You will be killed there."

He seemed disappointed by her answer, but he brushed it off and smiled his arrogant smirk. "You have so little faith in me?"

"It's too dangerous. All for a Galvasir title? It's not worth it."

"I will only be at the Borderlands for a few months."

"I will go with you."

He shook his head. "You know you can't. You are King Dale's heir."

"Tell me the truth," Coralie snapped. "Tell me it's because I was born a woman."

There was barely any space between them. Mordon reached out and tucked a strand of loose hair behind her ear. "No, you were born to be a queen."

54

VELAMIR
KINGDOM OF VERIN
THE KARAKAN'S LAIR

VELAMIR MADE OUT the cave in the distance. It was shadowed by trees and unsettling stillness. Not even birds dared fly near it. He halted and dismounted, looking up at Kasdeya. He held out a hand to help her, but she shook her head. She swung her leg over Vandal's back. Velamir stepped forward and wrapped his hands around her waist. He lifted her from the saddle and set her gently on her feet.

"There was no need for that. I could have dismounted myself," she told him.

Velamir smiled at the flush blooming across her cheeks. "I know."

She glanced up, lips parting to speak but he turned away, leaving her flustered as he approached Latimus and Finnean.

He passed the princess on his way. She took a seat on a log, and he noticed her handmaidens stayed away from her. He wondered why there was such tension between them. Earlier, when Kasdeya told the princess to listen to him, it almost seemed as if she was threatening her. Velamir couldn't help but wonder what hold Kasdeya had over her mistress.

"Are you going to leave us here alone?" the princess called after him as he joined Latimus and Finnean.

Latimus glanced at her. "She's right. What if someone attacks them?"

"Like Vykus?" Finnean muttered under his breath.

"Yes! Who knows what lurks around?"

"I'm guessing you think you would be the perfect bodyguard?" Velamir smiled.

Latimus scratched his head. "I never said that . . ."

Finnean sniffed. "It's better if you stay. You will slow us down if you come with."

Latimus frowned at the insult. "It's not as if I'm getting the easy task." He motioned to the princess, who was staring at them through narrowed eyes, although she was too far to hear their discussion.

"We have wasted enough time," Finnean grumbled, casting a sidelong look at Velamir. "Let's move."

A small flame burned on the end of the makeshift torch he'd crafted during their conversation. Velamir followed Finnean. When they entered the cave, they would have been cast in complete darkness if not for the torchlight. They crept through. Velamir could make out a glow against one of the walls.

"Bring the light here."

Finnean came by his side and shone the torch over the cave wall. Glowing blue flowers grew along the cracks. Velamir smiled and reached out, carefully picking them. Their glow seemed to dim as soon as he broke the stem.

"Jax said their effect would weaken after being plucked. We need to return to the castle when they're most potent."

"The more powerful ones are farther in the back," Finnean said.

"Wait." But it was too late. Finnean was venturing deeper into the cave.

Velamir picked more ovaline and walked to the front of the cave. He waited outside for Finnean, but a minute passed without any sign of him. Latimus waved at him in the distance, and Velamir held up the bag. He set it down at the entrance and returned inside. He was blind without any light. The farther he went the more worried he became. Where was Finnean? There was a long rumbling sound that echoed around the cave every few seconds. It vibrated, raising the hairs on Velamir's neck. Something was wrong.

He saw the torchlight in the distance. It illuminated the metal of Finnean's sword. Why had he drawn his weapon? Velamir glanced at the shape that clarified under the torch's glow, and his heart dropped like a stone to the bottom of his stomach. It was the Karakan. It was large, horrifyingly massive. Velamir's eyes trailed the length of its body. He could make out its tail near his boot. It was at least three times the size of a normal rumlok. He recalled Latimus's warnings.

"Finnean," Velamir whispered. "Don't do any-thing rash."

Finnean glanced at Velamir. "I have to do this."

He held the torch in a tight grip as he brought his blade closer to the rumlok in slow agonizing seconds. Velamir reached out, moving closer, trying to stop the inevitable. Finnean's sword pierced the Karakan's hide, again, and again, and again. Brutal, merciless strikes. Velamir tasted metal, in the air and on his tongue, as drops of blood splattered onto him. A large red eye opened. The following roar pierced Velamir's ears, and he wouldn't doubt if it could be heard all the way to the castle. Finnean smashed his crimson-coated sword onto the Karakan's head. Giant canines flashed as the rumlok caught the blade between its teeth. The beast swung its head, and the sword smacked the cave wall. Finnean's eyes were wide, and he shook his head in horror.

"Run!" he screamed at Velamir. "Run!"

They took off toward the opening of the cave, the Karakan's heavy paws pounding behind them. Finnean lost the torch along the way, and the sudden blackness was blinding. Velamir saw the cave opening appear ahead, terror in every rushed breath. Finnean was just behind him. He wouldn't make it unless Velamir did something. Velamir paused for a second, allowing Finnean to pass him. He drew his sword and pressed his back against the wall. As soon as the Karakan drew near, he pushed off the wall and pointed his sword at the approaching beast. It punctured the Karakan's chest. The rumlok reared with a gruesome howl. When it stood up on its feet, it was at least twice as tall as Velamir. The rumlok slashed a paw across Velamir's chest. Anguish struck Velamir's core as the razor-sharp claws pierced his flesh. His cry rivaled the Karakan's. Adrenaline kept him moving. The rumlok swiped at him again, but he ducked under the blow. Velamir grabbed the thick fur on the Karakan's arm. He hauled himself onto the beast's back. The Karakan charged out of the cave, and the wind blew its thick, mangled fur back. Velamir heard screaming, and his immediate thought was Kasdeya. He couldn't let the Karakan hurt her. The rumlok rose into the air again, and Velamir lost his grip. He crashed onto the ground, the breath knocked from him. A wave of dizziness crossed his vision. The Karakan's front paws smacked down near his face. The beast growled, and Velamir closed his eyes, awaiting the killing blow.

NATASSA
KINGDOM OF VERIN
THE KARAKAN'S LAIR

Natassa stared after Finnean and Velamir, watching until they disappeared into the mouth of the cave. She recalled how Velamir lifted her off his horse, with a grin and the audacity to tell her he knew she could dismount herself. Natassa heard footfalls beside her and a soft laugh.

"You're blushing," Krea said.

The heat in Natassa's cheeks increased. "I'm not."

Krea's smile widened. "He's the one you were painting. You've met him before?"

"Not exactly. Unless you count dreams as a meeting

place." Natassa turned to face her. "There is something else I need to tell you about, something important."

Krea's brow creased in worry. Natassa took her arm and pulled her farther away from Kasdeya and Latimus. She told her everything, about Thorsten's death, about her power. She brushed her hair aside to show her birthmark.

Krea shook her head in wonderment. "You're a Shadow Manos."

"But I somehow command two shadows."

Krea gasped. "But that's impossible. Kasdeya doesn't know . . . right?"

"I didn't tell her."

Krea let out a sigh of relief. "Good."

Kasdeya bustled over to them, a frown marring her features. Natassa and Krea stopped speaking as soon as she came.

"What do you want?" Natassa asked, her posture defensive.

"I am your princess, as you know." Kasdeya smirked. "You should attend to me, not amuse yourself with useless conversations."

"You will never be a princess, not a true one anyway," Krea spat at her sister.

Kasdeya kept her gaze fixed on Natassa. "Do not forget our agreement. I will save you from the responsibilities of being a princess. I will save you from Draven. But you will. Not. Tell. Anyone. About. Me." Kasdeya stressed each word.

A loud roar startled them, and they glanced at the cave. Latimus unsheathed his sword, looking at them.

"Stay back," he called.

It seemed like endless minutes passed. All Natassa could hear were howls and shouts. Finnean ran out of the cave. He tripped and crashed onto the ground, his face stricken. Another roar erupted, and the largest monster Natassa had ever seen exploded out of the cave, muscles rippling under thick fur matted with blood. This must be the Karakan.

"Four kingdoms," Latimus breathed.

The monster let out another murderous howl, rising onto his hind legs. Something fell from his back.

"That's Velamir," Natassa gasped.

Velamir rolled over, and the rumlok dropped beside him, jaws opening. Natassa lifted her skirt and ran, ignoring Krea's screams. She stepped in the Karakan's path, blocking his way to Velamir. The beast growled and lowered his fangs near her face. Natassa closed her eyes, seeking her shadows. It was easier to reach them. They drew on either side of her. Ghostly hands clasped onto her shoulders.

Speak to him, Natassa, a voice told her.

Connect with his mind, the other said.

Natassa concentrated. A pulsing heat grew at her forehead. The Karakan's hot breath blew her hair back. She searched for a connection and found it. She was in the Karakan's mind. A cry slipped past her lips as she saw the torture and agony the animal had gone through. The mutilation and loss.

"I'm sorry," she whispered, reaching out.

Her hand brushed blood-soaked fur. The rumlok whined, low and pitiful.

"We won't hurt you."

She sensed a deep thirst in him to kill, but that had been drilled into him. It wasn't who he was. Her shadows helped her delve into his mind. She filtered through the rumlok's memories, revealing things the beast itself had closed away. A moment of the rumlok running in Savoria, protecting his human family.

You weren't meant to be this way, she whispered in his mind.

Natassa continued patting him until the beast's anger receded. She kept her lids closed, picturing him as he used to be.

"You can change." A rush of energy flooded through her. It was the Lure. Her shadow was giving her strength.

You must do everything for them first. Earn their loyalty.

Her mother's words echoed in her mind. They were whispers in her ears; they were power behind her actions. She was Princess Natassa Hartinza, and she would face her fears.

55

VELAMIR
KINGDOM OF VERIN
THE KARAKAN'S LAIR

"OPEN YOUR EYES, Velamir!" The shout seemed far away. "Damn you!"

Hands prodded him, tearing his shirt. He groaned. The scent of warm blood sent nausea up his throat. He blinked back the weakness and opened his eyes. Latimus smiled when he saw him awake, and Finnean's expression held guilt. Velamir glanced past them, staring at Kasdeya, and his heart almost stopped. She stood before the Karakan. The beast seemed to be in a trance and lowered itself before her, almost in deference. Her lips were pressed tight, her brows squeezed together, and eyes closed in concentration. The rumlok's breath ruffled her hair, and the lighter strands in the brown mass glowed gold. There was a mark on her forehead. A phoenix just like Jax's. He remembered Jax pulling up his sleeve.

This is who I am, Vel.

She was a Shadow Manos. A gleaming light emanated from the mark. Velamir glanced at her hand, where it was placed against the rumlok's fur. The Karakan turned away from her and retreated into the cave. Its head hung low.

"What in the Empire was that?" Latimus asked.

Velamir continued watching Kasdeya as she approached them. He didn't know any Shadow Manos who had the power to control animals. What was she, or rather, *who* was she? She dropped beside him, peering at his chest. Velamir glanced down, seeing the blood pooling across his skin.

"It looks bad," Kasdeya whispered, reaching out and then freezing, breaths from touching his wound.

Velamir winced at the ache in his midsection. He clenched his jaw. Kasdeya pulled her hand back, touching her hair instead, dragging a thick strand over her mark. Velamir caught her fingers in his, and she stared at him with wide eyes.

"Thank you," he said softly.

If she hadn't stepped in the rumlok's path, he would've been killed. She stared into his eyes for a long moment. "I—" She winced and hunched her shoulders.

He sat up, ignoring the pain that tore through his middle. "Kasdeya?"

She sagged against him, collapsing on his bloody chest. "Kasdeya!" He cupped her cheeks.

He looked up, locking eyes with Finnean, who was the closest to him. "Help me!"

Finnean stared, slack-jawed, frozen in place. Velamir glanced past him at Latimus and the princess and Kasdeya's twin. Latimus was backing away. The princess was shaking her head with wide eyes. Kasdeya's twin rushed forward.

"Wake up! Na—Deya, open your eyes." Her lips trembled as she glanced at Velamir. "I don't know what to do."

"Did you know?" Velamir asked her.

She hesitated and then nodded.

"Has she ever done something like that before?"

"I'm not sure," Krea told him. She checked Kasdeya's pulse and said, "I think she just needs rest."

Latimus gained courage and approached them. "We don't have time to wait. We have to bring the ovaline back."

"We will remain here till she's better. You can ride ahead."

Latimus looked uncertain. "So you can go off on your own? I'm not going to let you get away, Velamir. You're coming to Verintown."

Finnean stood before Velamir could respond. "I'm here, Latimus. You are not the only one entrusted with this mission. If anyone will ensure Velamir's return, it would be me."

Latimus scoffed. "You were almost killed by the Karakan. I'm certain it was your foolish actions that led to the encounter."

"At least I was brave enough to fight it instead of staying behind."

Latimus fumed, his fists clenching.

Velamir spoke. "I will return to the castle, Latimus. You have my word. I don't break my promises."

Latimus held his stare for a long moment and then glanced down at Kasdeya's prone form, distrust evident in his glare.

"The bag with the ovaline is by the cave entrance," Velamir told him.

Latimus went to retrieve it, and the princess followed. "Take me with you. I don't want to be stuck here with that witch."

Krea gasped. "How could you say that?"

The princess's lips twisted in disgust. "To think she was hiding this right under my nose."

Krea stormed to the princess, yanking her away to speak to her in private. Velamir returned his attention to Kasdeya and examined her. Her eyes were closed, thick lashes brushing over pale cheeks. Despite being unconscious, her face held its worried state. Lips pressed tightly, brow furrowed.

"I need to cauterize your chest, Velamir," Finnean told him.

Velamir nodded, tearing his gaze from Kasdeya. Finnean built a fire and then extended one of his swords, placing it into the flames.

"When you were lying here, unmoving, it was like seeing my brother all over again." His words surprised Velamir. "You probably don't know what happened to him."

Finnean's fingers dug into the dirt, his face downcast.

"Latimus told me," Velamir said.

"I felt like I failed again." Finnean ran a hand through his short wavy hair, coating it in dirt. "I thought I caused another death."

"But you didn't kill your brother," Velamir told him.

"I dared him. I told him until he was brave enough to fight the damn Karakan, there was no way he could come with me on my missions." A tear slipped down his face. "I didn't know he would go . . . I didn't."

Velamir winced. "I'm sorry."

"As you lay there, I contemplated killing myself." Finnean's eyes were bloodshot when he looked up. "But I'm still here, and I pray every day that my death comes."

Velamir didn't know what to say. He watched Latimus ride away, shaking his head at the princess, refusing to bring her with him. Velamir turned back to Finnean, seeing a plea in his stare, desperation in the slump of his posture.

"We all make mistakes. Mistakes are easy. What's hard is changing the mistakes to something good. Instead of burying yourself in self-pity, help others. Take your mind off it."

"You think I haven't tried? Nothing works."

"Then you haven't tried hard enough."

Finnean took his blade from the fire and brought it to Velamir's chest. Krea came to assist, gently placing Kasdeya's head onto her lap. Velamir braced himself for the pain. Excruciating minutes later, Velamir attempted to fix his leather armor and battered shirt over his cauterized wounds. Large tears drove through the leather.

The princess stormed over to them. She pointed overhead. "It's getting dark. I don't want to stay here all night."

Velamir glanced down at Kasdeya. She was still unconscious.

"We should go," Krea said. "The rumlok might decide to emerge again."

Velamir hefted Kasdeya in his arms, bringing her to Vandal. He draped her over the saddle and mounted up behind her, turning her over and pulling her up into his arms. He winced as his movements tugged at his chest wounds. He took the reins and glanced back. Finnean held the reins of his horse, leading it forward. Krea and the princess sat in the saddle.

They traveled at a slow pace so Finnean could keep up. Hours passed, and darkness covered them, the only light coming from the stars and moon. Velamir felt movement against his chest and the intake of breath. She was awake.

NATASSA
KINGDOM OF VERIN

Natassa blinked, darkness enveloping her. Hoofbeats sounded in her ear, and her head bounced against something rigid. She reached out, her hand wrapping around the pommel of the saddle. Dark shapes of trees passed by. She looked down and noticed an arm wrapped around her waist, holding her in place. She gasped and straightened.

"Steady, you're all right." Velamir's voice rumbled near her ear.

"What happened?"

"You fainted. We are riding to Castle Verin."

He looked past her, his face closed off, and she knew he saw something in the distance. She turned to look, but Velamir pulled the horse to a halt. She fell against him at the rough movement, and she reached out to catch herself, her hands gripping his shoulders. Natassa shoved away. A second too late, she realized she moved back too far. Her balance was lost. She was falling, falling, and then his arm was there, locking behind her with unfathomable strength.

"Careful there," he said, pulling her up.

"Sorry." She was sure her entire face was on fire.

"Don't apologize. I don't mind."

Natassa wanted to fan herself. She had blushed in this single day more than she had in her entire life. She adjusted herself in the saddle, sitting upright so Velamir no longer carried her weight on his arm.

"Who goes there?" a voice called.

Natassa peered into the distance. Moonlight shone on several men on horseback. They rode closer, and Natassa's heart froze. It was Draven. She sank back, closer to Velamir. He glanced down, released the reins with one hand, and tightened his arm around her.

"Are you all right?"

Natassa nodded, breathing deeply. She had to pull herself together.

She almost jumped out of her skin at a sudden shriek. A shape hurtled past them, rushing to Draven.

The prince dismounted just as the figure plunged into his arms. It was Kasdeya, it had to be. She sobbed hysterically. Natassa had to close her open mouth. If this was how Kasdeya thought she would act, then she did not know her at all.

"Princess!" Prince Draven stumbled over his words, unable to comprehend what was happening. "What-why-how-how are you here?"

Kasdeya pulled away but kept a firm grip on his arms. "Oh, it was awful! This mercenary, Vykus, kidnapped us on our way to your kingdom."

The moonlight shone on the couple, highlighting them as though it knew how much Draven loved being the center of attention.

"Kidnapped? Vykus?"

His voice hardened when he said Vykus's name. Natassa realized he must know him.

"We must get married at once," Prince Draven said, his eyes glazed and unfocused as he thought of something else.

He isn't even concerned for her well-being, Natassa thought. *He wants to ensure his position on the throne.*

"I agree, my love," Kasdeya said ardently.

Draven's eyes bore down on her. "Are you feeling well, Princess?"

Kasdeya fluttered her lashes. "Now that I am with you, I've never been better."

Natassa felt Velamir shake with laughter. She shook her head. Kasdeya was taking things too far.

Draven seemed confused. "I . . . I am glad you are better disposed to me, Princess." He winked at Kasdeya.

Natassa's stomach swirled, and she felt like throwing up what little she had inside.

"It's Natassa to you." Kasdeya let out a tinkling laugh.

"Of course, Natassa." Draven nodded. "Let us be off to my kingdom. I am in a hurry to be wed." He sent Kasdeya another wink.

He pulled her to his horse, lifting her onto the saddle. Kasdeya met Natassa's eyes in the small distance separating them. Her smirk grew. Natassa looked away, not wanting to see Kasdeya a second longer. Draven mounted behind her. His gaze swept over the rest of them. For a moment, his eyes lingered on Natassa. Her heart almost stopped when his eyes narrowed.

He knows.

But then he addressed Kasdeya. "Natassa, my dear, aren't you forgetting your handmaidens?"

Kasdeya sniffed. "They have disappointed me thoroughly during our trip. I have no use for them any longer. They can work as scullery maids in Castle Verin. They deserve it after everything I have done for them."

"Why did you leave the castle so soon? Scared you would be thrown in the dungeons?" Velamir called to the prince.

Draven's horse shifted restlessly. "I wouldn't be worried about me, if I were you." He lifted his fist. "Let us be off!"

They rode in single file past them, raising a cloud of dust in their wake. Natassa watched them leave. She felt a prick of pain in her heart when she thought of Kasdeya's betrayal, but she was grateful. Because, in a way,

Kasdeya had saved her from a terrible fate. Draven's piercing stare rose in her mind. Did he know something was different? What if he knew Natassa was playing him? But why wouldn't he confront her if he knew?

Then you might as well call this farewell our last, because I will be dead before that happens.

Those had been her last words to him. Surely, he was suspicious of the princess's suddenly docile behavior.

Finnean rode up beside Velamir. Krea sat in the saddle behind him. "Shall we be off?"

They continued riding, traveling for so long, Natassa felt her head bobbing along with the horse's rhythm.

"You saved me from the Karakan." After so much stillness, Velamir's voice startled her.

"I couldn't let you die," she responded. "Besides, you saved me first."

He leaned closer to her, his breath brushing her neck, causing her stomach to flutter. "I guess we're even, then."

She had never felt sensations such as these before. Natassa could only think it couldn't be healthy to have her heart racing faster than a lancer horse. She evened her breath, focusing ahead to see a castle in the distance. They rode through the town, and Natassa thought it was strange when she didn't see a single person. She stared up at the castle as they crossed the drawbridge. It was beautiful, but nothing compared to the palace she had called her home. They dismounted by the royal stables. The stable hands rushed out and took their horses. They were about to enter the keep when a squadron of soldiers surrounded them. Natassa's hand instinctively reached for her knife belt, feeling only the plain work dress. Krea stood stiffly beside her. Velamir appeared resigned.

"How can I help you?" he asked the soldiers.

A tall, broad-shouldered man with piercing green eyes and a thick scar on his face brushed through the circle of soldiers.

His lip curled as he addressed Velamir. "You are under arrest and sentenced to death for working against the Empire."

56

CORALIE
KINGDOM OF VERIN
CASTLE VERIN

CORALIE JERKED AWAKE when she heard voices. Latimus was in the room, playing with an empty bowl across from Jax, who was crushing ingredients together. She stood and rushed to them, nearly ripping Latimus's arm from his socket as she yanked him toward her.

"Did you find it? Where is Velamir?"

Latimus winced and touched his arm. "I came ahead."

Jax turned, holding a bowl filled with a thick-looking liquid. He walked past her, heading to Mordon's bed. Coralie released Latimus's arm and followed Jax, wringing her hands. Jax lifted the wooden spoon from the bowl, scraping excess liquid off the rim of the dish. He opened Mordon's mouth and slipped the spoon inside. Coralie assisted him. Jax repeated the process several times. Boltrex took that moment to enter.

"Will he live?"

Jax shook his head. "It is too early to say for certain."

"How long until we know?" Coralie asked.

"I will give him the antidote again in a short while. We should know soon."

Mordon's skin was less pale and his breathing more regular, but he still hadn't regained consciousness. Coralie returned to Latimus's side as Boltrex took the seat she had been in earlier.

"Where is Velamir?" she asked again.

Latimus fidgeted. "He was injured during the fight with the Karakan. We also had a setback. We ran into Vykus along the way."

Coralie seethed. "Vykus is a problem we don't need right now. He's a rotten seed that grew quickly, his allies spread all around, roots to keep him grounded."

Latimus cleared his throat, bringing her attention back to him. "We saved some women he held captive. But they weren't just any hostages." Latimus paused. "I mean . . . one of them is the emperor's daughter."

Coralie drew in a sharp breath. "Princess Natassa?"

Her fists clenched. If Vykus dared to take even the emperor's own child, it meant Prolus had made his way into the palace. Vykus couldn't have done it alone. Prolus hadn't just taken Ayleth using Draven, his darkness had seeped into Hearcross too.

Latimus nodded. "Finnean and Velamir are bringing her here. She learned Prince Draven was in the castle and wanted to reunite with him."

Coralie laughed. "He is long gone."

"There's also the matter of her handmaidens. One of them . . ." Latimus trailed off, looking uneasy. Coralie saw his eyes follow Jax's movements behind her.

She urged him to continue but he hesitated, shifting his feet.

The chair creaked as Boltrex stood. "Captain Blayton!" he called. "I need to speak with you."

Latimus sent her an apologetic glance, and Coralie waved him off. She watched them step into the hall, wondering what Latimus had been about to tell her. She returned to the bed, observing Jax care for Mordon. The Shadow Manos looked up.

"Your general will kill me."

It was so unexpected, Coralie didn't know what to say.

"I was taken against my will and brought to Tariqi. I was raised by them, but I fought against their hold every day. If I told you I would change, that I would help this kingdom, would you believe me?"

She searched his earnest blue eyes, the hood that was falling back exposing blond curls. She fell into the seat with a less than graceful thump.

"How can I trust you?" she asked him.

"You slept for hours. I was the only one in this room. I could have killed you at any moment."

But I didn't. The unspoken words hung in the air.

"I know Velamir would say the same. He has always chased the right path."

Coralie's smile was sad. "Even if I wanted to, I can't pardon you. My uncle is the king."

"You are the princess. That must count for something. I've seen the way you command a room. I watched you kill a rumlok. I know you can get your way. You already rule."

Coralie rubbed her forehead. "How will you prove to me you mean what you say?"

"Prolus will arrive in a day or less. You have mere hours to evacuate the people from the town and shelter them in the castle. Do not leave them in the town. They will not be spared."

Coralie remembered the note sent to Draven. "You heard me speaking with my maid. I know Prolus is coming."

"But you didn't know how long you had. I'm telling you, he will be here before dawn."

Coralie hesitated. Should she trust him? He seemed to sense her thoughts.

"You were one of our targets. I could've completed at least part of my mission by killing you." He looked down at Mordon. "But I didn't kill you because I wanted your forgiveness or mercy. I've just . . . I've never seen anyone look at someone the way you look at him."

"What?" she stuttered.

"When you love someone, you would do anything and chance sacrificing your life for them. When you and Mordon fought the rumlok that day, I saw it in his face just as I see it in yours. You don't have to hide it. I know you love him just as he loves you. And I won't be the one who kills that. We are living in war. The bloodshed doesn't end. Love is the only way to heal those open wounds."

Coralie looked at her lap, examining the calluses on her palms. Warmth rushed through her at his words. Could Mordon possibly love her? She stared at his limp form, his strong face. He'd been through so much. He'd lost family just as she had. But he always hid behind something. He cloaked himself in anger and never let anyone past that to see the vulnerable heart within. But she knew it was there, she had glimpsed it. She cleared her throat. "Even if I let you stay, you'll never be safe in the Empire, not until a new rule is established."

"I am ready for a change," he said.

"If you are willing to face the challenges, I might give you a chance."

A slow smile spread across his face. "Thank you."

Coralie shifted in the seat, unable to look at Mordon without thinking about what Jax had said. She thought of a distraction and hoped Boltrex was still in the hall, because she had to inform him about Prolus. She was halfway standing in her seat when a groan of pain brought her attention to Mordon. His eyes were still closed, but he seemed to regain consciousness. She gripped his hand, entwining her fingers with his.

"Coralie," he whispered, and opened his eyes.

She smiled, tears blurring her vision. "Mordon."

Jax helped her prop up the pillows behind him. Mordon moaned, sinking back. She glanced at Jax, who nodded.

"He's fighting the poison."

Mordon sank in and out of fevered sleep for an hour. Coralie stayed beside him, giving orders and calling for food. A maid entered the room and set a tray with soup and bread on the side table. She curtsied to Coralie before leaving. Jax added a tonic to the soup.

"What is that?" Coralie asked him.

"It will speed his recovery. We make this for Deedan soldiers in Tariqi," Jax responded.

Mordon shifted and awakened, a sheen of sweat on his skin. Coralie was happy to see color return to his face, and the glassy look in his eyes was gone. Mordon gave her one of his half smiles. She brought the tray closer to the bed, lifting the bowl of soup and handing it to him.

"Beautiful," he mumbled, staring at her.

Coralie froze. "What did you say?"

He broke eye contact to look at the bowl. "The soup looks good."

She gave him a spoon, perhaps a little rougher than necessary.

"I don't think my hands work anymore," Mordon said. "Would you?" He motioned at the bowl.

Coralie heard Jax's retreating footsteps and glanced back to see him peering at his journal. He was smiling and definitely not paying attention to whatever was written on the pages. Coralie turned back to Mordon.

"I am not feeding you."

Mordon looked dejected and lifted the spoon, dropping soup onto the sheets and himself. Coralie fought a smile when he exaggerated each of his movements. His hand was shaking so hard that the soup kept splashing off the spoon.

She rolled her eyes and sighed before reaching for the bowl. "Give it to me."

Mordon's full smirk unleashed. Coralie dipped the spoon into the bowl and brought it to Mordon's mouth. He watched her boldly, and Coralie returned his stare.

"Were you grieved during my perilous state?"

"Everyone was."

Mordon searched her eyes. "But were you perhaps more worried?"

Coralie couldn't stop thinking about what Jax said. She found it hard to hold his gaze without fearing giving away her thoughts.

"What are you trying to say?"

"I was simply wondering, since you've been very attentive with my health and well-being . . ."

Coralie's lips pressed into a thin line. "Don't be ridiculous. Of course I care." She changed the subject. "You are probably wondering who poisoned you."

The door opened, and Boltrex stepped inside. "I can explain all that."

Mordon smiled at his father, but it was strained, half-hearted.

"How soon will he be up?" Boltrex asked.

Jax spoke. "I recommend he stay off his feet for a day or two at least."

Boltrex's forehead creased with disapproval.

"I will be up in no time, Father," Mordon reassured him, all playfulness gone. He took the bowl from Coralie.

"Princess, I need to speak with you," Boltrex told her.

He motioned to the door, and they stepped out into the hall.

"What is it?" Coralie asked.

"I just received news that all the families in the town

have been evacuated to the castle and are now in the Stone Chamber. Can you explain this?"

"I issued the order. Prolus will be here in a matter of hours."

Boltrex's lips thinned. "And how do you know this?"

Coralie hesitated. "The Shadow Manos told me."

"We cannot trust his word. I should put him in the dungeons with Velamir."

"Velamir is in the dungeons?"

"He just arrived."

Coralie's eyes caught on the key ring strung to his belt. "I don't think Jax is lying to me. He wants to help us."

"In exchange for what?" Boltrex crossed his arms.

"In exchange for being here, as a free man. He never wanted to be part of Tariqi's army."

"He might be playing another trick. And I'm not a fool to fall for it."

"Even if he is, I had to act. I cannot risk the safety of my people."

"I need to meet with King Dale to discuss this further."

Coralie straightened her shoulders. "I think you are forgetting something, General."

His brow creased in confusion.

"I don't need your permission."

They locked gazes for a long moment until Boltrex nodded. "As you wish." He waved a hand at the guard stationed in the corridor. "Send for Commander Rolix."

The guard rushed off, and Boltrex walked back into the healing chamber. Jax stepped out minutes later, joining Coralie in the hall.

"He was shooting me death glares," Jax told her, and she knew he was speaking of Boltrex.

Commander Rolix walked down the hall along with a scout. They bowed at the sight of her.

"What news do you bring?"

"The Dark Lord Prolus's army is approaching." The scout's voice wavered. "We only have a short time to prepare."

"How many men?"

"Three thousand at least," the scout replied. He ducked into the healing chamber with the commander.

Coralie turned to Jax. "Let's gather the remaining servants and bring them to the Stone Chamber. It's beginning."

57

VELAMIR
KINGDOM OF VERIN
CASTLE VERIN

THE CELL DOOR clanged shut behind Velamir. He spun around and grabbed the iron bars in his fists. Boltrex held Velamir's sword. He stared at it as if it was a treasured belonging before placing the sword on a shelf filled with other weapons.

"I have much to ask you, but it will have to wait."

"Why put me here? Why not kill me now?" Velamir asked.

"I have a feeling you are important to Prolus and the Savagelanders." Boltrex examined him. "And I want to find out why."

He turned and walked up the stairs leading out of the dungeons.

"You're making a mistake!" Velamir shouted.

He grunted in frustration and pulled away from the bars. Prolus would be here soon, and people would die. Velamir could prevent that. He could reason with Prolus or convince Dale to surrender. There was no chance Verin would emerge from this victorious. The dungeon door closed at the top as Boltrex left. Velamir sank to the ground and closed his eyes.

A maniacal laugh sounded from the cell across from him. Velamir peered into the darkness and saw a dirty man leaning against the bars. He was holding an arm over his thin stomach, trying to contain his laughter. As Velamir's vision adjusted to the dark, he could make out the rips and holes in the man's clothes.

"It's just us here!" he screeched.

Velamir was alarmed by the psychotic gleam in his eyes. He peered at the other cells.

"Where are the other prisoners?"

"They were executed weeks ago. It's been me . . . just me . . ."

Velamir heard sadness in his voice. "Who are you?"

"It doesn't matter who I am or who I was," he said with a faraway look in his eyes. "No one bothered. I have been here for years and never got out."

"What did you do?"

The man chuckled again. "I was put here for a deed I didn't commit. I was framed. But here I am, still burdened with another's sins."

His words were too eloquent to belong to a servant or someone of the lower class. Velamir examined him. He had been someone of importance once.

The man stared at him, and his eyes widened as if seeing him for the first time. "You look just like him," he murmured so quietly Velamir had to lean forward as far as he could and strain his ears to hear.

"Like who?" Velamir asked.

"Your father. He must be your father," the man said, nodding to himself.

Velamir gripped the bars again. "Did you know my father? I have no memory of him. I was orphaned when I was a child. My name is Velamir."

The man looked at him, confusion creasing lines into his wrinkled face. "Velamir? No, no, no. His son's name was Alaric . . . Maybe I am mistaken."

"What is the name of the man you believe to be my father?"

The man continued muttering, "Orphan? If I am right, you are no orphan. Your father is alive."

Velamir sat back. How could it be? Emotions flitted through him. What would it be like for him to meet his actual father?

"What is his name?" Velamir repeated.

The old man backed away, suddenly shaking. He huddled in the corner of his cell and wouldn't answer any more of Velamir's questions. Velamir sighed in defeat and paced the cell. Hours passed. He wondered how the others fared. Jax, Lissa, but most of all, Kasdeya. She had a unique power, one that would endanger her in the Empire. Velamir wasn't sure he could trust Latimus or Princess Natassa not to reveal what they had seen her do. Finnean . . . he looked like he could keep a secret. Velamir pressed his forehead against the grimy cell wall.

A second later, he heard the horn. Loud and blaring. A warning.

CORALIE
CASTLE VERIN

Coralie surveyed the inside of the Stone Chamber with a satisfied nod. She had gotten all the women who weren't part of the guard inside, as well as the children and her uncle. King Dale looked weaker than ever before and had sunken into one of the chairs in the chamber. His three loyal bodyguards surrounded him along with Advisor Welix. The general had ordered most of the men to fight. No matter what occupation they had, farmers or blacksmith or cooks. Women clustered in corners of the chamber, holding their children. The sound of the horn blowing brought a few people to tears. That could only mean one thing: Prolus's army had arrived.

Coralie hoped she could keep the people in the chamber safe. The Stone Chamber doors were strong enough to withstand a battering ram, and they blended in with the walls of the corridor, making the entryway of the chamber hard to spot. The best way for her to protect the people was to be outside the chamber, fighting. She wanted to be out there. It was a chance to attack the army that killed her parents.

She glanced at the two women beside her. They had introduced themselves as Kasdeya and Krea, the women Velamir and Finnean brought when they had returned. Coralie had been stunned when she first saw them because they looked exactly like Princess Natassa. Coralie wondered where the princess had gone, and they told her they had met with Prince Draven on the road. Coralie noticed they weren't doing anything, so she had recruited them to help.

"I need to check on something," she told the closest woman. She couldn't remember which twin she was. "Keep an eye on things here."

She nodded, and Coralie walked past her, eyes on the chamber door.

"Coralie," someone called behind her.

King Dale leaned out of his chair and held his hand toward her. He fell into a heap of coughs, his chest heaving with choked breaths. Coralie rushed to him, looking at his bodyguards, but they didn't seem concerned. They watched as if this was a daily occurrence.

"Uncle!" Coralie grabbed his shoulder. "What's wrong?"

He clutched her arm. "Don't—don't leave. It is too dangerous."

"I won't be gone long. Don't fret, I can take care of myself."

He gave her a tired smile. "I know, but that won't stop me from worrying."

She patted his shoulder and stepped back. "I will return as soon as I can."

Coralie turned to leave and found Advisor Welix standing in her way. He motioned for her to follow him and stepped out of earshot of her uncle, glancing over her shoulder at the king.

"Princess, the king has hidden his illness from you.

He ordered me not to say anything, but you must know the truth. He is very sick."

Coralie nodded. She had guessed. "How long will it take for him to recover?"

"That is the thing, Princess, we don't think he will recover." Advisor Welix had sympathy in his eyes. "After the stress of the war and then this sickness . . . it is too much for him."

Coralie shook her head in denial. "I will find a way."

The advisor wore a pitying look. "There is no stopping fate, Princess. You are his heir. You must marry to ensure this kingdom will stand."

Coralie was outraged. "You speak of marriage when we have war at our doors. Forget marriage. There is a high chance we won't survive this battle!"

There was silence.

Coralie realized her mistake as soon as she heard moaning and crying from the people in the chamber. She, the princess, was supposed to give them hope. Instead, she had crushed anything they had left and threw it out the window. What kind of leader was she? The wailing grew louder, and Coralie wanted to cover her ears.

Someone shouted, "Stop!"

Silence filled the chamber again. Coralie looked around, trying to find the person who had spoken. It was one of the twins.

"Don't you see? Crying won't help. Your husbands and sons, our brothers, our loved ones are fighting out there. Would you want them to see you like this?" Her twin stood behind her like a pillar of rock.

The girl continued her speech. "We have to be a

beacon of hope! We must see the light no matter what. You all have weapons. If they break through those doors, we will not crumble. We will fight. For our lives, our family, and our kingdom!" Determination lit her features, and she spoke like she was part of Verin even though she had just arrived a few hours ago.

The women nodded at the girl's words and picked up their swords, holding them in their fists. A wave of calmness fell over Coralie, and she felt rejuvenated by the girl's speech.

"It is true. There is a fire against us. And in the end, the fire could burn us, or ignite us into an unstoppable force. What choice do you make?" The girl looked each person in the eye, pulling back some of the hair spilling over her face.

Coralie glanced at Advisor Welix and noticed the impressed expression he wore. She went to stand beside the girl.

"My people, just now, I was hopeless. And that is a wretched feeling. I apologize to all of you. A leader should always have hope. And I will. From now on, I promise you." Coralie turned to look at the girl. "And my choice? I choose to fight."

The girl smiled at her. One woman in the crowd raised her sword. "I choose to fight!"

Slowly, all the people raised their weapons, fortitude in their stances.

"Thank you," Coralie said to the girl.

She nodded, touching her head with a frown. Her twin stepped closer. "Are you all right, Kasdeya?"

Kasdeya nodded again and smiled. "Yes, don't worry."

Coralie watched them for a second, wondering if she should say something, but they turned away to speak privately.

Coralie returned to the advisor. "I need to leave. Can you handle things for a while?"

"As long as you leave her here." He motioned to Kasdeya.

As soon as Coralie stepped out of the chamber, the sounds of shouting and chaos met her ears. Soldiers ran everywhere, their boots echoing in the halls. Standing in front of the Stone Chamber doors were at least ten guards, along with Jax. He looked nervous. Coralie walked to him.

"I need you to do something."

He nodded in acceptance, and she pulled out the ring of keys that she had snagged from Boltrex earlier.

"Get Velamir out of the dungeons."

58

VELAMIR
KINGDOM OF VERIN
CASTLE VERIN

THE DOOR TO the dungeon creaked open, and someone hurried down the steps. Velamir smiled when Jax came into view.

Jax held up the dungeon cell keys. "I came to get you out."

Velamir was astonished at the sight. "How?"

"The princess. She thinks you can help. The battle has started, Vel."

Jax opened the cell door, and Velamir stepped out, moving fast toward the weapon shelf. He sheathed his sword and grabbed his dagger. Pain rippled across his chest at his rough movements. Jax handed him a vial.

"I overheard Latimus saying you were injured."

Velamir nodded his thanks and gulped

the bitter contents down. The pain receded to a faint ache. Jax took a few steps up the stairs, and Velamir moved to follow him but paused.

He turned back, staring into the old man's cell. "Come with us."

The prisoner didn't move from his spot in the corner.

"He's safer here, Vel," Jax said quietly.

After a moment, Velamir said, "I will come back. You hold the answer to an important question."

This time the old man responded, his voice scratchy. "Then let's hope I am still alive to answer."

"We have to go," Jax urged him.

They rushed up the stairs into a corridor. Velamir heard shouting, and several guards entered the hall, running past them.

"Prolus is attacking! Prolus is attacking!"

"Where is Cora?" Velamir asked.

"She was heading to the entrance of the keep, last I saw."

They had taken two steps when someone stumbled into the corridor before them. Velamir tensed, and unease filled him at the sight of Mordon. The same wariness reflected in Mordon's face. Velamir noted Mordon was armored lightly for battle, perhaps to retain some of the stamina that the poison had stolen away.

"I see you have recovered sufficiently."

Mordon shook his head. "You thought you could infiltrate and kill us one by one? Your game was foiled." He drew his sword. "My father was right about the Shadow Manos. He rescued you from the dungeons so you can continue playing your game, but I won't allow it."

Velamir held up his hands. "I don't want to fight you. The enemy is at your door. Cora sent Jax to get me out. She said she needed my help."

"You're lying," Mordon sneered. "She wouldn't do that." He advanced. "So tell me, who are you? You aren't the Cavalier or Winston's son. My father suspects you're from the Savagelands."

"We need to get to the gates. If you want to fight, fight there."

Mordon laughed. "You think I'm going to fall for that? I know you are planning something the moment my back is turned. I'm not a fool to believe you will help Verin."

Velamir stepped back, but Mordon kept advancing.

"You chose Tariqi, and now you will die because of your choice." Mordon swung his sword at Velamir's head.

Velamir unsheathed his blade and Mordon's clanged on top of it.

"Believe me, I wanted to fight you. I wanted to kill you," Velamir told him, smashing his sword away. "But I realized revenge wouldn't satisfy me."

"What do you mean?" Mordon circled him.

"You killed the only father I ever knew!" Velamir spat out, pointing his sword at Mordon.

Mordon's eyes widened. "What?"

"Winston, you fool! You killed Winston!"

Realization dawned on Mordon's face. "You knew?"

"I saw you that night." Velamir spoke through gritted teeth.

He glanced to his side and noticed Jax had disappeared. Mordon took that moment to attack. He rushed at Velamir, slicing at his midsection. Velamir brought his sword down against his, and Mordon's blade dragged along the stone floor. Velamir didn't retreat. He threw blow after blow at Mordon. The pain and hurt he had suffered the night Winston died came rushing back full force.

They fought down the corridor and into the next one. Velamir swung his sword wildly, and Mordon ducked under it. Velamir's sword carried over Mordon's head and slashed through an elaborate tapestry on the wall. Sweat ran down Velamir's back, but he kept persisting, anger a powerful fuel that drove him on. Mordon landed a jab on Velamir's chin, and he stumbled, blood pouring from his busted lip. Mordon grinned, taunting Velamir into furious action. He drove Mordon to a curving staircase that led up to a watchtower.

Mordon proceeded upward, gaining the higher ground. Velamir bit back a curse as he was forced to go on the defensive. Mordon's powerful strikes sent tremors through his arms at each block. As they continued up the stairs, Velamir saw an opening in Mordon's guard and thrust at it. Mordon gasped when the sword sliced through his leather armor into his shoulder. He tripped, blood streaming down his arm. Mordon rushed up the remaining stairs and stepped onto the tower with Velamir following behind.

Mordon was panting, and Velamir knew the poisoning had placed a heavy strain on his stamina. He lunged forward, and Mordon took a step back, lifting his arm to block the strike. But he raised his blade too slowly, and Velamir's sword cut down his face. Mordon roared in agony and staggered against the crenellations of the tower. He covered his face, blood running through his fingers. Through his fury-filled haze, Velamir pressed forward. Mordon saw him coming and retreated another pace. But he stepped too far and stumbled, falling backward off the tower.

CORALIE
CASTLE VERIN

Coralie made her way to the keep doors, her eyes widening when she saw they were thrown open. Soldiers rushed inside, and Coralie looked out the doors, her heart thumping at the number of men wearing black and red. They were everywhere. Deedans yelled as they chased the castle soldiers inside. Boltrex dashed through with some of his men. As soon as they entered, the keep doors were slammed shut and barred. Boltrex sagged against them, sweat running down his face. His chest heaved with breaths. He pulled himself up and shouted orders. His eyes landed on Coralie, and lines formed between his brow, showing his displeasure. He stormed her way.

"Princess, what are you doing here?"

"We aren't faring well, are we?" Coralie said instead of answering his question.

Boltrex sighed, and Coralie noticed he was covered in blood. He looked back at the entrance, where the soldiers were holding their body weight against the doors.

There was a booming sound signifying the use of a battering ram. They would be in soon.

"We have suffered heavy losses," Boltrex said. "These are the only men we have left."

Coralie scanned the soldiers, recognizing many of them. Galva Blayton was there, along with Latimus. Finnean stood beside Latimus, his swords slick with blood. Many others were there, but they could not have equaled over two hundred and fifty soldiers. Despair washed over Coralie. They were done for.

Boltrex saw her expression. "They burned the town. It was good that we brought the citizens in."

Coralie nodded, but she didn't have the heart to acknowledge the praise. She heard screaming from behind the closed doors, and the battering ram stopped for a blessed moment.

"We put the townsmen on the parapets," Boltrex explained. "They have arrows and hot oil."

Coralie's head throbbed, and she rubbed it, trying to block out the hopelessness filling her. She took a deep breath and remembered her words to the people in the Stone Chamber. She had promised them she would not give up. Coralie drew her sword. Boltrex raised his eyebrows, but before he could protest, Jax ran up to them, panting.

"Princess! We need to stop them."

Boltrex stared at him with impatience. "What is it?"

"Mordon," he wheezed.

Coralie's and Boltrex's eyes sharpened on him.

"What of him?" Coralie asked.

"He is fighting Velamir!"

Boltrex brushed past him.

"They were heading to the south watchtower!" Jax called after him and moved to follow.

"Stay here," she instructed him.

Coralie rushed after Boltrex. The sound of the battering ram resumed. They did not have time to waste over useless fights. She caught up with Boltrex and broke into a run, passing him. She rushed up the steps of the watchtower and stepped onto the tower. A strangled scream escaped her throat. Mordon was hanging off the tower. Velamir was gripping his arm, the only thing keeping him from plummeting to his death.

59

VELAMIR
CASTLE VERIN

VELAMIR GRITTED HIS teeth, straining to keep his hold on Mordon. He was surprised he had even managed to grab him when he fell. Velamir could see Prolus's large army fighting below. He wondered why they hadn't tried scaling the walls yet and then noticed they appeared to be moving into the castle. Velamir could only hope they had not broken into the keep.

"Let me go," Mordon said as he hung below. "All I ever wanted was"—he gasped a choked breath—"was my father's approval. But I know I will never receive it."

Velamir was startled by the pity that over-whelmed him. He knew how it felt to want the approval of a father. Winston had done his best, but Velamir still had a gaping hole inside him. A hole that could never be filled, since his family was long dead.

Your father is alive.

Velamir banished the words. There was no use in hoping. Mordon's arm slid down his sweaty hand. Velamir wanted to grab him with his other hand but knew if he shifted his weight, he would fall straight off the tower with Mordon.

Someone screamed behind him, but Velamir didn't dare look. Just as Mordon's arm slipped to his fingers, someone darted next him and grabbed hold of Mordon.

"I've got you, boy." Boltrex's voice was gruff.

Together, they hauled him over the crenellations. Mordon sank down, his head leaning against the stone wall. Coralie had been standing behind them, but as soon as Mordon settled, she rushed forward and sat beside him, sucking in a breath when she saw his face. The wound bled profusely, and blood swirled in Mordon's eye, but he seemed to be able to see through it. Boltrex surveyed his son's injuries and turned on Velamir, his expression furious.

"You are a menace, like Winston."

Velamir retrieved his sword from the ground and pointed it at Boltrex. "Don't you dare say his name."

Boltrex spat on the ground. "He is the devil himself."

Velamir roared and charged at Boltrex. Boltrex stepped out of his way, and Velamir turned, charging back at him again. Boltrex's sword was slick with blood from Prolus's men. He parried Velamir's assault with ease. Velamir's rage built, and his attacks became wilder. Boltrex sent a hard blow to Velamir's skull with his sword hilt. Velamir staggered back, and Boltrex raised his sword.

"No!" Coralie screamed, blocking Boltrex's blade with her own.

Velamir stared at her in disbelief.

"Step away, Princess. So I can finish this villain," Boltrex growled.

"Don't do this, General."

"Coralie?" Mordon said in a broken voice. "Why do you take his side?"

Coralie glanced at him and opened her mouth to respond. Velamir saw his opportune moment and reached into his boot while the others' attentions were diverted. He wrapped his fingers around the handle of his dagger and rushed forward. Boltrex's eyes widened, and he tried to step back, but Velamir was too quick. In an instant, his dagger was pressed against Boltrex's jugular vein.

"Give me one reason why I shouldn't end you now," Velamir whispered.

Boltrex stared straight ahead, mouth tight. Velamir didn't see even a flicker of fear in his eyes.

"Stop this," Coralie pleaded, her sword still raised.

The sound of slow clapping drew their attention. Deedans rushed onto the watchtower and surrounded them. The clapping continued, and a man walked onto the tower. He wore a long cloak, and a hood concealed his features.

"Well, isn't this lovely?" the man said, giving one last clap.

Velamir's jaw slackened, and his heart chilled. He knew that voice. Boltrex paled as the man reached up to remove his hood.

"It can't be," Mordon breathed.

It was Winston.

EPILOGUE

THE MAN PULLED on his reins, halting his horse. His second-in-command raised a fist, and the cavalry behind them stopped. The horses shifted at the interruption. The man smiled. They anticipated the battle as much as he did. His eyes narrowed, focusing on the scout riding hard in their direction. The scout slowed as he neared, sweat dripping from his face despite the chilly Verin air. The man had always despised Verin's weather, finding the heat in Ondalar much more preferable.

The scout raised a curled hand over his chest, saluting him with the emperor's symbol. That was another thing the man loathed, and something he was going to change.

"General, they are breaking into the castle," the scout informed him, his breaths heavy.

The general sniffed, inhaling the smoky air.

The scout nodded. "They burned the town."

His second-in-command looked at him. "General Zenrelius, what is your order?"

"We will raze them to the ground," the general spat. "Let's finish this."

He glanced back at his men, all cold-blooded killers. They stared stoically, awaiting his directive.

"Are we to assist Verin as your cousin ordered?" his second-in-command asked, a heavy frown on his face.

Zenrelius contemplated the question. He imagined racing to the rescue of that old fool, Dale, and having praise heaped upon him. Zenrelius's mouth quirked upward. He liked playing hero. But then an image of him slicing through the soldiers, finishing them off like the slugs they were, rushed through his mind, and he realized he liked being a villain far more.

ACKNOWLEDGMENTS

It used to be a dream, and I can't believe it's come this far. I've been carrying this story in me for so long it almost seems surreal to be at this point. But I couldn't have done this alone. I want to start by thanking my mom for believing in me and encouraging me from the very beginning. I love you, Mom. A shower of thanks to my siblings, for being there for me and cheering me on every step of the way. Special thanks to my Padar jan and all my relatives who have supported me. A load of gratitude to my beta readers. Elena, you are always my mejor amiga; and Cristina, you are going to be an amazing nurse. Immense love and appreciation to my grandparents. All four of you. My grandpa for actually really enjoying my book after reading the first draft, and my grandma, I love you to the moon and back. To Bibi jan, I treasure every moment I have with you and Boba jan—I wish you could've been here to see this. Massive thanks to Diego Zaldivar for the fantastic composition crafted for my book, and thank you for your patience. The journey to getting this published has taken a long time, but it's finally here. Thank you, Mandi Andrejka, for showing me how much potential my book had. Many thanks to Tanya Oemig. You are an awesome editor, and I appreciate all your help and guidance. I'm super glad to have found the team at Enchanted Ink. You guys are wonderful, and I can't think of a better editing team to trust my book with. Thank you to Damonza for the fantastic cover design. And last but not least, thank YOU for taking a chance on this book and going on the ride with Velamir and Natassa. This book wouldn't be possible without readers, so you are my personal cavaliers. Stay tuned for Book 2. Until then, mavaalin.